PERFECT COUPLE

Derek Hansen is a former advertising man who walked away at the peak of his career to pursue a lifelong ambition to write novels. His first novel, *Lunch with the Generals*, became an immediate bestseller, followed by *Lunch with Mussolini*, *Sole Survivor* and *Blockade*, and the short story collections *Dead Fishy* and *Psycho Cat*.

Derek Hansen's work has been published in America, Great Britain, Europe and the Republic of China. He is married with two adult children and lives on Sydney's northern beaches.

DEREK HANSEN

PERFECT COUPLE

Penguin Books

Penguin Books Australia Ltd
487 Maroondah Highway, PO Box 257
Ringwood, Victoria 3134, Australia
Penguin Books Ltd
Harmondsworth, Middlesex, England
Penguin Putnam Inc.
375 Hudson Street, New York, New York 10014, USA
Penguin Books Canada Limited
10 Alcorn Avenue, Toronto, Ontario, Canada M4V 3B2
Penguin Books (NZ) Ltd
Cnr Rosedale and Airborne Roads, Albany, Auckland, New Zealand
Penguin Books (South Africa) (Pty) Ltd
24 Sturdee Avenue, Rosebank, Johannesburg 2196, South Africa
Penguin Books India (P) Ltd
11, Community Centre, Panchsheel Park, New Delhi 110 017, India

First published by Penguin Books Australia Ltd 2000
This edition published by Penguin Books Australia Ltd 2001

1 3 5 7 9 10 8 6 4 2

Copyright © Derek Hansen 2001

The moral right of the author has been asserted

All rights reserved. Without limiting the rights under copyright reserved above, no part of this publication may be reproduced, stored in or introduced into a retrieval system, or transmitted, in any form or by any means (electronic, mechanical, photocopying, recording or otherwise), without the prior written permission of both the copyright owner and the above publisher of this book.

Cover design by David Altheim, Penguin Design Studio
Text design by Melissa Fraser, Penguin Design Studio
Cover photography by Tim De Neefe
Typeset in Scala by Midland Typesetters, Maryborough, Victoria
Printed and bound in Australia by McPherson's Printing Group, Maryborough, Victoria

National Library of Australia
Cataloguing-in-Publication data:

Hansen, Derek, 1944–

Perfect couple.

ISBN 0 14 029246 2.

1. Man-woman relationships – Fiction. I. Title.

A823.3

www.penguin.com.au

Acknowledgements

It is fair to say that a lot of people who contributed to this book did so unwittingly, but that is true of all books. My advertising characters are everybody and nobody, composites of people I worked with over thirty years and three countries. My fictitious agency is typical of many aggressive, burgeoning agencies, but based on none.

Friends in Fiji provided general background to complement my own observations and others responded generously to my requests for specialised information. Physiotherapists and chiropractors also helped with books, diagrams and answers to my tedious questioning.

Every book also needs professional, expert assistance and in this department I was well served by my agent, Margaret Connolly, publisher, Clare Forster, and editor, Sandy Webster.

I thank them all.

Part I

Temptation

One

The idea of exacting revenge did not sit easily with Sandra Madison, nor did the prospect of divine retribution. If Rowan, her husband, fell under a bus, however deserving of his fate, she knew her grief would be bottomless and their two daughters inconsolable. Yet to do nothing struck her as pathetic and weak. Revenge seemed the only viable alternative and the opportunity to seize it lay all but naked in front of her.

She hadn't met him before and he certainly hadn't tried to hit on her, but she'd been aware of his eyes and their silent appraisal, and she didn't doubt that he liked what he'd seen. Then again, what was there to dislike? Sandra's Norwegian grandfather had bequeathed her hair that streaked from honey to light brown, blue eyes that drifted to mauve, and flawless skin that fell just shy of olive. Her body was beautifully proportioned for her height, which was perhaps her only physical demerit. Some men, if pressed, might consider she was built a touch close to the ground. But that was one of the things that had originally attracted Rowan to her. He always claimed that the best things came in small packages.

Whether or not the young man lying on the table had actually made any assessment at all of Sandra, she had certainly made an assessment of him. If she was to exact her revenge, she could hardly have picked a more suitable candidate. He was a triathlete, with a body sculpted in gyms and made lean by his disciplines. Sandra put him in his early twenties, around fifteen years her junior.

'How does this feel?' she asked.

'Good,' he said. He lay flat on his back with his hands behind his head, open and vulnerable, the privacy afforded by his Jockey briefs more illusory than actual. Justice beckoned, urged her to seize the opportunity and indulge herself as Rowan had. She gently pulled his right leg apart from his left.

'Ahh!' he said.

Sandra straightened his knee and set his leg back down on the table. 'When do you compete?'

'Five weeks. The Forster triathlon.'

'Your adductor muscle has a small tear as you suspected. I want you to rest for the next week to ten days and do gentle stretches every day. When you resume training, use your brain and ease into it. If what you do hurts, do something else. What concerns me most is not the tear itself, but why it tore. Talk to your trainer or see someone at the Institute of Sport. You could be over-striding, or it could be that the seat's too high on your bike. It's usually something simple.'

'Okay. Is that all?'

'No. I'm going to rub some gel over your groin and give you a bit of ultrasound.'

'What about sex?'

Sandra stopped dead in her tracks. Had she been so obvious? One quick and anxious glance at his face, however, and she relaxed. He still wore the same serious, watchful, matter-of-fact expression.

'Is it okay to have sex?'

Sandra laughed. 'Again, use your brain. If it hurts, swap places. Who's the lucky girl?'

'Lucy. First base.'

'Ah, so that's the connection.' Sandra had wondered what had brought the young man to her clinic. Lucy was one of the girls in her softball Under-19 regional representative team.

'My regular physio's booked out. You came highly recommended.'

'Nice to know.' Sandra began to move the sound-head slowly around his groin. She had two necks, a lower back and a knee still to go, then a break to play with the girls, bath and feed them. After dinner she had clinic for the softball girls – two haematomas from an outfield collision, a patella tendonitis and a hamstring.

She wondered if Rowan would come home for dinner as promised. After the heat of the previous night, the bitter accusations, the shamed apologies and promises of future fidelity, the chances were he would. She was glad she had the softball clinic so they wouldn't have to watch television together in awkward silence, or be insufferably polite in case one of them said something that set things off again. Everything that had to be said had been said, and all necessary undertakings made. Now they needed time to let the dust settle. Besides, she reasoned, it wouldn't do Rowan any harm to spend an evening with his daughters.

'All done,' she said. 'If you have any more problems or if it's slow to heal, give me a call and I'll fit you in.'

'Thanks.' The triathlete swung his legs over the side of the table and began to dress. Sandra had already turned away to clean the sound-head. In truth, revenge had never been more than a bitter thought. To have acted upon it would have been immoral and unethical. She'd lacked desire anyway. His near-nakedness hadn't aroused her in the least, nor had she expected it to. Just as athletes become so accustomed to people probing, manipulating and repairing their bodies that modesty ceases to be an issue, so it was with her. She'd planned dinner as she slid the sound-head around his joy toys. He'd read a magazine.

Yes, she had opportunity. Yes, she had motive. Yes, justice was on her side. But at the end of the day, Sandra was Sandra, and Sandra just didn't do that sort of thing.

'I'm afraid Rocky's inherited your ear, dear.'

'Hi Mum.' Sandra closed the door that linked her clinic to the rest of her home, wishing immediately that one of the car pool mothers had brought her girls home instead. Marion was one of those women euphemistically described as 'very capable'. Her principal characteristic was her determination to impose an order of her deciding upon the world, especially upon those within her orbit, whether they liked it or not.

Formidable was the word Rowan reserved for her, and he gave it a French pronunciation for emphasis.

'Thanks for playing taxi,' said Sandra graciously.

'On my way, dear. Sarah, I'm pleased to say, has talent.' Marion paused to listen to the tinkling of the piano. 'She's teaching Rocky what she's just learned. I think you should encourage poor Rocky to concentrate on sport.'

'I'm aware of each of my daughter's strong points.'

'Of course you are, dear.'

Sandra forced herself to remain pleasant. 'Can I make you a cup of tea?'

'Tea bags? No thanks.'

'How's Clive?'

'Clive is well, thank you. Why do you ask?'

'Courtesy.'

'Don't lie, dear. You never were any good at it. You're like everyone else. You want to know if our friendship has blossomed into a relationship so you can disapprove.'

'Has it?'

'Probably will this weekend. Clive's taking me to Ayers Rock.'

'Bit sudden, isn't it?' Sandra said weakly. When her father had died unexpectedly four years earlier, she'd thought her mother would settle into a retirement village and see out her days quietly playing bridge and going on coach tours like other widows. But once Marion had recovered from her loss it was as though she'd been reborn. She'd grabbed life with a determination to wring the best out of what was left. At first, Sandra was pleased when her mother began going out to plays, concerts and recitals. Her attitude changed when she became aware of the succession of men that accompanied Marion. Only Clive, however, had possessed the staying power to keep up with her.

'I know I said I'd babysit Saturday night but it can't be helped. You'll have to find someone else.'

'Terrific,' said Sandra. It was never easy to get babysitters at the last minute for Saturday nights but that was the least of her concerns. 'At least you've known Clive for, what is it now, almost two months?'

'More like forty years, dear. If he'd left the airforce a few weeks earlier he might have been your father.' She paused for a moment's reflection. 'God, you should have seen him in uniform.'

'Forty years?'

'More, actually, now that I think about it. Hadn't thought about him for ages and then he buys a unit in the village two doors down from mine. Anyway, mustn't keep you. Wish me bon voyage.'

'Now, both legs behind your head.'

The two girls copied their mother. Sandra often wondered how many other mothers insisted their offspring follow a regime of stretching. Her daughters had grown up believing yoga was as natural and as necessary as cleaning their teeth before bed. Sarah, her six-year-old, could tie herself up in knots and slip her legs behind her head without effort. Rochelle, her three-year-old, was giggling too much but Sandra made no effort to stop her. Instead she started giggling herself, knowing

Rocky would complete the exercise once she'd won a little bit of attention.

'Keep going,' she said encouragingly. 'Soon you'll be as good as Sarah. That's it. Now, what'll we do next?'

'That one where we do the splits and put our head on the ground,' said Sarah. 'I do that in dance class.'

Sandy even had Rowan doing yoga in the mornings, before he headed off to the gym. Rowan had always looked after his body and he only ever complained of stiffness as a consequence of stress and overwork. She could soothe that away with a back rub. It was the reckless stiffness in his nether regions that she wished would go away, never to return except at her bidding.

After bathing the girls she had twenty minutes to freshen up. As she stepped into the shower, she caught a glimpse of herself in the mirror and automatically turned away. Why? She stopped, forced herself to confront her image. What was so wrong with her that she couldn't bear to look at herself? What didn't she want to see? It wasn't her body, because her muscle tone was living testimony to her regime of exercises and stretches. Her breasts and buttocks still defied gravity and nothing sagged. The give-away was her face. She looked harried – that was the word that sprang into her mind – and, worse, unhappy. This was not the face that once had young men queuing to date her, that turned heads in the street, that endeared her to people. What scared her was the thought that when she looked into the mirror, she might also be looking into her future.

When Sandra and Rowan had first discussed getting married, she'd made it plain that she had no intention of giving up her professional life, which revolved around her physiotherapy practice. With the prospect of kids in the not too distant future, Sandra decided that the practice was only feasible if she could work from home. They'd had a clinic built on to the side of their home, with a separate entrance for clients. When Rowan decided to take the plunge and start his own advertising agency, it was largely her income that had kept them going through the first, difficult years. She was proud of the contribution she'd made, of having her salary help pay the mortgage, put food on the table and pay the bills.

Her business had made it possible for him to have a business, but she couldn't help feeling she'd also given him the means and opportunity to indulge in his stupid little infidelities. After all, if he got sprung on his sofa with one of the secretaries, he was hardly going to fire himself. It didn't matter that Rowan insisted he never meant to hurt her. It didn't matter that she believed him. He hurt her just the same. It wasn't that he didn't love her, because he clearly did, and he absolutely adored the girls. He genuinely didn't want to hurt any of them. The problem lay in his constant need to prove himself, despite her strident insistence that he had nothing to prove to anyone. Nothing she said could convince him, and he certainly could never convince himself. His vulnerability stood out like a missing front tooth.

'What did you think of Tony?'

Sandra forced herself to pay attention to the girl stretched out on the table before her. 'What?' she said.

'What did you think of Tony?'

'Who's Tony?'

'Jeez,' said the girl. 'It is true what they say about blondes. Tony's the guy Lucy sent to see you.'

'Oh.'

'Well?'

'Torn groin muscle.'

'Yeah, we know. What we want to know is, did you kiss it better?' The girl laughed and her injured friends joined in.

'That's what we would've done,' said one.

'Gone the Monica,' said another.

'What did you do?' asked the girl on the table.

'None of your business.'

The girls hooted.

'Anything that occurs between my patient and myself is strictly confidential. However, I took some Polaroids of his groin so that I can monitor improvement. If you win the regionals, I'll show them to you. Now hop it. You're finished. Disappear.'

'Are you serious?' asked the girl as she climbed off the table. 'You've got photos of his thing?' She had eyes like saucers.

Sandra just smiled and ushered them out. They chirped their thanks and took their frantic speculations out into the night, oblivious to the fact that Sandra didn't even own a Polaroid camera. She began the task of cleaning up and gathering towels for the laundry. She coached the girls and treated their injuries for free, and normally thrived on being party to their intrigues and gossip, but this time the dead spot had absorbed all her humour and all she felt was tired. She just hoped Rowan felt as flat as she did.

Sandra opened the door to the house, and was immediately assaulted by more giggling. She checked her watch. It was well past the girls' bedtime. When she looked into the living room her first instinct was to snap at them for being up, and at Rowan for keeping them up. But Sarah and Rocky had their father exactly where they wanted him – on his back on the carpet. They lay across his arms and legs and tried to tickle him, faces radiant as they shrieked with pleasure. So what if they should be in bed? So what if they were overexcited? So what if they'd be grumpy in the morning? They didn't see enough of their father and it was only fair they made the most of the times when they did. She tip-toed past the doorway to the kitchen, warmed milk for Milo and stuck crumpets in the toaster. The girls would get a real buzz out of staying up and having supper with Mummy and Daddy. Doubtless, tonight Daddy would get a buzz out of it as well. Only Mummy was miffed, miffed that Daddy could be so playful and full of fun while she felt so utterly brassed off.

'Every white woman at some stage in her life dreams of having sex with a black man.'

'Oh?' said Sandra doubtfully. She couldn't imagine a black man featuring next on her mother's agenda and there wasn't one knocking on the door of her own. She pressed her thumbs hard into the trapezius muscles on either side of her best friend's lower neck, feeling her squirm under the pressure. Caroline Pengelly was tall where Sandra was petite, dark-haired where Sandra was fair, and the romantic of the two. Caroline had always dreamed of a life far more exciting than the one she lived, her mind abuzz with exotic and risky adventures she'd done little to pursue. But her true character was revealed in her choice of husband. Mike was tall and handsome, though his soft body sign-posted the nature of his calling. Caroline had married an accountant.

'It's our most cherished fantasy,' said Caroline. 'Whether we admit it or not. Black men represent the ideal, the hope that totally satisfying sex does exist for a woman.'

'What about film stars and pop singers?'

'Film stars are people you have relationships with. Pop singers get busted in toilets or fry their brains on drugs. I'm not talking about relationships or even love. I'm talking about the pure, unfettered, animal act of sex. Uninhibited, no-holds-barred, endlessly orgasmic sex – the kind that sends you screaming off through the cosmos knowing that there is nothing more to be had nor to be wished for. I'm talking big bang theory. The truth is, when women imagine the ultimate bonk, it's always with a black man. Hey! That hurts!' Caroline lifted her head and glared accusingly at Sandra.

'These neck muscles should feel like soap sliding on glass, but you haven't been doing your stretches.' Sandra pushed Caroline's head back down. 'Instead they feel like I'm trying to push pumpkins through a pea-shooter. You work at the computer, you stretch. On the hour every hour. No exceptions, no excuses.' Sandra gently loosened the muscles down the sides of Caroline's vertebrae, from her ears to her shoulder-blades, waist and lower lumbar.

'Do you still fantasise about screwing a black man?'

'I'm not sure I ever did.'

'Oh, come on, Sandy! What about the nights when Rowan's away, or late home, and you've got that whole big bed to yourself? Don't you like to imagine the possibilities if you were still single – no husband, no kids, no conscience? Christ, it was all you ever used to talk about.'

'When?'

'When we were students.'

'Oh, way back then.'

'And since, and don't try to deny it. I bloody well still do. Do you know what my current fantasy is? I dream you have to go out suddenly and I have to come over and mind the shop for you. A big black guy comes in for a massage ...'

'I'm not a masseuse.'

'I know that, but he doesn't.'

'Go on.'

'He thinks I'm you and starts stripping. I know I should stop him but he's just so mind-numbingly beautiful. Before I know it, he's naked and lying face down on the table. Oh my God, you've never seen a body like it. Like a statue come alive, all rippling, glistening muscle.'

'Glistening?'

'Baby oil. He's got baby oil all over him.'

'Of course.'

'I can hardly breathe. He's just lying there, mine to do whatever I want with. I start on his shoulders and slowly work my way down. God, his body's hard and he has the tightest, tautest bum you can ever imagine. Like cantaloupes in cling wrap. I want to grab him and screw him till I die from ecstasy.

Next thing, my clothes are on the floor and I'm sliding naked up and down his body.'

'Let me guess what happens next. He turns over and you discover he's doing steroids. His balls have shrivelled up and his dick's a button mushroom.'

'No!'

Sandra started laughing helplessly.

'Stop it! What did you have to go and say that for?'

'Sorry, Caro, but I can't handle your fantasies right now. I've got customers waiting, people in pain, and the girls are due home from ballet in half an hour.'

'It's not fair, Sandy. If I can't tell you my fantasies, who can I tell? If I can't share them, there's no point having them.'

'I love hearing your fantasies. Just not when I'm working.'

'When then? How about you come around for coffee on your morning off? I'll tell you mine and you can tell me yours.'

'Sounds fair.'

'You do still have fantasies, don't you?'

Sandra took a moment to answer and her voice was flat when she did. 'I suppose so. Sometimes. Usually I'm too busy. Sometimes I think Rowan has them for me.'

'Uh-oh, I don't think I'll go into that.'

'No, I don't think you should.'

'But you must have fantasies sometimes. So what are they?'

'I don't know. Maybe spending a couple of months in Tuscany or France, renting a villa out in the countryside that has its own vines and a three-star Michelin restaurant twenty minutes down the road. Oh, and a housekeeper who is an angel and a superb cook.'

'Come on, Sandy.'

'Right now I'd settle for a week in a five-star hotel.'

'That's not the kind of fantasy I'm talking about and you know it.'

There had been a time when Sandra indulged in erotic fantasies and delighted in discussing them, but black men hadn't featured any more prominently than other men. It troubled her that it all seemed such a long time ago. As she recalled, black men had been Caroline's fantasy more so than hers, but she decided to take the line of least resistance to please her friend. 'I suppose my fantasies are the same as yours. Now, on your feet, you're done.'

'Knew it!' said Caroline triumphantly.

As Caroline dressed, Sandra prepared for her next appointment. She had one more neck and two lower backs, all women. Distracted, she nearly forgot to ask Caroline the all-important question.

'Mike made up his mind yet?'

'Still working on him.'

'I'll keep my fingers crossed.'

'I'm going to keep my legs crossed, to force the issue. And he better decide the right way or I'll have them welded together permanently.' Caroline handed Sandra a cheque. 'See you and lover boy on Saturday. In the meantime, I'm off to cruise the shopping mall in search of the perfect male buttocks, something interesting to follow around the supermarket aisles.'

'Good luck.' Sandra saw Caroline to the door and admitted the neck, a woman suffering from menopause-induced stress and headaches. The thirty-minute sessions brought the poor woman so much relief she often became teary before drifting off to sleep. It was at times like these that Sandra really did believe she had healing hands. Her fingers sought out and found the bunched and spasming muscles and soothed them into pliancy. Her hands worked automatically, as if all of Sandra's knowledge resided within them. The trouble was, her knowing fingers left her mind free to wander when it needed to be occupied. She tried to think of ways to help Caroline coax her husband back to the IVF clinic but nothing would lock in. No, the black hole had her firmly in its thrall, suppressing all thoughts but the one she most wanted to avoid.

'You do still have fantasies, don't you?' Caroline had asked. The question had stunned her and, momentarily, she'd been lost for words. What had happened to the young woman whose mind had been a whirl of possibilities and speculation, of intense passions and even more intense sex? When had she stopped dreaming? Had she? Was she just going through a lull? Or, at the age of thirty-eight, had all her fantasies abandoned her for someone younger?

Two

Rowan strode the platform that ran the full width of the boardroom. It was only twenty centimetres high and one metre wide, but he cherished it. Being up on the platform, he claimed, was his favourite position. At least, while he still had his trousers on. It was his great equaliser, his domain, his stage, and scene of his finest performances. It was here that he presented strategies and creative concepts to clients, and used his formidable presentation skills to dazzle them with the agency's collective brilliance. It was here that he pitched new business. The value of the platform could easily be measured. Rowan was twice as likely to win a new account if the presentation was held in his boardroom, rather than in the prospective client's. It was also here that he made his 'state of the nation' addresses to his staff and wound them up for greater effort.

Rowan was passionate in his belief that an agency's greatest asset was its people, and he was convinced people worked best when they were kept informed. He told them everything it was prudent to tell them and sometimes even things that weren't. People liked to belong to something, he insisted, liked to know where they stood and liked to be told when they'd done well or stuffed up. He was convinced people didn't want democracy but a benevolent dictatorship, a kindly but nonetheless strict father figure, someone to hold their hand, be arbiter of taste and tactics, and guide them through their working day.

He paused at the end of the platform and scanned the twenty-two faces in front of him. Only Glynis, the receptionist, was missing, still at her post manning the phones.

'This is the rarest of opportunities,' he began. 'This is like checking into a hotel and finding you have to share a bed with Jennifer Aniston or Brad Pitt.' He paused and looked around the room. Did he have everyone's attention? Did Jesus, when he gave his Sermon on the Mount? He could tell from the looks of anticipation that all his staff wanted was confirmation of the rumour they'd heard. He lowered his voice so they had to strain to hear him. He spoke with reverence, not just for effect but because he, too, was in awe of the news. 'We have been invited to pitch for Lavalle.'

'Yes!' screamed his junior creative team. Others whistled, some even applauded. No one was unmoved. Rowan waited patiently for the excitement to die.

'We have good clients but they're not first rank. Hell, let's be honest, some would even struggle for fourth. Lavalle, as you all know, is the gold standard. Win this account and every account worth having will want to talk to us. Win and every other agency in town will want to talk to you. Win and it won't be the last time we win big. But if we lose ...' Rowan paused and scanned the room once more, taking in the rapt faces staring back. 'If we lose, we may as well all rack our cues and get a job in a bank. Advertising has no place for losers. And, for that matter, neither have I. So for the next three weeks, I don't care if you've got a private life, I don't care if your mum drops dead or your kid gets hit by a bus. I don't care if your dog rips your bloody leg off. I don't care if your boyfriend comes out of the closet or your girlfriend tells you she's got AIDS. You will spend twenty-four hours a day thinking about Lavalle and twice as long in here at your bloody desks.

'I don't want a lot, I want everything. Now, I want the first cut at the brief tomorrow morning, and first ideas five minutes later. We'll work nights and weekends until we're absolutely certain we've blown the other agencies out of the water. I'll be here and if I'm not you can ring me at home. Any time of the day or night. Anyone unhappy can fuck off now. Any takers?'

Once again he scanned his audience. The lights were on in every eye he gazed into. If he'd asked them to give up drink, drugs and sex for life they would have. People loved pressure, loved feeling indispensable, loved being part of the team.

'Get some product from Blake and start sucking, but remember, the key to this presentation will be the new flavours – the Cola and the Ginger Mint. Anybody has an idea, I want to hear it and I don't care who has it.' He turned his gaze to the office junior. 'You're closest to the target group. I want your opinion on everything we do. Tell me or Blake. You've got ability or I wouldn't have hired you.' The junior glowed. 'Okay, everybody get your freebies.'

Rowan stepped down from his platform and strode purposefully back to his office. Nobody had seen him move any other way. He gave the impression of being a man who knew exactly where he wanted to be and was impatient to get there. As he left the room he heard Blake, his account director, trying to get some order into the handing out of the sweets. Blake didn't have a chance. It didn't matter how much agency people were paid – and Rowan paid them well – they were like pigs in a trough when it came to freebies.

At his desk Rowan checked his messages. There was nothing that couldn't wait. He checked through his diary so that he could reschedule client meetings to give him more time to spend on the pitch. He'd never wanted to win so badly. Sure, the revenue was important, but to win Lavalle would lift the agency into the big league. Every award book had its share of Lavalle commercials. Commercials that had won Palm d'Ors at Cannes and Venice, gold at London's D & AD, gold at New York's Art Directors' Show, gold at Clio. It was heady stuff. They'd come to him and two other agencies purely on the strength of their creative work. One of the most enlightened and aggressive clients in the world had invited *his* agency to pitch because they admired his work. It was the happiest day of his professional life but Rowan had no illusions about where his agency ranked in the pecking order. The other two agencies occupied the territory he aspired to. He'd have to come from behind to win.

'Jesus.'

'You called?' Rowan looked up as Blake wandered into his office.

'Jesus,' Blake said again. 'I'd rather dip my dick in piranha-infested custard than go through that again. I managed to save half a dozen packs for you even though I know you don't eat the stuff. There you go.' He tossed the packets onto Rowan's desk. 'Peppermint, Cola, Ginger Mint, Citrus and Aniseed.'

'Thanks.'

'How're things at home?'

Rowan smiled thinly. 'Thawing.'

'How'd she get on to you?'

'It's pushing midnight, right? Sandra rings to see when I'm coming home. Stupid Glynis answers the phone. I guess it was habit, but you'd reckon with both of us lying naked on the couch, normal office procedure would not apply.'

'Ouch.'

'Yeah. As soon as Glynis heard Sandra's voice she realised what she'd done. She dropped the handset like it was burning hot. I don't know why she didn't just say, "Hi Sandra, I'll pass you over to Rowan as soon as he finishes wiping his dick."'

Blake started to laugh. 'You bloody ask for it. Tell you what, though, you've still got problems there. That girl's got ambitions.'

'I know. They're all the bloody same. They all want the short cut to the easy life. She's good but she'll have to go. Sandy's insisting on that. But after the presentation, of course.'

'Good luck,' said Blake. 'Can you afford another strike against your name?'

'Probably not but that's irrelevant. I'm giving myself one hundred per cent to the pitch. Now, when are we going to start work on the brief?'

'It's going to take us two hours to read all the stuff they sent us. How about the boardroom at four?'

'Got me,' said Rowan. 'Anyone else know about what happened with Glynis?'

'Nobody,' said Blake. 'At least, nobody outside the industry.' Blake turned away so that Rowan wouldn't see the smirk on his face.

'I'll do my best,' said Rowan, but he could see that Sandra wasn't impressed.

'Not good enough,' she said. They sat at the dinner table, their dirty plates still in front of them, the dregs of a bottle of pinot noir in their glasses. Sandra had marinated two pieces of tuna in lime and rock salt, and barely seared them so that the middle fell just shy of sashimi. It was one of their favourite meals and one intended to heal rifts. 'Caroline arranged this dinner weeks ago. We're not cancelling now.'

'You go.'

'No, Rowan, we both go. We've accepted. She's planned the menu and bought the food.'

'For Christ's sake!' said Rowan. 'Don't you realise what this account means to me? It's my reward! It's my reward for all the effort, all the scratching and scraping. It'll make people sit up and look at me. Look at the agency. Put us on their list. It'll give me breathing space, Sandy. If I lose an account now I'll have to fire people. Start firing people and others will get nervous and start leaving, and God only knows where I'll find people to replace them. If I win Lavalle I'll have a buffer. We can relax, take holidays.'

'It's a scratched record, Rowan.'

'Damn it, Sandy, this is different. My Xerox breaks down every second week, half of my computers are secondhand and past their use-by date. My senior team are looking around because they know – and I know – there's always someone who'll pay them more. The future of the agency hinges on this account. I need it!'

'And I need you on Saturday night.'

'Look, if this was just another account I'd back off now. But this is Lavalle.' Rowan could see he was getting nowhere. He thought he'd chosen his moment well. Outside of bed, the most intimate times of their marriage occurred around the dinner table, during dinner and often for hours afterwards when they exchanged news, brought each other up to date, planned holidays and even engaged in a bit of flirting. Sandra had made an effort with the pinot noir and tuna but he was wrong in assuming the wounds had healed over. The more he tried to reason with her, the more thin-lipped she became. His only hope was a compromise. 'How about a deal? I pop in after dinner for a couple of hours?'

'No. The call is seven-thirty for eight. I don't care how early you get to the office or how hard you work while you're there. But at five o'clock you get in your car, you come home, you shower, you change, you come with me to Caroline's. You come home or don't bother coming home again.' Sandra pushed her chair back, grabbed their plates and stormed off into the kitchen.

Rowan stared at the table mat in front of him. One of the pieces of advice he gave his staff was to always know exactly where the last trench was, so that they didn't end up in it. The last trench loomed large in front of him. He gathered up the serving dishes and slowly made his way into the kitchen. Sandra had her back to him as she rinsed dishes in the sink.

'Okay,' he said. 'Unconditional surrender. I'll skip breakfast, I'll skip lunch and I'll be a total bloody martyr. But I'll be here by six Saturday and you can dress me for dinner. I will not be surly or resentful. I'll be in good humour, bright and witty. Shall I open another bottle to celebrate your overwhelming victory?'

'Don't bother,' said Sandra.

Later, when they were in bed and Rowan made tentative overtures about beginning the process of creating a son, she said exactly the same thing.

'Don't bother.'

Rowan reached the gym impatient to do powerful things. He'd slept badly, risen early and completed his yoga in the dark. The gym was practically deserted. There were no aerobics classes, no fit young businesswomen working out to leaven the pain of his exertions, and no waiting to get on any apparatus. It didn't matter that there were no young women because he only had eyes for the heavy bag. He wanted to lay into it and thump the stuffing out of it. But first he had his routine. Bicycle, Nautilus, step machine, speed ball, then heavy bag before warming down with treadmill and stretches.

In any conflict it was Rowan's nature to play the man, to prove that he was not just the equal of his adversary but better. It was an attitude that had got him into the rugby first 15 at school, the cricket first 11 and more fights than he could remember. On the football field they called him 'Mad Man' because of his fearlessness and determination to overcome anyone foolish enough to stand in his way. His coach used to say he was a stroppy little rooster and, though he meant well, Rowan hated him for it. He didn't mind being called stroppy, but the coach had no right to go calling him little.

Rowan's lack of height was an intolerable burden he carried with burning resentment. From his first day at school he was made aware that being short made him less of a human being. When kids chose sides for games he was never the first picked, and the humiliation of waiting in the diminishing line while other kids, bigger kids who weren't as tough or as fast, were picked ahead of him lit bitter fires deep inside his soul that would never dim. He'd been too small to play in the forwards, too short to be a fast bowler, and lacked the stature to play the lead in school dramatics. As he grew older he discovered that pretty girls didn't want boyfriends shorter than themselves. Every knock-back, every disappointment added fuel to the fires. He saw himself as the hero destined always to be cast in support roles.

Rowan was convinced nature had intended him to be a big man, that he was a big man trapped inside a small man's body. He had the build of a boxer, well-muscled with broad shoulders that seemed to bypass the formality of a neck and grow straight up to his ears. To the rest of the world he looked powerful, even intimidating, but Rowan could only see that he'd been short-changed in the neck department by important centimetres. His legs were another problem. They were too short for his build. He believed that a genetic malfunction had robbed him of his birthright. Once, while Sandra was massaging his back, she'd commented that his discs felt compacted, and that the gaps between his vertebrae were narrower than normal. Rowan had seized on her innocent remark and claimed it as further evidence that God had intended him to be tall. She was talking millimetres. Rowan heard centimetres. He was convinced he was meant to be 190 centimetres tall, and not the meagre 172.5 centimetres his misbegotten genes had stuck him with.

The Managing Directors of the agencies he was competing against for Lavalle were both tall and handsome, with the easy charm that comes with height, affluence and an expensive education. Before they even opened their mouths, their sheer presence claimed trust. Clients trusted them, trusted them with millions of dollars, trusted them to guide their companies to one success after another. Rowan resented his competitors for the advantage they gained so effortlessly and accepted so casually, as if it were their birthright.

He buried a right rip into the heavy bag, felt the shock of the blow ripple through his shoulder and down to the soles of his feet.

'Hey! That bag call you a poof or something?' The gym instructor grabbed hold of the bag and held his weight against it to provide more resistance to Rowan's punches. 'This thing's only hanging from hardened steel set in reinforced concrete. It's only bomb-proof. You wanna leave something for someone else to hit?'

Rowan smiled for the first time that day and unleashed a

five-punch combination that he believed would have sat a heavyweight on the deck.

'I've been watching you,' said the instructor. 'You've got a good punch, and good combinations. Whoever taught you, taught you well.'

Rowan threw one last punch and stepped back. 'Police Boys Club. How are you going?'

'Good, mate,' said the instructor. He grabbed hold of Rowan's hands and began pulling the gloves off. 'You got one of them new business things?'

'Yeah,' said Rowan. 'How'd you know?'

'Obvious. You're here early and you're trying to break my equipment. You did that last time, when you were after the Fiji Tourist Board.'

'We got it,' said Rowan.

'Good on yer,' said the instructor. 'Just a thought, in case you're interested. Mason's gym's being demolished. From today half a dozen of his boxers are coming down here to train. We're moving some gear and putting a ring in out the back. If you fancy a bit of sparring come along in the evenings. Blokes are always looking for someone to spar with. Might help burn off some of your aggression.'

'You want me to come and spar against pros?'

'Yeah, if you want. I reckon you could handle it.'

'What divisions?'

'All divisions. Some big boys.'

'Count me in,' said Rowan.

'Good man,' said the instructor. He patted Rowan on the buttocks like a football coach and left Rowan with a smile as wide as the Harbour Bridge. The instructor also had a bit of a grin on his face. He'd worked around small men all his life and knew exactly what not to say to them. Never qualify their ability with their size. Never say 'for a bloke your size', and never say 'pound for pound, you're the best'. Never, ever, remind small men of their size. Especially not stroppy little roosters like Rowan.

Rowan slumped back in his chair. Despite all his years in advertising, despite all the campaigns he'd worked on, he still felt a frisson of fear every time he started a new project. This time the stakes were higher than they'd ever been. What if they weren't good enough? What if they didn't come up with an idea? What if he got the strategy wrong? His fear, his nightmare, was to be exposed in the middle of a presentation, caught in a lie or in ignorance; to dry up, stammer, stutter, lose confidence, lose his nerve and blow it publicly up there on his platform with nowhere to run and nowhere to hide. To be shown up for the small man he was. This was the fear he lived with.

It was one thing to blow it in front of a normal client. It had never happened, but that hadn't stopped him wondering how he'd cope if it ever did. In his heart he knew he could battle through the humiliation, plead sickness and live to fight another day. But with Lavalle there could be no excuses. He'd be under the microscope, under the scrutiny of some of the sharpest marketing brains in the business, people so accustomed to success that they had no tolerance for failure nor use for excuses. He had one chance and only one chance. For two hours the future of his business would depend on his tap-dancing skills, on his ability to persuade and convince, but most of all on his ability to ignite their imagination and make their nipples go hard.

They'd want brilliance and conviction, a business partner as convinced of his supremacy in advertising as they were of their supremacy in marketing. The truth was, every other presentation he'd ever made had only been a rehearsal for this, the main event. This was the real thing. *The real thing?* The line bounced around his brain, firing up transmitters and activating receptors. *The real thing!* He leapt from his chair and raced screaming out into the corridor. 'Where's Mark? Where's Elaine?' He could have offered free cocaine and had no takers. The agency was deserted. He raced down to the creative department and back around to reception. The elevator opened and Blake stepped out grinning.

'I could hear you three floors down.'

'Where's Mark and Elaine?'

'They were here until well after ten last night so I wouldn't expect to see either of them before ten this morning. Unless they're still here . . .'

'No. I went past their office. Bugger me, Blake, there's no one here. Most important bloody presentation we'll ever see and there's no one here!'

'It's only five to eight. Why don't you tell me what's on your mind and I'll tell you where I got to with Mark and Elaine last night.' Blake strolled into his office and pushed out a chair for Rowan, knowing there was absolutely no chance he'd ever sit on it.

'Let's do it in my office,' said Rowan.

Blake watched Rowan go and smiled. He dumped his bag and dutifully followed his boss into his office, Rowan's chair was adjustable, and screwed up to its maximum height. Rowan even had to be tall sitting down. Blake slumped into a chair opposite him. 'Okay, let's have it.'

'I've got a line for Cola.'

'I thought you had a cure for cancer.'

'How about this. New Cola Frisks, they're just like the real thing.'

Blake's features drifted into a broad smile. He thumped his fist into his hand. 'Bloody brilliant! When did Coke stop using "It's the real thing"?'

'Who gives a shit. Lavalle will love it.'

'And Coke will hate it. Probably sue.'

'Probably only threaten and that won't do sales any harm at all.'

'What's the execution?'

'Buggered if I know. That's why we pay creative people. Christ, I only thought of the line a minute ago.'

'Why don't you give it to the junior team? Give it to Ken and Chris.'

'Stuff that. It's a great line and I want my top team on it.'

'Mark and Elaine are already working on an idea for Ginger Mint.'

'Go on.'

'Couple of ideas, actually. I should let them tell you themselves.'

'Screw them, Blake! If they were here they could tell me.

They're not, so you tell me. If the ideas are any good they'll get the credit.'

Blake shifted uncomfortably. 'They'll probably kill me for this, but here goes. They've got this Chinese guy eating in a restaurant in China, so it's the absolute, authentic real thing, and he orders in Chinese. He orders napalm with everything. The translation of what he orders is supered underneath. He orders and the super reads, "Double chilli ginger duck". The plate curls up and melts because the dish is so hot. His chopsticks dissolve, but he is unmoved and keeps eating. He orders another dish. "Habanero chilli chowder". The tablecloth catches fire in a ring around his plate, but he still carries on eating like it's mother's chicken soup. Cut a long story short, he leaves the restaurant and decides to freshen his mouth with a Ginger Mint Frisk. As soon as he puts it in his mouth, sweat breaks out on his forehead and his eyes water. Flames come out his mouth. A voice-over comes on and says, "Ginger Mint Frisks. Made from lava."'

Rowan laughed and rocked back on his chair. 'Yeah, like it,' he said. 'Probably more than the original.'

'What do you mean?'

'Tic-tac did it in London back in the late sixties or early seventies. Only they had a Frenchman eating a Spanish onion, then wimping out when he sucks a peppermint Tic-tac.'

'I don't remember it,' said Blake defensively.

'Lavalle will. Tic-tac won awards for it and Tic-tac is, after all, their major competitor.'

'Well shoot me now.'

'"Made from lava" isn't original either. It was done in

Scotland for Irn Bru. Remember? "Irn Bru. Made from girders?"'

'You're right.'

'Yeah, and you're right too, Blake.'

'How come?'

'I'm giving my idea to the junior team. That way I might get something original.'

Rowan was halfway through structuring a series of major and minor promotions for the Fiji Tourist Board – a digression he'd hoped to avoid – when Glynis slipped into his office and perched nervously on a chair in front of his desk.

'Am I interrupting?'

'Yes, but go on.' Rowan looked up but his fingers remained on his keyboard.

'Fancy a drink after work?'

'No.'

'We need to talk.'

'Do we?' Rowan allowed a little of his impatience to show. 'Fine. Any time you like.'

'I like tonight.'

'Any time you like after the presentation to Lavalle.'

'That's two weeks away.'

'Yep.'

'It's important.'

'No it isn't, Glynis. You don't know the meaning of the word. The only thing that's important to me right now is Lavalle. People are depending on me and I'm not going to let them down. I'd like to be selfish. There are lots of things I'd rather do than spend sixteen hours a day in this office for the next two weeks. But that's my job, and I'm going to do it to the best of my ability, even if it means everything else is excluded. And I do mean everything. It's not a matter of choice. Am I communicating?'

Glynis bit her lip.

'I've got to do my bit and you've got to do yours. Okay? Now let's both get back to work.'

Glynis thought for a moment, rose and wasted a hurt, accusing look at Rowan. He'd already focussed his attention back on the screen. She turned abruptly and left his office. Rowan sneaked a quick glance at her retreating figure and felt an immediate pang of regret. She really did have a great arse.

Three

Saturday had its rituals and it irritated Sandra that Rowan excluded himself from them. They both ran businesses but apparently he thought the house ran itself. She gathered up the dirty clothes that lay scattered around the house, the sheets off the beds and towels off the rails. She turned on the washing machine and went gathering magazines, newspapers and toys. The girls were tidying up their room as they did every Saturday morning, before helping with the vacuuming. Rochelle did the edges with the special attachment while Sarah imperiously vacuumed everything in between. When they were finished Sandra gave them their pocket money, some of which they could spend when their mother took them shopping.

Sandra wondered if she had the right to complain. After all, Rowan was off earning the money that paid the mortgage and promised a future immeasurably brighter than their present. She never used to feel irritated when he worked weekends, and puzzled over what had changed. It went beyond her bitterness and the depth of her feelings over his fling with Glynis. Clearly, Rowan enjoyed going to the office. He loved his work and he loved it most when they were generating new campaigns. The thought caused her to flinch. Did she really resent his absence simply because he was enjoying himself and she wasn't? Would she be happier if he didn't enjoy his work? One of Rowan's old jokes sprang into her mind. He'd hit her with it one night when she'd faked a headache to get out of bedroom duties. It had stung her at the time.

'Why do women close their eyes when they make love?' he'd asked her. And the answer? 'Because they can't stand to see a man enjoying himself.'

No, she decided, that wasn't why she resented his absence. Saturday was family day and he should be with his family. There were things they needed to discuss. The fact that the girls managed to spread their toys and clothes from one end of the house to the other suggested they'd outgrown it. It was a nice house, Wyong Road was a nice street and Mosman a nice suburb, but three bedrooms, lounge, dining room, and a breakfast room that doubled as the family room didn't leave them much room to grow. If they moved, where would they move to? And what about the girls' schooling? What about her business? She knew that as soon as she resolved any issue Rowan would suggest an alternative she hadn't considered, which, in turn, would only lead to more delays.

She didn't mind when Rowan worked weekends but he'd taken to working part or all of every weekend. That was the problem. The exception had become the rule. She needed the back-and-forth, needed to trade ideas, needed to discuss things. Above all, she needed not to be ignored.

'Get a move on!' she called to the girls. 'If we don't get to the shops soon we'll be late for softball.' Softball was the highlight of the week and her escape. As soon as they got back from shopping, she'd dress the girls in their mini Pittwater Pythons softball kit, pack her glove, bat, sweat band, helmet, pads and bottles of iced water and set out for the field. In her heyday she'd made second pitcher for the state, but now she was content to pitch open division District and coach her Under 19 reps. She loved the atmosphere, camaraderie and competitiveness. The fact that it also brought substantial business was almost irrelevant.

Sarah and Rochelle were the mascots and led the team on to the field between innings, and headed the line-up for the post-match handshake. They sat in the dugout with the big girls and joined in all the chants. They adored softball and wouldn't miss it for the world. Sandra heard the giggling stop, cupboard doors open and a frantic scurrying. At least the girls still made her smile.

Sandra showered and slipped on a tracksuit while she made dinner for the girls. Five-thirty came and went. Would he or wouldn't he? The litany accompanied her everywhere she went and in everything she did. She supervised the girls' bath and contrived to make it fun though, in truth, she felt more like hitting someone. Somewhere, way out west, her mother was sitting down to dinner with her latest lover, watching the sun set over the Olgas or play light games on Ayers Rock.

Six-thirty came and went. Would he or wouldn't he? She

dressed and sat down to finish her make-up. At seven o'clock she decided enough was enough and rang him. He answered almost immediately.

'I'm coming,' he said.

'It's seven o'clock.'

'I'm sorry but I couldn't leave earlier. The problem's fixed and I'm on my way. Ring Caro and tell her we'll be there at eight.'

'You ring her yourself.'

'Jesus, Sandy, I'm late enough already.'

Sandra hung up and dialled Caroline's number. 'Hi,' she said. 'He's on his way. We'll be there around eight.'

'Well done,' said Caroline.

'Sorry we're late,' said Rowan. 'My fault.' He walked straight up to Caroline, threw his arms around her and kissed her on the lips. 'Are your tits getting bigger or are my arms getting shorter?'

Caroline laughed, took his hand and led him into the lounge where her husband and another couple were sipping drinks. Sandra followed along behind. Even after thirteen years of marriage, Rowan still had the capacity to surprise her. She thought of all the threats and nagging it had taken to get him to Caroline's, how she'd practically dragged him along, and yet he made it seem as though there was nowhere else in the world he would rather be. Sandra could only shake her head at the irony as they greeted him like a homecoming hero.

Caroline, Mike and the third couple, Rhonda and Arnold, welcomed her just as enthusiastically. The fact that they had held up dinner was not an issue. People always forgave them their transgressions because she and Rowan were often the star turn, the most outspoken, the most enthusiastic debaters, the couple most capable of the grand gesture. When Rowan had become particularly sexist at one of Caroline and Mike's dinner parties, Sandra had calmly got up and dumped her bowl of pasta over his head. Everyone had sat stunned, looked on horrified until Rowan had started laughing.

'What took you so long?' he'd said. People still talked about it.

If they played charades, Sandra and Rowan always got the biggest laughs, and if it was a warm night, they were always the first to strip off and dive naked into the pool. People envied them and looked forward to an evening in their company. They thought Rowan and Sandra were the perfect couple.

Things started to go wrong after the mint crab Vietnamese rolls. Caroline was in the kitchen getting ready to serve the coral trout she'd bought from the fish market when the phone rang.

'For you, Rowan. Want to take it in the hall?'

'Babysitter?' asked Sandra.

'Someone from the office,' said Caroline. 'He was very apologetic.'

Rowan pushed his chair back with a shrug of resignation.

'Five minutes, Rowan,' warned Sandra. 'Tell whoever it is that dinner's on the table. Tell him he's got five minutes to say his piece and hang up.'

'No worries,' said Rowan. Conversation which had been

bubbling along prior to the phone call seemed to follow Rowan out of the room. Sandra smiled at Mike and shrugged helplessly, but inside she was seething. It was one thing to bring work home, another entirely to take it out to dinner. Mike and Arnold began discussing the wood-chipping of old-growth forests, an issue Sandra felt very strongly about, but she couldn't bring herself to contribute. She sat with eyes glued to the door, her resentment growing with every passing minute.

'Ta daa!' Caroline had managed to sit the coral trout upright on a bed of mint leaves and parsley. It glistened with the chilli ginger Thai sauce she'd poured over it. Sandra led the applause. 'Shall I serve now or wait for Rowan?'

'Serve now,' said Sandra. 'You could be waiting all night.'

It was another thirty minutes before Rowan joined them. 'Sorry,' he said. 'I pay three hundred thousand dollars for a creative team and they do anything except what I ask them to do. I dunno whether they're stupid or stubborn. Christ! What have I been missing? That looks fabulous.'

'You should have seen it half an hour ago,' said Sandra.

'Can I warm it up for you?' said Caroline.

'No, it's fine. I sometimes think I prefer Thai fish cold.'

'I'll nuke the bok choy for you.'

'Thanks Caroline,' said Rowan appreciatively. 'It's more than I deserve.'

'Yes,' said Sandra. 'It is.'

'Sensational!' said Rowan. As if to compensate for the fact that he was last to finish the trout, he was first to finish his crème caramel. 'Can't I convince you to open a restaurant instead of just writing about them?'

Caroline smiled. 'Restaurant kitchens are sweat shops. You work long hours, work while others play, get paid peanuts and get so sick of food that you eat badly. On the other hand, writing articles for food magazines pays badly, but it makes restaurants tax deductible and we eat like kings.'

'I can't fault your logic but your cooking is a loss to the world,' said Arnold. 'Rowan's right. The entire meal was sensational. I loved the crab rolls and the crème caramel, but the fish was special. There's something magic about reef fish.'

'We were tossing up between the coral trout and a red emperor,' said Mike. 'It turned out that the trout was more tax deductible than the red emperor.' Mike was one of those rare accountants who could laugh at himself and enjoyed aping the stereotype of his profession. In fact, he'd progressed well beyond the daily grind of balancing books and had become general manager of a company that supplied plastic components to car manufacturers. Every Ford and Holden on the road carried his company's products.

'God, what a choice,' said Rowan. 'When I finally get sick of advertising I want to make that choice a daily event.'

'What do you mean?' asked Caroline.

'It's his fantasy,' said Sandra.

'Fantasy! Then you've got to tell,' said Caroline. 'Sandy and I were just discussing fantasies the other day.'

'I don't think this one will turn you on,' said Sandra.

'So it's not sharing a bed with twins who just happen to

be nymphomaniacs?' said Caroline. 'I know, the Babe Watch brigade naked on a trampoline.'

'Let me tell it,' said Rowan. 'It's my fantasy. Advertising is people and stress and impossible deadlines. It's having to come up with ideas to order, whether you feel up to it or not. It's a constant battle of conflicting opinions, needs and egos. I've always figured that when I make the break I'll do something as far removed from advertising and pressure as possible. When we won the Fiji Tourist Board account I went there on a familiarisation tour. That's when I discovered my dream. I met a man doing the job I want to do when I finally quit.

'I'd been taken out to look at Coralhaven, that new luxury resort at the north end of the Yasawa islands. It's a sensational place, only fourteen *bures*, with a chef who trained under Roger Vergé at Moulin de Mougin, and a cocktail barman from Manhattan. One day this guy shows up in a twin-hull fly-bridge cruiser rigged out for game fishing. He took two guys fishing for the day. Guess how much? One thousand dollars US. Turns out he runs charters from all the upmarket islands. He only skippers when he feels like it, which he says is never more than three days a week, except when there's a tournament. On other days, his Fijian skipper handles the boat. He fishes when he wants, goes diving when he wants, the boat pays for itself and he has a magnificent house surrounded by palms and hibiscus on a nearby island. He lives the life of Riley. His wife, by the way, paints and designs *sulus* for rich tourists to wrap around their pampered bodies. I think about him and his lifestyle whenever the job gets too much and whenever I have trouble sleeping. I told him when they get bored we want first option on buying his business.'

'Sounds fantastic,' said Arnold.

'Paradise,' said Mike.

'Sounds boring,' said Caroline. 'That's not a fantasy. Only a man could waste good fantasies dreaming of retirement. How pathetic! You'd have done better if you'd stuck with the nymphomaniac twins. Sandy and I have much better fantasies than that.'

'Oh?' said Rowan. He looked enquiringly at Sandra. 'Let's hear them.'

'Off you go, Sandy,' said Caroline.

'Oh no you don't,' said Sandra. 'It's your fantasy, not mine.'

'Well,' said Caroline, 'I'm convinced that every white woman secretly harbours the desire to make love to a black man at least once in her lifetime.'

'I don't,' said Rhonda. 'I'm not sure any of my friends do either.'

'What about you, Sandy?' said Rowan.

'What's the matter, Rowan?' asked Mike. 'Worried you might have a bit of competition there?'

'Why would I worry? Skin colour has nothing to do with dick size or bedroom performance.'

'Codswallop!' said Caroline. 'Who on earth told you that? I've never heard of black women boasting about sleeping with white men but I've heard plenty of white women boasting about the black guy they slept with. Just mention the subject and they trip over themselves in their eagerness to brag about their exploits. They flaunt them like a trophy.'

'There's a well-researched argument,' said Rowan. 'I assume fifty per cent of the women in these discussions were black?'

'Oh don't be such a bore, Rowan. Face reality and accept the truth. White's all right, but once you try black, you never come back.' She started laughing. Mike and Arnold joined in. It wasn't often they had Rowan on the back foot.

'That is pure myth,' said Rowan doggedly. 'I've never read anything that proves black men have bigger pricks than white men nor found any evidence to suggest that they're any better in bed.'

'You obviously don't read women's magazines,' said Caroline. 'There's plenty of evidence there.'

'Bullshit,' said Rowan. 'Black guys suffer just as much from impotence, brewer's droop, premature ejaculation and the button mushroom syndrome. I might also point out that an equal percentage of them are gay.'

'Got him!' said Arnold.

'I wouldn't like Caro to sleep with a black man,' said Mike. 'I freely admit it. I don't want to spend the rest of my life in the shadow of unfavourable comparison. But it's good to see that at least one of us is capable of rising to the challenge. Do we take it you're volunteering Sandy for comparative performance testing?'

'Why would I volunteer Sandy to sleep with any other man, black or white? I'm not aware of any complaints. Besides, that's not the issue. I simply asked Sandy a question.'

'What was the question?' asked Sandra.

'Do you also fantasise about being screwed by a black man?'

'What makes you think he'd screw me? Why can't I screw him?'

'So you do?'

Sandra laughed. 'Not particularly. But I do the way Caroline tells it.'

'So tell it,' said Rhonda. 'Make me change my mind.'

'Here we go again,' said Mike wearily. 'Some husbands just have to wear a Batman cape to please their wives. I have to cover myself in cocoa and sing "Old Man River".'

'I have this dream,' said Caroline, 'where Sandy asks me to look after the clinic because she has to dash off somewhere. In comes this gorgeous hunk of a black man for a massage. Muscles on his eyelashes, you know the type. He thinks I'm Sandy and starts to strip off ... oh damn!' The phone began ringing out in the hallway.

'I'll get it,' said Mike. 'You carry on.'

'He lies down on my table,' said Sandra. 'Caroline covers him in baby oil and uses him as a slippery-dip.'

'Butt out! This is my fantasy.' Caroline took a long sip of wine to settle herself for the task. 'I watch him strip off and he lies face down on Sandy's table and ... what is it?' Mike stood in the doorway, phone in his hand.

'Sorry Caro. Rowan, it's the office again.'

'Bloody hell,' said Rowan. 'I'll make it quick.'

'You'd better,' said Sandra.

On the drive home Sandra ignored all of Rowan's attempts to apologise or engage her in conversation. She sat stonily silent, filled with the fury that had built while Caroline served coffee and cheese. Once again Rowan had made himself conspicuous by his absence. The others had tried to make excuses for him and to sympathise with her for the workload he was under. But as far as Sandra was concerned, there were no excuses for the inexcusable. The evening had ended both early and lamely.

Rowan had hoped that the food and wine might put Sandra in the mood to commence production of the son he longed for, but she ignored him. He said he might as well tie a knot in his dick. She said she wished he would.

Four

'Let's hear it,' said Rowan. He sat in the boardroom with Blake by his side, a mug of black coffee sitting in front of him and a plate of chocolate croissants he'd picked up from a French patisserie. 'Help yourselves,' he said expansively. 'The croissants are for everyone.'

'Great,' said Ken, the junior writer. 'First the script. We've got this young dude, right, thinks he's real cool, got the haircut, the clothes and the Nikes. He's in one of these places that has virtual reality games.'

'Like it,' said Rowan.

'He becomes a gridiron quarterback. Every time he gets the ball he gets sacked. We alternate between what he sees and what we see of him, and vision of him ducking and diving with the headset on. The defence slams him and when we cut back we see him flying through the air and crashing into other machines. He wrecks the joint.'

'Got it. Then what?' Rowan was smiling and impatient.

The young team read the signs as encouraging and powered on.

'He takes the headset off and he's got black eyes, his nose is bleeding, his ear's half torn off. We cut to a pack shot and a thumb flips up the top. Two Frisks roll out. The voice-over says, "New Cola Frisks. They're just like the real thing." Cut back to the kid and he's sitting on an outside step, like in front of one of those New York brownstones. He sticks a Frisk in his mouth and solemnly nods. What do you think?'

'Great,' said Rowan. 'But the ending sucks. Do something a bit cleverer with the pack shot and the voice-over. It feels like you're talking to me, not the youth market. Act your age, not mine. Make my tits go hard. Make my scrotum scrunch. You've got a licence to thrill, so use it. Do me two more executions. Well done, both of you, you've earned your croissants.'

'There's one more thing,' said Chris, Ken's partner. 'Blake gave us a copy of the brief for Lavalle's Chocolate Jam. We've got a great idea for that.'

'You're on a roll,' said Rowan.

'Jam roll,' said Blake.

'We've got a kid,' said Chris, 'seven or eight years old. Bit punky and surly with it. He's sitting at the kitchen table with his arms folded in front of him, his chin down on his arms. We hear his voice-over. It says, "My name's Fred, I don't like bread. I'd much rather eat cake instead." We cut to his mum spreading Chocolate Jam on a thick slice of fresh bread. She puts it in front of the boy. He eyes it suspiciously, sniffs it, then sinks his teeth into it. His eyebrows shoot up in delight.

We freeze frame. His voice-over continues, "My name's Fred, forget what I said." And we super "Chocolate Jam. It's what you put in your cake hole." What do you reckon?'

Rowan sat stunned, then started clapping. 'Jesus,' he said. 'It's great to be sitting where I'm sitting when a young team comes of age. I didn't know you kids were that good. It's fantastic. Done right, mums will love it. Make sure you slice the bread thick. None of that sliced white. Use real bread. Okay?'

'Okay to storyboard?' asked Blake.

'Do it.'

'Tell Rowan about your freebie.'

'Friends of ours are opening a Greek brasserie and tapas bar at Manly Beach,' said Chris. 'They asked us to help them come up with a name.'

'And?' said Rowan.

'Ouzone.'

'Perfect,' said Rowan. 'Hope you charged them.'

The phone rang and Blake answered it. 'It's somebody called Caroline for you.'

'Get it put through to my office.' Rowan stood and shook hands with his young team. 'You're doing bloody well and I'm proud of you.' If God had reached down and patted them on the back they couldn't have felt happier.

Rowan powered along to his office and whipped the handset off its cradle.

'Hi, Caro. Great night. Meant to ring earlier and apologise. Sorry I stuffed it up. What can I do for you?'

'I've just had Sandra on the phone,' said Caroline. 'She's

not happy, Rowan, and a wise man would do something about it.'

'Ah, she's just upset because of the phone calls. She'll get over it once we've done the pitch. She always does.'

'You're probably right, Rowan, and I'm not going to tell you how to handle your own wife. But it sounded serious to me, more serious than I think you realise.'

'Serious?' Doubt began to creep into his voice.

'Very serious. Like I said, I don't want to interfere, but in my experience these sorts of problems are best dealt with sooner rather than later.'

'Flowers?'

'Not enough.'

'That serious?'

'Yep,' said Caroline. 'That serious.'

'You're kidding. Dinner-at-Tetsuya's serious?' Tetsuya's was the best restaurant in town and Sandra's favourite.

'I'd say new start serious.'

'New start serious ... ?' Rowan's voice began to falter.

'I'd say so, if you want to stay married.'

'Oh Christ, Caro, have I been that bad?'

'You tell me.'

Rowan closed his eyes and sat silently, trying to absorb what he was hearing.

'Sandy told me about Glynis and your earlier flings. That's not like her. She normally keeps those sort of things pretty close to her chest. Says nothing or just skates over them. You might think she's forgiven and forgotten, Rowan, but she hasn't. Not entirely. Then you let her down when she needs you. She hardly sees you, the girls hardly see you. All these things have a habit of aggregating. She's unhappy, Rowan, intensely unhappy, and you're not doing anything to make her feel better.'

'Oh Jesus, Caro, there's no chance you're over-reacting, is there? You're not reading too much into the situation, are you?' Rowan knew the answers without Caroline having to say a thing. How bad did things have to be for Caroline to take the unprecedented step of ringing him?

'I'm not enjoying being the messenger,' she said, breaking the silence. 'I rang because I can't bear the thought of you and Sandy splitting up.'

'Splitting up!'

'That's what happens, Rowan.'

'Surely things haven't come to that?'

'The thought has been voiced.'

'Jesus,' said Rowan. 'Oh, Christ Almighty. Okay. I hear what you say. Your warning is timely and will not be ignored. You're a good friend, Caroline, to Sandy and to me. I appreciate your call. I'm really sorry I've put you in this position.'

'Good luck,' said Caroline.

Rowan slowly hung up, mind reeling. Sandra had actually talked about splitting up? He sat back in his chair and tried to take stock. He'd never regarded Caroline as a drama queen and wondered how much courage it had taken her to make the call. Paper was stacking up in his in-tray and his senior team were still wheel-spinning and getting nowhere. But Ken and Chris had excelled and Blake was quietly getting on with the presentation document, which detailed research, marketing and media strategies. Even so, there was a mountain of work he needed to do.

He picked up the phone and pressed the speed dial. It took a few minutes of wheedling to get what he wanted, then he rang home.

'Sandy?'

'What's up?' Her voice was flat, as if anticipating bad news.

'I want to try out an idea on you.'

'Is that all?'

'Wait till you hear the idea. I've rung the Flower Drum. They're holding a table for us, provided we get there by twelve. Do you and the girls fancy some yum cha? Maybe a movie afterwards?'

'Are you serious?'

'How quickly can you get dressed? I'm leaving here in five minutes. Pick you up at the gate in fifteen.'

'What about the pitch?'

'Fuck the pitch!'

'Rowan?'

'Yeah?'

'It's the best idea you've had in months.'

'Can't we get the girls forks?' asked Rowan. He waved to the waitress piloting a trolley stacked high with prawns and scallops in steamers.

'No,' said Sandra. 'If they're going to eat Chinese, they have to learn to use chopsticks.'

'Can't we get Rocky chopsticks with the rubber bands on the end?'

'Yes,' said Rochelle.

'No,' said Sandra. 'You watch her. She won't miss out on anything.'

Rowan barely had time to lift the lid off the steamed prawn dumplings before his daughters struck, stabbing the dumplings with their chopsticks. 'I guess you're right,' he said. 'You have to be quick around here.'

'Imagine them with forks,' said Sandra.

'I've got another idea,' said Rowan. 'Do you want to hear it?'

'Is it as good as your last idea?'

'Better. I think it would be nice if the girls had a little brother who they could teach to use chopsticks.'

'I've heard that idea before.'

'Not quite. I think little brothers are a serious undertaking and deserving of proper commitment on our part.'

'Still sounds awfully familiar.'

'Well, it's been hard to get any commitment at all lately, and I take the blame for that. I give too much to work and not enough to you and the girls.'

'You've noticed?'

'Yeah, I've noticed. I can't help being the man I am, Sandy. I can't help wanting to succeed. Sometimes the agency demands one hundred and ten per cent of me, all I have to give and more, and that leaves nothing for you and the girls. I admit I love it. I love the drama and the challenge, but don't ever think I don't love you more or love the girls more. If I ever have to choose, I'll choose you. Don't ever doubt it. But there are limits and I'm the first to admit that I've exceeded them. I've been a bastard to you and neglectful of the girls. It hurts me to know that I've hurt you and I'm deeply sorry.'

Rowan could see that he had Sandra's entire attention and he noted with relief the subtle unfreezing in her demeanour. 'I want to make it up to you, Sandy, I really do. I want you to have the one hundred and ten per cent for a change, and stuff the agency.' He took her hands in his. 'My idea is that, as soon as the pitch to Lavalle is over, we farm the girls out to your mum and you and I go to Coralhaven for ten days.'

'Coralhaven? In Fiji? For ten days?' The proposal was so unexpected, and so grand, it slipped right through Sandy's weakened defences. She tried to sound practical but couldn't hide the excitement in her voice. Only multi-millionaires went to Coralhaven. 'Can we afford it?'

'Of course we can't, but stuff it! You've been through the mill and you deserve the best. The best resort, the best chef and the best cocktail barman this side of Manhattan. What do you say?'

'I'm overwhelmed, stunned. How do you do it, Rowan? I'm so pissed off with you, I walk around the house at night crying. Then you just ring up, bring me here and sweep me right off my feet. How do you do it?' She tried to sound angry but she was far too excited. Her face lit up for the first time in ages. 'Do you really want to do this?'

'Absolutely. Castration couldn't make me change my mind. You deserve it, Sandy, for putting up with me and all my faults. And by the time the pitch is over, I think I'll deserve it too.'

'Ten days of sun and sea and nothing to do but enjoy it?'

'That's right. Barring sickness, accidents or coups.'

'Coups?'

'No chance. They learned their lesson last time.'

'Is there entertainment at night?'

'Not a lot, but I'll think of something.'

'Oh, I'm sure you will,' said Sandra.

'Is that a problem?'

'Not any more,' said Sandra. 'Not unless you were serious about castration.' She gave him a look that let him know he was back in favour.

Rowan breathed a profound sigh of relief and thanked God that He'd seen fit to put people like Caroline on earth to save poor sinners. It didn't matter that he had to go to Fiji on business anyway, or that Coralhaven probably wouldn't charge him or that, if they did, his tab would be written off against the Tourist Board account. The important thing was for Sandra to believe that he was prepared to spend an outrageous sum of money on her, for her to feel valued and loved, and to be pampered like she'd never been pampered before. He wanted to make certain Sandy realised that he still loved her and didn't want to lose her.

Once they were on the island, he could break the news to her that he had to fly the seaplane back into Nadi for a day to attend the Tourist Board's annual marketing meeting. He could always convince her that the idea for the holiday preceded their request for the meeting. Besides, he figured, she'd probably welcome having a day in paradise all to herself.

Their good humour lasted through lunch, the movie, takeaways from McDonald's and right through the evening. That night they broke the drought and took the first step towards making a young brother for their daughters. Rowan thought their problems were over.

Five

When Rowan worked on a new business pitch there was no middle ground. Things were either brilliant or crap, and he was either ecstatic or raging. Nobody was ever in doubt which way the pendulum had swung and this particular morning was no exception. Rowan stormed out of the boardroom and down the corridor into his office. Everyone within range found work that required their total concentration or ducked for cover.

One week to the presentation and his senior team still hadn't come up with an idea for Ginger Mint, and Ken and Chris thought it would be funny if they had a guy watching porn movies and simulating an orgasm before popping a Cola Frisk into his mouth. Just like the real thing? Porn movies? A guy jerking off? He'd probably over-reacted but Rowan wasn't sure it was even possible to over-react to such appalling taste and stupidity. That was the thing about creative people – they were either incredibly clever or incredibly dumb and you never knew from one day to the next what you were going to get.

Ken and Chris got a kick up the arse and never was it more deserved.

Rowan hardly looked up as Blake came into his office and slumped down in the chair opposite him.

'Can you believe that?' asked Rowan.

'It's not like they were joking,' said Blake.

'What the hell are we going to do? Fire them? Get freelancers?'

'Get smarter,' said Blake carefully. 'You're no use to anyone right now. You've given the studio the shits for throwing your handbag just because they misspelled Lavalle.'

'It's only the client's name, for fuck's sake!'

'It was only a literal. They probably made the mistake at two this morning because they were tired. You've given Mark and Elaine the shits and they're too scared to commit themselves to paper in case you jump down their throats. You had Elaine in tears last night. As for the secretaries, well, expect a thankyou note from Kleenex. You've done wonders for the sales of tissues.'

Rowan closed his eyes. New business pitches were always a trying time for all. Late nights, coffee and pizza, high emotions, hair-trigger tempers. This time the stakes were higher and his volatility had increased accordingly. Nothing worked for him, not yoga or alcohol. Nothing assuaged his fear of failure, of being caught on his platform with nothing to show and nothing to say. He tried to imagine the machine at the gym that measured blood pressure. He pictured the gauge dropping. One hundred and fifty, 145, 140, 130. He thought he could feel himself calming down. One-twenty.

Everything Blake said was probably true. After all, Blake had no reason to lie or mislead him. On the contrary, he was the agency's rock, his office a pool of calm in the midst of a raging sea. Rowan had hired him originally not just for his reputation as a strategist and marketing man, but because he was tall and had presence. Rowan was convinced he needed somebody on his side who could counter the impressive MDs of competing agencies, and Blake fitted the bill to perfection. Right from the start he'd added weight and substance to their presentations and clients were automatically inclined to trust him. Given the freedom denied him in more structured agencies, Blake had blossomed. He was astute and capable of extraordinary insights and, Rowan excepted, nobody was better at pulling a document together. God had given Blake many gifts but had stopped short at the one that Rowan treasured most. Blake lacked ambition. He was born to be a second-in-command, a bridesmaid and never the bride.

'What do you want me to do?' asked Rowan.

'Piss off for a while. Go down to the gym and take your anger out on the heavy bag or whatever it is you do there. Just get off our backs. We know what's required of us and we need the time to get on and do it, to make mistakes and fix them without being abused along the way. I need more concepts to put into research if the research is to have any credibility at all. I've got strategies for Jam and for Cola that aren't brilliant but are extremely sound. If I was Lavalle, before I committed millions of dollars to an off-the-wall idea, I'd first want to see how it stacked up against conventional approaches. I want to put the concepts to bed without interference. Ginger Mint is still a problem but that just needs time thrown at it. While you're beating the bag to bits, we might have a quick think tank and share thoughts. Your analysis is a good place to start.'

'Thanks for remembering to tickle my ego. You almost had me resigning on the grounds of incompetence.'

Blake laughed. 'Just piss off.'

'Thanks mate,' said Rowan.

'By the way,' said Blake, 'I'm pleased to see you're back on side with Sandy.'

'Not as pleased as me. I've even got my son back on the agenda.'

'Well done. What if you have another daughter?'

'Don't, for Christ's sake. Don't get me wrong, I love the girls, but I refuse to even think of having anything but a son this time. I want a son I can teach to play rugby and cricket. I want to see my son score the winning try or the winning runs, win the one hundred metres or the fifteen hundred. I don't care which, so long as everyone knows who his dad is. I can just see him, you know? Father and son, inseparable. He looks exactly like me, only he's as tall as you, a natural breakaway or lock. He's going to play rugby for Australia, I can feel it in my bones. He's also going to be as clever as all buggery and creative. He's going to shit on Mark and Elaine, make them look like hacks. Imagine it, Madison Partners and Son.'

'I like the partners bit.'

'It'll happen. Let's get Lavalle first. Jesus, I don't know what I want more, a son or Lavalle. Yes I do, I want a son. No bugger it, I want both. God gave us two hands so we could grab with both. Why should I choose?'

'Why indeed. Now, are you going to piss off or not?'

'Okay. I'll see you in a couple of hours. Oh, one more thing. Get Ken and Chris to consider surfing for Cola. Get some kid wired up, then cut to footage of the big waves in Hawaii. I'm talking tow-in waves, fifty-footers.'

Rowan packed his bag and strode out towards the lift. Glynis glanced up as he passed through reception.

'Just going down to the gym,' he said. 'Anyone wants me, I'll be back between seven-thirty and eight.' He stepped into the elevator.

'Break a leg,' said Glynis. She gave him the same twinkling smile that had resulted in them bonking on his sofa. Rowan couldn't resist the thought that fifteen minutes with Glynis would do more to de-stress him than two hours in the gym.

The ten-minute drive took twenty-five, courtesy of rush hour traffic. He wished he'd had the foresight to change and jog. Inside the gym, his ears were assaulted by conflicting soundtracks. Two groups of costumed figures leapt about in the frantic ballet of aerobics. Normally Rowan would join in with the advanced class but he wasn't in the mood. He needed something more physical. Just as he stripped down, the gym instructor wandered into the changing room.

'Thought it was you,' said the instructor. 'Come for a spar?'

'What?'

'You know, a couple of rounds. A few of the lads have dropped in. One of them's boring himself witless shadow boxing. Problem is, his shadow's better than he is.'

'I was going to work out on the bag.'

'Keep that for the wife,' said the instructor. 'Well, are you on?'

'Why not?' said Rowan. 'Where do you keep your protectors?'

'Come with me.'

Rowan followed the instructor out the back. One guy was working on the heavy bag, another was doing sit-ups while a third bounced a medicine ball off his six-pack stomach. The instructor pointed to a boxer still wearing his sweatshirt who danced and weaved and floored imaginary opponents.

'His name's Trevor, but he thinks his name sucks. Unless you want your teeth shaking hands with your toes, it's best to call him Tiger.' The instructor grinned. 'Light-heavy. Reckon you're up to it?'

'Size isn't everything,' said Rowan.

'Here's your kit. I'll go have a word with the kid. Do your gear up tight. I'll come back and tape your laces. Tiger's got a fight in three weeks and I don't want any cuts.'

'Sure,' said Rowan. He gave the young fighter the once-over as he kitted up. Tiger was strong and looked fast for a light-heavy, but anybody could be quick chasing shadows. He held his hands too high, which made a big target of his body. Overall, Rowan figured he'd acquit himself okay and maybe even give the kid a couple of rib-ticklers to think about. He saw

Tiger throw a disdainful look in his direction and wondered what the instructor had said.

'You gotta be jokin', mate,' said the kid. 'I'll fuckin' stand on him. He wouldn't make ninety kilos.'

'Keep thinking like that and you'll end on your arse,' said the instructor. 'He's short but he's built like a brick shit-house, got fast hands and he's quick on his feet. He can also throw a good punch. He hasn't sparred for a while so he'll be a bit rusty. Shouldn't take you long to work him out.'

'I'm scared to hit him. He looks like he might break.' The prospect brought a grin to Tiger's face.

'You might be right,' said the instructor. 'So here are the rules and I want you to stick to them. Use him to sharpen your defence. He'll work to your body and you can certainly sharpen up your defence there. Jab when you have to, if he starts getting too cocky, but hold back with the right hand, okay? Hit him, but not hard. Use him to sharpen your timing. Here he comes. Show some gratitude. You need the work, not him.'

'How're ya goin'?' said Tiger.

'Good. How about you, Trevor?' said Rowan. Tiger's eyes narrowed. The instructor rolled his.

'Me name's Tiger. Thanks for offering to spar. You little blokes are good for speed work.'

'You big blokes make a change from the heavy bag,' said Rowan. 'And you're almost as fast.' He climbed through the ropes.

'Keep your gloves up and your elbows in,' said the instructor. 'And if you get hit, just sit down. Okay?'

'You talking to me or Trevor?' said Rowan. He'd had a bad

day. Blake had kicked him out of his own office and now these two jerks were treating him like some wimpy Neville Nobody. So he was only good for speed work. Had to sit down if he got hit. He tucked his chin into his gloves and advanced. The kid saw him coming and smiled.

Tiger missed with his first jab. Missed with the second, missed with the third, missed with the fourth. He tried to quarter the ring and cut Rowan off but was too slow. He chased and Rowan danced. Tiger had had more success chasing shadows.

'I did warn you,' said the instructor and laughed. The kid glanced angrily at him. Rowan moved in, set his feet and blasted a solid right up under Tiger's ribs. The fighter's mouthguard shot out over Rowan's shoulder and bounced on the mat. Rowan stepped back. Tiger looked shocked. The instructor climbed into the ring and shoved Tiger's mouthguard back in. 'Like I said.' The instructor had a grin all over his face.

Rowan dodged as Tiger came after him, this time more purposefully. He ducked a jab, ducked another and fired his own left hand hard at Tiger's chin. The next thing he knew he was sitting on the deck.

'Right hand,' said the instructor to Tiger. 'Fuck did I tell you?'

'I tripped,' said Rowan.

'Yeah,' said the instructor. 'Over your guard. Keep them up.'

The two boxers circled each other looking for an opening. Rowan ducked more jabs as he bobbed and weaved, but the law of averages caught up with him and he took a few full in the face. They stung, but Rowan had expected them to hurt, really hurt. Rather than lose heart, he gained confidence. He led with a left, another left and ducked so that Tiger's right whistled over his head. He seized his chance and stepped in for a five-punch combination to the body. He landed three before his bum once more kissed canvas.

'You left yourself wide open for a left hook,' said the instructor sympathetically. 'Take a minute's break while I talk to Tiger.'

Rowan slumped on the stool, puffing and hurting, but also elated. He knew his body punches had hurt Tiger. He had heard the air forced out of his lungs and seen him double up involuntarily. Across the ring the instructor was showing Tiger how to use his elbows and forearms to protect his stomach. Rowan stood and wriggled his shoulders to loosen them, keen to get on with the fight. He believed he'd taken the best punches a light-heavy could throw at him and bounced back.

'One more thing,' said the instructor to Tiger. He checked to see that Rowan couldn't overhear. 'I told you to pull your punches. He's no use to you lying on the canvas. If you get clipped, it's your own bloody fault. This guy can help you prepare and I don't want you knocking him senseless.'

'Hardly fuckin' touched him,' said Tiger. 'I hit me girlfriend harder.'

'You heard me,' said the instructor. He looked towards Rowan. 'Okay, to go again?'

'I'm ready if Trevor is,' said Rowan.

'Oh Jesus,' said the instructor.

Rowan and Tiger danced around each other for another two rounds. As much as Rowan ducked and moved, Tiger's jab found its target increasingly often. It was always there in his face, a constant irritation, pushing him off balance and forcing him on the defensive. On the few occasions he managed to slip in close, his body punches failed to penetrate Tiger's protective screen of elbows. But he took good punches and stayed on his feet and was proud of the fact. When the instructor called time, he'd had enough.

'What do you reckon?' asked the instructor.

'You tell me,' said Rowan. He leaned agaitst the ropes for support.

'I reckon you done okay. What do you reckon, Tiger?'

'Yeah,' said Tiger grudgingly. 'He done good.'

'Come back for more?' asked the instructor.

'Sure. If you want.'

'We want. You've got Tiger guarding his guts. Nobody else has managed to make him do that. All we've got to do now is find some way to stop you leading with your chin.'

Rowan drove back to the agency feeling on top of the world. He'd forced a light-heavy, a pro, to change his technique. That was something. He parked under the building and momentarily considered running up the stairs. But he'd showered and changed and didn't want to get sweaty again. He stepped out of the lift expecting to hear noise and see people bustling. The lights were on but it looked like no one was home.

'Hello!' he called. An icy anger began to settle on him, the cold, implacable fury his staff feared most. Rowan felt betrayed.

'I still here.'

Rowan forced a smile. The Armenian cleaner stuck his head around the corner and smiled back.

'Everybodies on other side. Terrible mess, Mr Rowan. Garbages everywheres. Don't let me touch nothing.'

'Bunch of wankers,' said Rowan dismissively, and set off towards the creative department. He found Blake sitting in with Mark and Elaine. 'How's it going?'

'We've got some good positioning statements for Ginger Mint, one of which shows real promise. The guys are pretty keen on it but want to sleep on it overnight. Everybody else is in the studio mounting storyboards and layouts. The research company is coming in at eight.'

'Great,' said Rowan, trying to muster enthusiasm. 'Want to tell me about Ginger Mint?'

'No,' said Blake. 'Not till we're good and ready.'

'What's the deadline for concepts?'

'The research company has given us an extension on Ginger Mint. We've got until tomorrow night.'

'Concept boards or storyboards?'

'No time for storyboards.'

'Jesus Christ, Blake.'

Elaine put down her squeaker pens and left the room.

'Concept boards will be fine,' said Blake.

'I hope for your sake you're right.' Rowan turned to Mark. 'Blake's gone to the wall for you. You fuck up, he goes with you.' He turned and marched out of their office. The sickening hollow feeling crept back into his stomach. What if he was putting his trust in fools? What if their ideas sucked? What if they bombed in research? What if he had to stand up on his platform with nothing to show but a hatful of promises and a bag of hot air?

He strode into the studio. His junior team were helping the production guys mount storyboards. Glynis was pounding away on the spare Mac. The Mac operator had five dried-up coffee cups around his keyboard and an old film can filled with cigarette butts. One of the secretaries had stayed back and was binding the first stage of his report. The place crackled with activity and energy and Rowan fed on it like a drug.

'Are we going to make it?' he asked.

'We'll have most if not all,' said his production manager. 'We've got Art Rending working through the night. So long as they keep to schedule we're laughing.'

'Art Rending?' said Rowan.

'Our competitors have got the other studios tied up. Art Rending was the best I could do.'

'Okay,' said Rowan. 'Tell me what you want for dinner and I'll send out for it.'

'Laksas,' said the Mac operator. 'And a truck-load of beer.'

'Prawn laksa,' said Chris.

'Chicken laksa,' said Ken.

'Vegetable laksa,' said the secretary. 'And a Diet Coke.'

'One day,' said Rowan, 'surprise me by agreeing on something.'

'We agreed on laksas,' said the Mac operator.

Rowan turned back to his office. Muscles ached from unaccustomed exercise and his face and upper arms felt bruised and raw. But the real pain came from doubt, the nagging feeling that they were out of their league. Art Rending were second-string. Why hadn't he tied up the studios in advance? It was such an obvious move. Once again he'd handed his competitors an advantage. How far ahead of him were they? He had two creative teams, they each had half a dozen and Mac studios that left his for dead. His agency was good but they were out-gunned. He just hoped that when the day came, they wouldn't get blown out of the water for want of resources.

As he picked up the phone he heard the lift doors open, saw a flash of grape-coloured pants and a bomber jacket. Mark and Elaine, his precious senior team, leaving. Gone to contemplate their navels and their next job while everyone else worked their guts out. His temper flared. He was tempted to race out and fire them, but dialled the Malaya restaurant instead. As the phone rang he looked at the pile of paper stacked in his in-tray and tried to guess how many hours of work lay ahead of him. The restaurant answered and he placed his order with a promise of a tip if the food arrived hot. He hung up and dialled home to say goodnight to the girls. They'd already gone to bed. Sandra sounded unimpressed.

'Get you anything?'

Rowan looked up. It was two in the morning. 'What are you still doing here?'

Glynis smiled. 'Blake sent everybody home. They have to

be back on deck at six. I don't have to be here till eight so I volunteered to stay and clean up.'

'Very noble,' said Rowan.

'I'm going to pour myself a vodka and tonic,' said Glynis. 'Can I get you a scotch?'

'Good idea,' said Rowan. But it wasn't. Within thirty minutes he was back on the sofa with Glynis's legs wrapped around him, stirring the pot for all he was worth.

Six

It is one of life's paradoxes that even the most capable of women are unable to buy a swimsuit on their own. Caroline insisted Sandra buy two. They raced from shop to shop with the enthusiasm of schoolgirls preparing for their graduation formal, finally settling on a one-piece and a bikini.

'You're going to need new shorts and tops,' said Caroline.

'No,' said Sandra. 'Apparently everybody on the island is encouraged to put away their clothes, their jewellery and their watches and just wear *sulus* and sandals. According to Rowan, we buy the *sulus* there.'

'Then you're going to need sandals,' said Caroline. 'Come on.'

They found a café for lunch shortly after they'd found two pairs of sandals they could both agree on. It was the sort of café that had large palms, small tables and spindly chairs that discouraged overeating and lingering over coffee. Sandra ordered smoked salmon on a bagel, Caroline a spinach and prosciutto omelette. Both got the impression that the waitress disapproved of them for not ordering vegetarian.

'God, I envy you,' said Caroline, as they waited for their meal to arrive.

'You have no cause,' said Sandra.

'Hey, it's not me who's being whisked away to Club Melanoma for ten days. I'm not the one buying the swimsuits. That's the trouble with Mike, he just hasn't got any grand gestures left in him.'

'I didn't think Rowan had either.'

'That was guilt. God, I wish Mike would play around so we could go with you.'

'No, you don't,' said Sandra.

'No, I don't,' agreed Caroline apologetically. 'Can I take my foot out of my mouth now?'

Sandra laughed.

'I'm sure he doesn't mean to hurt you.'

'I'm sure I don't want to talk about it, not now, not with my arms full of shopping he has generously donated.'

'Even so, I envy you,' said Caroline. 'You've both got your own businesses, you've got a nice life and your two adorable girls.'

'We've been fortunate,' said Sandra cautiously. There was a touch of self-pity creeping into Caroline's voice. 'How'd you go with Mike?' she asked tentatively.

'He's still not sure.'

'Wavering?'

'Maybe. It's not just the money, it's the disappointment. Mike still hasn't got over the first try. As far as he was concerned, it was all a formality, a mechanical process. They pop in the embryo and nine months later a baby pops out. He wouldn't listen to the doctors and dismissed the odds. Failure never entered his head. He was shattered when I miscarried.'

'So were you,' said Sandra sympathetically. 'But you've had two years to get over it.'

'He says he doesn't want to put me through it again, when really he's the one who can't face it. The clinic is anxious for our decision, and I'm scared that if we let it go this time we won't get another chance.'

'What are you going to do?'

Caroline looked up at Sandra and her eyes were pleading. 'Could I ask a big favour?'

'Of course.'

'When you go to Fiji, could you leave the girls with us? Mike's crazy about them, as you know, and I thought having them live with us for ten days might make him clucky. In fact I'm sure it would. What do you think?'

'I think it's a great idea. The girls will leap at it and so will Marion. She has other things on her mind right now. The girls are baggage she can do without.'

'Oh God, Sandy, it'll be fabulous having them.'

'Just make sure they do their stretches every morning.'

'Don't worry, I'll do my stretches with them.' Caroline leaned back to allow the waitress to serve their salads. 'Am I allowed to ask how Rowan's behaved since the night of the long phone calls?'

'I suppose so. Saturday you know about. I was about to give him up for good when he rang. You've got to hand it to

Rowan, he's got a sixth sense where those sorts of things are concerned. His timing was impeccable. He was at work all day Sunday and Monday and didn't come home until four this morning, though he did ring – too late – to say goodnight to the girls.'

'At least he's trying.'

'He was up at six this morning and gone by quarter past.'

'No shower?'

'He had a shower when he got home last night. That's what woke me up.'

'He came home late and had a shower?' Caroline allowed her suspicions to show.

'I know what you're thinking, but he always showers when he's late home. Says he doesn't want to come to bed stinking of booze, cigarettes and bad ideas.'

'If Mike ever did that I'd be up first thing in the morning checking his clothes for evidence.'

'Rowan wouldn't risk it. Not now. Not for a very long while. C'mon, finish your salad, I've got to get to work.'

'Is that triathlete you told me about coming in?'

'Yes, and I'll be treating his groin for a good half an hour.'

'Oh God, I dream about things like that. I have to keep my hands outside the blankets.'

'It has no effect on me,' said Sandra.

'Really?'

'Really.'

'God, that is a worry,' said Caroline. She laughed but Sandra struggled to crack a smile.

Sandra worked through the afternoon, mainly on necks and backs, for which she was gaining something of a reputation. People continually complained that there seemed to be no specific cause for the pain in their backs and necks, that they just woke up one day feeling sore. But Sandra knew she was treating the effect of years without stretching or exercising. Her solution was uncomplicated. First treat the symptoms, then treat the cause. Her patients tended to begin their set exercises cautiously, becoming zealots when the pain went away and stayed away. They sent their friends and clamoured for her to run night exercise classes, but Sandra resisted. There wasn't enough time in her day as it was.

The schoolkids with tennis elbow, twisted ankles and torn muscles dribbled in from three o'clock on. It was five before she got around to treating her triathlete. She left him alone to change and returned to find him in his briefs, lying flat on his back on the table. What would Caroline give for this? she wondered.

'Okay, let's see how much mobility you've got.' She lifted his leg and bent it outwards. 'Tell me when it hurts.'

'No worries. After you've done the ultrasound, would you have time to give my back muscles a bit of a rub as well?'

'I'll make time.' Sandra concentrated on her work but part of her couldn't help wondering why he didn't turn her on – not while she was treating him, but afterwards, when she was alone in bed. Caroline was right. On the nights when Rowan didn't come home it would be so easy to summon up an image of the athlete, his hard body and enviable equipment, and indulge in flights of erotic fantasy. But she never did. She went to bed thinking of jobs she still had to do, people she had to ring and speculating on what time Rowan would get home. It all seemed so predictable, dull and mundane. She couldn't help wondering if this was the pattern for the rest of her life.

Sandra didn't see much of Rowan at the best of times but as the week went by she hardly saw him at all. He came home in the small hours of the morning, rose at six and was gone by half past. Some days he rang, others he forgot. On Friday night he surprised her by arriving home at seven. She opened a bottle of red to celebrate and made him dinner, but he scarcely touched either. He was in bed by eight-thirty and slept right through till six. As far as Sandra was concerned, she was no better off than if he'd stayed out all night.

Later that morning she baked some chocolate chip cookies. As soon as softball had finished, she raced home, showered, bathed the girls and drove them to the agency to see their father. There was nobody manning reception so she walked straight around to Rowan's office. The sight of him left her speechless. His skin was grey and his hair tousled, like he'd forgotten to comb it after his shower. Blake, sitting opposite him, looked no better. Both of their faces lit up as the girls charged into the room.

'Hey!' said Rowan. Sarah and Rochelle leapt at him, screaming for attention.

'Hi Sandra,' said Blake. He stood and hugged her. 'I don't know what brought you here but thanks for coming. We need a reality check.'

'I've brought some choc chip cookies,' said Sandra.

'Wonderful! The troops will love you.'

'I figured coming here was the only way the girls would get to see their father until the presentation's over. How's it going?'

'Great, but it needs to be sensational.' He nodded towards Rowan who was listening to an entire week of his daughters' adventures, and loving it. 'He's raised the bar but people are rising to it. Win, lose or draw, we'll have a lot to be proud of.'

'Wrong. Rowan will never be proud of second. You should know that.'

'We've got some of the stuff up on the wall in the boardroom. Would you like to see it?'

'I'd love to.'

'We come too,' shouted Rochelle.

'Your father can bring you,' said Sandra. She walked past frantic secretaries who barely glanced up from their keyboards, entered the boardroom and stopped stone dead, stunned by the sheer volume of work. 'My God, you've done all this in what, two weeks?'

'That's not all of it,' said Blake. 'Like I said, Rowan's raised the bar.'

Sarah and Rochelle barrelled into the boardroom.

'Don't touch anything,' warned Rowan.

The girls stopped and looked around. The room was formal and solemn feeling. They didn't like it at all. It was nowhere near as much fun as the finished art studio where they could draw and play video games. They turned and took off down the corridor.

'Want me to go after them?' asked Sandra.

'No need. There are twenty people out there who'd love a diversion. Well, what do you think?'

'Love this,' she said, and walked over to get a better look at the Chocolate Jam poster. 'Who thought of the line?'

'Ken and Chris,' said Blake.

'Cute. If it gets kids eating bread, mums all over Australia will love you for it.'

Rowan put his arm around Sandra and gave her a kiss. 'Do you know what I love about you, Sandy? You're such a fine judge of advertising. Come and I'll show you the rest.' He led her down the corridor to the studio, which was crowded with staff mounting layouts, scanning and printing pictures. The girls were in their element, being fussed over and indulged. Everyone smiled when Sandra walked in, except Glynis, who had Rochelle on her knee. She looked Sandra up and down dismissively, was brazen enough to make eye contact.

Sandra slipped her arm around Rowan and gazed enthusiastically at the work piled up against every available inch of wall. 'I've got a good feeling about this,' she said. 'It's all fabulous.' But what she said and what she was thinking were two different things entirely. Glynis was still around and openly practising being Rochelle's mother. She was outraged and wanted to scream at the gold-digging, opportunistic slut, tell her to find her own husband and have her own daughters.

'C'mon,' said Rowan. 'We can't hold up the works. I'll walk you to the lift.'

'Bye!' chorused the girls. Glynis gave Rochelle a farewell kiss and hug.

'You look dreadful, Rowan,' said Sandra softly. 'Come home with us. I'll run you a bath and give you a full massage.'

'Body massage?' asked Rowan.

'Sure you're up to it? You need another good night's sleep or you're simply not going to perform on Tuesday. People who are exhausted and sleep-deprived say stupid things. Is that what you want?'

'I can't leave Blake. He's been working as hard as me.'

'Send him home as well.'

'Okay,' said Rowan wearily. 'I think we're ahead of the game at last. How about I come home in an hour?'

'Deal,' said Sandra. 'Oh, one more thing. You told me you were going to fire that stupid girl, Glynis. She's not Rocky's mum and never will be. Tell the little bitch she failed the audition and send her on her way.' She stepped into the elevator and turned to face Rowan, lips thin and jaw set. There was just time for her to see a chastened nod of agreement as the doors closed. She smiled grimly.

True to his word, Rowan arrived home an hour after Sandra. He hopped straight into a hot bath and didn't try to stop the girls when they wanted to shampoo his hair. The hot water soaked away tension and eased tired muscles. Once the girls had played themselves out and gone to get ready for bed, he had to fight to stay awake. He couldn't remember when he'd last soaked in a bath without reading a magazine or listening to the radio. Inactivity did not normally come easily. When thoughts of work crept into his head, he closed his eyes and concentrated on the blood pressure monitor at the gym, and the falling red line. One hundred and thirty, one-twenty-five, one-twenty. His eyelids closed and stayed there. Only when he felt Sandy's hand on his chest did he open his eyes.

'Dinner is ready,' she said. 'Lamb fillets on Chinese noodles.' She glanced at his limp penis, barely visible beneath the cloudy water. 'I think the poor thing's drowned. Pity, I've been off the pill all week.'

Rowan dragged himself out of the bath and into the towel Sandra held open for him. It felt really good to be home.

Seven

Rowan strode the platform, a man as much in command of his audience as Sir Laurence Olivier in his heyday, and as certain of himself as Chrysler's Lee Iacocca. He felt ten feet tall. He kept the agency introduction short, cut the showreel down to their five best spots and only displayed press ads that had won awards. He figured that a client as sharp as Lavalle would have done their homework on him, and he didn't want to waste valuable time showing them stuff they'd already seen. He looked into the eyes of each of Lavalle's three representatives and gave them equal attention. It was tempting to concentrate on the senior man, the International Marketing Director who'd flown in from Paris for the presentation, but Rowan knew better than to alienate the other two. For a start, he didn't know who would make the final decision, whether the man from Paris would impose his decision on the local team, or whether they each had an equal vote. He'd arranged a tag-team tactic, with Blake presenting marketing and research analysis, himself presenting strategy and creative, and Blake coming back with the results of concept testing. He was just getting ready to flick to Blake when the Marketing Director cut in.

'Before you start addressing our business, what is the most successful advertisement your agency has produced?'

'We're just about to get to it,' said Rowan without batting an eyelid. 'It's one of yours, so I'm afraid you'll have to be patient.'

All three clients laughed immediately. So they like cheek, thought Rowan. He decided to ride the wave, discard the rest of his preamble and hand over to Blake. Momentum was everything in presentations. He settled back to watch Blake and covertly assess the reaction of the three men opposite him. He could tell immediately that they liked Blake, and more than that, he could see they liked his brain. They fired questions at him, not to test or throw him off his rhythm, but out of genuine interest. Blake departed from the script and fielded their questions confidently and enthusiastically, as if he'd suddenly discovered like minds. Rowan watched in awe. He was the showman and Blake the rock, but on this day the rock had become as showy as a diamond.

The client reacted enthusiastically and appreciatively to Chocolate Jam and they loved Cola. The final hurdle was Ginger Mint. Blake set the scene and Rowan reviewed strategies. But when it came time to present the creative execution he stopped, stepped down from his platform and sat. Three faces turned to him, clearly taken aback.

'I'm not going to tell you what the execution is,' said Rowan. 'You've heard enough from me. Mark and Elaine came up with this idea and when they told me what it was they nearly blew my socks off. You asked me earlier what is the most successful advertising this agency has ever produced. Well, gentlemen, this is it. I'm going to let the two people who created the ads tell you about them.'

Mark and Elaine, who'd sat silently throughout the presentation, looked at each other nervously. Mark had a rough head and even rougher accent but he had talent and passion. Elaine was all class, although she did her best to hide it, a product of private schools and Enmore Tech. She managed to dress down and conservatively at the same time, and hadn't lost her born-of-privilege imperiousness, the look that suggested everybody was somehow beneath her or, at the very least, had dog shit on their shoe.

His senior team rose unwillingly. Rowan sensed a quickening of interest from the clients. He'd guessed that a client as sophisticated as Lavalle would want to have direct access to creative people and want to feel involved in the creative process. Mark and Elaine weren't great presenters, but he figured he'd bought them a little leeway with his introduction. They were passionate about their ideas, and passion translated easily into conviction.

'We have three things going for us,' said Mark. He did his best to sound positive and aggressive but there was a nervous quaver in his voice. 'It's a different taste, it's an intense taste and it's a refreshing taste.'

Rowan began to relax. Mark had sat through all the rehearsals, had heard Rowan's pitch and was simply parroting it. The clients were listening attentively. Elaine chipped in on cue, explaining the difficulties of creating good advertising without a solid base to build on, and how Blake had opened the door for them with his positioning line. For the first time, Rowan noticed that Elaine wasn't wearing a bra, and that her top was quite low cut. He wanted to burst out laughing. Elaine always wore bras that looked like they'd been cast in metal and she never wore low-cut tops. Her zeppelin breasts embarrassed her and, normally, she was Miss Uptight personified. One way or the other, she was determined that Lavalle would like their idea. He looked to see if the client had noticed. They had. Their eyes followed her as she bent over to hit the play button on the VCR.

Berlin's hit song, 'Take My Breath Away', suddenly boomed around the boardroom from quad speakers. Images flashed up onto the screen just long enough to be recognised, just long enough to shock or amuse. There were cuts of world leaders artfully edited to make it appear they were gasping for breath – Ronald Reagan after one of his stumbles, George Bush puking at the banquet in China, Bob Hawke stopping a cricket ball with his head – close-ups of marathon runners collapsing at the finishing line, high divers slamming into the water, a motorbike racer smashing into a fence, a nuclear explosion, high chimneys toppling, aircraft colliding in mid-air, clips from *Funniest Home Videos* of men being hit in the balls, a bullfighter copping a horn in the groin, people in North Sulawesi eating chilli rat, Frenchmen eating snails, people eating snakes, lizards and bêche-de-mer. Intercut throughout were extreme close-ups of people popping Ginger Mints into their mouths, and all of it happening to Berlin's powerhouse sound. The commercial was engaging and its message seductive. Frisks tasted great, cleaned your breath and, above all, they were cooler than Lenny DiCaprio.

'Take my breath away.' That's what the song said, that's what the images did, and they offered no respite. Mark and Elaine had wanted to cut the footage to sixty seconds but Rowan had insisted they cut to the full three and a half minutes. He and Blake had argued passionately about it and Rowan had refused to buckle. By the time the clip had finished the client was stunned. And breathless.

'Of course we don't suggest you run the full song,' said Rowan, timing his entry. 'Just two minutes. In prime time.'

'Two minutes?' said the advertising manager. He had to look around to find Rowan because Rowan was back on his platform, poised like a big cat ready to pounce.

'Do you want to kick arse or just tickle it?' snapped Rowan. 'Gentlemen, this agency is not in the tickling business.'

The man from Paris smiled. 'Your point is well taken. Indeed, you've made your point well throughout the entire presentation and constructed solid arguments. I would like to congratulate you and your agency on the quality of your work and your creative. I also admire your attitude and commitment.'

But, thought Rowan.

'I'll be frank with you. Your agency was our third choice. The first two were obvious. We put you on the list for the promise contained in the work you have done for your other clients – promise more so than the actual delivery.'

'I appreciate your comments,' said Rowan, though he

didn't altogether. The rider had stung. But he was on his feet, on his platform, in his territory and they looked up to him. He felt powerful, dominating, tall. Besides, he had a few points to make himself.

'What you say is obviously true. We're well aware we came into this pitch in third place, but I'd like you to look at that from our perspective. You want a new agency, we want fame, success, adulation, glory, envy, and for that we need first-rank clients. We're hungry and we're growing. We don't want to be our competitors, we want to beat them. We need you to get there and the ride won't do you any harm at all. Your business would give us the opportunity to excel, give us visibility and stature. Our competitors think they've got that already and maybe they have. They can afford not to win your business. We can't. In terms of commitment, they can't get close to us because they don't have as much to gain, or as much to lose. We need you, they don't. We need you, they merely want you. They are complacent.' Rowan spat the last word, managing to make complacent sound like a particularly nasty venereal disease.

'There is the question of resources,' said Lavalle's Australian MD.

'People are resources and they're the best resources.' Rowan was on familiar territory. He no longer stood still but prowled, so certain of his territory that he never once took his eyes off the three men from Lavalle. 'This agency is not a one-man band. You've seen that today. If you'd come in here two days ago you would have seen our receptionist working on the Mac in the studio; you would have seen Mark and Elaine mounting layouts and doing the work of studio juniors; you would have seen secretaries walking into my office with observations about what their friends think of your products; you would have seen twenty-three people working as one, with one objective. That did not happen at our competitors' studios. When our studio gets overloaded we contract out. When it's consistently overloaded we'll expand it, but not until then. We contract out media because the best media people work for the media consultancies. We run a lean and hungry TV department of one co-ordinator because we believe the best producers are the people who thought of the idea in the first place. When my creative teams work twelve hours a day every day, I'll hire another team, and I already know who I want to hire. The day you appoint us, we'll hire another team and a number two for Blake. We've met with him on three occasions already and he's made it plain he wants to work here. Resources aren't a problem.'

'Your competitors showed finished commercials. They had the same lead time as you. What do you say to that?'

Finished commercials? Rowan was gobsmacked but didn't let on and didn't let up. 'I'm sorry, I didn't realise you had trouble understanding what we showed you today.'

'Not at all,' cut in the man from Paris. His associates nodded agreement. 'You communicated your ideas well. We understood perfectly.'

'Then who needs finished commercials?' said Rowan. 'Sounds to me like the other agencies underestimated your ability to comprehend concepts. I'm surprised you didn't find that patronising.'

'Perhaps,' said the Frenchman, but it was clear he liked the answer. 'You've made things very difficult for us and for that I must thank you again and congratulate you. All three agencies have shown excellent work and each of you has come up with at least one stand-out idea. What are your terms?'

God help us, thought Rowan, if the decision comes down to percentages. There was no way he could fight his competitors on percentages. His agency was too small. Every client had to pay its way. 'Our terms are in the document, but I'll tell you now so you're under no illusions. We charge like wounded bulls.'

The clients smiled. They were developing a taste for Rowan's brand of cheek.

'We've put into the document the remuneration we need to consistently produce work of the standard you saw today. Quality costs. Perhaps we're not the most expensive agency in town, but it's certainly our ambition to become it. Cost is one issue, value is another. We like to think we give value. We'd welcome your input on our fees. We'd be happy to discuss them with you and if necessary negotiate, but you only get one shot at it.'

'What do you mean?' asked the advertising manager.

'Simply this. Our terms aren't figures we've plucked out of the air. We've thought about them very carefully. You can find agencies prepared to work for half what we charge but their work isn't half as good. We know exactly what it costs us to do business and what we need to earn. We run transparent accounts. Any time you want to check on us, you're free to walk in unannounced with auditors. We have a cost of doing business, below which it ceases to be feasible or worth our while. I won't have one client propped up by other clients. If we have differences that can't be resolved in one meeting, further talks are a waste of time.'

'I agree,' said the man from Paris. He rose and extended his hand to Rowan. 'Once again, congratulations. You've given us a lot to think about. We'll be back in touch in a few days. Thank you once more.'

'Our pleasure and privilege,' said Rowan. 'Thanks for the opportunity to present.' The meeting concluded in a round of handshakes, kisses from Elaine – who was really excelling herself in her commitment – and generous compliments, but Rowan gleaned no clue as to which way Lavalle would jump. All three agencies had at least one stand-out idea, so where did that leave him? He saw his guests to the door before slumping back in his chair as if someone had pulled his plug.

'That was fantastic,' said Mark. 'What do you reckon?'

'We've one chance in three,' said Rowan. 'Realistically, the objective of the presentation today was to stay in the game. After the best presentation we've ever done, after the best work we've ever done, after Elaine selflessly sacrificed her modesty to the cause, all we can do is stand up and say with pride, "Hey everybody, look at us. We're still in the game!" Now, somebody pour me a beer.'

The rest of the agency drifted into the boardroom to find out how the presentation had gone and bathe in the afterglow. Normally Rowan would lead the celebrations and take everybody down to Chinatown for dinner, but instead he sat quietly and merely watched proceedings. He wasn't sure how he should feel. For all his brave face and speech about remaining in the game, he felt he should've got at least one of the clients to openly commit to their work. Yet the presentation had gone brilliantly, the work was on target and had clearly rung Lavalle's chimes. What had he overlooked? What had the other agencies done that he hadn't? Were the finished commercials the tip of the iceberg? What else had they done?

He thought of his competitors' advantages in creative teams, Mac studios and TV production and wondered if the shoestring resources of his agency hadn't stuck out like a secondhand gown at the ball. Was he just a little guy, out of his league and kidding himself, or were Lavalle just good poker players? After all the work everybody had put in, he had a nagging feeling that he'd failed them somewhere along the line.

Glynis sidled into the chair alongside him and used the excuse of congratulating him to kiss him on the cheek. Rowan barely acknowledged her, grabbed at his beer and swallowed savagely so that the icy liquid stung his throat. A bit of Chinese, a lot of wine, a couple of scotches afterwards and a good screw to conclude – there was the tried and true formula for getting rid of the post-presentation blues. Despite everything, he couldn't help smiling when Elaine wandered back into the boardroom. She'd reverted to iron maiden and put her bra back on. Rowan wondered if she hadn't provided the lead he should follow. He left Glynis sitting next to an empty seat and powered down the corridor to Blake's office. Blake was on the phone to his wife, telling her how things had gone. He was still riding his high. Rowan hesitated, uncertain how to proceed. There was a party brewing and down at the gym there were pro boxers hoping he'd show for a spar. Glynis wanted to wrap her long legs around him and screw him till there was no more paste left in the tube. He picked up his phone and hit speed dial.

'G'day,' he said. 'Remember me? Open a nice bottle of red. I'm coming home.'

Eight

Three days later Sandra entered the realm of the unlimited expense account. Rowan had booked business, but Air Pacific had upgraded them to first, as he thought they might. Air Pacific were also represented on the Tourist Board and were, indirectly, a client. Sandra wasn't aware of this and thought it was all part of the red carpet treatment Rowan was providing. He didn't disabuse her of the notion.

'It's all preparation for mingling with millionaires,' he said. 'You'd better get used to it.'

'Oh, I can,' said Sandra. She accepted the glass of French champagne handed to her on boarding and allowed the flight attendant to refill it. She had a glass of Montrachet with the canapés and lobster salad, an Haut-Brion with her rack of lamb, and a Chateau d'Yquem with dessert. Another three firsts for her. She scolded Rowan for making do with a single glass of Montrachet and tumblers of iced water.

'I don't drink on planes,' he said.

'You may be on a plane,' said Sandra, 'but you're also on holiday so you'd better get used to that. You've got nothing to do and nothing to worry about for the next ten days.'

Rowan smiled stiffly. When the wine began to take effect, Rowan suggested Sandra recline her seat, extend the leg rest and grab forty winks. A snooze in the middle of the day was another luxury Sandra seized upon. Rowan waited until she'd settled and her breathing had become regular before he dared to open his briefcase. Two and half hours into his holiday and he was already wondering whether he'd made a cataclysmic mistake.

Lavalle still hadn't contacted them and had met his polite enquiries with a stock response. The next step had not yet been determined, they'd said. From this Rowan had concluded there would be a next step. Maybe one agency eliminated and another assignment to determine a winner. Maybe they'd want them to run through the presentation again, or come in and interrogate them on the detail or hassle over finances. Rowan didn't know what they'd do but knew he ought to be at the helm of his agency when they did it. The ten days stretched ahead of him like a prison sentence.

He opened a Fiji Tourist Board research analysis to refresh his memory prior to the annual marketing meeting. That was another bridge he had to cross, and he couldn't help wondering how Sandra would respond when she found out about it. In hindsight, he regretted not telling her prior to their departure. She was so up and excited he was sure she would have just accepted that he'd be gone for a day and dismiss it. He only wished he'd been as sure then as he was now. Sandra stirred and he slipped his folders back into his briefcase. He couldn't concentrate anyway. He caught the flight attendant's attention and requested a scotch. He was on holiday after all, an enforced holiday maybe, but still on holiday.

On landing, they were met by representatives of Air Pacific who escorted them through immigration and cleared their bags. Sandra looked at the long queues forming behind her and squeezed Rowan's hand. Being privileged was fun and she was loving every second of it. It was her intention to reward Rowan with some early practice on the son he wanted the instant they were alone. She momentarily regretted her selfishness in bringing the packets of condoms.

Their escorts took them down a long corridor that Sandra assumed led to their transport. She was unprepared when they were ushered into an office.

'Welcome to Fiji!'

Before her stood the largest human being she'd ever seen, wearing a smile you could park cars in. When he shook hands with Rowan, she expected to see her husband's feet leave the floor and his head hit the ceiling.

'You've lost weight, Tiny,' said Rowan, and the big man roared with laughter, his white teeth brilliant against his dark skin. 'Sandra, I'd like you to meet a special friend of mine, Timocy Nadruku.'

Sandra placed her hand inside his giant fist and to her surprise he kissed it.

'Welcome to Fiji, Mrs Madison. I hope you enjoy your stay. If you don't, tell me who is responsible and I'll have them cooked.' He roared again.

'Thank you, and please call me Sandra.'

'Please call me Tiny,' said the big man. He turned to Rowan. 'My driver is waiting to take you to the seaplane. I've taken the liberty of putting together a folder with the agenda and latest statistics for you to look at prior to Friday's meeting.' He picked up a thick manila folder from his desk and handed it to Rowan.

'Ta,' said Rowan. 'Any surprises?'

Any surprises? thought Sandra. Her hands clenched involuntarily.

'No,' said Tiny. 'Japanese numbers are slightly down but Australia and New Zealand are holding.' Behind him, a Japan Airlines 747 lumbered down the runway, the roar of its engines muted by double glazing. 'Come along now, we don't want anyone else flying off in your seaplane.' He led the way down the corridor.

'You bastard,' Sandra whispered furiously. 'Tell me about Friday.'

'Later,' said Rowan.

'Well?' said Sandra.

Rowan watched the amphibious seaplane taxiing towards the slipway. He knew the pilot would rev the plane's single motor to drag it free of the water and up the steep ramp. If he played his cards right, he could keep the conversation mercifully short. The engine began to roar. Sandra's lips had drawn back to a thin line, a sure sign that she was not amused. 'Tiny sprung it on me when I told him we were coming to Coralhaven. It's no big deal. It's courtesy to attend and this way the agency can pick up some of the cost of the holiday.'

'How long have you known?'

'A couple of days, but it wasn't confirmed. It's no big deal, I'll only be gone a day. I'll have breakfast with you and be home for dinner.'

'Is that it? One day, nothing else?' Sandra's eyes bored into him, defying him to tell a lie.

He hedged instead. 'They want me for a day.' He thought if he mentioned Lavalle right then she might just turn around and go home. The seaplane dragged itself clear of the water and the pilot gave the throttle a final squirt to make sure everyone within ten kilometres was aware of his arrival. Rowan decided it was time to accent the positive. 'Look on the bright side,' he shouted. 'You get a day all to yourself to do whatever you like. Doesn't sound too bad to me.'

But Sandra was no longer listening. A horrible thought had just occurred to her, as Rowan had anticipated. She stood transfixed, immobile as a mouse before a cobra. It had just dawned on her that the tiny seaplane was their plane.

'We're flying this to Coralhaven?' she asked.

'That's what planes do,' said Rowan. 'Fly.'

'It's tiny.'

'Yes,' said Rowan. 'I'll give you that.' He noticed that Sandra's lips had drawn even thinner and her skin had paled. 'I did warn you to go easy on the champagne.' He glanced towards the seaplane. 'I hope you packed light.'

The sea beneath them sparkled in the late afternoon sun, turned dark indigo away in the deep and turquoise where reefs and atolls thrust upwards. Sandra was too apprehensive to be impressed. Over the pilot's shoulder she could see a dark spot on the horizon, which she assumed was Coralhaven. She silently urged the plane on, deafened by the bludgeoning waves of noise from the overworked engine, sickened by the buffeting from thermals, and stunned by the suddenness of the transition from first class to aerial cattle truck. When the plane began its descent, she prayed that it was intentional. When it ran up onto the white sand beach and almost into the coconut palms, she nearly cried with relief. When the pilot turned off the engine, she wanted to hug him. She stepped out of the plane, head thumping, totally disoriented, and shaking, to be greeted by two guitars, a ukelele and the welcoming voices of the assembled staff harmonised in song. She looked about her. People had no right to be so happy nor the island so tranquil so soon after the plane. She needed time to adjust. A young girl waited to place hibiscus leis around their necks. Behind the staff, guests curious to see the new arrivals smiled sympathetically, themselves recent passengers. Sandra smiled back. She hadn't expected millionaires to be quite as friendly. She bent forward so the young girl could place the lei around her neck.

'*Bula!*' cried the staff.

'Thank you,' said Sandra.

'*Bula!*' said Rowan. '*Vinaka vuka levu.*' He stepped forward, shook the manager's hand and introduced Sandra.

'Leave your things where they are,' said the manager. 'The boys will take care of them. I'll take you straight to your *bure* so you can freshen up before dinner.'

'Lovely,' said Sandra. Freshening up sounded fine but collapsing was more what she had in mind.

The manager showed them their bathroom, how to work the spa in their private little garden, and left them to it. Sandra lay down on the enormous bed. She heard the boys arrive with their bags and Rowan joking with them. Her head swam with wine and new experiences. When she opened her eyes she saw a massive fan revolving silently above her bed. Coconut palm beams towered above it, supporting a thatched roof. Intricately woven cane panels lined the walls between hand-hewn support beams. Beautiful rugs lay scattered over darkly polished timbbers. Quilted armchairs didn't so much invite as demand people curl up in them. A coffee table supported a bowl crammed with papaya, pineapple and limes. Red, white and pink hibiscus peeped into every window and framed their garden courtyard and spa. Fingers of sunlight reached through palm trees, making patterns on the floor and on her bed. She'd landed in paradise but somehow it still seemed a touch beyond her grasp.

'Sit up,' said Rowan.

'What's that?' said Sandra.

'A complimentary cocktail,' said Rowan. 'A fluffy duck, to be precise, made to a formula designed to ensure that every guest forgets that another world exists beyond the sanctuary of this island.'

Sandra took a sip, and then another. 'Works for me,' she said, then looked hard at Rowan. 'But will it work for you?'

The first faxes were brought to them as they took their place at the breakfast table. Rowan thanked the young woman who brought them and placed them face-down on the table.

'For goodness sake,' said Sandra. 'Something else you forgot to tell me about?'

'Like the condoms,' said Rowan.

Sandra had explained how, if she conceived during their holiday, there was a strong chance that the baby would be born during Christmas week, or even on Christmas Day. All she wanted was for Rowan to allow a month's grace so that they could have a proper Christmas together with the girls. The condoms were necessary, she'd argued, because she'd just come off the pill and didn't want to go back on again or use a 'morning after' pill. Rowan had not been impressed with the condoms, but that hadn't prevented him from test-driving two of them.

'You're not being fair,' said Sandra, trying hard to keep her voice even and her anger in check. 'I want to know now, Rowan, if this is a holiday or your Fijian office.'

'This is reality, Sandy,' said Rowan. 'I don't have a business where I can just close the door and walk away. I wish I did, but I don't. I have a small business in which I am the linchpin. I expect the office will try to contact me every single day we're here. I might sort out their queries in half an hour, but if Lavalle ring with a list of demands, it might take two hours out of my day. That's how it is, and there's not a bloody thing I can do about it.'

'Our day,' corrected Sandra.

'Okay, our day,' agreed Rowan.

'No more than two hours?'

'Two hours max.'

'Promise?'

'I promise.'

'And you'll do your utmost to ensure it doesn't spoil our holiday?'

'Scout's honour.'

'Then you may as well get on with it,' said Sandy. She nodded towards the sheaf of faxes.

'Bugger them,' said Rowan. 'They can wait till I've had breakfast. And maybe till after I've had a swim.'

'Now you're thinking,' said Sandra.

'Have you tried the papaya with lime and ginger?'

'Nice?'

'Like Chateau d'Yquem is nice.'

Sandra laughed and Rowan joined in. Sandra might have forgotten that Fiji was two hours ahead of Sydney but Rowan hadn't. Leaving the faxes meant nothing. His office wouldn't be open for another hour.

'I thought eggs Benedict to follow.'

'Whatever you say,' said Sandy. 'And Rowan? Thank you for bringing me here.'

'I'm sorry about the faxes,' said Rowan. 'And I'm sorry about the meeting in Nadi. I really am.'

'Forget it,' said Sandra. 'So long as you don't forget why we're here.'

Rowan took her hand. 'Any chance you could forget the condoms?'

'Not a chance,' said Sandra.

By mid-afternoon they'd swum out to a nearby reef and snorkelled for half an hour, paddled around the island in a two-person kayak, and met a couple from California with whom they'd arranged to join for pre-dinner drinks. They returned to their *bure*, flopped down on their bed and managed to further deplete their stock of condoms before dozing off. When Sandra awoke, Rowan was reading a report on Fijian tourism. She decided not to make an issue of it. Some people read books, others magazines. What difference did it make to her if Rowan chose to read reports? The sun filtered through the coconut palms and rested warmly and indolently on her back. Like a cat on a windowsill, she stretched and slipped blissfully back to sleep.

The following morning Sandra lay on the beach, trying to adjust to the fact that eight and a half days of paradise stretched ahead of her, and there was absolutely no urgency for her to do anything. The beach would still be there tomorrow, and the next day and so on. So would the coral and the exquisitely coloured fish. If she wanted to go sailing, there were catamarans and sailboards. If they wanted to go fishing or snorkelling on an outer reef, somebody would always take them. There was nothing for her to do but relax and indulge herself in whatever took her fancy. One hundred metres out from shore, Rowan was duck-diving on fish and taking photos with a disposable underwater camera. Up by the breakwater, the Californian couple waved lazily to her, content in the shade of overhanging palms. Down the beach, two young Fijian men were bringing a water-logged outrigger canoe into the shallows where another two of their friends waited to help them pull it ashore. Attracted by their laughter, she turned to watch.

The men wore floral *sulus*, which they'd tucked up like loin cloths. Clearly they'd done it so that the wet *sulus* wouldn't impede their movements, but it had the effect of highlighting their magnificent physiques, their axe-handle shoulders, washboard stomachs and powerful thighs. Something long dormant stirred within Sandra and she felt a quickening of interest. The two men in the canoe threw down their paddles and joined their friends in the shallows. One man tripped and fell face first into the water. Their laughter was so spontaneous and full of joy, Sandra couldn't resist smiling. Water glistened off black skin as the four men hauled the canoe up onto dry sand, their muscles so hard and clearly defined it was as though Michelangelo had lent a hand in shaping them. Sandra felt her nipples harden and her stomach tense.

'Allellujah,' she whispered triumphantly. Caroline would be pleased. It hadn't taken long, just two days of absolute luxury and indolence, two days away from tensions, suspicions and daily routine. She glanced down at her bikini top and was relieved to discover her interest hadn't become too obvious. There was a splash out deep and she heard her name called. Rowan was yelling something about a painted lobster. She smiled and waved to humour him. She had other fish to fry. The Fijians were doubled over, scooping water out of the canoe. What would they think, she wondered, if she strolled over and offered to help? A tremor raced through her body, which she took as encouragement. She decided to find out.

'Hi,' she said.

The Fijians turned towards her. 'Helloo,' they said softly, dragging out the o. Despite their size, the Fijians seemed to have an almost childlike shyness, which Sandra found endearing.

'Mind if I watch?'

They smiled. They all had perfect teeth except for one who was the eldest, tallest and, in tough competition, also the most handsome. Sandra thought he was the best-looking man she'd ever seen, but couldn't help noticing that his upper two front teeth were missing. Their absence didn't disfigure so much as add character.

'Do you have a hole in your canoe?' asked Sandra.

Gap-tooth stood up, leaving the other three the job of draining the water. He towered over her. Sandra had never felt so small in her life. It wasn't just his height but the breadth of his shoulders and, she suspected, the darkness of his skin. He was almost jet black.

'I am Siti,' he said, and held out his hand to her. 'This one here ...' he pointed to one of the other men who grinned foolishly, '... this one tie the mooring rope too short so waves splash in and swamp canoe.'

The canoe had a hollowed trunk for a hull, but the sides were built up with planking and caulked. Even so, there was not a lot of freeboard and Sandra could see how easily the canoe could become swamped. The supports for the single outrigger bisected the canoe fore and aft, and were woven onto the gunwales. The cords were dyed so that they made geometric Polynesian patterns. It looked like something Sandra had seen in a museum, but she'd never expected to see one in use.

'Where do you go in it?' asked Sandra.

'In the *waqavoce*? Everywhere. Other islands, fishing. This is my own canoe, not belong to the resort. See? I put mast here for sail. If wind no good I paddle. I show you.' He rattled off some Fijian to his friends. They lifted the canoe onto its side so the last of the water drained out, then carried it back into the water. 'This one, Tomu, he come too. You sit in the middle.'

Sandra squealed in surprise as Siti scooped her up in his massive arms, held her briefly as though she weighed no more than a child, before lowering her gently into the canoe. Sandra thought she knew exactly how Jessica Lange must have felt in the remake of *King Kong*.

Siti hopped in at the bow while Tomu, by far the youngest of the men, pushed off at the stern. The two men dipped their paddles into the water and the canoe quickly gathered speed. The muscles in Siti's shoulders and back rippled every time he paddled and the pleasant excitement Sandra had experienced earlier on the beach returned. They passed within metres of Rowan.

'Hi,' she said as he surfaced. His snorkel and mask hid his expression but she could well imagine his surprise. Two days on Coralhaven and she was being carried out to sea by two gorgeous black men. She wondered what she'd say in her postcard to Caroline, and sat back to admire the undulations rippling through Siti's trapezius muscles, his deltoids and *latissimus dorsi*. His arms moved with the rhythm of centuries of seafaring. Siti really did have the most amazing body.

When she and Rowan lay down that afternoon, she stunned him – and herself – with the urgency of her love-making and the intensity of her orgasm. She'd forgotten that it could be so all-enveloping and overwhelming. How long had it been since she'd felt that way? she wondered. More to the point, how long had she been putting up with second- and even third-best, and fooling herself that she was satisfied? Good sex was as much mental as physical, she knew. There'd never been any problem physically so maybe at last her brain was coming back into line. The thought pleased her.

'Holiday seems to be agreeing with you,' said Rowan.

'It's the condoms,' said Sandra. 'I'm into rubber.'

'Bullshit,' said Rowan amiably. 'That was the most fun I've had in a long time.'

Did that include Glynis, wondered Sandra?

'Where have you been?' asked Sandra sleepily.

'The office,' said Rowan. 'You were asleep so I thought I'd get some work done.'

'Finished?'

'Yep.'

'What time is it?'

'Monday.'

Sandra smiled. 'Can you be a bit more precise?'

'Afternoon.'

'I guess that's close enough. Any word on Lavalle?'

'Not a dicky bird. Now, look what I've brought back.'

'Fluffy ducks!'

'The perfect accompaniment to a spa. Come on.'

'I thought you were running a bath.' Sandra dragged herself out of bed and walked sleepily over to the spa.

'God, you've got a great body,' said Rowan.

Sandra stepped into the spa and lay back. She picked up her fluffy duck and slipped the straw between her lips. She closed her eyes, slowly sucked and swallowed. 'Why can't we live like this all the time?'

'We will, when I finish with advertising,' said Rowan. He stepped in alongside her.

'Your fantasy,' said Sandra.

'My fantasy,' agreed Rowan.

The following day Rowan went game fishing off the outer reefs with his new friend from California, leaving Sandra and Leanne – the other half of the couple – to hit the beach.

'I'm watching you,' said Sandra.

Leanne was pretending to read, but her eyes were keeping tabs on the Fijian men rigging the sailboards and catamarans in case any of the guests shook off their lethargy long enough to use them.

'No, you're not,' said Leanne drily. 'You're watching what I'm watching.'

Sandra smiled.

Leanne rolled over to face her. 'Do you ever wish you'd left your husband at home?'

'It is tempting.'

'Which one do you think has the nicest arse?'

'Siti,' said Sandra without hesitation.

'First-name terms?' Leanne raised an eyebrow and sat up to get a better look. 'Which one's Siti?'

'The one giving instructions.'

'Right,' said Leanne. 'The one with the love gap in his teeth. I'd claw your eyes out if you ever came between us.'

'The what in his teeth?'

'Don't tell me you don't know.'

Sandra thought she was about to find out when a shadow fell across them. Both women turned to see who it was.

'Helloo ... Would you like me to show you how to make Fijian baskets? Fijian hats for the sun? Yes?' The woman was huge and seemed to smile compulsively. Sandra guessed she'd be in her thirties and pushing 100 kilos. Her *sulu* only accentuated her bulk. She showed them a basket she'd woven.

'My God, it's beautiful,' said Leanne.

'I show you how to make.'

'What do you think, Sandy?'

'No charge,' said the woman.

'Why not?' asked Sandra.

'Ayyyyy!' said the big woman delightedly. 'You come with me. My name is Finau. You call me Fi.' She escorted them down the beach to a clearing covered with newly woven palm mats. Other guests joined them. Finau made them sit in a semi-circle facing her. 'First, we have island milkshake. Taitusi, fetch us some island milkshake.'

The young man grinned shyly, put his hands around a coconut palm and began to climb. Taitusi wore a *sulu* over his swimming costume, but the women saw a lot of his costume as he climbed.

'Nice botty,' said Finau gleefully.

'I think she means great arse,' said Leanne.

Taitusi gently threw down the young green coconuts he'd picked, and descended. He stripped and split them, before handing each of the women a little coconut cup filled with the cool clear milk.

'See?' said Finau. 'Island milkshake.'

'Don't drink it all,' warned Sandra. 'Rowan says it's a mild laxative.'

'You worry too much,' said Leanne. 'Relax, go with the flow.'

'Drink,' said Finau. Sandra drank the coconut cup dry. 'Now we weave.'

Sandra and Leanne sat enthralled as Finau showed them how to shape the baskets and weave in the patterns. When Sandra finished her first basket, Finau held it aloft so everyone could see it.

'Ayyyyy,' she said. 'Look how good it is!'

'You're a cow,' said Leanne. 'God I hate you.'

They idled away the afternoon learning Finau's tricks of the trade and exchanging gossip. Because she was on holiday, it took Sandra most of the afternoon before she realised Finau was favouring her right arm. When the group split up and Leanne and Sandra volunteered to help Finau pack up, her disability became more obvious.

'Let me have a look at your arm,' said Sandra. A worried look crossed Finau's face. She reminded Sandra of a hurt child fearing that ointment might make a wound sting worse. 'It's okay, I won't hurt you.'

Finau tentatively held out her arm.

'How far can you straighten it? Is that all?'

The big woman nodded fearfully.

Sandra pressed on the tendons attached to her elbow. 'Does this hurt?'

'Yes,' said Finau in a voice Sandra had to strain to hear.

'And this?'

'Yes.'

'How long has your arm been like this? One month?'

'Yes.'

'I think longer. Three months?'

Finau bowed her head. 'Yes.'

'It's just tendonitis, Fi. Come to my *bure* in half an hour and I will treat it. Before I go back to Australia it will be as good as new. Will you do that?'

'Yes,' said Finau. Her fear turned into a shy smile.

'Is this our holiday or your Fijian clinic?' demanded Rowan. 'If it's your clinic, I want to know now.' He stood in the doorway of the *bure* with a smile that spoke of success with the rod and reel, and an excess of Fiji Bitter.

'Welcome back,' said Sandra. 'Where are the fish?'

'The kitchen,' said Rowan proudly. 'Half a dozen yellowfin tuna and a monster wahoo. Now, are you going to introduce me to our lovely guest?'

'Fi, this is my husband, Rowan.'

'Helloo,' said Finau.

'*Bula*,' said Rowan. 'What's the problem?'

'Fi has tendonitis in her elbow. She has more scar tissue along the tendons and nerves than I've seen in any softball or tennis player I've ever treated. I'm just finishing for today.'

Finau got up off her chair and took the three anti-inflammatory tablets Sandra handed to her.

'I want you to put ice on your elbow and take two tablets before you go to bed tonight, and the other one in the morning. I want to see you again tomorrow afternoon. Okay?'

'*Vinaka*,' said Finau. '*Vinaka vuka levu.*'

'*Moce*, Fi,' said Rowan as Sandra walked her to the door. 'Goodbye.'

Rowan began stripping off and turned on the water for the spa. His back ached pleasantly from fighting the fish on light gear, and he was looking forward to a long soak followed by a massage. While the spa filled he helped himself to a can of Fiji Bitter from the room fridge. When he judged the water to be deep enough, he hit the button to start the spa pumps. They'd barely kicked in when he heard a loud thunk and the pumps fell silent. 'Damn!'

'What's up?' asked Sandra. He told her. 'So come and have a shower,' she said. 'There's room for two.'

Later that night, when Sandra closed her eyes to sleep, Siti crept into her head. On one hand she felt guilty because Rowan was lying in bed alongside her and she was still flushed from their love-making, but on the other she felt a flood of relief and pleasure that her fantasy life had been reactivated. A tremor ran through her body, which she hoped Rowan would not notice. Siti placed his enormous hands on her shoulders and stared into her eyes. His skin was wet as if he'd just stepped straight from the water and his *sulu* clung to his thighs. He smiled, a flash of white in the darkest of faces, and his smile revealed the love gap in his teeth. Why had Leanne called it the love gap? Sandra let her imagination run free as it explored possible reasons.

Nine

Breakfast brought more faxes but there was no mention of Lavalle. Rowan wanted to rip them into shreds, ball them up and throw them at somebody, anybody. Instead, he pushed them aside dismissively and smiled to hide his frustration. There was a fist in his stomach tightening its grip. In his experience, reality contradicted popular wisdom. No news was not good news. No news was never good news but inevitably bad. Good news was always impatient, eager and anxious for release. Bad news always dragged its feet. He needed distraction, something physical and challenging to occupy body and mind and prevent futile speculations.

'How about we grab a Hobie cat after breakfast?'

'Can you sail?' asked Sandra.

'Anyone can sail a Hobie. Yes or no?'

'Okay, so long as you promise not to show off.'

'Slow down!' screamed Sandra, but her voice was filled more with excitement than fear. Rowan tightened the sheet so the windward hull lifted clear of the water.

'Lean back!' shouted Rowan. The catamaran surged forward as if straining at a leash. Spray reared up and stung Rowan's eyes but nothing could wipe the smile off his face. Ahead of them, flying fish broke the surface in panic and fled to safer waters. What made it even more special for him was the sound of Sandra laughing.

As they'd glided out through the quiet waters of the lagoon in front of the resort, Sandra had found herself wishing she'd brought a book or magazine with her. When Rowan had sailed out through the gap in the reef into open water, she understood immediately why he'd insisted she clip herself into a harness. The breeze had picked up strength the instant they'd cleared the lee of the island and Rowan had taken full advantage of it. Spray had kicked up over the bow and drenched her. When she'd turned to Rowan to object, she'd found him watching her and laughing like a big mischievous kid. She'd forced a smile and hung on for dear life, unwilling to spoil his fun.

'Get ready to come about,' yelled Rowan.

Once more Sandra prepared to duck the boom and cross over. When she glanced back over her shoulder, Coralhaven seemed a long way away.

'Are we safe out here?' Sandra asked.

'Safer in deep water than shallow,' Rowan said. He hauled on the sheet and the cat leapt in response, accelerating hard as it jumped waves. 'Last thing you want to do is hit coral.'

For more than an hour Rowan raced the cat back and

forwards in front of the island, each time a little more daring, a little faster, and each tack took them further and further out to sea. Sandra had overcome her fear of capsizing or pitchpoling and begun to revel in the thrill of the ride. But the growing distance from shore also began to nag at her. What if something went wrong? What if something broke?

'I'm getting tired,' she said at last.

'Me too,' said Rowan. He turned the cat on to a tack that would begin the sail home. Once more the little Hobie accelerated. Sandra relaxed and again began to enjoy herself, scanning the water ahead for glimpses of flying fish and tail-walking long-tom. When they came about for the starboard tack, she was surprised at how far away the island still appeared to be – she'd expected it to be a lot closer and stole a quick glance at Rowan. He didn't seem the least bit concerned. Bracing her legs as the cat gathered speed, she tried looking over her shoulder to see how much closer they were getting to the island but copped a face-full of spray for her trouble. Behind her Rowan laughed. When they turned on to the port tack the island was closer, but only marginally. Worse, she could feel the wind blowing the Hobie backwards as they stalled in their turn.

'Bugger it!' said Rowan. 'Tide's turned.'

'What does that mean?' said Sandra.

'Just going to slow us down a bit, that's all.'

They completed the port tack but, again, much of the ground they'd made up was lost in the turn.

'Longer tacks,' said Rowan. 'I'll try and head more into the wind. Could be a wet trip.'

Confidence breeds confidence, and suddenly Rowan didn't

seem quite so confident any more. The more he turned into the wind, the more speed he lost. He decided to bear away. The wind immediately filled the sail and forced him to ease off the sheet.

'Wind's picking up,' he said. 'Hold on.' Rowan wanted to let the cat go and use its speed to close the gap between them and the island. But the rising wind had also lifted the waves and increased the risk of the hull digging in and pitching them head over heels. Once more he had to ease the sheet. When they came about, the island was no closer.

'Bugger!' he said.

Sandra began to worry. Clearly Rowan was struggling to make any headway and she was beginning to feel the chill of the wind on her wet body. She tightened her life jacket but if offered little warmth.

'Hurry up. I'm getting cold,' she said.

'I'm doing my best,' said Rowan. He turned on to a port tack but now his sailing was tentative. Waves kicked up over the bows, drenching them both. When he tightened the sheet, the cat leaned over alarmingly. When he turned back to starboard, water raced beneath them but he knew it wasn't so much their hull speed as the current from the outgoing tide. Coralhaven still remained frustratingly distant. The sail crackled like thunder as they crossed under the boom and the singing in the rigging passed on more news he didn't want to know. The breeze was freshening.

'What are we going to do?' asked Sandra.

'More of the same,' said Rowan. He tightened up on the sheet and the cat leapt forward, lifting the windward hull clear.

He held fast, waiting for the cat to steady, but still the hull rose.

'Rowan!'

Rowan eased the sheet the instant the mast reached the point of no return. The Hobie capsized, catapaulting them into the water. Sandra had rehearsed in her mind exactly what she'd do in the event of capsizing, but her rehearsals amounted to nothing. She had absolutely no control over where she went or landed. Her one hope was that she'd miss the mast. She felt herself flying through the air and expected to plunge deep into the sea but instead landed on the sail. Before she had time to unclip, Rowan was by her side.

'You okay?'

'A bit winded. What do we do now?'

'Try and get her upright. Stand on the hull and haul the mast up.'

Sandra climbed the webbing and joined Rowan on the upturned hull. He planted his feet and began to haul the mast clear of the water. Water spilled out of the sail as the mast slowly began to lift.

'Here she comes,' said Rowan.

But as the mast rose upright, the wind caught the sail, got beneath it and pushed the mast beyond the vertical. To her horror, Sandy realised that the cat was going to continue its roll and capsize over them. She let go and dived clear. When she surfaced, there was no sign of Rowan.

'Rowan!'

Wind whipped spray off the top of the chop and into her eyes.

'Rowan!'

He popped up alongside her, gasping and spitting sea water.

'Rowan, are you all right?'

He looked anything but.

'Sail came down on top of me.'

'What are we going to do?'

'Try again.' Rowan's attempt to sound confident collapsed as he gagged and coughed up more sea water.

They tried again and again and again, but to no avail.

'What are we going to do now?' Sandra was scared and didn't bother hiding the fact.

'Rest for a while. I told one of the boatboys what we were doing. Just hope like hell someone's awake on the beach.'

'That's all?'

'Have you got a better idea?'

Sandra looked around anxiously. 'Are there any sharks out here?'

'No, they hang around drop-offs and the seaward side of reefs.'

'Honestly?'

'Yeah. But I guess we should climb up onto the hull just in case.'

Once out of the water, Sandra was again exposed to the wind and she felt it keenly. She grew colder and more frightened with every passing minute. When she looked to Rowan for reassurance, she realised how much the effort of trying to right the cat had taken out of him. He looked exhausted. Fearing the worst, she turned towards the island, desperate for any sign that help was on its way. Spray kicked up in the distance.

'At bloody last,' said Rowan. 'Here comes the cavalry.'

It took a good ten minutes for the powerboat to reach them, by which time Sandra was almost overwhelmed and teary with relief. When she realised who her rescuer was, she wanted to hug and kiss him in gratitude. Siti had come to her once more.

'My hero,' she said. 'Am I ever glad to see you.'

The big man lifted her into his boat, smiled shyly when she threw her arms around him and hugged him.

'You're cold,' he said. He wrapped a large beach towel around her like a father would a child stepping from a bath, felt her cheek and grabbed another towel to make a windbreak around her head. He seemed genuinely concerned for her well-being. If the second towel was intended for Rowan, he never said. He helped Rowan right the Hobie, fixed a tow-line and left him aboard the cat so his weight could give it stability.

The powerboat was long and narrow, as most Fijian boats are, to handle the short, steep chop. It had a narrow splash guard in front of the centre console to protect the driver. Two people could shelter behind it from the spray and wind but only if they squeezed up close together. When Siti offered Sandra room she didn't hesitate. Despite the sun and towels she was still shivering and her hands and feet were white with cold.

Sandra could see it was going to be no quick trip back with the Hobie in tow. Wind whipped spray over the bow and she huddled in close to Siti for protection. To her surprise, he began singing softly in Fijian. He smiled at her as he sang. There was something wistful in the melody, something ineffably beautiful and sad. She couldn't help being touched by it.

'That was lovely,' she said when he'd finished. 'What's the song about?'

'It is the song of *lawedua*,' he said. 'It tells the story of a young man who rescues a princess from another village who has been carried away out to sea in her boat. She is very beautiful and he is very strong and handsome. They fall in love but cannot marry because the chiefs of their villages are fighting with each other. One night he sneaks into her village and they sail away together in his *waqavoce*. But someone sees them and the chief gives chase. While his warriors fight with the young man, the chief grabs his daughter from the young man's canoe. Suddenly a storm comes and blows the canoes apart. The young man escapes into the night but he is never seen or heard from again. In her grief the princess turns into a beautiful white seabird and spends forever searching the ocean for her lost love. She is the *lawedua*. You can see her now. See, up there? *Lawedua* still searches.'

Sandra looked up. Hovering high in the sky above them was a solitary white bird like a cross, with an exquisitely long tail.

'My God, it's beautiful,' she said.

'Yes, she is beautiful,' said Siti. He turned and held her eyes. 'You are like *lawedua*.'

Sandra smiled and squeezed Siti's arm. No one had flirted with her for what seemed like light years. Certainly no one as handsome as Siti, and she enjoyed the feeling immensely.

Once back in the *bure*, Rowan just wanted a hot spa to warm his tired body and pummel away the aches. His gratitude to Siti was tempered by the fact that it had taken the Fijian so long to come to their rescue. His mood didn't improve when he realised nobody had come to fix the spa pump. In the end he settled for a hot bath and a massage but fell asleep well before Sandra's soothing hands had finished their work. Sandra lay back and thought about the story Siti had told her and the beautiful white bird that had held station above them in its endless, futile quest. She dozed off, dreaming about the beautiful princess who became the *lawedua*, and Siti's sweet gap-toothed smile.

Ten

The waitress brought the fax to their table as soon as they sat down for breakfast. Sandra smiled. Some people had tea or coffee brought to their table first thing, they had faxes.

'Only one?' she said. 'They must know we're going to visit your fisherman friend.'

'Yeah,' said Rowan. He unfolded the fax and read it. 'Uh-oh.'

'What's the matter?'

'Blake wants me to ring him.'

'Why?'

'Doesn't say.'

Sandra thought for a few seconds. 'Could be good news.'

'Don't, Sandy. Don't try to second-guess.'

'Lavalle?'

'Sandy, don't. Look at the fax, look what it says. Three words. Ring me. Blake. What does that tell you? Maybe the agency's burned down, maybe the staff's walked out, maybe we've lost all our accounts.'

'Maybe you've won Lavalle.'

'Can you see the word congratulations anywhere?'

'Calm down. All I'm saying is, don't assume the news is bad.'

'And if it is?'

'You've got two hours to deal with it. Then you, me, Marty and Leanne are going to visit your friend on his beautiful island. You're going to introduce me to your fantasy, right?'

'Maybe.'

'No maybe about it. We've got a deal and I'm holding you to it. Good news or bad, you've got two hours, Rowan. No extensions.' Sandra smiled but it was her thin-lipped smile. 'Now I'm going to get some papaya and, if you know what's good for you, so will you.'

Rowan rose slowly to his feet. 'Guess there's no point worrying until I know what I'm worrying about.'

'That's my boy. Do you know the Fijians believe that if you eat a lot of papaya, you're almost guaranteed to have a son?'

'First you have to unwrap the papaya,' said Rowan.

'Blake, it's Rowan.' Rowan got through to the agency on only his third attempt.

'G'day, how's the happy holiday-maker?'

'You tell me.'

'Do you want the good news or the good news?'

'You better give me the good news.'

'I'll give it to you in bullet points. Lavalle loved our

presentation. They loved our work, our thinking, our strategies, our executions.'

'But?' said Rowan.

'They said the same thing to Glengarry and Associates.'

'So?'

'They want to split the business between us and them. How about that?' Blake started to laugh.

'Jesus, Blake, you're a bastard. You had me thinking the worst and nearly started a blue between me and Sandy.'

'All I said was ring me.'

'That's right, that's all you said. Now, before I break out the champagne, tell me the deal. What products do we get?'

'All of them.'

'What?'

'So do Glengarry.'

'What?'

'Both agencies get briefed on every assignment and the best solution wins. Full fees to the successful agency, two-and-a-half times head hours to the unsuccessful agency. It was a split decision. They couldn't decide who to give the business to so they're leaving us to fight it out.'

'Fucking nice of them!'

'What?' It was Blake's turn to be stunned.

'Tell them no deal.'

'What?'

'Figure it out, for Christ's sake. They get the two best agencies in town working on their business for the price of one plus the cost of a good dinner. Bugger them. I'm not buying it and neither should Glengarry.'

'You can't be serious. You're going to tell Lavalle to get stuffed?'

'If necessary. Give me Nathan Glengarry's number and I'll ring him.'

'Bloody hell, I hope you know what you're doing.' Blake gave Rowan the number and waited until he read it back.

'Now, what was the good news?' asked Rowan.

'Glynis has resigned. I had a chat with her.'

'Thought you might.'

'I just pointed out that you and Sandy had gone to Fiji for the noblest of reasons, and were hard at it creating a son. I don't know what you'd promised her but she was genuinely stunned. She didn't believe me at first. I think she thought your next child would look like her. I pointed out that she was just the latest in a succession of nubile young women to whom your dick has taken a fancy, that to win over your dick was easy but your heart nigh impossible. I told her Sandy had that bit and wasn't open to negotiations.'

'How'd she take it?'

'Tears, temper, tantrum. Everything you'd expect. I commiserated with her, told her you were an arsehole, and told her I'd give her a month's pay whether she worked out her notice or not.'

'A more than generous offer, if you don't mind me saying.'

'She leaves Friday.'

'So I don't even get to kiss her goodbye?'

'Don't be a bigger arsehole than normal. She worked bloody hard for us. Now, are you going to kiss Lavalle goodbye or not?'

'I'll get back to you.' Rowan hung up. He stared at the phone for a full twenty minutes as he pondered his next step.

'Bad news?'

Rowan looked up as the resort manager, Maurice, wandered into the business centre.

'I don't know,' said Rowan. 'I have to make another call to find out.'

'Good luck.' Maurice walked back outside as if he hadn't a care in the world. And he probably hadn't. Rowan punched numbers and waited for his call to connect.

'Mr Glengarry's office.'

'Rowan Madison. I need to speak to Nat urgently.'

'Can I say where you're from?'

'Lady, if you don't know, you're in the wrong job.'

'One moment please.'

Rowan counted to five. If Glengarry didn't come on in five it meant he'd ducked his call.

'Nathan Glengarry.'

'It's Rowan, Nat.'

'Thought you'd ring.'

'You've spoken to Lavalle?'

'Of course.'

'You're buying it?'

'Thinking about it.'

'That shouldn't take long. The deal sucks. I'm turning it down. You should too.'

'We're pretty confident of winning the bulk of the business.'

'As I recall, you were pretty confident of blowing me out

of the water when we pitched, but here I am. Maybe you're too casual about where you place your confidence.'

Nathan laughed. 'I knew straightaway you wouldn't buy the deal. I've got my people doing the sums.'

'What's to do? Even if you win eighty per cent of the business – which you won't – you're still taking a seventeen to eighteen per cent cut in fees. Can you afford to do business on those terms?'

'We could. What do you propose?'

'Split the account down the middle and review after eighteen months, with the intention of consolidating with one agency. By then they ought to have a good grasp on who's delivering and who isn't.'

'Full fees?'

'Do you really want a price-cutting competition?'

'Let me think about it and I'll get back to you.'

'Don't take all day and don't play tricks with me. You know I have to get back to them. I've played straight with you, I deserve nothing less in return. I want to know what your commitment is before either of us speak to Lavalle again. Fair enough?'

'I'll get back to you the moment we make a decision. Where can I reach you? You're in Fiji somewhere, aren't you?'

'You could send a fax to the resort but I might be out. I'll ring you at two-thirty. Will you be in the office?'

'Should be.'

'I'll give you my fax number here. And Nat?'

'Yeah?'

'Don't you think we're both too good to be pushed around?'

'Absolutely.' Nathan began laughing gently, which Rowan took as a good sign. 'By the way, how's the fishing?'

Rowan wasted valuable minutes on pleasantries. He had barely hung up when Sandra appeared in the doorway, skin oiled, hair brushed and her new, hand-woven beach basket over her arm.

'Marty and Leanne are already on the boat and wondering where we are. I've packed your things.'

'I'll be five minutes, no more, I promise. I have to ring Blake again. You go on ahead. Make sure there's plenty of Fiji Bitter on board. Oh, and better grab a bottle of champagne from the manager to take as a gift. Tell him to add it to our bill. Okay?'

'Five minutes,' said Sandra. 'After that you go without sex for a day for every minute you're late.' She turned and wiggled her bottom at him. 'Your choice.'

Rowan wasted valuable seconds watching her walk away, eyes locked on to the exaggerated, sassy swing of her hips. His jaw had dropped open. He couldn't begin to understand what had got into her, what had changed her back into the sex machine she'd been in her younger days, when she'd blown his lights out. All he knew was that he liked what he saw and wanted more. His fingers punched buttons furiously.

'So, are you going to tell us?'

'What?' said Rowan.

Marty opened another Fiji Bitter and passed it to Rowan. 'All the phone calls. Good news or bad?'

'Just business.'

The four of them sat beneath the flybridge, away from the spray, as Coralhaven's twin-hull cruiser sped across the light chop towards Koru Island, where the owner of the game-fishing boat had made his home.

'Are you going to think about it all day or talk to us?' asked Sandra.

'I'm sorry. Have I been bad company?'

'No,' said Sandra. 'You haven't been any kind of company. Let us know when you're going to join us.'

'Okay, I get the message. Let me be tour guide. The island straight ahead is Koru, but we have to motor around to the other side to find the channel through the reef that surrounds it. The channel leads into Homestead Bay, so named because that is where Dean and Van built their homestead.'

'Van?' asked Marty.

'Short for Vanessa.'

'Did you finish your business?' asked Leanne.

'No, but I've still got fifty minutes to go. Right, Sandy?'

'I suppose so,' said Sandra.

Ten minutes later the twin-hull nosed inside the reef and around the headland that sheltered Homestead Bay.

'My God, it's gorgeous,' said Leanne.

'Fabulous,' said Sandra.

'What you're looking at,' said Rowan, 'is my future.'

'Our future,' said Sandra. 'Your fantasy, our future.'

Dean and Van saw the boat come in and met their visitors at the jetty. Vanessa showed Sandra, Marty and Leanne around the gardens and homestead while Dean showed Rowan to the phone. Rowan joined them for drinks, then disappeared back to the phone. He rejoined them for the lunch of painted crays that Dean had caught that morning, and a barbecued coral trout he'd caught the night before. Rowan returned to the phone the instant he'd finished eating.

'He's impossible,' said Sandra.

'He reminds me of me when I was younger,' said Dean. 'I drove Van to distraction, but it got us this. When you know this is where you're going to end up, it's all worthwhile.'

'Wanna bet?' said Sandra.

'What's the verdict?' asked Rowan.

'We're going to accept their terms,' said Nathan. 'Sorry, Rowan, but we've looked at the figures and I have enough confidence in my people to believe that we can make it work.'

'You're crazy,' said Rowan. 'My way you'd get the same income for half the work.'

'My way we might get all the business,' said Nathan. 'What are you going to do?'

'I guess now that's between me and Lavalle. I know we're competitors, but sometimes it's in our best interests to take an industry approach. I think you've done the industry a disservice today, Nat. I'm disappointed in your response.'

'It's business, Rowan, and in my opinion good business. Let me know how you get on.'

'Get stuffed, Nat.' Rowan hung up and dialled Blake. As he listened to the clicks of his call trying to negotiate the Fijian telephone exchange, Sandra ghosted up alongside him.

'Your two hours are up.' She slipped her arm around his waist. 'It's time to join the party.'

'I need another five minutes,' said Rowan. 'Then I can relax.'

'Good, then maybe I can as well,' said Sandra.

'For Christ's sake, Sandy, will you get off my fucking back!'

Sandra flinched, stunned by his sudden outburst. She let go of his waist. 'Sure,' she said, turned and walked away. This time her bottom didn't wiggle at all.

Rowan closed his eyes and clenched his teeth in sheer frustration. He tried to picture the blood-pressure gauge at the gym and the red line falling, falling, falling. But it held steady at 150 and Rowan could feel himself getting angrier by the second. He saw the heavy bag and wanted to blast it off its bomb-proof mounts. His agency faced its biggest crisis and all Sandy could do was play stupid games. He hung up and redialled, hoping the Nadi exchange would get it right this time. He had to talk to the man from Paris, convince him to change his mind and get him to divide the account up fifty-fifty. He only wished he could give himself a fifty-fifty chance of success. The light breeze carried the sounds of laughter from the veranda. At least somebody was having a good time.

Rowan rose at six, showered and dressed to meet the seaplane that would fly him back to Nadi for his meeting with the Tourist Board. Sandra stayed in bed and only grunted when he said goodbye.

'Damn you,' she said softly as the door closed behind him. Rowan had hardly spoken to her – or anyone – since his outburst. She lay still, trying not to get angry, trying to go back to sleep. But sleep was no longer possible. She got out of bed, did her stretches, showered and, in the process of showering, determined not to allow anything Rowan did to spoil her holiday. From now on, she decided, Rowan could do what he liked and she'd do what she liked. If he also wanted to do what she wanted to do, terrific. If not, too bad. She dried herself and moisturised her skin from head to toe, slipped into her new bikini and wrapped herself in a freshly pressed *sulu*. On the way to breakfast she picked a hibiscus blossom and threaded the stem into her hair above her ear. On the whole, she felt she looked pretty gorgeous.

She scanned the dining area, hoping that Marty and Leanne were up, but there was nobody she knew or, at least, knew well enough to join. She sat down at her usual table and waited for the waitress to bring her a bundle of faxes. The waitress brought a pot of tea instead.

'That's better,' Sandra said, and smiled.

The waitress shyly returned her smile. 'I give fax to Mr Rowan. We have fresh island grapefruit this morning.'

'Thanks, but I'll stick with papaya. Tell me, is it true that if I eat lots of papaya my next child will be a boy?'

'Ooooh,' said the waitress, and momentarily hid her face behind her hands. 'Maybe Mr Rowan eat lots papaya, too.' She giggled and made her way back to the kitchen.

Sandra smiled. As far as she was concerned, Rowan could eat whatever he liked for the rest of their holiday, one small papaya or a whole mountain of them. He had a lot of ground to make up before she'd play bun to his hotdog. She took her time and followed up the papaya with a plate of bacon, eggs and hash browns, a combination she'd never consider back home in Australia. When Marty and Leanne still failed to show, she decided to walk along the beach back to her *bure*, and then catch up on her reading for an hour or so until the rest of the island caught up with her.

The Fijians were already up and about, cleaning and preparing the boats and sailcraft for the guests. Some still had their *sulus* wrapped around their hips, but most just wore their swimming costumes. Water glistened off their backs and arms and they needed no excuse to dive into the still, crystal-clear water of the lagoon. Obviously, this hour of the morning allowed as much time for recreation as work. Their chatter and laughter was incessant, and they swam canoes into shore when they could have paddled them in more easily. Sandra unwrapped her *sulu*, spread it on the sand and sat down to watch them, waving back when they spotted her.

One of the men called out to her, '*Bula! Marama totaka!*'

The rest burst into ribald laughter. Sandra wondered if it was a joke and whether it was at her expense. She decided it didn't matter if it was. She watched three young men drag a canoe up onto the beach, convinced they were showing off for her benefit.

'Nice botty,' she said under her breath. Said it again as another emerged from the water. She looked for Siti but it seemed he had the day off. She wanted to see the gap in his teeth and wonder again at its purpose, though she figured she now had that well and truly pinned down. Did he have his front teeth removed for that specific purpose? Sandra wondered. If so, it was a noble sacrifice, and somewhere on the island there was a very grateful lucky girl. The waitress? Their housemaid?

She couldn't help speculating on who the lucky girl might be. Maybe Siti was generous with his favours and they were all lucky.

The sun finally rose high enough for Sandra to feel its heat and remember she had yet to apply sunscreen. Reluctantly, she dragged herself to her feet and headed back to her *bure*. Rowan had told her about the women exercising at the gym while he worked out. Watching Fijian men prepare boats, she decided, was infinitely more stimulating.

She opened the doors that led on to their private courtyard and spa, letting the morning sun flood in through the hibiscuses. She pulled the double bed towards the courtyard and into the sun, and propped up pillows so that she could sunbathe while she read. Remembering to apply sunscreen, she slipped off her *sulu* and bikini top and wandered into the bathroom. She couldn't help a wry smile when she noticed how far her nipples were sticking out.

She'd barely finished one chapter of her book when she heard a knock on the door. Her first thought was that Leanne had come to invite her to join them in whatever they had planned. Even so, she took the precaution of putting on her bikini top. When she opened the door she wished she'd put on her *sulu* as well.

'Helloo,' said Siti. He smiled his gap-toothed smile. 'Mr Rowan ask me to fix spa pump. Okay I come in or maybe I come back later?'

As Sandra recovered from her surprise, she noticed Siti carried a bag of tools and wore a white T-shirt in addition to his *sulu*, clearly the official uniform of the island tradesman.

'You'd better come in. I'm sure Rowan would love a spa when he gets back from Nadi.' She stood aside and let Siti step timidly inside. 'I assume you know the way.'

'Thank you,' said Siti. He walked straight past her into the courtyard and opened the pump box. Sandra stood watching him, hands on hips. So what if she was only wearing her bikini? She'd only been wearing a bikini when he'd rescued them and he'd seen her in her bikini often enough on the beach.

'You okay if I keep reading?'

'Yes,' said Siti. 'Please.'

Sandra lay belly down on the bed, her chest propped up on her stack of pillows to take the weight off her elbows, and pretended to ignore his presence. Siti was crouched down on his haunches with his back to her. Her interest quickened when he straightened, pulled his T-shirt off over his head and, without so much as a glance at her, threw it to one side. That's better, she thought. Siti had magnificent shoulders and the taper of his back to his waist and hips would make a nun renounce her vows. Siti appeared to have difficulty fitting a spanner and moved so that he worked side-on to her.

'Siti, what does ...' Sandra hesitated as she tried to recall the pronunciation. 'What does *marama totaka* mean?'

'*Marama totaka*? Who said this to you?'

'Some of your friends.'

'It means "beautiful woman". They say you are a beautiful woman.' Siti stared at her with such intensity, Sandra felt her blood abandon the rest of her body and race hotly to her face. 'You are a beautiful woman.'

'Oh,' she said weakly.

As the minutes passed, Sandra tried to ignore Siti but found herself helplessly alternating between her book and stealing glances at him. Already the heat in the courtyard had caused him to sweat. It glistened on his shoulders and upper arms. Sandra felt a tensing in her stomach and smiled inwardly in acknowledgement. What would Caroline give to swap places? she wondered. Siti reached into the pump box and appeared to flinch as he lifted out the electric motor.

'You weren't down at the beach this morning,' said Sandra.

'Nooo ... not this morning.' He flinched again as he picked up the replacement motor.

'Are you all right?'

'It's nothing,' said Siti.

'So why did you flinch? Something must be hurting you.'

'Sometimes the speedboat is hard to push back into the water.'

'Did you hurt your back?'

'A little bit. So I do not go down to the beach this morning.'

'I see. Would you like me to look at it before you go?'

'Yes please.' He spoke so softly Sandra had to strain to hear him. 'Fi says you are very good doctor.'

'Not doctor, physiotherapist.'

'First I put in the new motor.'

'Be careful.'

Sandra watched to see that he was careful – at least, that was her excuse. Siti was the most beautiful man she'd ever seen. For all his size, the man had a cat-like grace and sensuality. What would Caroline think? she wondered again. Hell, she knew exactly what Caroline would think. As she propped on her elbow watching the show, it slowly dawned on her that she had the perfect opportunity to live out Caroline's fantasy. But it was no longer just Caroline's fantasy. Siti had also featured in her dreams, not because he was black but because he was beautiful, gentle and his missing front teeth hinted at exquisite, illicit pleasures.

God knows Rowan had certainly given her cause to pursue her fantasy. She'd spent the day before indulging his fantasy, maybe it was time to indulge in her own, to get even with him for the phone calls, for Glynis and for all the rest of his hurtful little humiliations. The idea aroused her. Who would know? Certainly not Rowan, not ever. This time she could indulge her fantasy. And the best part was, nobody would get hurt. It would be victimless.

But thinking about it was one thing, actually committing herself to having sex with Siti was something else entirely. She was Sandra, she reminded herself, wife and mother, professional physiotherapist, and she just didn't do that sort of thing no matter how justified she felt. But would it hurt? Just once? To find out? To finally find out what it was like to have sex with a gorgeous black man, instead of spending a lifetime wondering? She'd never have a chance like it again. But even so, to actually do it . . . She felt a further tightening in her lower belly. The spa pump burst into life, startling her.

'All fix,' said Siti proudly. As he smiled he pushed his tongue against his top teeth so that it showed through his love gap.

Sandra was fascinated. She had trouble finding her voice and had to swallow hard. 'You'd better come up here and lie down so I can look at your back.' Her voice sounded strange, different. She stood up and pushed the pillows off the bed. Siti undid his *sulu*. 'Wait,' she said. 'I'll get some towels for you to lie on.'

Sandra grabbed two towels from the bathroom and spread them along the bed, close to the edge. She looked up to see Siti towering above her. Nothing in all her years of physiotherapy had prepared her for being so close to such a large and beautiful body. 'Lie down,' she said, her voice strangely thickened. She sprinkled a little baby oil along his spine and across the broad of his shoulders. She had no cause to put oil on his shoulders at all but couldn't resist the temptation to rub her hands over as much of him as possible. What harm would it do?

'Feels good,' said Siti.

Oh God, thought Sandra, you're not wrong there. She slowly worked her way down his spine, pushing the muscle away from the bone, feeling for any tightness or constriction, trying hard to be professional. 'Is this where it hurts?'

'Noo,' said Siti. He reached behind and indicated an area below the line of his swimming costume. She rolled his costume down as she'd done a thousand times before with other patients.

'There?'

'Yes,' said Siti. 'There.'

'Are you sure? I can't feel anything.'

'Yes, I'm sure.'

'Does this hurt?' She pushed down gently with her thumbs.

'No.'

'This?' She increased pressure.

'No.'

'No?'

'Good, feels good.'

Sandra pushed down and out across his buttocks, feeling them suddenly tense beneath her hands. She did it again for the same result.

'Ahhh . . .' said Siti.

She did it yet again, not for any professional reason but simply because she couldn't stop. She rolled her wrists so that her hands slid straight down his buttocks and slipped along the crevice between them. She repeated the action, but more slowly. What had Caroline said? Two cantaloupes in cling wrap? That didn't even come close. She felt Siti's hand close around her wrist, saw his head turn and his eyes look into hers.

'*Lawedua*,' he said.

She didn't move when he rolled over and casually pulled off his swimming costume. Even then Sandra knew it was not too late, that she could get off the bus right there and then. But she did nothing. Siti took hold of her arm again and gently pulled her towards him. She turned away from his eyes, but the movement only directed her gaze towards his penis, which was rising like the trunk of an enraged elephant and still growing. Siti pushed his tongue hard against his upper teeth so that the tip protruded through his love gap. He swung his legs over the side of the bed. His hand let go of her arm and slipped inside the back of her bikini bottom, his fingers beginning gentle exploration.

Oh God, thought Sandra. Oh God! It was too late. She knew she was going to let him do what he wanted – what she wanted – felt herself flush hotly, weaken and slip downwards towards the bed. She barely had the presence of mind to reach into the drawer of her bedside table and grab a handful of condoms. Condoms were never part of her fantasies, but this wasn't a fantasy, this was the real thing. She didn't ask, she just ripped open a pack and slipped one onto his penis, rolling it down as far as it would go and trying to push it further. It didn't seem to go very far down his penis at all. Oh Christ, thought Sandra again. She just hoped that the condom makers had taken people like Siti into consideration when they made their products.

Siti stood suddenly, picked her up as if she weighed no more than one of her pillows, and placed her gently on the bed. He put his knees either side of her and crouched over her, dwarfing her, removing first her bikini top, then her bikini bottom. He cupped her breasts in his massive hands, kissed them, sucked them, then slowly worked his way down her body to where she knew he'd pause. She felt the teeth on either side of his love gap exactly where she expected to find them, felt his tongue begin its work. Her excitement began to rise to the point where screaming seemed the only possible outcome. Oh God, she thought again. Oh God, oh God, oh God! Caroline!

Sandra picked up the condoms the moment Siti closed the door behind him. Four of them. Four! In what, an hour and a half? She wondered if Rowan would notice the missing condoms and briefly panicked. No. He didn't know how many she had to start with so how could he know if any were missing? She hurriedly flushed them away down the toilet, even though the sign said such things should be disposed of in the bags provided. She stepped into the shower and scrubbed every inch of her body, as though washing away evidence, careful around her groin, which was both tender and tingling.

She hoped everything would be back to normal before Rowan got home, even though their current state of pique meant that he wouldn't arrive home with his hopes up, or anything else up for that matter.

She was determined not to feel guilty, arguing that what she'd done was a once only, once-in-a-lifetime indiscretion in which nobody got hurt. It was a victimless crime, if indeed it was a crime. She told herself she'd only done what Rowan had done more times than she'd ever know. Had Rowan felt guilty or filled with remorse? No, he'd probably felt like he'd scored a goal. She was certain his feelings of guilt and remorse had only come as a consequence of exposure, on the rare occasions he'd been caught. All she'd done, she assured herself, was take one small step towards redressing the balance. But infidelities were typical of Rowan and not at all typical of her.

Her image in the mirror appeared no different, though when she looked closely, her face appeared a little flushed and her eyes a little wild. That, she figured, was only to be expected. A thrill ran through her body as some of the excitement returned. She immediately felt guilty, despite her intentions to the contrary, as if thinking about it – and enjoying thinking about it – was a greater sin than the commission. She fought the guilt because it was too soon and she wasn't ready for it. Guilt would settle on her sooner or later, she was sure of that, but in the meantime she decided to enjoy the afterglow.

She only had to touch herself to set the aftershocks rolling again. Oh God! It had been amazing! Not just amazing but mind-blowing, gob-smacking, incredible, all the better for being illicit. She couldn't wait to tell Caroline the full chapter and verse, particularly the bit about the love gap. She just knew Caroline would go off her brain.

It was late morning when Sandra finally met up with Marty and Leanne to spend the day swimming, snorkelling and sunbathing. Around mid-afternoon, after they'd moved back into the shade of the palms to escape the sun, Siti turned up at the beach and sauntered down to the shoreline where the island's work-boat was beached. Sandra watched to see if he'd notice her and wave, sat up stunned as he single-handedly lifted a 30-horsepower Yamaha outboard up off the work-boat's transom, and carted it along the shore to the maintenance hut. Sandra was about to yell at him to be careful of his injured back when she noticed Leanne looking at her curiously. She slumped back onto her elbows, and shifted her gaze aimlessly out to sea, trying hard to keep her face expressionless. But inside her head, her synapses went into overload. Behind the innocence and small-boy mannerisms, was Siti just another calculating opportunist? Was she just the latest in a succession of foolish guests who'd become his conquests? What did Siti say to the boat boys that made them glance her way and laugh? Had he said something about her? A cloud seemed to pass in front of the sun. One thing was for sure, Siti's injured back had got better in a real hurry.

Sandra excused herself and returned to her *bure*. The bed had been made and pushed back against the wall. All the bathroom towels had been replaced and the floors swept. There were fresh flowers in the vase on the coffee table. Everything was exactly as it had been whenever she and Rowan had returned to their *bure* in the late afternoon. But this time it felt different, as though all the charm had been drained away. With her complicity, their *bure* had been invaded, violated, used, and it seemed coldly impersonal when before it had been a cheerful, sun-filled sanctuary and love nest. It was a millionaire's retreat yet she felt cheap in it, cheapened at any rate.

Rowan arrived home gleefully intoxicated, carrying flowers, two champagne glasses, a bottle of Dom Perignon in an ice bucket, and wearing a smile of pure happiness. He stopped at the door and dropped onto his knees.

'Forgive me, for I have sinned,' he begged.

Sandra forced a smile. 'What have you done, you silly bugger?'

'I've slain the dragon.' He handed Sandra the flowers, champagne and glasses and dragged himself to his feet. 'No more work for the rest of our holiday. No faxes, no phone calls, nothing. Just you, me and a drawerful of condoms.'

Sandra's eyes widened. 'What's happened?'

'Tell you in the spa. Oh jeez, did Siti come and fix it?'

'Yes, he came.'

'Good man! You get the taps running, I'll open the Dom. By the way, we're having dinner with Maurice and his wife tonight. Marty and Leanne are also invited.'

'What?'

'Maurice came with me to the meeting. He's on the board representing the resorts. We had a drink or three together afterwards. It's his idea that we celebrate with him.'

'What are we celebrating?'

'I'll tell you in the spa. Now give your returning hero a hug and a kiss.' He threw his arms around her and Sandra hugged him back as hard as she could. In the end he almost had to push her away, frowned when he noticed her brush away a small tear.

'I missed you,' she said, before he could say anything. 'Go on, get unchanged.'

Sandra switched on the courtyard light and turned on the spa taps. When she wandered back inside to undress and get towels, she noticed Rowan's trousers had been thrown onto the bed along with his shirt and tie. His shoes had been tossed in the general direction of the closet. His socks sat on the floor like stepping stones leading to the bathroom. Under any other circumstances she'd have yelled at him, but instead she smiled. In an instant, the *bure* had become less alien, less tidy but also less sullied, more normal looking. The toilet flushed and Rowan started singing the theme from one of the *Rocky* movies.

She loved Rowan in this mood, loved him anyway, and wondered what in the world had possessed her to do what she'd done with Siti. It seemed so unreal, so unlikely, to be no more rooted in reality than a movie or a dream. Yet it had happened, and there was nothing she could do to change that. She'd been selfish and disloyal, and what she'd done had been sheer madness and unjustified, but it was over. Over and done with. History. She decided the sooner she forgot the whole episode, the better. Guilt had returned and stood banging on the door, demanding admission.

Rowan left the bathroom wearing nothing but a smile, and paused to open the champagne before making a beeline for the spa. 'Come on, Sandy,' he yelled. 'The bubbly's getting warm and the spa's getting cold.'

'Exercises.'

'Afterwards.'

Sandra stripped and climbed in beside him.

'That's better,' he said. 'First a toast to me, then I'll turn on the pumps.' He handed her a glass of champagne. 'Sip it with respect. It's two hundred bucks a bottle here.'

'Two hundred bucks!' said Sandra. 'What are we celebrating?' She took a sip. 'Oh my goodness, it makes the champagne on the plane taste like lolly water. Come on, tell me what this is all about.'

'There are two things. First, I blew everyone away at the marketing meeting and actually managed to get them to increase their budget. Another half-million. You know, when I finished my presentation everyone stood and applauded?'

'Well done.'

'Yeah. But the big news is Lavalle. I managed to convince them to change their mind and award us half of their business outright. In fact, we ended up with more like sixty per cent. Yesterday it looked like we'd end up with nothing.' He told her all about the previous day's dramas.

'So that's what all the phone calls were about when we were over on Koru?'

'Yeah. I'm sorry I snapped at you but my balls were in a vice.'

'Why didn't you say something?'

'I didn't want to spoil your holiday. I owe it to you, and it's been a long time since I've seen you so happy.'

Sandra closed her eyes as if hit by sudden pain.

'Oh God, I feel terrible.'

'Don't. No harm done.'

No harm done? Sandra felt sick.

'Hey,' said Rowan. 'All's well that ends well, right? Let's get stuck into the champers.'

Sandra threw her arms around Rowan's neck and hugged him as tightly as she could.

'I'm really sorry,' she said. 'I can be a stupid bitch sometimes.'

Eleven

'You did what?' said Caroline. Her eyebrows sat up like McDonald's arches, framing eyes stretched wide with disbelief. They stayed that way, hardly blinking, throughout Sandra's tale. 'More detail,' she begged, but Sandra kept doggedly to the facts, speaking softly so no one else in the café could possibly overhear.

'I'm only telling you because I feel I owe it to you. Believe me, it wasn't worth it. It might have been the ride of a lifetime but the admission price was too high.'

'Oh come on! I'm so damn jealous I'm getting horny just listening to you.'

'Don't,' said Sandra. 'I'm not joking, Caro. I've been on a massive guilt jag. Sometimes I really hate myself. I go through periods where I feel nothing but disgust for myself. I really don't know what got into me. If I had the time over again there's no way I'd do it.'

'But you did do it,' said Caroline. 'Unlike me, you're not

going to die wondering. Now, I want to know all about this love gap. Tell me and don't hold back.'

Sandra told her, trying hard to remain objective and dispassionate, but she soon got caught up in Caroline's enthusiasm. Caroline made her feel like she'd done something sensational for the cause of womankind everywhere, and it felt good riding along on the wave.

'So what did you do when Rowan got back?'

'I made it up to him in every way that I could.'

'You're joking!'

'I let him unpeel his papaya.'

'What?'

'Left the condoms in the drawer.'

'Did he wonder why?'

'You know Rowan. He thinks everything I do somehow relates to something he's done. He just thought I was making up for giving him a hard time when we went to visit his fisherman friend.'

'That would be right. Oh God, Sandy, I want your life, I really do. You're a bitch, you know, an absolute bitch. You get the holiday and the full-on raging animal rut with a gorgeous black man, and what do I get? I get to stay home and babysit your kids.'

'You asked for them, as I recall.'

'Yeah, I did. And do you know what?'

'Don't tell me!'

'Take two. Twelve weeks from today.'

'Fantastic!'

'I knew Mike would get clucky.'

'That's fantastic news.'

'It'll be fantastic news if it works. I don't know what I'll do if it doesn't. I'm excited and scared all at the same time.'

'I know exactly how that feels,' said Sandra emphatically. 'Oh boy, do I ever!' She caught Caroline's eye and both of them burst out laughing. 'I never suspected they came in that size. Tell you what . . .'

They leant back in their chairs and laughed so hard that their waitress had to dodge around them to serve their second cups of coffee. She looked at them quizzically, appeared poised to enquire what the joke was, then apparently thought better of it.

'Sandra, can I ask a big favour?'

'Sure.' Sandra looked closely at her friend. Caroline's mood had changed, as though a cold breeze had suddenly sprung up and found its way into the café. Her smile had gone, replaced by nervous anxiety. 'What's the matter?'

'Will you come with me?'

'What?'

'Will you come with me to the clinic when the embryos are implanted?'

'What about Mike?'

'He said he'd take me, hold my hand and so forth, but you can see he really doesn't want to. He's too scared to hope, and I don't want that when the implants are being done. I want it to be a happy occasion, joyful even. We should be positive and optimistic, not fearful. Sandy, I want to be relaxed, not tense. I think it makes a difference to the chances of success, and I want to do everything in my power to make sure it's a success this time. There won't be another if it doesn't work. I want you to be with me, Sandy. I want a cheer squad. Will you do it?'

'Of course!' Sandra took Caroline's hand.

'I knew you would.'

'If one of Rowan's little swimmers hits the spot, we could have a race to see whose baby pops out first.'

'God, I love it when you talk like that.'

'One condition.'

'What?'

'That you never mention what I just told you ever again.'

'Are you serious?'

'Deadly.'

'Not even to you?'

'Not even to me.'

'Okay, but it seems a bit of a waste.'

'Promise me.'

'I promise. Am I allowed to think about it in bed?'

'No! I want you to forget about it altogether, okay?'

'Okay, it's forgotten.'

'As far as I'm concerned, it never happened, and I don't want any reminders.'

'No reminders,' said Caroline.

'Absolutely no reminders,' said Sandra.

Part II

Revelation

Twelve

The instant the lift doors closed, Rowan turned and strode purposefully back towards his office. He had dozens of things to do before going home but nothing could wipe the smile off his face. The receptionist picked up on his mood.

'How'd it go?'

'If only I had the same effect on women,' said Rowan. 'We can't make any announcements yet but the agency's just won itself a Christmas present.'

Claudine parted her lips in a smile that lit up a face most people believed belonged more properly on the front cover of magazines than behind an advertising agency's front desk. She wore a little red Santa hat, and not even that could look foolish on her. If anything, she dignified it and the gaudy, tinselled tree with its flashing fairy lights alongside her. 'I took down two messages for you while your line was engaged.'

'Thanks,' said Rowan, taking the slips from her. 'You

know, Claudine, when you smile like that I wonder why we bother with the tree.'

'Go away,' she said. 'You'll make me blush.'

'How would I tell?' he said.

Claudine was just one of many hirings he and Blake had been forced to make to keep pace with their expanding business. Born to a Mauritian mother and a French Legionnaire father, she had the dark, exotic beauty that Rowan would normally have found irresistible, and that would have given Sandra grave cause for concern. Tall and lithe, she moved with an elegance and grace that was both sexy and stylish. Yet Rowan had done no more than give her a kiss and a cuddle on her birthday, flirted innocently and playfully, and made no attempt to manoeuvre her anywhere near his sofa.

Blake stood waiting for him at his office door. 'Go wash your hands,' he said.

'Why?'

'You've had Capital Mutual eating out of them for the last hour and a half. Slobbering, actually. It was disgusting to watch.'

'You did your share of talking.'

'Yeah, but you're the legend. It was you they wanted to hear.'

'Not true,' said Rowan loyally.

'Are they coming aboard?'

'I could've unzipped and pissed in their coffee and they'd still give us their business.'

'Bloody fantastic! If this is a dream, I hope I die in my sleep.'

'Chalk it up. Our seventh new business win since Lavalle. They're telling the other agencies tomorrow. More drinks in the boardroom. Will you get Barth to organise it, or will I tell Margaret?'

'Barth can do it. I think Margaret's got other plans for you. Catch you later.'

Rowan turned around and found his secretary standing behind him with a pile of letters and documents in her hands, immovable and undeniable. 'Give me a break,' he snapped, but his petulance was all part of a game they played. She kept him on the ball, and Rowan liked to let her think she could boss him around. Shortly after the Fiji trip, when their shared secretary had resigned, Rowan and Blake had decided they each needed a secretary of their own, and over a drunken dinner agreed to hire each other's. Blake hired Margaret for Rowan, a short, slightly plump woman in her late forties who dressed early thirties, blonded her hair and wore enough perfume to be accused of waging chemical warfare. A shared ride in a lift almost induced suffocation, to which she alone seemed immune. However, her secretarial skills were exceptional, and she had both the strength to stand up to him and to shield him from people who were determined to waste his time. No mother bear was ever more protective of her cubs. She also had about as much chance as a mother grizzly of ending up on Rowan's sofa.

In return, Rowan had hired Bartholomew for Blake, and introduced the first male secretary to the agency. Blake was initially taken aback, but was quickly won over by Barth's efficiency, intelligence and uncanny ability to anticipate his needs.

Blake's trust had grown to the point where he allowed Barth to choose his new shirts and ties, and even a new suit. The young man had impeccable taste.

Both Blake and Rowan maintained they had simply chosen the best applicant, and perhaps they had, although no one believed them.

Margaret followed Rowan around to his side of the desk, stood while he sat. 'I've rung Sandra,' she said. 'Told her you were in a new business meeting and would phone the moment you were free. She's fine and doesn't think anything's going to happen for another week at least. I've ordered some flowers to be delivered here at five o'clock for you to take home to her.'

'Why?' asked Rowan. 'What have I forgotten this time?'

'It's your anniversary.'

'No it's not. That was two or three months ago. I remembered that myself and booked Tetsuya's.'

'That was your wedding anniversary. This is the anniversary of the day you first met.'

'How do you know that?'

'Sandra mentioned it one time while we were chatting on the phone, so I made a note of the date in your diary. It was at a Christmas party thrown by one of your university friends.'

'Amazing.' Rowan shook his head to reflect the amazement he felt. 'Now can we get on with some work?'

'Here are your letters to sign, here's your list of people to ring ranked by urgency, and these are reports you have to read before tomorrow's meetings. First things first, ring Sandra. Sarah and Rocky also have important news they're dying to tell you.'

'What's that?' said Rowan.

'Their letter to Santa,' said Margaret. 'I'll go get you a coffee while you work out where you can buy a giant panda for Rochelle.'

Rowan smiled as he picked up the phone and hit Sandra's speed dial number. He would have smiled if he'd picked up the phone to ring his dentist. When he looked through the glass partition of his office, he saw plenty of reasons to keep smiling. New faces worked behind new work stations on new computers, aided by new faxes, copiers and colour printers. Down in the creative department, two new teams were pushing their talents to the limit, revelling in the opportunities they'd been given, desperate to be the new Mark and Elaine and see their names up in lights.

In the nine months since returning from Fiji, he'd added ten new staff and nearly doubled the agency's billings. On the walls, newly framed certificates informed passers-by that his agency had won awards for the best commercial of the year, best campaign, best print campaign, and best poster. A framed letter from Lavalle congratulated the agency on the most successful new product launch they'd ever had. In pride of place alongside reception, two plaques proclaimed Rowan's triumph in winning both Agency of the Year and Advertising Man of the Year. They were the talk of the town, the subject of stories in the leading dailies and even scored a snippet on the TV news. Life, as far as Rowan was concerned, could not get any better. And best of all, Sandra was within days of giving him the son he wanted. The baby's sex had been confirmed, and a framed Polaroid of the ultrasound sat on his desk, alongside pictures of Sandra and the girls.

'Hi,' he said as Sandra answered the phone. 'It's your loving husband. I hear you're still smuggling footballs under your dress.'

Sandra hung up the phone and lay down on her bed. The bedroom was the only airconditioned room in the house and the only place she felt moderately comfortable. Even though it was after five o'clock, the north-west breeze kept the temperatures outside up around 35 degrees, and not much cooler inside. She lay on her back and cradled her swollen belly in her hands. This was the biggest she'd ever been. Neither of her two previous pregnancies had even come close. She dreaded to think of the pain ahead of her and the stretch marks her little boy would leave behind. But the thought also caused her to smile. Her little boy wasn't little at all. Rochelle had been the biggest of the two girls, with a birth weight of 3.4 kilos. Her doctor had warned her to expect the new baby to weigh at least one kilo more, a fact which had delighted Rowan. He didn't just want a son, he wanted a big, strapping boy who'd grow to the height that had been denied him, and excel at every sport he turned his hand to. He wanted a footballer, not a poet, and the baby's weight encouraged him to believe he was well on the way to getting what he wanted.

Despite her discomfort, Sandra had to concede that getting pregnant again – especially with a boy – was probably the smartest thing she'd done in her life. Along with the Lavalle win, it had been the catalyst for a change in Rowan that not only made her forget the bad times, but doubt that there'd ever been a problem. She'd loved him before, but she adored the man he'd become. He still rose at six every morning, still went to the gym, still worked hard, but most nights he was home by seven-thirty and happy to be there. He seemed to have grown in stature and confidence, and with the confidence had come contentment. She knew with absolute certainty there were no more Glynises in his life. Of course, he still went out on wild celebratory nights with the staff – and they'd had plenty to celebrate – but the four a.m. homecomings had pulled back to one a.m., and he was responsible enough to leave his car at the office and come home by taxi. As she lay on her bed, she thanked God for her little boy, for Lavalle, and for the fact that she'd seen off the bad times without flipping her lid and doing something irreversible.

A car pulled into her driveway and stopped. She heard doors open and bang shut, followed by Rochelle's high-pitched squeals. With schools closed for the Christmas holidays and ballet, music and drama lessons also in recess, the girls had become bored, hot and irritable. They'd begged her to take them down to Balmoral Beach for a swim. Sandra hadn't been up to it and had rung Caroline, who'd leapt at the chance to play stand-in mum. She felt guilty about dumping the girls on Caroline, but also knew her friend wouldn't have it any other way.

Caroline doted on the girls and took them to the movies and McDonald's every chance she got. There'd been a time when Sandra had even worried whether Caroline's interest in her daughters was healthy. Caroline saw too much of them, and even rang them most nights before bedtime to wish them sweet dreams. In the end, Sandra didn't have the heart to speak out and was glad she hadn't. Because of the heat and her monstrously swollen belly, she'd relied on Caroline to do her Christmas shopping for her. She thought briefly about putting on a pot of coffee, but decided on a bottle of sauvignon blanc instead. She braced herself as the front door burst open and tiny feet hurtled her way.

'Hi,' called Caroline.

Sarah and Rochelle burst into the kitchen and threw themselves at her, both talking at once.

'We found a puffer fish,' said Sarah.

'It was alive,' said Rochelle. 'Blowed up like a balloon.'

'Like Mummy,' said Sandra. 'Ugh! Your hair's still wet and you're all covered in sand. Shower first, then tell me all about it.'

'Want me to supervise?' asked Caroline.

'Do pregnant women waddle? Just make sure the water's not too hot, then leave them to it. They know if they touch the taps they lose their pocket money. I'll open the wine.'

'Should you be drinking?' asked Caroline warily.

'Do you think it's going to make any difference at this stage?'

'No, probably not. Back in two minutes.'

Sandra opened the fridge door and let the cool air wash over her, glad that Rowan wasn't home to tell her off. Without the fridge to stand by and the bedroom airconditioner, she thought she would have expired in the heat. She made a note never to fall pregnant again when El Niño was due. The shelves were stacked with food for Christmas Day. She looked enviously at the prawns and oysters, the 3 kilogram red emperor Rowan planned to barbecue, the tray of perfect Queensland mangoes and the bottles of champagne and wine, and wondered if she'd still be in one piece to share it. What did hospitals serve mothers with new babies? Cold turkey and roast potatoes with brown sludge for gravy? Would she be allowed to drink alcohol?

'Okay, where's the wine?' Caroline wandered back into the kitchen. 'You haven't even taken it out of the fridge.'

'I didn't want it getting warm in the glass,' said Sandy lamely. She handed the bottle to Caroline to open, closed the fridge door and heaved herself up onto a stool. Caroline was wearing a thin cotton wrap over her costume, which became see-through against the afternoon light beaming in through the kitchen window. Sandra looked enviously at her friend's trim figure and wondered if she'd ever be that shape again. She was tempted to compliment Caroline on how slim she was looking, then thought better of it. Caroline would swap roles in an instant.

'Have you and Mike agreed upon a country yet?'

'We'd pretty much agreed on Colombia, but last night we met a couple who adopted a baby girl from Korea three years ago. She's absolutely gorgeous. Like a little china doll.'

'Does it matter which country you adopt from?'

'No, not really. In a lot of countries you have to bribe officials, and that sort of goes against the grain. But if that's what we have to do, that's what we have to do.'

'So it's Korea now?'

'We'd already put our names down for both Colombia and

Korea. Boy or girl, doesn't matter so long as it's a baby.'

'And Mike's fully committed?'

'Absolutely. Once he accepted it was the only option left to us, he's backed me one hundred per cent. He even handled the paperwork. He couldn't take his eyes off the little girl last night, and she seemed to take a shine to him. Now he's getting impatient.'

'Typical. How long do you think it'll be before they'll have a child for you?'

'A year, maybe less. But it could be as long as two years.' Caroline's shoulders sagged.

'But it could be sooner?'

'Hope so.' Caroline smiled weakly. 'You know, if you hadn't let me take your two out and play with them, I think I'd have gone mad. I'll just go and check on them.'

Sandra took a long sip on her wine and wondered at the injustice of it all. There had to be millions of babies around the world desperate for loving parents and the chance of a good life. And there were Caroline and Mike, desperate for a child and having to wait up to two years. It didn't seem right or fair. What was Christmas without children to share it with? She heard screams of delight coming from the bathroom and assumed Caroline was tickling the girls as she dried them. She felt tears come to her eyes for her friend. Poor Caro, she thought.

Sandra and the two girls waited until Rowan had come home so that they could all do their stretches together. The girls got a buzz out of it and so did Rowan. It wasn't just that they liked to compete against each other, some of Sandra's attempts to do even basic stretches reduced them all to fits of laughter. At the end of the stretches, the three of them clustered around her outsized stomach, put their hands on it to feel the baby's kicks and their ears to try to hear his little heartbeat. Sandra loved the closeness of it all, loved being the centre of attention and object of wonder, loved it even more when Rowan surprised her with flowers. Once people had thought she and Rowan were the perfect couple. That was the old days. Now they were the perfect family.

'Are you okay?' asked Rowan. He glanced at the bedside clock glowing in the dark alongside him. Two fifty-five a.m.

'Just another pee,' said Sandra.

'How many is that tonight?'

'Who's counting? I wish the little bloke would get a move on so I can get a good night's sleep.'

'Would you like me to make you a cup of tea?'

'God no! I'll be up peeing all night.'

'Anything I can do?'

'Rub my back.'

'You know something, Sandy? I don't think I've ever been happier in my life. I didn't know it was possible to feel this happy.'

'I didn't know it was possible to feel this fat.' Sandra lowered herself gingerly back onto the bed. 'I'm happy too. But I'll be a bloody sight happier once this bloke stops using me as his trampoline.'

At six o'clock Rowan silenced the alarm, rolled over and

went back to sleep until seven. He tried to slip out of bed without waking Sandra, but failed.

'Stay put,' he said. 'I'll get the girls up and dressed, feed them and point them at the telly. Can I get you anything?'

'I'll have that cup of tea now.'

'Anything happening?'

'You'll be the second to know.'

'Want me to stay home?'

'No way. Babies this size give plenty of warning. If anything happens you'll have time to drive home, change, have a coffee or even dinner if you like. No matter what time you get me to the hospital, I guarantee you'll be standing around twiddling your thumbs for at least six hours. But thanks for offering.'

'What if there's an emergency?'

'Caroline's on standby.'

'What if she's on the phone?'

'She's got call-waiting.'

'What if her car won't start?'

'She'll get a taxi here and use mine. Failing that, there's always Mum. I'm sure she could put Clive down for a moment to help out.'

'Yeah, but what if –'

'Shut up, Rowan. Just make me a cup of tea and go.'

'Anything happening?'

'No. Go back into your meeting.' Margaret managed to sound bored even though her first instinct was to laugh. Rowan had been in and out of meetings all day asking the same question. Barth was timing Rowan's appearances, comparing them to contractions, and making bets with the other staff on what time he'd appear next. They thought Rowan was behaving more like a first-time father than someone who already had two beautiful, healthy girls. What they failed to take into consideration was the fact that he hadn't had a son before. When Rowan's direct line rang, Margaret intercepted the call.

'Hi,' said Sandra. 'How's your baby?'

'He's doing fine,' said Margaret, 'but he's coming out of meetings every twenty minutes now. How's yours?'

'I think he's just realised it's Christmas and doesn't want to miss out on the presents. The contractions started coming on strong an hour or so ago.'

'Where are you?'

'At the hospital,' said Sandra. 'Caroline brought me when she picked the girls up. Saved her doing two trips. There's a cool change coming and bringing a thunderstorm with it. I thought I'd beat it to the hospital in case there was a traffic jam.'

'Do you want me to get Rowan?'

'Good heavens no. This is going to take ages.'

'Ouch.'

'Just ask Rowan to call me when he has a free moment, and above all tell him not to hurry over. Call on my mobile.'

'No problem. Would you like me to send over some magazines?'

'No. Just keep Rowan hosed down and occupied while I try to grab some sleep. Tell him Caroline's got the girls.'

'Good luck.' She hung up and turned towards Barth just as Rowan reappeared.

'Anything happening?'

'Nothing to get excited about,' said Margaret. 'And nothing to keep you out of your meeting.'

'Where's Sandy?'

'At the hospital trying to catch up on sleep. Anything else you want to know?'

'Hospital? Is everything okay?'

'Everything's fine.'

'I'll go there straightaway.'

'No need.'

'Sure?'

'Absolutely. Sandy went early, to beat the traffic and the storm.'

'Any news on Sandy's new Volvo?' Sandra loved her Peugeot 306 despite the fact that it seemed to start every week with a new problem, or not start at all. The time had come to trade it in and Christmas seemed the perfect opportunity. Besides, Rowan wanted a safer car for his daughters and new son.

'It's ready and waiting, baby capsule fitted.'

'Tell them to deliver it now and reverse it into the garage. I want it facing out when Sandy sees it for the first time. Don't forget to remind them about the ribbons. It has to look like a present.'

'That's all been taken care of. Now go back to your meeting.'

'Call me if anything happens.' Rowan turned and reluctantly shuffled back to the boardroom.

'They never grow up, do they?' said Margaret to no one in particular.

'How're you going?' asked Rowan. There were two other women in the ward besides Sandra, one a young, tearful girl of Mediterranean origin and her grim-faced, black-attired mother who offered no sympathy and spoke only to the rosary clutched in her clawing hands; the other a large, bored woman with her equally large, bored husband. She read *Women's Weekly* while he read the form guide. His beer gut hung so far over his belt he appeared more pregnant than his wife. They all looked up as Rowan burst into the ward. 'Aren't you supposed to have a private room?' said Rowan.

'That comes later,' said Sandra. 'This is the waiting room.' She leaned forward so that Rowan could kiss her. 'You're wet.'

'Thunderstorm. Everything all right?'

'Everything is happening exactly as it should, except that I can't remember ever feeling so completely stretched out of shape. I swear, Rowan, this is going to be the last.'

'Sure,' said Rowan.

'I mean it,' said Sandra. 'I've been warned to expect a lot of stitches.'

'Problem?'

'No. It's just that he's a bigger baby. Big and strong with a head the size of a football.'

'My boy,' said Rowan.

'My problem,' said Sandra. She squeezed her eyes shut and arched her back as a contraction took hold.

'Want me to call the doctor?'

'Yeah. In about four hours.'

Rowan's jaw dropped. 'Can't you hurry things along a bit?'

'Can't I what?'

'You know, push a bit harder or something. Go from latent to active.'

'Latent to active!' Sandra burst out laughing. 'My God, this is serious. You've been reading the book.'

'Can't they induce it, or something?' said Rowan doggedly.

'No. Not until mother nature's had first crack.'

'When did the doctor last come by?'

'Ten minutes before you did.'

'What did he say?'

'He said I'm going to have a baby.'

'Come on, Sandy ...'

'He said my cervix has dilated three centimetres.'

'Three centimetres.'

'Which means I've got another seven or so to go before your little bruiser sets out on his journey and they cut me in places no woman should ever be cut. Happy now?'

Rowan looked away and found the mother in black staring at him accusingly, and the big woman glaring at him over her *Women's Weekly*. The strange thing was he felt guilty even though he was damned if he knew what he was supposed to have done wrong. He felt guilty for putting his wife in this predicament, guilty for causing her so much pain. 'I'm sorry,' he said.

'You weren't at the time,' said Sandra. She started laughing again. 'As a matter of fact, you were feeling pretty pleased with yourself, reckoned you could feel your darts hitting the board.'

The big woman's big husband looked up at the analogy, as if he'd just heard something he could relate to. He gave Rowan a wink. 'Good one,' he said.

'Jesus, can't we get a private room?' asked Rowan as softly as he could.

'Doesn't work that way, I told you. We just get stack parked until the baby enters the drop zone.' Sandra tensed once more at another contraction.

'You're supposed to relax.' said Rowan. 'It hurts less.'

'This one's going to hurt no matter what I do. Je-eeesus!'

'You okay?'

'Yeah, yeah ... Rowan, why don't you go find the canteen, sit down, have a cup of coffee and leave me to my second thoughts.'

'What if something happens?'

'You'll hear me scream from there.'

Rowan sat in the cafeteria wondering how hospitals could possibly hope to cure patients of cancer when they couldn't even make a decent cup of coffee. Four hours, Sandra had said. What the hell was he going to do for four hours? The coloured lights on the plastic Christmas tree in the middle of the cafeteria blinked away the seconds. He'd seen traffic lights with more cheer. He took another sip from his polystyrene cup and once again wondered what they used instead of coffee. The last time he'd had anything that tasted as foul was when Sarah had made coffee for him one morning as he lay in bed with a hangover. She'd added two spoonfuls of tea to a plunger filled with used coffee grounds from the previous night's festivities. That brew at least had a vague resemblance to coffee, even though it had almost caused him to puke.

The thought of Sarah made him check his watch. The minute hand had moved all the way from nine-forty-nine to nine-fifty. He decided to wander outside and phone Caroline on his mobile. Maybe his girls were still up.

'Hello Caro?' The rain had stopped but the air was still heavy with moisture. A ribbon of cars snaked up the Pacific Highway, eager to beat Santa to their homes.

'Rowan!' The excitement in Caroline's voice made him flinch. 'Well . . .? How's the baby? How's Sandra?'

'Whoa!' said Rowan. 'Not so fast. Things are still happening here, and happening bloody slowly at that. Sandy's sent me out because she wants to suffer in silence. I just rang to say goodnight to the girls.'

'Oh.'

'Can you put them on?'

'They're in bed fast asleep. It's nearly ten o'clock.'

'I know what time it is. I guessed as much. Thought I'd ring on the off-chance.'

'Sorry, Rowan.'

'Hey, no worries. How's Mike?'

'Seventh heaven. He read bedtime stories to the girls. They kept him reading for over an hour. They put him to sleep as well. He's unconscious on the sofa, snoring his head off.'

'Good for him. Anything arranged with the girls' presents?'

'I brought some over here but left most at your place. They have to wake up to something on Christmas Day. I'll tell them Santa left the rest of their presents by their beds at home.'

'Thanks, Caro. I don't know how we'd have managed without you.'

'Don't mention it. You all right?'

'Just fed up with the waiting. I just want Sandy to get on with it and have the kid so that I can see him. See how much he looks like me, see how big he is, hold him, let him know that he's in for one hell of an exciting life.'

'I can't wait,' said Caroline.

'I have no choice,' said Rowan. 'I want him here, I want him here now!'

'I'm sure if Sandy could pop him out she would. How is she, anyway?'

'Bit scared. She thinks it's going to hurt like hell. They've warned her that she'll need a lot of stitches.'

'Ouch! Poor thing.'

'Yeah, she's spent a lifetime stretching every part of her but the bit that matters right now. What the heck, it'll all be over in a few hours. By morning she'll have forgotten all about the pain.'

'Let's hope,' said Caroline doubtfully. 'In the meantime, you look after her. Okay?'

'No worries,' said Rowan. 'It's not as if we haven't been down this road before. Once the baby's born she'll be on top of the world. Once the lump ceases being a lump and becomes a living, breathing human being, she'll be as right as rain. God, Caro, I can hardly wait. I just want to ... Jesus ... I don't even know what I want to do. I just want to do something, anything! I want that kid!'

He thought of the heavy bag, of taking a swing and knocking it flying. Yes! That's what every hospital should have. A heavy bag for expectant fathers. And a heavy-duty winch to help reluctant babies along.

Sandra tried her best to stay positive and relaxed but the pain of each successive contraction was worse than the one before, inconceivably worse, and had reached the point where she wanted to scream the house down. She clenched her teeth and fought against the onset of the next contraction. She wasn't ready for it, wasn't ready for the pain, wasn't ready to once more suppress the urge to scream. She didn't scream, wasn't a screamer, had no time for women who were.

'Uh ... uh ... agghhhhh ...!' she groaned. 'Oh ... oh ... ohhhhh!' This through clenched teeth.

'Push!' said Rowan.

'Relax,' urged the nurse.

'It hurts!' said Sandra. 'Oh God it hurts!'

'How about an epidural?' said Rowan.

'She won't have one,' said the nurse.

'What about pethidine?'

'We've given her a shot and she refuses any more. She says she wants all her wits about her when she holds the baby for the first time.'

'Agghhhh!' said Sandra.

'How about giving her some Syntocinon to help things along?'

'Induce her? What do you think's happening here?' The nurse gave Rowan a withering look. 'Why don't you stop trying to medicate and do what you're here to do – encourage, sympathise, share the burden.'

'I think what Sister is saying is that your wife is doing very nicely.' The gynaecologist looked up from his privileged position between Sandra's legs to give Rowan the benefit of his opinion. 'In fact, if I may make an observation, I'd say your son appears to have inherited at least one of your characteristics.'

'Yeah?' said Rowan. His face lit up.

'Yes. Your impatience.' The doctor returned to his task at hand. The nurse sniggered.

'Agghhhh!' Sandra moaned as her baby renewed his efforts to force entry. 'Aggghhhh!'

'Push!' said Rowan. 'Push! Push! Push!'

'Push yourself!' snapped Sandra. 'OH, OH, OH GOD!' Despite her best intentions Sandra's scream ripped through the delivery rooms. A chorus of screams followed as other mothers-to-be seized on the precedent.

'Here he comes,' said the doctor. 'I'm going to have to do an episiotomy, just a small incision to make things easier. Nurse?' A second nurse moved in to assist.

'Let me see!' said Rowan.

'Stay where you are and hold your wife,' said the doctor calmly. 'I don't need your help, she does. Here he comes, here comes the head. Push for me now, Sandy, push ... push ... that's the girl!'

'Ah-ah-AHHHH!'

'Here he comes,' said the doctor. 'Head's clear.'

'Let me see,' said Rowan.

'Stay where you are!' said the doctor. No, not said, ordered. He glanced sharply at the nurse, whose lips suddenly tightened.

'What's the matter?' said Rowan. He'd sat through enough presentations, read enough expressions, seen enough looks exchanged to realise something was up.

'Everything's fine,' said the doctor. 'C'mon, Sandy, give me the shoulders.'

'Ohhhh!' said Sandra.

'That's the girl! Head rotating nicely. Well done!'

'What's up, for Christ's sake?' said Rowan.

'Everything's fine,' said the doctor, but he couldn't meet Rowan's eyes. 'Shoulders through ... Come on, Sandy! One last push.'

'Let me see!' Rowan let go of Sandra's arms and raced around behind the nurse to see his son. She tried to hold him back but he brushed her aside. He had to stand on tip-toes to see past the doctor, to see the baby boy he'd wanted for longer than he could remember, to see the doctor's expert hands cradle the baby at the instant of birth, to see what was wrong, see why they were concerned. Rowan fully expected to see a monster with two heads or a baby with missing limbs. What he saw shocked him even more. It left him dumbfounded, stunned, wounded beyond all measure of pain. 'Oh God!' he said. 'Oh God, no!' He spun around and glared incredulously at Sandra. Looked once more at the baby. 'Oh Christ ...' he moaned.

'What's happening? What's happening?' screamed Sandra. 'What's wrong?' But Rowan had gone, fled away down the corridor. She turned to the doctor. 'What's wrong? What's wrong with my baby?' She heard a cry, almost like the bleat of a lamb, and knew instantly what it was. Her instinct to smile momentarily overcame her fears.

'All yours, nurse,' said the doctor. He finished tying the cord and handed the baby over.

'What's wrong with him?' demanded Sandra. 'Please! I have a right to know!'

'Nothing, nothing at all,' said the doctor, but he didn't smile at her or look up from his suturing. 'Listen to him. He's a perfectly healthy baby boy.'

The nurse wasn't smiling as she wiped down the baby, wrapped him and placed him on Sandra's breast. Sandra forced her head up off her pillow, hungry for a first glimpse of her son. Whatever she intended to say went unsaid. The words froze on her lips. There was no mistaking the baby's features, his tight little fuzz of hair, or the colour of his skin.

'Oh my God . . . !' said Sandra.

'Waaaaaa,' cried the baby, crying for comfort, crying for love, a stranger in an alien world.

The nurse checked the watch pinned to the front of her uniform, and entered eleven-fifty-nine as the time of birth, 24 December as the date. As she double-checked her watch it ticked over to midnight.

'Merry Christmas,' she said.

Thirteen

Rowan ran. He ran down corridors, past faces that stared and yelled at him to watch out. He ran past the cafeteria with its cheerless Christmas tree and undrinkable coffee. He ran from the looks the doctor had exchanged with the nurses, ran from their embarrassment, ran from the tiny dark face that proclaimed his cuckolding, ran from his shame, ran from a life that was tumbling down around him, ran out across the car park.

Fallen rain lay trapped in puddles that flooded his shoes and soaked his trouser cuffs. He didn't notice. Trapped rain showered over him as he wrenched the driver's door open. He didn't notice. Rain distorted his view of the world as he looked through the windshield, made streaks of tail-lights, turned headlights into showers of molten metal. He didn't notice. His hands gripped the top of the steering wheel and he clung to it as if to do otherwise would result in his slipping to oblivion.

His head fell onto his hands. There was a sound like

sobbing, a groan like pain, a cry like despair. Then nothing. His senses shut down. He sat unfeeling, unhearing, unseeing, waiting, waiting, waiting for his mind to recover from its shock and tell him what to do next. He could no longer comprehend or even glimpse the shape and form of the life ahead of him, couldn't even guess at what the cornerstones might be, where he might find shelter, where he might find comfort, where he might hide.

When feelings returned they came in the form of bitterness and shame. He could hear the sniggers and innuendos, feel the pitying looks and see the smiles on the faces of his opposition. How could he face his staff? How could he face anyone? What would he say to his girls? In an instant, he'd gone from Advertising Man of the Year to Joke of the Century and there wasn't a damn thing he could do about it.

He started his car, switched on lights and wipers, slowly edged out of the car park and stopped at the traffic lights. Someone tooted their horn and when he looked, the red light had become green. He turned left towards Mosman and home, then right towards Caroline and his girls. *His girls!* Tortured windshield wipers screeched and scraped, begging to be relieved of the task of wiping away rain that had long ceased falling. He turned into the street where Caroline and Mike lived, where his girls were tucked up in bed dreaming of Christmas, Santa Claus and stockings filled with sweets and presents. Some houses still had lights on but Caroline and Mike's was in darkness. He stopped outside, wondered momentarily what he was going to say, then decided there was nothing he could say. Rowan rang the bell twice before

Mike opened the door, Caroline behind him, both looking worried.

'Rowan!' said Caroline. She looked closely at his face. 'What's the matter?'

'I've come for the girls.'

'What?' said Caroline. 'It's after one o'clock. You can't wake them now. How's Sandy? What's up? Is something wrong?'

'Sandy's fine. Baby's fine. A big healthy boy, ten fingers, ten toes.' His voice belied the sentiment.

'Congratulations!' said Mike, grabbing his hand and shaking it.

'Fantastic!' said Caroline. 'Come on in, come on in and tell us all about it.' She kissed him but he didn't respond.

'I'd rather not.'

'Rubbish!' said Mike. 'Come on in and have a drink. Wet the baby's head.'

'Not tonight.'

'Are you all right?' said Caroline.

Rowan saw them staring at him like he was a specimen in a jar, and a pretty poor specimen at that – a man who couldn't satisfy his wife, who sent her looking elsewhere, to bigger, taller men, for her gratification. He didn't know what to say and knew only that he didn't want to say anything. Humiliation burned like raw flame in his blood. 'I'm fine,' he said. 'Really. Forget about the girls. You're quite right. I'll come by in the morning.' He turned to go.

'Wait!' said Caroline. 'You can't just go! How much did he weigh?'

'I don't know,' said Rowan.

'Come on! Don't leave us in the dark. Who does he take after?' said Caroline, trying desperately to draw him out. 'Does he look like his father?'

'Yes,' said Rowan. 'As a matter of fact he does.'

The phone was ringing when Rowan arrived home. He ignored it, walked straight to his liquor cabinet and broke the neck seal on a bottle of Johnny Walker Black. He cracked ice from the freezer, poured a triple and didn't bother adding water. The liquor hit the back of his throat like a bullet. The phone began ringing once more.

'Rowan Madison.'

'Rowan, it's Mike. We're worried about you. Is everything okay?'

'Everything's fine, Mike. Thanks for calling.'

'Don't hang up!'

'Look, Mike, Sandy's fine, the baby's fine. His crying is probably keeping half of Sydney awake. If you don't believe me, ring the hospital.'

'We believe you. We've rung the hospital. Mother and baby both doing well. It's you we're worried about. For Christ's sake, tell me what's wrong?'

'I'm tired, Mike. It's been a big night. In fact, it's been a big fucking year. I'm having a quiet scotch and then I'm going to bed.'

'You sure you're okay?'

'I'm sure. Why wouldn't I be? I appreciate your concern but there's no cause for it. Now can I go to bed?'

'You're absolutely sure you're okay? You're not sick or anything? Not hiding something?'

'Mike, I'm fine. Really. Now goodnight.'

'Well, you don't sound right to me. If you need me, just call. I'll come over in the morning anyway with the girls.'

'Appreciate it.' Rowan hung up, looked in his glass and wondered where all the scotch had gone. He added more ice and poured, didn't bother stopping at a triple. The ice crackled, a sound that evoked memories of new accounts and celebrations. Rowan smiled grimly. He made a call to Sandra's mother, to keep a promise, left a message on her answering machine, then switched on his own.

He headed for the lounge, where Sandra had left the Christmas tree's lights on. They shone on the circle of presents clustered around its base and were light enough for him. Cards full of cheer draped over a ribbon hung the length of the lounge wall. Rochelle's metre-high stuffed panda stared at him gleefully, buttoned eyes gleaming maniacally every time the coloured lights flashed. Rowan slumped down on the sofa and pushed his shoes off. His feet were cold, his socks soaking wet and he didn't give a shit. The fridge motor cut in, the only sound in an otherwise silent house. It was the season of goodwill towards all mankind, but there was a woman in hospital he could never forgive. And over in Fiji, a black bastard he could happily kill.

Sandra cried as they wheeled her away from the delivery room to her private ward. She cried when they took her baby away from her to lie in the crib alongside her, fearing they'd punish her for her sins and not bring him back. She cried as she lay back against her pillows, sleepless and distraught, overwhelmed by shock, experiencing simultaneously the weight of her guilt and enormous upwellings of love for her new little baby boy. But she felt resentment too, swirling in the emotional mélange, and a sense of unfairness and of being cheated. Why couldn't he be Rowan's child? What had happened? What had gone wrong? Her breasts had begun to lactate and make wet patches on her nightie as she alternated between visions of Rowan storming out of the delivery room and the sight of the helpless, sleeping, tiny dark face that depended so absolutely upon her, and deserved her utmost affection.

Sandra flicked on her bedside lamp and pulled the crib gingerly towards her so that she could see him more clearly. He appeared to smile, as if aware of her attentions, and she responded automatically. How could she feel resentment before such innocence? For once in her life she didn't know how to react or how to feel. Her mind cannoned from elation to utter despair, ignoring all points in between. She wanted to give her little son every ounce of love she could muster, reassure him that he was welcome and wanted, but was restrained by wave after wave of guilt and shame. The duty nurse kept looking in to check up on her and encourage her to sleep. When Sandra complained about the pain from the stitches in her perineum, the nurse said she'd get her some aspirin and slipped her a Mogadon as well. Sandra drifted into uneasy sleep and, later, barely managed to keep her eyes open when her son was placed on her breast to be fed.

Though Christmas Day dawned bright and clear, Sandra awoke with a feeling of dread. It was a day for confrontation, confession and consequences. A day for counting the victims of her victimless sin. Somewhere down the corridor someone's TV or radio played carols. The day nurse burst in, filled with hearty good cheer to gush over her and her little interloper. The nurse gave her an apparatus to express her excess milk but nothing that would help ease her growing sense of dread.

Sandra swung her legs over the side of the bed, determined to use her toilet rather than the metal bottle, and abruptly changed her mind as she felt a sharp sting from her stitches. The bottle would do for the moment, she decided. Episiotomies were known as the unkindest cut of all, but in truth, they weren't the cruellest. That honour went to the occupant of the crib alongside her, the beautiful little boy who'd begun to stir and screw his tiny face up as he tried to come to terms with this new sensation called hunger. Loveable as he was, he was the cuckoo in the robin's nest, the baby that shouldn't have been there, the product of sperm that had escaped and defied all odds.

Sandra reached over to pick her son up and feed him. Maybe they could give each other comfort until Rowan came to visit. Would he bring the girls, she wondered, and how would she explain if he did?

The sun woke Rowan just after seven. It came through the gap Sandra had left in the curtains so that their Christmas tree could be seen from the street and contribute to the seasonal gaiety. His empty glass and whisky bottle cast tall shadows across the coffee table. He sat up lethargically, waited for the jackhammers to start in his head, was pleasantly surprised when they didn't. Maybe they had Christmas Day off. He looked at the rings his glass had left in the table's polished veneer, wondering if he should sponge them immediately or later. Before he'd reached any decision, his mind dragged him to contemplate the larger issue.

Rowan took stock of all the things around him, the memories, feelings and experiences the room contained, rose and began a tour of his home. He baulked at entering his own bedroom – his and Sandra's bedroom – and wandered instead to the girls' room. Their lives and personalities were inscribed indelibly in their paintings and pictures hanging on the wall, in the toys in their toy box, in the dolls and stuffed animals that occupied privileged positions on their beds, in the wardrobes and drawers stuffed with little girls' clothes.

He took stock of everything he stood to lose and tried to gauge how painful the loss would be. When he wandered back to the kitchen he found notices advising of the recommencement of ballet, drama, music and softball stuck to the fridge door by magnets shaped like elephants and monkeys. Rowan had worked hard for the right to have those notices, had built his life around the necessity for them, could not begin to imagine life without them. He opened the door to shelves stacked with seafood and fruit, and remembered his Christmas Day obligations. Christmas dinner for the family, Sandra's mother, her friend Clive, and Caroline and Mike, at home if Sandra hadn't gone into hospital, at Caroline and Mike's place if she had. How could he possibly endure such a day?

He reached for the coffee jar, let the cupboard door swing back behind him. As he boiled the water, he ran through his immediate options. Hopping into his car and driving off into the sunset appealed but he had the girls to consider. Taking the girls to hospital to see their mother and their new little brother didn't appeal at all. But how could he not? At any moment he expected to hear a car pull up, little feet run up the drive, and a mini tornado, generated by two little girls, ripping apart the wrapping on the presents under the Christmas tree. He expected Caroline and Mike to be standing mere centimetres behind them, asking questions he had no inclination to answer. He spooned more grounds than necessary into the jug and added hot water, enough for two large mugs. There was only one card he could play and he figured it would be consistent with his behaviour of the previous night. If he played it well, it might even excuse him for the rest of the day. But then he still had the girls to consider and it was, after all, Christmas Day. Maybe his ploy could keep him on the bench until lunchtime, when the nigger would be well and truly out of the woodpile.

He poured two mugs of coffee and took both to bed with him. After undressing, he grabbed the thermometer out of the bedroom cupboard and placed it in a glass of water beside his bed. Unwashed, unshaven, pale and hungover, he figured the thermometer was the only prop he'd need. He'd finished one coffee and was halfway through the second when he heard Mike's car pull up and turn into the drive. He dipped the thermometer into the coffee and withdrew it immediately before the mercury blew. Thirty-nine degrees would do nicely if Caroline got nosy. He listened to the doorbell ring, and let it ring, knowing that sooner or later Caroline would use her own key to get in.

'Yoo-hoo,' called Caroline.

'In here,' he called back. Little feet pounded down the hallway towards him.

'Daddy! Look!' screamed Sarah. She was wearing new clothes and blowing on a mouth organ, which she insisted on blowing directly into his ear as he cuddled her. It didn't matter. It was all he could do not to choke up and he didn't want to let her go.

'Me! Me! Look at me!' screamed Rochelle. She climbed onto his bed and smothered him in kisses. The two girls jockeyed for position as they brought him up to date with Santa's largesse.

'Okay if we come in?' said Mike. 'We've been up since five.'

'And loving every minute,' said Caroline. 'I thought you'd be up and ready to visit Sandy.' She spotted the thermometer, picked it up and twisted it to read the temperature. 'Are you all right?'

'Yeah,' said Rowan wearily.

'What's wrong?'

'Bit of a fever, headache.'

'Are you all right to visit Sandy?'

'I'm not sure that would be a good thing. Might have a virus. I don't think Sandy would thank me if I passed it on to her. I was hoping you'd take the girls.'

'Of course,' said Mike.

'Happy to,' said Caroline.

'Did Santa leave any presents for me and Rocky?' asked Sarah.

'Did he?' echoed Rochelle.

'Did he what,' said Rowan. 'Go look under the tree.' The two girls took off like rockets.

'Mind if we go and watch?' asked Caroline.

'Somebody should,' said Rowan.

'Get you anything?' asked Mike.

'I've just had a coffee,' said Rowan. 'Thanks anyway. You go with the girls.'

As Caroline and Mike headed off to the lounge, Rowan remembered the empty bottle of scotch on the coffee table. What the hell, he thought, they'd find out soon enough.

'Congratulations!'

Sandra looked up to see Caroline standing in the doorway holding a bunch of flowers, Mike alongside her, holding Sarah and Rochelle.

'Congratulations!' echoed Mike.

'Mummy, look what Santa brought me!' said Sarah.

'Look at me!' screamed Rochelle.

Caroline walked straight over to the bed and kissed Sandy on the cheek. Mike stood by awkwardly, unsure what to do with the girls.

'Put them down, Mike,' said Sandra. 'Girls, just be careful, Mummy's a bit sore.'

'Where's the baby?' asked Sarah, staring into the empty crib.

'They've just taken him to be weighed. They'll bring him back in a minute. Where's Rowan?'

'He's got a virus,' said Caroline.

'A hangover more likely,' said Mike. 'I found an empty bottle of scotch. Looks like he spent the night celebrating.'

Sandra flinched.

'How are you feeling?' asked Caroline. 'You seem a bit down.'

'Childbirth does that to you.'

'I gotta bear,' said Rochelle. 'A pandy.'

'I got a bike,' said Sarah. 'It's pink and it's got trainer wheels. What did you get?'

Before Sandra could answer, the day nurse breezed into the ward carrying her precious bundle. The little dark face was framed in a cream-coloured woollen blanket.

'Oh, would you look at that!' said Caroline. 'What a sweetie! Hope your baby's as cute.'

'Caroline, he is my baby.' Sandra turned away, unable to face her friend, her daughters or her shame.

'Wha . . . ?' Caroline looked from baby to mother, not once, not twice but three times. It seemed to take an eternity but finally comprehension dawned. Blood drained from her face. She opened her mouth in horror, looked again at the baby, looked back at Sandy. Rowan's strange behaviour. The bottle of scotch. The tears starting to course down Sandra's cheeks. 'Oh God no!' Caroline said, her voice barely a whisper. Her arms crossed in front of her, her hands clasped her shoulders protectively. 'Oh dear God!'

Mike stood bewildered, confused. Sandra could no longer

bear the shame and covered her face with her hands. Her shoulders shook. Her tears found passage through the crevices in her fingers.

'Nice day for it,' said the nurse as she tucked the baby into its crib. 'Nice to have a dry Christmas Day for a change.' Sandy's crying didn't strike her as in the least bit unusual. New mothers did the oddest things. She swung around and left.

'What's wrong, Mummy?' asked Sarah. Rochelle just stared, wondering what she was missing out on this time.

'Whose baby did you say that was?' said Mike. No one answered. Caroline had begun crying as well. Mike didn't know exactly what was happening but knew enough to realise that a strategic withdrawal was called for. 'Come on, Sarah, Rocky,' he said. 'I know where we can get ice-creams.'

Caroline sat down on the edge of the bed, put her arms around Sandra and waited for her friend's sobbing to ease. She gently prised Sandra's hands apart.

'I'm so sorry, Sandy,' she said. 'So sorry.'

'Bloody condoms!' said Sandra bitterly.

'What are you going to do?'

'I don't know. I haven't a clue.'

'What did Rowan say?'

'He took one look at the baby and bolted.'

'He must be shattered. Oh God. What are you going to do?'

'I don't know! I don't even know if I still have a husband. I don't know if I still have a family or a house to go home to. I don't know what I'm going to do! I don't know!' She burst into tears again and this time her sorrow and fears could not be contained. She grabbed hold of Caroline and wept on her shoulders, shuddering as great sobs wracked her body. 'What am I going to do, Caro? What's going to happen to me?'

As Caroline waited for Sandra to calm down, she felt riven by pangs of guilt at her possible role in the catastrophe. How much of the blame lay with her? After all, screwing a black man had been her fantasy. She'd been the promoter, the advocate, the urger.

Mike returned with the girls, figuring fifteen minutes was long enough for Caroline and Sandra to cover whatever territory needed covering. He didn't like to see Caroline cry, and the black baby in the crib had him wondering. No matter how he looked at it, he couldn't find a rational explanation that brought him any joy. Unhappily, the least probable explanation also seemed the most likely. Life held many surprises but he doubted he'd ever experience another remotely comparable. He opened the door, took one look and wondered how on earth he could distract the girls a second time. How many ice-creams could a grown man eat?

'I feel like it's my fault, Sandy. I feel like I put you up to this. Let me speak to Rowan. I'll explain what happened. I'll make him listen.'

'I have to talk to him,' said Sandra.

'Of course, but let me talk to him first. Pave the way for you. Tell him it wasn't your fault. He loves you, Sandy, that's important. That has to count for something.'

The baby started whimpering.

'Oh, listen to him,' said Caroline. She reached into the crib and gently lifted the baby up. 'Would you look at him. He's so adorable!' She cradled him and held him against her chest, reached down and kissed his tiny forehead. The baby's lips smacked together and he made little sucking noises. Reluctantly she passed him over to Sandra, watched as her friend slipped the strap of her nightie and the baby latched onto her breast. It was too much for Caroline and she had to look away. The tears that began to flow weren't for Sandra but for herself, and they were tears bitter with irony. All she wanted from life was a baby of her own, a baby to love, to cuddle and to mother; and there were Sandra and Rowan with a perfect little baby boy, arguing over the colour.

Marion and Clive came to visit shortly after Caroline and Mike had left with the girls. They came bearing flowers and gifts, hearty in their cheer, her mother clearly excited at the prospect of seeing her new grandson. The message Rowan had left on their answering machine had done nothing to prepare them. Their cheer evaporated with one glance in the crib.

'Good grief!' said Marion. 'Sandy, what have you done?'

'It wasn't meant to happen like this.'

'I should hope not,' said Marion. 'Especially with a black man!'

'What's being black got to do with it?'

'Oh, Sandy, grow up! Poor Rowan,' her mother said. 'That's who I feel sorry for. Poor old Rowan. You with a black man, Sandy. Really!' Marion couldn't bring herself to do any more than glance at the baby, as if she couldn't face the evidence of her daughter's crime, denying the slightest possibility that the baby in the crib could be related to her in any way at all. She made no attempt to pick him up or touch him. Once she'd recovered from her shock, she glared angrily at Sandra and set about imposing her solution.

'You'll give it up for adoption, of course.'

'No!'

'Don't be silly, girl! That's what people do.'

'He's my son!'

'Yes, that is the problem, dear. Give it up now before you get attached to it. That's what any sensible person would do. Give it up and then apologise to Rowan.'

'No. No way.' Sandy reached into the crib and lifted the baby up and onto her breast.

'Give it up or you'll live to regret it, you mark my words. I know about these things, dear.'

'Yes, she does,' chipped in Clive. 'My word. You should listen to your mother, you know.'

'What do you mean?' said Sandra.

'Just give it up,' insisted Marion. 'Put it behind you and salvage what you can. That's all you can do.'

'No! He's my baby. He's my baby!' She clung to him protectively.

'You seriously want to risk your marriage for this?' Marion's nose turned up as she glanced at Sandy's unwelcome little bundle.

'He's my baby! I can't abandon him.'

'Come on, Clive, we're leaving,' said Marion disgustedly. 'There's no talking sense to her. There's no point in trying to help people who won't be helped.'

'Just hold it there,' said Sandy. 'What makes you the almighty authority on these things?'

Marion ignored her, grabbed Clive's arm and began to pull him away. Clive hesitated and, to Sandra's bewilderment, threw her a parting wink and a wry smile.

'No doubt about it,' he said. 'You're your mother's daughter.'

'I can't believe Sandra would do something like that,' said Mike to break the silence. 'What on earth possessed her?' He always drove slowly with the girls in the car and a succession of red lights hadn't helped. Caroline glared at him. Too late, he remembered the girls and changed tack. 'What do you think of your little brother?'

'He's cute,' said Sarah. 'I like his hair. It's all frizzy.'

'Like Pandy,' said Rochelle.

'When Mummy brings him home, I'm going to show him my new bike.'

'I show him Pandy,' said Rochelle.

'What do you think we should call him?' asked Mike.

'Ernie Dingo,' said Rochelle.

Caroline burst out laughing. Mike had to wrestle with the steering. Ernie Dingo was an Aboriginal actor.

'Rowan Junior,' said Sarah. 'Mummy told me before she went into hospital.'

Caroline stopped laughing.

'Maybe we should just call him Junior,' said Mike. And more softly, 'Sammy Davis Junior.'

When they reached Rowan's, they found him waiting

on the front steps, the seafood and wines in eskies at his feet.

Caroline turned to the girls. 'You two wait in the car.'

'I want to see Daddy,' said Sarah, unbuckling.

'Me too,' said Rochelle.

Any hopes Caroline had entertained for quiet commiserations were dashed as the girls leapt out of the car and raced over to Rowan. She was pleased to see Rowan's face light up, see him hold out his arms and embrace both girls as they reached him. Maybe, just maybe, he was softening.

'Daddy, you should see him,' said Sarah. 'He's got frizzy hair.'

'Has he?' said Rowan.

'His name's Juni,' said Rochelle.

'How about that?' said Rowan. He looked up as Caroline and Mike approached. 'Marion rang from the hospital. Wanted to know if Christmas dinner was still on. They want to come for the sake of the girls.' Rowan smiled thinly.

'Do you think you could put the girls down and give me a hug?' said Caroline.

'Sure. Just don't say anything, okay? Not now.' He stood slowly and turned to the girls. 'Sarah, Rocky, go get your swimming costumes.' He waited until they'd dashed indoors before opening his arms to Caroline.

'Jesus, Rowan, I'm so sorry.'

'So am I.'

'I don't know what to say.'

'Say nothing.'

'I feel partly to blame.'

'Don't see why. It only takes two to tango, Caro, and you weren't even there.'

'I just can't believe it,' said Mike. 'It's just not like Sandy to do something like that.'

'Apparently it is.'

'What are you going to do?' asked Mike.

'Enjoy lunch.'

'After that?'

'See if the gym's open.'

'You know what I mean. You're going to have to talk to Sandy,' said Caroline.

'Is that right?' Rowan turned away from Caroline and picked up one of the eskies to carry to the car. 'Sometimes actions speak louder than words. Sometimes actions leave nothing left to say. I've got a feeling this is one of those times.' He started walking to the car.

Caroline followed, pleading. 'You can't just walk away from it, Rowan, you've got to talk about it, talk to Sandy, hear her side. What happened was just . . . I don't know . . . an aberration, a freak accident.'

'Sure,' said Rowan. 'The kind of thing that could happen getting in to bed.'

'You can't just turn your back on her. You've got to talk to her. She hasn't stopped crying since the baby was born. This is the worst day of her life, too, you know.'

'Yeah. It's a black day all round.'

'Stop it, Rowan! Stop it!' Caroline burst into tears, so upset that Rowan dropped the esky and put a comforting arm around her. Sarah and Rochelle appeared at the front door and stopped dead in their tracks.

Mike came rushing to Caroline's assistance. 'For Christ's sake, Rowan! What are you doing to her?'

'Sorry Mike, sorry Caro. I shouldn't take it out on you.'

'Promise me you'll go see Sandy after lunch, Rowan. Promise me!' Caroline pulled away from Rowan and stood glaring at him.

He put his hand up in mock surrender. 'Okay, I guess I owe you that. I'll go see her. Talk to her. But I don't expect it'll solve anything.'

'Thanks, Rowan.' Caroline wiped her eyes.

'Now can we drop the subject?' Rowan felt small hands latch tentatively onto his own, glanced down and saw his two daughters looking up at him reproachfully.

'Why is Auntie Caroline crying, Daddy?' asked Sarah.

'I don't know,' said Rowan. He forced himself to smile, although the smile was grim. 'Maybe Santa brought her a present she doesn't like. But she's lucky, she can take hers back.'

Rowan did not visit Sandra that afternoon. He played with Sarah and Rochelle in the swimming pool before lunch and afterwards listened patiently to Caroline's explanation of how Sandra came to be carrying a Fijian baby. Her explanation changed nothing. Every time he looked up, he'd catch Marion watching him and would have to endure another sympathetic smile. She felt sorry for him, Mike and Caroline felt sorry for him, even Clive felt sorry for him.

'Got to watch those blackfellas,' said Clive, in what he

imagined were words of sympathy. 'My oath, you do. Bloody insatiable.'

It burned Rowan that people like Clive felt sorry for him, felt superior because they'd escaped misfortune and he hadn't. Maybe soon the whole bloody world would feel sorry for him. Rowan hated that prospect more than anything. He would be humiliated, emasculated and, above all, belittled. It was something he could never tolerate. He endured by drinking himself into a paralytic mess. He drank with anger and bitterness and it didn't matter much what was poured into his glass. Mike tried to slow him up with beer but Rowan just drank more quickly. Wine hardly touched the sides. When he became too drunk to stand, Mike helped him into the guest bedroom, where he collapsed into a dead sleep. Later that evening, Mike and Caroline drove him and the girls home, put the girls to bed and left Rowan to fend for himself. They went on to the hospital to visit Sandra. Rowan went straight to the liquor cabinet and cracked open another Johnny Walker Black.

He flicked on the TV for distraction. Eddie Murphy played a Hollywood cop on one channel, Whoopi Goldberg wise-cracked on another. When he flicked to the ABC, Jessye Norman was singing opera. SBS was re-running *Black Orpheus.*

'Jesus!' he said. 'Whatever happened to white Christmases?'

Colour and race had never been an issue with Rowan. People were clever or stupid, good-looking or ugly, rich or poor, and the colour of their skin a total irrelevance. Tolerance was not a conscious decision, rather a decision that had never had to be made. Yet as he channel-hopped from one black face to another, it was easy to feel that he wasn't a victim of coincidence but of a conspiracy to remind him of the colour of the baby that had stolen its way into Sandy's womb and that, one way or another, he was being mocked. He switched off.

A few kilometres away, in North Sydney, there was a gym with a heavy bag just waiting for him to beat the crap out of it, and he deeply regretted the fact that he hadn't made it there.

Fourteen

Some time during the early hours of Boxing Day morning, Sandra made a decision. She lay in bed, her swollen breasts aching, her stitches complaining, mentally and physically wrung dry. Rowan's non-appearance had convinced her that if the situation was to be resolved in the near future – or even at all – it was up to her to take the initiative. She'd suffered Rowan's flirtations and flings in silence until she'd learned to speak out, and she'd revelled in the benefits of speaking out right up until the moment her little imposter had entered the world. The problem could be talked through, she was convinced of that. She loved Rowan and believed with all her heart that he loved her equally. Both of them had too much to lose. What was her single hour of disgrace measured against their thirteen years of married life, the best interests of their daughters and their future together?

Sandra believed she could make Rowan see reason, provided she seized the initiative, but to do that, she first had to get herself together. Over the twenty-six hours since giving birth she'd been pathetic, she thought grimly. Given the shock, perhaps she'd had every right to be. Now she had to make herself strong and work out some of the weariness and stiffness, regain her confidence, so that she could think clearly and positively. In short, she had to get out of bed, get moving again, get back on her feet.

Nothing in her room offered encouragement. Her curtains were drawn and the only relief from gloom and total darkness came from cracks of light around her door, which had been left slightly ajar. Weak as it was, the light at least provided an objective, a temporary destination.

She swung her legs over the side of the bed, gritted her teeth against the pain and stood. She didn't feel too bad, just a touch light-headed from lying down too long. Her little baby slept peacefully in his crib, two hours short of feeding time. She stepped out into the dimly lit corridor. A pool of light halfway to the lifts indicated the nurses' station, her next objective. As she inched closer, crab-like in her episiotomy shuffle, she heard soft voices, the night nurses gossiping or exchanging notes on patients. Further down, someone was up watching TV, its flickering blue glow infiltrating the hall.

One of the nurses looked up as she crept past. 'Can I help you?'

Could anyone? Sandra smiled ruefully. 'Can't sleep. Just thought I'd go for a jog.' The nurses smiled sympathetically.

Sandra set herself the target of reaching the lifts at the end of the corridor, a small step for mankind but an epic journey for a woman whose two halves were held together by stitches.

As she passed by the ward where the TV was still operating, she glanced inside to see what fellow sufferer was still up and watching. The TV provided the only light. Three women were asleep but the fourth, a very large or very pregnant woman, was sitting propped up against pillows. She couldn't see the woman clearly, not as clearly as the woman could see her, and was caught by surprise when the woman seemed suddenly to sit up straighter and wave. Sandra didn't wave back but simply acknowledged the woman's greeting with a nod. In a strange way, she found the simple gesture encouraging, an act of solidarity between sisters.

She shuffled on to the lifts, touched the doors like a swimmer doing laps, as if to do otherwise would negate her journey, and shuffled back to her bed. Her baby hadn't stirred, but something had stirred deep inside her. She'd had no need to get up, no need to push herself all the way to the lifts, but she had. Accomplishment fed her growing determination. Her life had changed at one minute to midnight on Christmas Eve and it could change again on Boxing Day. Nothing was fixed, nothing was certain. Sandra began to feel like her old self. By morning she was determined to be strong, to be confident and ready to confront Rowan.

Some time during the early hours of Boxing Day morning, the cold woke Rowan. He discovered he was naked and lying on the floor of his bedroom. This puzzled him. There were dim memories of finally pushing the bottle away, a noble gesture diminished by the fact that there were only a few drops left in the bottom. He distinctly remembered undressing, leaving his clothes where they fell and climbing into bed. What had happened? As he dragged himself up into a sitting position, waves of nausea assailed him. He knew he had to throw up and the knowledge jogged his memory. He'd thrown up earlier. Something touched his hand as he tried to stand, something round and broken. Sandra's bedside lamp. More memories stirred, but he didn't have time to pursue them. His stomach began to heave and he stumbled to the bathroom, hit the light switch and threw himself at the toilet. He retched loudly and wetly and vomited into the bowl. At least his aim was good. So why did his feet feel wet? Clearly, at another time during the night, his aim had not been so good, which accounted for the smell and the poisonous taste in his mouth.

He lurched over to the hand basin and cupped his hands under the cold tap. Just as he was about to splash the water on his face, he caught sight of his reflection in the mirror. Blood had caked in his eyebrows and hairline, and an angry graze covered half of his forehead and one side of his nose. There was also a graze on the point of his right shoulder and more blood. On the way back from his first visit to the bathroom his sensibilities must have given up on him, and he'd passed out and kissed the carpet. He groaned as the memory came back. The frantic, futile clutching to prevent himself falling, his hand dragging the lamp, the crash as it hit the floor.

The tap was still running as he put the plug in the basin and let it fill so that he could clean himself up. Unfortunately, his body had nowhere near exacted final retribution for the alcohol he'd consumed. His head began pounding, not dully but sharply, spiking every time he tried to move it. Plunging his head into the basin was no longer an option. He doubted he'd survive to pull it back out again. He soaked his face washer and gingerly applied it to his forehead. Slowly the water in the basin coloured, turned pinkish, then unmistakably red. How much blood had he lost? How much blood was on the carpet? How would he get it off? Even thinking made his head hurt. He unplugged the basin and watched the water swirl away. Could he run a toothbrush around his mouth without causing massive cerebral haemorrhages? Unlikely. He found a glass and a compromise, rinsed his mouth out instead. Beyond any doubt, he knew there was only one place for him and that was bed.

He tip-toed out of the bathroom, his upper body as immobile as an Easter Island statue, skirted wide in case there were any sharp shards of broken pottery in his way. Relieved, he lowered himself gently onto the bed and slipped between the sheets, tucking the blanket up under his chin. He lay shivering, hoping that the bed-spins had spun themselves out. They hadn't. Once again the nausea returned and Rowan realised he'd been premature in returning to bed.

'God help me!' he said earnestly, partly from self-pity but also from sheer frustration. His life was a mess, he was a mess and it was high time he did something about both. Like a million drunks before him, he swore off the booze. But his regrets were way too late to prevent ramifications. His feet hit the floor and he staggered to the toilet as best he could, with no consideration whatsoever for wayward pieces of pottery. The toilet bowl made a large target, and needed to.

A hangover as profound as it was deserved woke him at

seven. He looked in on the girls on his way to the kitchen to make a life-saving cup of coffee. They were dead to the world, as fast asleep as only drunks and children can be. Rowan gave himself an hour to an hour and a half to clean up the bedroom and bathroom, and do what he had to do. Then he'd have to begin serving Coco Pops or, heaven forbid, the girls' favourite – scrambled eggs and tomato – after which, he'd have to dress them to visit their mother.

Sandra showered, washed her hair and applied lipstick. She changed into a clean nightie and matching peignoir. There were shadows under her eyes that no make-up could disguise, but overall she thought she looked rather presentable. Her achievement was in looking better than she felt.

She tried to keep herself occupied but there was a limit to the number of things she was required to do. Despite her efforts, she clock-watched, not knowing what time Rowan would show but knowing that every passing second brought the confrontation closer.

She kept her door more closed than open, for the sake of privacy. Her pulse rate accelerated every time it opened, in anticipation of the reckoning that had to come, only to see a nurse enter or the woman who brought her meals and cups of tea. When the door began to ease open shortly after ten, she braced herself to expect Rowan, knowing the routine well enough to realise it was unlikely to be staff. It wasn't staff, but it wasn't Rowan either. It was the woman who'd waved to her on her epic journey to the lifts.

'Helloo,' she said shyly.

It took a moment for Sandra to recognise the face and overcome her surprise. 'Fi!' she said.

'I come in, please?'

'Of course. You're not here because of your arm?'

'Noo . . . my arm good now, thank you. I see you last night.' Finau stood timidly at the end of Sandra's bed. 'I want to call out to you, say I am here, say Fi is here. I am all alone here. Family all in Fiji.'

'What's wrong, Fi? Nothing serious, I hope?'

'Something burst inside, Mrs Sandy. Doctor say ectopic pregnancy. Hospital in Fiji send me here.'

'I'm sorry, Fi. Are you all right?'

'Very sick before but now I am better. I have no more babies. Babies all finish.'

'Oh, Fi.'

'It's okay, I have five children. Five children enough. You have baby?'

The question was reasonable and asked in all innocence. Sandra's carefully constructed facade began to crumble when she realised there was no way of hiding. She bit her lip and willed herself to reply. She had to be strong, had to face reality. She just wished she could begin with someone else, someone removed from the scene of her crime.

'Yes,' she said softly and glanced towards the crib.

'I look now?' said Finau. The big woman had put all her troubles aside to share the joy of her friend. A smile spread from ear to ear as she edged forward and bent over the crib, then froze there. She turned slowly around to face Sandra, her expression slowly melting to one of sorrow and apprehension.

'Ohhhh, Mrs Sandy,' she keened. 'Ohhhh, Mrs Sandy.' Her eyes were filled with pity, shining with nascent tears. 'Does Mr Rowan know?'

'He knows. I'm expecting him any minute.' Sandra found it hard to meet Finau's eyes.

'Ohhhh, Mrs Sandy. I go now.' The big woman wrung her hands, her distress etched in her face. 'Maybe talk later.'

Sandra nodded, not trusting herself to speak. The moment Finau had pulled the door closed behind her, Sandra squeezed her eyes shut to block the flow of tears. Her shoulders heaved and a mighty sob racked her body. Oh God, this was not how she wanted the day to begin. She had to be strong. Strong!

She'd barely wiped a tissue across her eyes when Sarah and Rochelle burst through the doorway and hurtled towards her. If she'd been away for a year, their joy could not have been greater. They brought her flowers purchased from the stall downstairs and little presents they'd wrapped themselves. There were chocolates individually wrapped in Christmas paper they'd recycled, a little Lego baby in a little Lego cot – at least, that's what Sandra guessed the construction to be – and hand-drawn cards confessing undying love and affection. They'd done paintings of their little brother in his crib. In one his face was red, in another it was Bart Simpson yellow. The girls fought for her attention and she had to give it, prattled non-stop and she had to listen, asked questions and she had to answer. She was aware of Rowan hovering in the background and looked up to meet his eyes. Her brow creased in concern when she saw the livid graze on his face and nose, but his expression gave nothing away.

'Hi,' she said cautiously.

He merely nodded in reply.

'I wanna see Juni,' said Rochelle.

'Me too,' said Sarah. They slid off Sandra's bed and peered intently into the crib. 'Look, Daddy.' Sarah turned to her father imploringly. 'Come and look at his frizzy hair. It's funny.'

'I can see from here,' said Rowan, though it was plain he couldn't.

'I want to hold him,' said Sarah. 'Can I?'

'If you're very, very careful,' said Sandra.

'Can you pick him up for me, please, Daddy?' asked Sarah.

'I might drop him,' said Rowan, without a trace of humour. 'Get your mother to do it.'

'Here,' said Sandra. She swung her feet stiffly out of the bed so that she sat on the edge, reached in and gently lifted her little son. 'Come and hold him over the bed,' she said. 'Just to be on the safe side.' She placed the sleeping baby delicately in Sarah's arms. 'Make sure you support his head. Remember how you used to hold Rocky?'

Sarah held her little brother in her arms, speechless with awe, her face registering delight every time his expression changed. 'Look at his tiny fingers,' she whispered.

'Me see!' begged Rochelle.

'Look, Daddy,' said Sarah.

'I saw them before,' said Rowan. He sat down on the visitor's chair, against the wall by the door, and started thumbing through one of Sandra's magazines.

Sandra kept smiling, trying hard to match her daughters' excitement and delight, but Rowan's determined disinterest had brought her doubts flooding back and, with them, wave upon wave of apprehension. Her hopes withered with each covert glance she stole. She recognised his mood as one both she and his staff had come to dread, when his anger was beyond shouting and a coldness descended over his eyes like a third lid – when he put himself a step beyond the reach of the rest of humanity. At such times there was no reasoning with him, and no point to even the most cleverly constructed argument.

The girls played pass-the-parcel with Junior until he began crying to be fed. They watched fascinated as their mother cradled him across her chest and offered him the right nipple.

'Look, Daddy,' said Rochelle. 'Look what Juni doing.'

But Daddy took no notice.

'Yuk! What does it taste like?' asked Sarah.

'Try some.' Sandra eased Junior onto her other breast. Droplets of milk hung on her right breast. Sarah leant forward and cautiously licked them.

'Oh yuk!' she said.

'Me too! Me too!' demanded Rochelle. She stood on her tip-toes and reached over the edge of the bed.

'It's warm!' she said. As far as she was concerned, milk came from the fridge and was always cold. 'It's yucky!'

'You try, Daddy,' said Sarah.

'I've lost the taste for it,' said Rowan.

Sandra winced as though stung by a bee. There'd been a time, particularly after Sarah was born, when Rowan had suckled on her breasts almost as hungrily as his new daughter, when he'd followed up by making love to her tenderly and beautifully, when he made her feel like a goddess and his love had bordered on worship. It had been the same when Rochelle was born. Nothing else in their relationship even came close to the intimacy and sheer magic of those moments. Throughout her pregnancy she'd been looking forward to repeat performances. His words pierced her heart and even penetrated her soul.

He put his magazine down and stood. 'Come on, girls, we've been here long enough. Your mother's tired. Kiss her goodbye and let's hit the road. Buy you McDonald's on the way home.' He added the bribe as a means of cutting short the farewell.

'Yeah!' squealed Sarah. The girls wasted no time saying their goodbyes.

'We have to talk,' said Sandra. She kept her desperation out of her voice but her eyes were pleading.

'Call me this afternoon,' said Rowan.

'You want to do this over the phone?' said Sandra incredulously. She thought her spirits had sunk as low as it was possible for them to go. Once again, he had proved her wrong. And he still wasn't finished.

'Might be the only way to ensure privacy,' Rowan said. 'Oh, I've brought you something to read.' He pulled a sealed envelope out of his pocket and placed it on her bedside table. 'You might like to read it before you call.'

'What's this?' said Sandra. She smiled, but inside, her newly kindled hope flickered and died. A sense of dread enveloped her. 'Are you giving me my notice?'

'Call after three.' Rowan turned abruptly and followed the

girls into the corridor. No kiss, no goodbye, no nothing.

No nothing.

Sandra didn't even need to glance at the envelope to know she'd been judged, found guilty and sentenced without being given the chance to enter a plea. Could she appeal, she wondered? Did she have grounds? Would he listen? Tears that had threatened from the moment Rowan had stepped into her room now flowed freely and there was no stopping them. They ran unchecked down her cheeks, gathered into large drops on the point of her chin, paused momentarily before tumbling onto the precious baby sucking contentedly on her breast.

Boxing Day's noon aerobics class was poorly patronised, attended only by the fanatical and the penitent, the latter anxious to atone for the excesses of Christmas Day. Rowan completed his stretches and warm-up exercises before joining them, quitting when he became aware of the rank, sour reek of his sweat. At the best of times gyms were not good places for sensitive noses, but Rowan felt his pungency far exceeded the norm and was loath to inflict it on others. He attacked the step machine like a man caught thigh-deep by a rapidly rising tide. His head pounded and stomach churned but he pushed on, determined to sweat out all the ills that beset him. It wasn't enough. He turned to the Nautilus machine, to lift, pull, push till every muscle swelled and throbbed with hard pumping blood. It wasn't enough.

Rowan was well aware of what he'd come for and everything else was just preparation. He stepped off the Nautilus, heart pounding, sweat streaming, smelling like an open sewer, and began stretching, buying time to allow the oxygen levels in his blood to recover and, equally important, for his hate to build. People were wrong, he thought, when they described hatred as burning. Hate didn't burn. Hate was icy, colder than the grave, colder than purgatory, cold as only imagination fuelled by genuine grievance could make it. Hate did not burn, didn't flare or spark, but moved with slow determination, relentlessly unstoppable, utterly unforgiving.

Rowan was no stranger to heavy bags and, in his travels, had thumped in to all makes and sizes. Some had been cherry red, others bright yellow, one bruise-blue and many of them tan. The one in front of him had been black when new, and had gradually greyed down as the surface had crazed. Still, it was black enough for Rowan. In fact, the colour suited him just fine. With aerobics finished, the sound of his first impact resounded around the near-empty gym, causing the few who remained to turn their heads towards the source. His second punch rocked the bag backwards, rattling its restraints. His third punch was on the way and timed to hit the bag the instant it resumed the vertical. His fourth, fifth and sixth punches caused it to defy gravity. Rowan felt the impact of his blows through his shoulders, down the muscles of his back, through his solar plexus, through his thighs, his calf muscles, through the soles of his feet, and they carried all the weight and force of the righteous. He punched, pummelled, battered, gaining a bemused audience but not the redemption he craved.

'Jesus Christ!' said the instructor. 'You gunna let the bag see in the new year?'

'I've finished,' said Rowan.

'Glad to hear it. What's the problem? Miss out on Christmas presents?'

'Fuck's it to you?'

'What?' The instructor's jaw dropped.

'I said, what the fuck is it to you?'

'Nothing,' said the instructor. His right foot automatically moved behind his left and his left shoulder dropped forward in case Rowan wanted to kick his hostility up a notch. 'Just making conversation.'

'Don't bother,' said Rowan.

'Pardon me for living,' said the instructor, relaxing his stance as Rowan climbed onto the exercise bike to warm down. 'By the way, in case no one's told you, you smell like dog fart.'

Sandra called at exactly three o'clock. Even though Rowan was sitting right beside the phone he let it ring five times before answering.

'Rowan Madison.'

'It's me, Rowan.'

'Thought it probably was.' He waited for her to continue, heard a shuffling and what sounded like a stifled sob.

'Can you talk?' she said eventually.

'Yeah, can you?'

'Where are the girls?'

'Marion and Clive are taking pity on them. Probably taken them to a nice exciting art gallery.'

'Rowan ... ?'

'Yeah?'

'I'm really sorry.'

'Join the club. Look, if you intend going over what happened, don't bother. Caro's already given me chapter and verse.'

'I was angry, Rowan, angry with you. I don't know why I did it – to get even with you, or what. The temptation was there and I succumbed. All I know is that I regretted it immediately and every day since, wished it had never happened.'

'So do I.'

'Please, Rowan, don't play games with me. I don't need any wisecracks and I don't need telling how stupid I've been. I'm sorry. I'm sorry a hundred, thousand, million times over. I'm sorry for you and your disappointment. If I could turn the clock back, I would. If I could change things, I would. I'd do anything, give anything, if things could be the way they were.'

'So would I,' said Rowan softly.

'I love you, Rowan,' she said, and he could hear that she was crying.

'Yes, I think you probably do.'

'Do you still love me?'

'Yes, I think I probably do.'

'Then why, Rowan, why throw everything away?'

Rowan pulled the phone away from his ear. Sandra was crying openly now and he couldn't bear to listen. Hard choices had to be made, painful choices, and caving into sentiment would only add to the pain. He waited for Sandra to regain her composure.

'I have no choice,' he said simply.

'Of course you have choice!' Sandra's voice rose sharply.

'No, I don't. I will not have that baby in my house. I will

not wake every day for the rest of my life to reminders of my inadequacy.'

'Your ... what?'

'I will not spend the rest of my life explaining to friends and strangers alike why my son doesn't look like me, why he's not even the same bloody colour!' All the anger and bitterness Rowan had been nurturing bubbled out, betrayed by his voice, the flush in his face and the shaking of his hands.

'Rowan! Stop it!'

But he was beyond stopping. 'I will not spend the rest of my life suffering their pity, being talked about, sniggered about behind my back, being the butt of sick jokes. Poor little short-arse. His wife likes dark meat and big servings, bigger than he can give her.'

'Stop it!' Sandra's scream cut through the phone. 'Stop it!'

Rowan stopped, not because Sandra had begged him to, but because he was shocked by his own words. All the dark, brooding thoughts that had been roiling around inside his head suddenly had expression and definition, and they bludgeoned him to silence.

Sandra stared at the phone, frozen in shock, trying desperately to come to terms with his outburst. Not once during the lonely hours she'd lain in bed testing and rehearsing arguments in her head had she considered that Rowan would link the baby to his obsession with his shortness. His height was not something they ever discussed nor something he ever mentioned. It was just there, like a dead body in the hall. No problem so long as everyone stepped around it. When he'd called himself a short-arse, he'd left her speechless. It was a word she'd never expected to hear from his lips. Nor had she ever expected to hear him expose his vulnerableness so blatantly. She had no arguments prepared, could think of no words to soothe wounds that cut so deeply into the core of his being. Slowly she began to comprehend the true extent of the hurt she'd caused him. What could she salvage? How could she even begin?

'You think all this is about you?' she began hesitantly. 'You think people will see the baby as a reflection on you?'

'Isn't it?' he snapped. 'I'm the joke who's had the little bastard's Polaroid on my desk for the past three months. I'm the sucker who had to face the reality of his wife giving birth to another man's son! Are you saying this has nothing to do with me?'

'No, I'm not saying that at all.' Sandra let her instincts take over, the instincts of a mother, wife and best friend called upon to help and somehow make things better. She recovered some of her composure and her voice took on a measured calm. 'When people look to see who to blame, they won't be looking at you, Rowan. You're blameless, innocent, the party that was wronged. All the world can see that. The buck stops squarely with me. I'm the stupid bitch who risked everything to indulge a sexual whim. I have to live with the spoken and unspoken accusations of everyone we know or simply pass in the street. Yes, people will feel sorry for you, Rowan, because I've put you in a situation where you deserve their sympathy. But that won't mean they think any the less of you. I'll be the one they think less of, and deservingly so. I will be the recipient of their scorn and contempt, not you.'

'I should be so lucky,' said Rowan bitterly. It didn't matter a damn what Sandra said. Rowan worked in an industry that rejoiced in cutting tall poppies down to size and he knew exactly how cruel his fellow advertising men and women could be. His competition would have a field day and not only his competition. There were people within his own agency who'd have a field day, too.

'Just give it time,' said Sandra, changing tack desperately. 'People will forget after a while, get bored. Time heals.'

'So long as nobody picks at the scab.'

'What do you mean?'

'Give me a break, Sandy. All my life I've had to fight my way out from under the shadow of taller men. It's a problem I can't run away from, nor ever defeat. I wake up with that handicap in front of me every single morning, like an itch I can't scratch, a wound that won't heal, a race I can't win. One handicap's enough, I can't face two. That kid will always be an open, festering sore to me, no matter what you say. A living testimony to your dissatisfaction with my bedroom performance. It doesn't matter how you dress it up, that's what it is and that's how the world will see it.'

'You're wrong, Rowan.'

He ignored her and continued, unstoppable in his anger. 'I won't have him in my face for the rest of my life. I won't have him in the house, not while I live in it. I don't want to have to look at him. Ever. The day you bring that little bastard home is the day I move out. I want no reminders of the bastard who planted his son in my son's place. Do you understand that?'

'Rowan –'

'Fuck you, Sandy. Do you understand that!' He was shouting now, standing and shouting, face twisted by bitterness and injustice, breathing harder than he ever did in the gym.

'Just give us a chance, please! Please, Rowan! We can work it through. I love you and –'

He didn't slam the phone down but placed it gently on the cradle. He cut Sandra off all the same.

Fifteen

'He can't walk out on you just like that.' Caroline's face was ashen as she put Rowan's note back down on the bedside table. 'Oh Sandy ...' Caroline put her arms around her friend's shoulders and hugged her. Sandra neither resisted nor responded. They sat side by side on the edge of the bed, the cause of their distress sleeping peacefully in his crib in front of them. 'There has to be something we can do.'

'What?'

'You both still love each other.'

'Obviously not enough.'

Caroline sighed helplessly. 'There must be something we can do,' she said, but her voice carried no conviction. She'd come in response to Sandra's distress call. Her friend needed comforting, but what comfort could she offer? Needed cheering up, but what the hell could she say? Needed reason to hope, but what hope was left? She looked instead at the baby, who was beginning to stir. His tiny brow furrowed and he whimpered. It was hard for her to believe that something so wonderful could cause so much desolation. She reached into the crib and touched the baby's hand lightly with her little finger, could not resist smiling when the tiny hand closed around it. 'Look at him,' she said. 'He's so gorgeous.'

'He cost me my husband.'

'Don't say that,' snapped Caroline. 'Don't even think it. He did nothing of the sort. You . . .' She stopped short as she realised where her words were heading. The look Sandra gave her was tinged with hurt.

'Go on. I'm the one who stuffed up. Is that what you were going to say? It's all my fault, like I wanted the condom to break?'

Caroline closed her eyes momentarily. 'Sorry, Sandy. Not much of a friend, am I? It's just that I don't think you should go blaming him or even start thinking that way. If there's one entirely innocent party here, it's him.'

'You're right, but it's hard sometimes. As much as I love him, I catch myself wishing he was someone else. God Almighty, I wish he was who he ought to be.'

'Maybe Mike and I should talk to Rowan, try to talk him around.'

'How?'

'I don't know but we'll think of something. Make him an offer he can't refuse. Look, think about this. In a couple of months' time you could be pregnant again, and nine months later give Rowan the son he wants. Wouldn't that change things, bring in a whole new perspective? Rowan gets what he wants, you get what you want. What do you think?'

'Maybe,' said Sandra. It wasn't much of a ray of hope but she seized on it in the absence of any other. The more she thought about it, the better it seemed.

'I think he's got wind,' said Caroline, desperate for a diversion. 'Maybe he's just feeling hungry. Can I pick him up?'

Sandra nodded, her thoughts elsewhere. 'You're right, Caro. If I got pregnant again, everything would change. Rowan wouldn't walk out on his own son. Maybe if Mike spoke to him. He might listen to Mike.'

Caroline reached into the crib and gently lifted the baby up and cradled him in her arms. His eyelids flickered and his face puckered up. For a moment she thought he was going to start crying. Whether it was simply a reaction to being picked up or the realisation that his head was resting on a breast, whatever the trigger, he responded by making little sucking noises and seeking out a nipple. Caroline yearned for him to chomp down on her through the thin cotton of her blouse. She even considered unbuttoning her blouse and putting the baby on her breast, just to see how it felt, just to experience the intimacy of feeding, however fleetingly. If she was honest with herself, she'd omitted wearing a bra not for any dictates of fashion or weather, although it was scorchingly hot outside, but for the chance to feel a newborn baby against her breast with as little impediment in between. 'Couldn't you just eat him!' she said.

'It works the other way around,' said Sandra, and finally managed a smile. 'Here, you'd better hand the little interloper over.'

'God, I envy you.'

'Do you?' said Sandra sharply.

'You know what I mean. I envy the fact that you've got him, got this beautiful, beautiful baby.'

'Yeah, it's life-changing.'

Waves of yearning washed over Caroline as the baby latched onto Sandy's breast and began sucking. A confusing mix of anger and jealousy came over her and grew until she could no longer contain it. 'Rowan's a fool, a prize ... stuffing ... idiot ...' Tears reddened her eyes. 'How could anyone turn their back on him? In the end it doesn't matter who the real father is. He's just a baby who needs a mummy and daddy to love him.' She turned away and began wiping her eyes with her handkerchief. 'Mike and I would kill to have him.'

'Come on, Caroline, you're supposed to be cheering me up.'

'It's not fair.'

'No, it's not. It's not fair to any of us.' She put her hand on Caroline's arm. 'Your time will come, Caro, probably sooner than you think.'

'I suppose so. But even then, I won't be able to do what you're doing.'

'Breast-feed? It hurts, you know.'

'I'd always imagined I'd have a baby feeding on my breast. I can't imagine anything more wonderful.' She brushed new tears away from her eyes. 'I'm really jealous of you, Sandy.'

'Save it,' said Sandy. 'Do you want to try?'

'What do you mean?'

'Unbutton your blouse and rub some milk around your

nipple. He's so sleepy he won't notice that the tap's stopped running.'

'Are you serious?'

'Here, take the little sucker.'

'Oh God, Sandy ...' Caroline took the baby in her arms and he immediately latched onto her nipple and began sucking. Love, both profound and abundant, welled up from her soul. Tears flowed down her cheeks but came from eyes now filled with ecstasy, as she devoured every little sensation and imprinted it indelibly upon her brain.

'You will talk to Mike, won't you?' said Sandra. 'Get him to talk to Rowan.'

'Of course. Oh, would you look at him!'

'As soon as you get home? If I could give Rowan a son I think everything would change.'

'Absolutely! I'll do anything for you, you know that. So will Mike. You're the best friend anyone could ever have. Oh, look at his little face, Sandy. Look, he's smiling! God, if you're listening, I want one!'

Sandra knew a gas smile when she saw one, but smiled anyway. She had her own reasons. Despite everything, there was still a glimmer of hope. Maybe, just maybe, she was still in with a chance.

As Caroline drove home, her whole body chemistry felt like it had changed forever, that if Mike made love to her right then and there she couldn't help but fall pregnant. Just thinking about Junior brought a tear to her eyes, the way his rosebud mouth had cupped her nipple, the way his tiny hands had pushed into the soft tissue of her breast, the way he'd seemed to look at her, lovingly, trustingly, dependent, accepting her as his mother. They had bonded. Yes! For those few precious minutes they had belonged to each other, as close as any mother and child could be. She turned into her street, into her driveway and parked. She was loath to get out in case she broke the spell, in case she left any of her experiences behind on the front seat, but finally she bowed to the inevitable. She found Mike scooping leaves from their swimming pool, soaking wet and wearing only his Speedo briefs.

'How'd you get on?' he asked. 'How's Sandy?'

'Never mind Sandy.' She threw her arms around him and kissed him passionately on the lips. 'How'd you like to get laid by the horniest girl in Sydney?' she whispered.

'What have I done?' he asked.

'It's not what you've done,' she said, taking his hand and leading him to their bedroom. 'It's what I've just done.' Caroline told him, his eyes widening by the second.

'God, Caro, I wish I'd been there.'

'If you'd been there, God only knows what would have happened. I'd have pushed Sandy off the bed and banged your brains out, and I wouldn't have cared a damn who saw us. Now lie down, lover boy, and give me your best shot.'

'I'm wet.'

'So am I.'

Mike liked to control the pace of their love-making but he wasn't given the option. Caroline knew exactly what she had to do and no one and nothing was going to get in her way. She pushed him back onto the bed and pulled down his Speedos.

His penis celebrated its freedom by springing up like a jack-in-a-box. She climbed on top of him and closed her eyes in concentration. She wanted him deep inside her, deeper than it was possible to go, defying those doctors who had declared her incapable of bearing children. She seesawed with the rhythm of their love-making, plunging and rising in blind determination, convinced that nursing Junior had changed something that changed everything. When they climaxed, her ecstasy was absolute, founded on her conviction that his sperm had negotiated the hitherto impenetrable and were homing in on their prize. Later, as they lay together on the sweat- and water-soaked bed, Mike gently reached across and took both her hands in his.

'Don't start,' he said. 'Please.'

'What do you mean?'

'You know exactly what I mean. Please don't start, because you'll only hurt yourself again. You know and I know – and the doctors know – it's not going to work, this time or any time.'

'But . . .'

'No buts, Caro. There are no ifs or buts. We can't change the way things are, no matter how much we might wish to. I'm glad Sandy let you nurse her baby, but that doesn't alter anything. You might think it did, but it didn't, because it can't. We both know this, sweetheart, and it's not going to do either of us any good if you start thinking otherwise. Okay?' He reached over, took a tissue from the box on the bedside table and brushed away her tears. He put his arms around her and left them there long after her sobbing had stopped.

'Helloo?'

'Hello Fi.' Sandra did her best to sound cheerful but groaned inwardly. She put down the magazine she'd been trying to read for distraction. As much as she tried, she couldn't get past one sentence before her mind started wandering off to the very subject she was trying to avoid. She couldn't see how Finau's arrival would help her cause.

'May I come in?'

'Of course. How are you today?'

'Good. No pain. I go home to Fiji in two days. How are you?'

Sandra swung her legs over the side of the bed so that she could sit up. Her stitches pulled painfully but not unexpectedly. 'I'm fine, Fi. Not quite up to dancing yet, but getting better. They'll probably send me home tomorrow.'

'I saw Mr Rowan.'

Sandra's interest quickened. 'Did he speak to you?'

'Noo. I was back in bed. He didn't see me.'

'You didn't miss anything. He wasn't exactly in the mood for talking.'

'The two girls. Your daughters?'

'Yes.'

'Very beautiful. What are their names?'

Sandra told her.

'Beautiful names. Do you have a name for your little boy?'

'Rowan Junior no longer seems appropriate.'

'Maybe give him Fiji name.'

'Maybe. Tell me a few Fiji names.'

'Timocy.'

'Mmm ...'

'Tomu.'

'No, he doesn't look a Tim or a Tom to me.'

'Mikeli.'

'What's that in English?'

'Michael.'

'No, my best friend's husband is a Michael.'

'Sitiveni.'

'God no.' Sandra realised her mistake the instant the words left her lips. When she looked up, she found Finau looking at her sadly.

'Siti is very bad man. Got six children in Fiji, all girls, three different mothers. His wife was your housemaid. She has four children.'

Sandra wasn't surprised to discover Siti had sown his seed so profligately. She'd suspected as much once she'd seen him lift the outboard motor. What sent her mind reeling back to Coralhaven were memories of the softly spoken housemaid who'd cleaned their room – who'd cleaned up after her and Siti. Had she realised, Sandra wondered, aghast at the possibility, had she discovered anything as she'd cleaned? She bowed her head in shame. 'I'm sorry,' she whispered.

Finau bent over the crib, lifted the sleeping baby up and cradled him against her cheek. Black skin on black skin looked so natural. If Finau turned and walked off with Junior in her arms nobody would bat an eyelid.

'Josetika,' said Finau. 'To me he feels like a Joseph.'

'Too Catholic,' said Sandra. 'What about Aaron?'

'Aaron is a white boy's name,' said Finau.

'Dad, why is Junior different to Rocky?'

'What do you mean?' Rowan smiled but was instantly on guard. It was inevitable that the questions would come but he still wasn't ready for them. He'd hoped the girls would hold off until Sandra could deal with them. It was her responsibility to answer their questions, not his.

'Rocky was pink when she was born.'

Rochelle struggled to open her eyes and tune into the conversation. Her panda lay wide-eyed alongside her.

'Well . . .' said Rowan. Sarah pinned him with her eyes. 'His hands are pink and so is the underneath of his feet. Why isn't he pink all over?'

'Maybe the angels hadn't finished painting him,' said Rowan.

'What do you mean?'

'Well, he was born a week early. Maybe the angels had run out of pink paint and were waiting for more when he was born. That's why he missed out.'

'That's silly,' said Sarah.

'Silly,' confirmed Rochelle.

'Well somebody slipped up,' said Rowan.

'Could we have got someone else's baby by mistake?' asked Sarah. The obvious worry in her eyes and the frown that wrinkled her forehead warned Rowan to tread carefully and not be flippant.

'Why do you say that?'

'He looks like an Aboriginal baby.'

'Like Ernie Dingo,' confirmed Rochelle.

'Don't you think Mummy would know if Junior wasn't her baby?' said Rowan.

'I suppose so,' said Sarah reluctantly.

'If you're worried about it, you can ask Mummy tomorrow.'

'He looks like Pandy,' said Rochelle. 'I love Pandy.'

'Of course you do. Now go to sleep.' He kissed both girls and tucked in their sheets.

'When's Mummy coming home?' asked Sarah.

'Tomorrow.'

'Is she bringing Junior home?'

'Yes, I believe she is.'

'Good,' said Sarah. 'Dad?'

'What?'

'Do you love him?'

'Not as much as I love you,' said Rowan. He forced a laugh.

'Me too!' said Rochelle.

'And you,' said Rowan. He kissed both girls and switched off the light. He walked straight to the liquor cabinet, to drown his deceptions and evasions and the treachery he had planned. Memories of the previous night pulled him up short. He retreated to the kitchen to make coffee instead. What would Sarah and Rochelle think of him when he packed up and moved out? He could imagine their bewilderment, their reproachful looks and their tears, and wished there was something he could do about it. He thought briefly of taking the girls with him but just as quickly dismissed the idea as unworkable. How could he be mother and father when for days at a time he was barely even a father? He wanted to smash his fist into the cupboard doors and shatter benchtops but held back for fear of disturbing the girls. He stared at the stickers on the fridge and hated Sandy for what she'd done and for what she was forcing him to do.

He sat down and spread the real estate section of the previous Saturday's *Sydney Morning Herald* over the kitchen table. Did people move over the holiday period? he wondered. Apparently they did. There were fewer listings than usual, but enough to give him an idea of what was available, at what cost and who to contact. He circled advertisements for townhouses around Mosman and Cremorne that had harbour views. The prices were prohibitive but Rowan couldn't afford to look at anything cheaper. From time to time he had to entertain clients at home, and he couldn't do that in a shoebox stuck in some high-rise. His position made it mandatory that he impress. If he had an outside entertaining area he could get away with barbecues and salads. He decided to hand over the problem of financing to his accountant. As he swallowed the last of his coffee, the doorbell rang. He glanced curiously at the kitchen clock. Nine-thirty and he had visitors?

He rose and strode to the front door, half expecting to find Jehovah's Witnesses or earnest young Mormons. He began planning pithy ways of expressing dismissal so as to cause maximum offence. His jaw dropped when he realised who his visitors were. 'Jesus, what are you doing here?'

'Can we come in?' said Mike.

'Sure. Do you know what time it is?'

'Caro wanted to make sure the girls were asleep in bed.'

Rowan looked quizzically at Caroline but she stared steadfastly past him. 'Can I get you a coffee?'

'I'd prefer a red if you've got one open,' said Mike.

'I can open one easily enough. Caro?'

'Whatever.'

'Make yourselves comfortable in the lounge. Get three glasses from the cabinet.' Rowan diverted to the kitchen, grabbed a Yarra Valley cabernet merlot and set about extracting the cork on his way to the lounge. 'Is there a point to this call beyond the obvious? I've about had all the commiserations I can handle.'

'There's a point,' said Mike, with a sigh.

'Let's hear it.' Rowan poured the wine. 'Caro went to see Sandy this afternoon. You know why so I'll cut to the chase. We don't like what's happening. We like you both enormously, as individuals, but especially as a couple. Recent developments aside, you are the perfect couple, and as friends we can't stand by and watch you two self-destruct – not when we think there's something we can do about it.'

'I appreciate what you're saying, Mike, but I think you're on dangerous ground. Do you really want to go on with this?'

'Yes,' said Caroline flatly. 'He does.'

'No,' said Mike. 'Frankly I think we're interfering.'

'But?'

'Friendships and duties. You could make this easier for me, you know.'

'Sorry, you're on your own. I can't think of a single thing you could say to change my mind. Just don't put our friendship in jeopardy, okay? I've lost enough as it is.'

'All right, in the spirit of eternal friendship, I'll put this as nicely as I can. Rowan, why are you behaving like such an arsehole?'

'Why am I what!'

'Shut up and listen for once in your life. You've got a fabulous wife who worships the ground you walk on. God knows why, after the way you've apparently thrown your willy around, but she does! You've got two precious, beautiful, wonderful daughters who think you're the greatest dad in the world. You've got a home-life that damn near every man in the world would swap for. I envy it, for Christ's sake! Why throw it all away? All I'm asking is that you cool down and use your brain to find some way of coping with what has happened. So Sandy has had a kid under the most bizarre and unfortunate circumstances. Think of all the times you've waved your dick about and Sandra's forgiven you. Wouldn't she have forgiven you if you'd come home with a bastard child your shagging around had produced? How about reciprocating and taking your turn at forgiveness?'

'I didn't hand her a little black bastard as a souvenir.'

'Do you think that's how Sandy wanted things to turn out?'

'Not for a second. But that's how things did turn out and nothing can change that.'

'What if Sandy got pregnant again?'

'Again? Bloody hell! Is there something else she forgot to tell me?'

'What if she got pregnant again?' said Mike patiently. 'What if she got pregnant by you, as you both had planned? What if nine months down the road she hands you a tiny little Rowan? Would you still want to walk out on her and your daughters? Would you want to walk out on your son? Try and see the big picture here, Rowan. A year or so from now, you and Sandra could be back to where you were the instant before Junior stuck his head out. You could be watching the birth of your own son, holding him, cuddling him. Walk away, and you could be walking away from that opportunity forever. You could be walking away from your own son! Think about it. As for Junior, you don't have the capacity to sustain hate, and you don't have the capacity to hate little babies, regardless of their origin. In a year's time you could have four children, two boys and two girls. Caro and I can't even imagine the joy that would bring. Think about it, Rowan. You and Sandy, your two girls and two boys. Now why in God's name would you – or anybody – walk away from that?'

Rowan closed his eyes and slumped forward, his head buried in his hands. Some truths were undeniable and inescapable. More than anything else he wanted to turn the clock back to the way things were, yet Mike had shown him a way forward with almost the same result. He wouldn't have to leave Sandra or the girls, and she'd give him a son. That was what he wanted with all his heart. The more he thought about it, the more he wanted it. Only one thing would change. He'd have two sons, not one, and one of them would be his. He tried to project ahead and imagine them walking down the road as a family, Sandra with a baby on her back, the two girls holding her hands, he pushing a stroller carrying a black toddler.

'Well?' said Mike.

Rowan dropped his hands and looked up. He didn't mind that Mike and Caroline would see his anguish and that his eyes were red-rimmed and moist. 'I can't do it.'

'Why not?' demanded Mike. 'Don't tell me it's not what you want, you dumb bastard, because I can see it is. You don't want to go, so don't go! Don't be so bloody-minded. Christ Almighty, how many times has Sandy forgiven you? Can't you be a man and forgive her just once? Aren't you man enough to do that?'

'I won't have him in my house.'

'Oh for Christ's sake!'

'Take the bastard out of the deal and you've got me one hundred per cent. You're right, Mike, that's what I want. To go on as before. To start again, and this time make sure the baby boy she carries is my son. But I can't do it waking up to someone else's son every day for the rest of my life. I won't have that indictment of me, of my manhood for Christ's sake, living in this house and reminding me daily of my failure to father my own fucking son!'

'So let us adopt him,' said Caro.

If a Tomahawk missile had burst through the window at that moment, nobody would have noticed.

'What?' said Mike. 'What did you say?'

'Say that again,' said Rowan. Both he and Mike stared at her, mouths agape, as if she'd just entered from another dimension.

'Let us adopt him.'

'Jesus,' said Mike. 'You're way out of line, Caro.' He wiped his forehead and tried not to look as stunned as he felt. 'I'm sorry, Rowan, I had no idea she was going to spring this on you – or me, for that matter! Bloody hell! We've said what we came to say and I think it's time we went.'

'No!' Caroline leapt to her feet, eyes blazing, hands clenched so tightly that they blotched pink and white.

'Let Caro speak,' said Rowan wearily. 'You've had your turn and I've had mine. If nothing else, let's get it all out into the open.'

'Think about it,' said Caroline. Her voice was sharp and strident and her eyes aflame. She paced the room as though possessed of divine vision. 'It's the best possible solution. You don't want to leave, Sandy and the girls don't want you to leave. My way, you don't have to leave because you won't have to face Junior every day. Oh, you'll still see him occasionally, but there'll be no mistaking who he belongs to, who his mother and father are. Us! Mike and me. You get the chance to forgive and forget, Sandy keeps her family together and we get the baby we always wanted.'

'I'm not sure Sandy would give up Junior,' said Mike.

'It's not as though Sandy would lose contact. It's not as though he's being adopted by total strangers. Think about it, Rowan. She can watch her baby grow up and she'll have the satisfaction of knowing he's in a good home where he's loved and wanted and probably spoilt rotten. But on the other hand, if either you or Sandy still can't handle the proximity, we'll move away. If that's the way you want it, you need never set eyes on us or Junior again.' She stopped pacing and stared intently at Rowan, waiting for a response.

'That wouldn't be necessary.'

'So you agree?'

'Let's just say I'm not opposed to the idea.' Rowan drained his glass and refilled it, occupying time to give himself a chance to think. 'In fact, I think it has merit.'

'Jesus,' said Mike. 'This is scary. Let's not run too fast with this.'

'Do you want the kid?' asked Rowan.

'Do I want the kid? Where have you been, Rowan? Of course I want the kid. We want the kid. Your kid, anybody's kid. Black, yellow, white or polka-dotted. To have Junior would be better than anything we could have hoped for. If you're saying this is a real prospect, and it comes to fruition, then I don't know how we'll ever thank you. Do I want the kid, God Almighty . . .'

'It would solve a lot of problems.'

'Oh Rowan!' Caroline sat on his lap and threw her arms around him. 'I know it's the right thing to do, I just know it! It was meant to happen this way. It's like Sandy has had my child for me because I can't have him myself. Don't you see? It's predestined.'

'How do you think Sandy will feel, Rowan?' asked Mike cautiously.

'I'm sure she'll agree,' cut in Caroline. 'Sandy's my best friend. She'll see that Junior was meant for us.'

'I'm not so sure. She's still the kid's mother,' said Mike.

'True, but I don't see that she has much option,' said Rowan. 'I'll speak to her.'

'No,' said Caroline. 'That's my job. It was my idea.'

'I'm her husband.'

'I'm her best friend.'

'And they're reasons which exclude you both,' cut in Mike heavily. 'It's a big thing for any mother to give away her child. If she doesn't go along with the idea, she may never forgive either of you for even raising it. The end result could be she loses her husband or her best friend at a time when she's going to need both of you.'

'So what do you suggest?' said Caroline.

'I pick up the short straw,' said Mike unhappily. 'I talk to her. I'm the only one who's expendable.'

'Sandy would never consider you expendable,' said Rowan. 'And neither would I. All the same, you're probably right. You carry an air of neutrality. Sandy's always listened to you.'

'Rowan's right. You can make her see reason,' said Caroline. 'See that it was meant to be.'

'I think I need my head read,' said Mike.

The three of them stared into their wine glasses, their minds ablaze with possibilities, each of them daring to hope for the best.

Sixteen

Somewhere out in the corridor two trolleys collided and someone tried to stifle a laugh. The sound reverberated off the walls, singled out Sandra's room and came rushing in like a wave upon rocks. She groaned, turned over and tried to focus on the numbers on the digital clock. Four-fifty-nine. Not even five! Sandra surrendered to the inevitable, and eased out of bed to visit the toilet, legs leaden and head swimming. Had Mike spoken to Rowan? Had Rowan changed his mind? Hope flared, and died just as quickly. Her thoughts were in tumult, a continual scrolling of options, all without foundation, all dependent upon the outcome of a conversation that might not even have taken place, each adding to the deadweight of her gloom and fuelling her sense of apprehension. In truth, the noise hadn't woken her. Despite her overwhelming tiredness, sleep had eluded her and she'd spent the long night tossing and turning.

She stumbled back to bed, using the white light of her call

button and the two green lights that glowed on the panel above the bedhead for bearings. How would her stay in hospital end? Would Rowan come to take her and Junior home?

She snuggled back under the blankets, desperate to salvage some sleep before another trolley brought cups of tea and little mouths cried out to be fed. She tried to think of happier times, of flowers and waterfalls, picnics and long days spent knocking softballs around parks, but the hour of the day seemed to prohibit it. Her mind and vital functions seemed in recess and her spirit at its lowest ebb. This was the death hour, when the long-term and critically ill were at their most vulnerable, when wills weakened and the reaper harvested the wards. This was the time when thoughts blurred and reactions dulled, when trolleys crashed in corridors and cars collided on streets.

A radio blared into life in a nearby ward – someone had forgotten to fit the ear-plug jack. Sandra caught the weather forecast. It promised an overcast day with showers. That seemed entirely appropriate to her homecoming. The main lights flicked on outside her door and the sounds and activities of a hospital waking up filled her room. Junior cried out plaintively in his crib. Would Rowan come for her? Would anyone come? Or would she be left alone to stand on the hospital steps, her shame cradled in her arms, waiting for a taxi?

Caroline woke Mike at seven o'clock with a cup of tea and a milk arrowroot biscuit. He looked on dazedly and helplessly as she chose clothes for him to wear and ironed him a shirt. She was talking to him, prompting him, telling him what to say, words spilling ceaselessly one after the other. He tried not to listen. She stopped mid-sentence and glared at him when he flicked on the TV at the foot of the bed, ostensibly so that he could catch the news.

The words of the newsreader were equally meaningless but served their purpose in silencing Caroline. He needed time to think and gather his wits, to try to counter his growing doubts. As they'd lain in bed waiting for sleep to bring respite, he and Caroline had managed to convince each other of the rightness of his mission. He'd put aside his doubts then. But what had seemed a great idea hours earlier now seemed overly optimistic, and its outcome no longer cut and dried. Had their judgement been affected by the passions of the moment and the prospect of what he and Caroline stood to gain and Rowan retain? In the cold light of day there was no escaping the grim reality of the task ahead and the true burden of his duties.

Could logical argument sever a bond as profound and fundamental as that between mother and newborn? Nothing in Sandra's make-up gave him cause for hope. In fact, he didn't doubt Sandra would defend her girls to her last breath, lay down her life for them if necessary. Why would she react any differently with Junior? Yet if he backed out, he'd have to face Caroline and he couldn't bear the thought of that. She was beyond his reach, beyond reason and argument, having convinced herself that possession of Junior and immediate motherhood were mere formalities, predestined. On the other hand, if he went ahead he'd have to face Sandra and the pain and distress he'd cause her, especially if he succeeded in his mission. But if he failed, no one would be spared, not Sandra, not Rowan, not Caroline, not even himself. But especially not Caroline. He dreaded to think how she would react. He must have groaned aloud because Caroline looked up from her ironing.

'What?' she said.

'Nothing. Just thinking.'

Caroline's face lit up. 'So was I. By tonight you could be a daddy.'

'I'm going to have a shower.'

When he finally sat down to breakfast he discovered that Caroline had made him fried eggs, bacon and sausages with extra toast and marmalade. In earlier times wives sent their husbands off to battle in just this manner. They laid out their husbands' battledress and prepared one last meal to fortify them before sending them on their way. The irony drew a faint smile.

'You might have to borrow Rowan's car,' said Caroline.

'Why?'

'You'll need a baby capsule.'

'Can't I just borrow one and put it in my car?'

'Rowan said it's easier if you borrowed his car. They have to be fitted.'

'When did he say that?'

'I rang him this morning.'

'He say anything else?'

'Only that he was counting on you and that he'd be waiting at home when you bring Sandy back.'

'Noble of him.'

'Mike?'

'What?'

'You're not having second thoughts, are you?'

'You want the truth? Yes, I am. I don't think I have a snowball's chance in hell of pulling this off. But I said I'd speak to Sandy and I will.'

'Of course you will! It's the right thing, I know it is. It's predestined.'

Mike shuddered as she said that word again. 'Please, Caroline!' He lay down his knife and fork. 'I'm going to have a hard enough time facing Sandy. Please don't build your hopes up. Please don't give me reason to dread coming home.' He strode off to his study, closing the door behind him.

'Raurawa,' said Finau. 'My grandfather's name on my father's side.'

'I don't know,' said Sandy without interest. She sat on the edge of her bed, dressed, packed and totally distracted, awaiting the final okay from her gynaecologist. Her discharge was a formality. She had her little blue book, sponsored by Johnson & Johnson, with Junior's growth charts, immunisation schedule and personal health records. Who would come for her? Rowan? Caroline? Marion? Would Rowan come even if Mike's talk had got nowhere? Would he come as a last act as her husband? Would Caroline come, assuming Rowan wouldn't? Why hadn't anyone rung to tell her what was happening? She glanced across at Finau and Junior, who was asleep on her enormous breasts.

'Pannapasa,' said Finau. 'My grandfather's name on my

mother's side. You like? Or Jamesa, my cousin's name.'

'I don't know,' said Sandra. 'Maybe he should have an Australian name.'

'But he is Fiji baby.'

'He is also my baby.'

Finau fell silent before changing the subject. 'You go home now?'

'Yes, as soon as I've seen the doctor.'

'Maybe I say goodbye now.'

'I'm sorry, Fi, I have a lot to think about today.'

'That's okay, Mrs Sandy.' Finau kissed Junior and placed him gently back in his crib. 'You a very lucky boy, Fiji baby. Very lucky boy. You have good mother and good life in Australia. Better life than Fiji.' She covered her face with her hands and to Sandra's surprise began sobbing.

Sandra shot to her feet, ignoring the sharp sting from her stitches. She put her arms around the big woman and held her as tightly as she could until her shoulders stopped heaving. 'Junior will have a good life here, Fi, I promise you. I'll make sure he does. I'll be a good mother. Our Fiji baby will have lots of love and lots of friends.'

Finau pulled herself away from Sandy, bent back over the crib and stroked Junior's hair one last time. 'Goodbye Fiji baby,' she said. 'Goodbye lucky boy.' She straightened, paused to touch Sandra lightly on the shoulder and left with tears rolling down her cheeks.

Oh God, thought Sandra. She slumped back down onto her bed. Is there anyone in the world I haven't upset by having this baby? She picked up a magazine she'd already read from cover to cover and began to flick through it. Nothing registered. Where was the blasted doctor? She heard a gentle knock on her door and turned expectantly towards it, was disappointed when Mike's head appeared but managed a smile anyway.

'Can I come in?'

'Thank God for the cavalry,' she said. Sandra rose to give him a hug and was surprised at Mike's reluctance to let go of her. 'Wow,' she said finally. 'That was some hug. That was done with feeling.'

'You're precious to us, Sandy.'

'As you are to me, Mike. No Rowan?'

'No.'

'Where's Caroline?'

'She didn't want to drive Rowan's car. It's got the baby capsule.'

Sandra frowned. Why hadn't Caroline come as a passenger? There was room. 'Is that the only reason?'

Mike shuffled and wouldn't meet her eyes. 'No, it's not the only reason.'

Sandra's last hopes foundered. 'I suppose you were sent because your last-ditch talk with Rowan went nowhere.'

'I wouldn't say that exactly,' said Mike.

'Well, what would you say? C'mon, Mike, I get the distinct feeling you'd rather be somewhere else.' She lifted her hand, placed it on his shoulder and rested her head against it. 'He's gone, hasn't he?'

'Not quite.'

'Not quite?'

'Not quite. Sit down, Sandra. There could be a happy ending to all this but it depends entirely on you.'

'Sounds ominous.'

'Just listen for a moment.' Mike sat down alongside her on the bed, turned so that his eyes held hers. 'He doesn't want to leave, you know, and for a moment there I thought we'd convinced him to stay. I had you giving him another son in a year's time.'

'Not with these stitches.' Sandra attempted a smile.

'Please, Sandy, let me finish. I thought I had him convinced that in time – and a very short time at that – he'd come to regard Junior as just another member of his family, that in nine months or so he'd have not just one son but two. Rowan was in tears.'

'And?'

'He almost bought it.' Mike took both of Sandy's hands in his. 'He desperately wants to stay but he flatly refuses to have Junior in the house. It's unreasonable and illogical but that's his position and a nuclear detonation won't budge him. He loves you dearly, loves the girls, wants to stay, wants you to give him a son, but he doesn't want Junior. There is the problem in a nutshell.'

'Thank you for trying.' Sandra could feel tears starting and stared down at her feet. 'I suspected all along it was too much to hope for.'

'I haven't finished. We had an idea last night, which at the time seemed quite reasonable. Inspired even.'

'Go on.'

Mike hesitated before asking. 'Would you consider having Junior adopted?'

'No! No way! We may have a problem with the father but there's no problem with the mother. He's my son. There's no way I'd give away my own son to strangers.'

'It wouldn't be to strangers.'

'What do you mean?'

'Come on, Sandy, do I have to spell it out for you? You'd still keep in contact, watch him grow up. Everybody would win, you see? You and Rowan would stay together, the girls wouldn't lose their father, we'd get what we've always wanted and Junior, well, you'd have the comfort of knowing he was being loved to death.'

'I don't believe I'm hearing this.'

'It's not a proposition made lightly, Sandy. It gives you the chance to turn the clock back. Isn't that what you want?'

'No!'

'At least take time to think it over. Talk to Rowan, talk to Caroline, talk to the girls. No one's asking you to make a decision right now.'

'No!' Sandra began to shake her head from side to side. 'No!'

'Your reaction is perfectly understandable. It's a big thing we're asking. But think what's best for the girls, what's best for Rowan and, most importantly, what's best for you. I know you want to hang on to Junior but look at the repercussions. The girls have a right to a live-in father.'

'No!' Sandra's shaking grew in intensity until Mike was obliged to throw his arms around her to calm her down. 'No! No! No!' she said, each denial adding to her determination. He held her tightly, stifling any resistance, and kept holding her until she calmed down.

'I'm sorry, Sandy, I'm really sorry. Nobody wants to hurt you, but we've had to look at all our options, however painful. You know we're acting in good faith. We only want what's best for everyone.'

Sandra pushed Mike away and stood up. 'Caro's behind this, isn't she? It was her idea. Do you really think I could let you and Caro take my own son away from me? Do you?'

Mike bowed his head. 'It's not like that, Sandy.'

'Yes it is! That's exactly how it is and don't try to deny it. You and Caro want a baby so you thought you'd take mine.' She reached down into the crib, picked up Junior and held him tightly against her chest in defiance.

'That's unfair. That's not how it is.'

'Caro's behind this, I can see her hand in it. I bet she's even got his room ready! Well, you can tell her no deal and, while you're at it, tell her to find another friend. There's something neither of you understand, Mike, something neither of you have considered. If I give Junior away, I give him away forever. But if I lose Rowan, there's always a chance I can win him back later. It may not seem likely right now, maybe even impossible. But while there's a chance I can keep my son and get my husband back, I'll take it. Rowan loves me, you've said so yourself. He loves me and I love him. That has to count for something.'

'I hope so,' said Mike grimly. 'I hope for your sake it does.'

Rowan listened as Mike relayed his conversation with Sandra, his hand wrapped so tightly around the phone that his knuckles turned white. A carpet of pine needles lay on the floor around the fading Christmas tree. Sandra still smiled at him from the photo on the wall but her smile now meant nothing. Away in the kitchen the girls were playing a game that had them shrieking with laughter. 'Any point in me talking to her?' he said finally.

'She's not going to give him away,' said Mike. 'Your call, but I think you'd be wasting your time.'

'Where is she?'

'Getting the final okay from her gynaecologist. I'm using her mobile.'

'Guess I'll just start packing.'

'Will you be there when I bring Sandy home?'

'Yeah. It'll take a day or two to organise somewhere to stay. I'll need temporary accommodation until I find something to buy. Have you told Caro?'

'No. God only knows how I'm going to handle that. She'd managed to convince herself that, beginning tonight, Junior would spend the next twenty years of his life sleeping in our courtyard bedroom.'

'Want me to go over and talk to her?'

'Thanks, but no. Keep well clear for at least a week. There'll be tears and tantrums and wrist-slashing despair but at least I've been down this road before. For us it's just another link in a chain of life's dirty tricks and disappointments. Sometimes life's a bitch.'

'Yeah,' said Rowan bitterly. 'And then you marry one.'

Part III

Retribution

Seventeen

The loss of Rowan had been devastating but to lose Caroline simultaneously had been catastrophic. A week after Sandra had brought Junior home from hospital, she and Caroline engaged in a screaming match over the phone, Caroline accusing her of being selfish and she accusing Caroline of trying to steal her baby. Both Rowan and Mike tried to broker a peace but the women rebuffed their attempts. Yet peace would have benefited both. Caroline lapsed into a deep depression requiring psychiatric counselling and drug therapy, while Sandra was at her wit's end trying to cope. Out of desperation she turned to her mother but was rewarded with a blunt reworking of the advice Marion had given her in hospital.

'Give him up and put your mistakes behind you,' she urged. 'You see him as your son, but the rest of the world sees him only as a monumental indiscretion. Why live with your shame when you can bundle it off somewhere else?'

If Sandra hadn't needed help, she would have hung up on her mother immediately.

In the aftermath of Rowan's departure, Sandra's circle of friends contracted alarmingly. It surprised her to discover how many of their friends were from the advertising industry, clients, colleagues or acquaintances of Rowan, and were more Rowan's friends than hers. Forced to choose between them, they'd remained loyal to Rowan following the split. Some of the wives rang with expressions of sympathy and some even called around with flowers and offers of assistance. But as with her own friends, many of whom were mothers of Sarah and Rochelle's schoolfriends, much of their sympathy and expressions of solidarity were no more than a disguise for curiosity, a deception to get a closer look at the evidence of her misdeed and gather fuel for gossip. Once their curiosity was satisfied, the offers of assistance dissipated and Sandra's sense of alienation and ostracism grew.

Worse was to follow as Sandra struggled to get by. She'd never had to cope as a single parent before, never had to combine her work with caring for a new baby, entertaining the girls and running the household without help. She'd made no contingency plans. Why would she have? With the summer holidays in full cry, there were no diversions or activities for the girls. No school, kindy, ballet, music or softball. Many of her good friends, people she'd grown up with and felt she could count on, were away up the coast or overseas, taking advantage of the Christmas break. She'd done a frantic ring-around of peripheral friends and barely acquainted mothers of the girls' schoolfriends only to discover that they, too, were out of town on holiday, working or unsympathetic. The cold rebuffs hurt her deeply. News of her indiscretion had spread and her reputation had been revised.

Not all her friends shunned her or were unavailable, and Sandra blessed the few occasions when the girls were taken off her hands for the day by friends who were genuinely caring. But that also carried a price, which soon became evident in Sarah's sullen, withdrawn silences. Occasionally she'd catch her daughter looking at her reproachfully and Sarah would burst into tears at the slightest provocation. Sandra didn't need a degree in psychology to know what was worrying her, and she realised she could no longer avoid the unavoidable. It was time to talk to the girls, to come clean about Junior and explain that Rowan wasn't his father. Of course Sarah would have some inkling, having overheard conversations or having had relayed to her conversations her little friends had overheard. It broke Sandra's heart to imagine what was said and the hurt Sarah must have felt. Up until that moment Sandra had thought her spirits had fallen as low as they could go, but now an abyss opened in front of her that seemed bottomless. She didn't know what she'd do if she also lost the respect of her daughters.

It took six months for Sandra to get her life back into some kind of order and that was only made possible through the unselfish and unstinting support of her softball girls. They had rallied around to help get her back on her feet. They organised a roster around each player's commitments, babysat, cooked, shopped and provided her with the uplifting company she desperately needed. Perhaps it was their youth and their general disregard for consequences that framed their attitude. Sandra wasn't criticised, but made the object of their collective awe. Naturally they wanted to know all about Siti and in gratitude Sandra didn't hold back, which only served to deepen their respect. She became their cause. With their help, Sandra had been able to reopen her clinic and restore routine and purpose to her life. She drew strength from them and surprised herself with her readiness to smile. She began to enjoy their futile but well-intentioned attempts to fix her up with a date and gradually reacquainted herself with the world beyond her immediate problems. She repaid her team for their kindness by treating their injuries.

Sandra fitted the interferential pads to Lucy's knee and dialled up the electric current. 'How's that?' she asked.

'You can goose it a bit,' said Lucy. 'Give it heaps if it'll get me fit for State sooner.' During the regional play-offs, Lucy had held her ground on first base against a desperate runner as the mid-fielder had rifled in a return. She'd gloved it and got the out the instant before the runner knocked her flying, knocked her patella out of alignment and tore enough tissue for her knee to blow up to twice its size. Sandra had been treating it every night for the past week so Lucy could play in the State finals in Lismore, up north by the Queensland border.

It was nine o'clock before the girls finally left and Sandra was faced with the prospect of putting Sarah, Rochelle and Junior to bed. She tidied up in preparation for the following day's patients – Friday was one of her busiest days – bundled up everything that needed washing and headed for the laundry. She glanced into the lounge as she passed by. Mel Gibson was wasting his time knocking the stuffing out of various bad guys. Junior was asleep on the floor, face down on his lamb's skin. Sarah and Rochelle were asleep on the sofa. The coffee table was littered with half-emptied glasses of orange juice and cordial. Whoever had been babysitting had been overgenerous with biscuits. Soggy remains and crumbs covered everything. A basket of ironing awaited her attention. It was the sort of scene that might have inspired Norman Rockwell to paint, and it dragged a reluctant smile to her face. It should have been the epitome of domestic bliss, but for the fact that a key element was missing.

When the phone rang she thought it was Rowan ringing, all too late, to wish the girls goodnight. Marion's voice caught her by surprise.

'Hello, Mum,' she said cautiously.

'Not interrupting anything, am I?' asked Marion.

'Like what?'

'I don't know, dear, and I wouldn't have the impertinence to ask.'

'What do you want, Mum?'

'Something you should know,' she said, matter-of-factly. 'Clive and I have decided to get married. No point paying for two apartments when we're only using one. Ceremony's on Hamilton Island, so we won't be plagued by family and friends. Then we're off on a Pacific Cruise for four weeks. No need for presents but you can send a card if you wish.'

Sandra's jaw dropped open but no sound emerged. She

was stunned, far too shocked to express her outrage. The thought of her mother marrying again was horrific enough, but her mother's reference to her and her children left her near speechless. 'Plague?' she'd said incredulously. 'We're a plague?'

'You know what I mean, dear.'

'No, I don't! Why do you do it, Mum, why? Just as I'm getting back on my feet, you have to do this to me.' Sandra didn't wait for a reply. She placed the phone back in its cradle when she really wanted to slam it down, her mind reeling under the twin blows of her mother's insensitivity and the fact that she was marrying Clive. She couldn't understand how her mother could be married to her father for so many years and not remain faithful to his memory. Didn't all the years they'd lived together mean anything any more? Besides, Clive was a flake. His spit wasn't fit to shine her late father's shoes. Her mother needed slapping.

The television cut to a commercial, which for some reason was twice as loud as the program. It woke Sarah, who sat up sleepily. Sandra stood her iron up and helped the seven-year-old to her feet. After a brief detour to the toilet, Sarah finally curled up in bed. She held her arms up for a goodnight kiss and wrapped them around her mother's neck.

'Love you,' said Sarah.

'Love you, too.'

'Mummy . . .'

'Yes?'

'Is Daddy ever coming home to stay?'

'I hope so, honey, I really do.' Sandra turned off the

bedside light and tip-toed out of the bedroom. How many times had the girls asked the same question? How many times had she given the same answer? How long would it be before they accepted that Rowan might never come home to stay? How long before she did? Even more importantly, how long before Rowan did?

Eighteen

Sandra didn't send a congratulatory card but received regular postcards from Marion, all with pictures of magical tropical destinations and happy, smiling people. Her mother had been impressed by the garlic coconut crab in Port Vila, amazed everyone by going snorkelling in Fiji and had cleaned up regularly at bridge. Apparently Clive had brought quite formidable card skills to the union. The arrival of the postcards had annoyed Sandra, but a little less each time. At least her mother was getting on with her life, which reminded Sandra that it was high time she did the same. She made a conscious effort to follow her mother's example.

It was Rowan's turn to have the girls for the weekend and she hoped they wouldn't come home with another new name on their lips, another of Daddy's friends who'd just happened to come to dinner and wake up in his bed. She hated the example he was setting Sarah and Rochelle, but more than anything, she bitterly resented the fact that Rowan had slipped so casually into a succession of relationships, and so quickly. After thirteen years of marriage he'd waited just two weeks before taking a girl home from the office. Sometimes she found herself wishing he'd find one girl he liked and form a stable relationship with her – stable, but not permanent. Permanence was the thing she dreaded, the one thing that could shatter the hope that Rowan would one day return to the fold. The hope that underpinned her recovery.

Marion had agreed to take Junior on Friday night and all day Saturday. Since marrying Clive, her mother had softened in her attitude towards Junior, and Clive seemed to thrive on his company. Sandra put it down to the fact that they had the same level of intellect.

With the Saturday competition between seasons, she had no softball commitments until Sunday morning rep training. She'd arranged to kick the weekend off with a girls' night, drinks followed by a movie and a late meal somewhere. She decided to doll herself up, dress young, sexy and single, and give her softball girls some competition. She'd get her hair and nails done, shop leisurely, bring something nice home for lunch, read magazines and have an afternoon sleep. Sandra looked forward to Friday night and Saturday with almost the same relish she'd once viewed her holiday in Coralhaven.

The weekend began early when the last of her Friday patients failed to show. She waited ten minutes, then closed up. With her afternoon babysitter, the sixteen-year-old daughter of her nearest neighbour, booked until five, she seized the opportunity for a long and luxurious shower. When she checked on the kids she found Sarah, Rochelle and the babysitter trying to encourage Junior to crawl by lying him on the floor and placing his favourite biscuits on a plate a metre and a half in front of him. Junior was lapping up the attention and doing his best but hadn't quite acquired the knack. He worked his arms and legs furiously like a stranded swimmer but, if anything, went backwards more often than forwards. Sarah and Rochelle were laughing their heads off, which in turn made Junior laugh. Whenever he laughed he had a habit of rolling over onto his back and covering his eyes with his tiny hands. He looked so cute, Sandra just wanted to eat him. The girls had both been good babies but Sandra thought Junior must be the happiest soul God had ever put on earth. He was certainly the smiliest baby she'd ever seen. She couldn't look at him without smiling herself, and with every smile she felt more justified in hanging on to him.

As the shower cascaded over her, she tried to think what to wear, what to pack for the girls and whether anything needed ironing. Fortunately Margaret had rung to give her an idea of the outings Rowan had planned for them, so she'd know what to pack. The girls loved their weekends with Rowan and had every reason to. There was hardly a minute when they weren't doing something. On Saturday alone, he had them visiting the Museum of Technology in the morning, having yum cha at the Flower Drum for lunch, riding the ferries to Manly in the afternoon and, in the evening, being fussed over in Channel 9's private box at the Sydney Sports Ground while Australia played rugby against New Zealand. Rowan made a big effort to entertain the girls, believing he did it out of love. Sandra knew better. He did it out of guilt for walking out on them.

She slipped into her dressing-gown, ran a bath for the girls and sent the babysitter home early. All going well, and provided Rowan turned up on time, she and the softball girls might just be able to knock back a leisurely cocktail before their movie. Once she took such things for granted, now it was an almost unimaginable luxury, a sweet reminder that she still had a life.

At seven-fifteen there was still no sign of Rowan. The girls sat watching TV half-heartedly, waiting for him, their bags packed and ready by their sides. Sandra began to worry that Rowan would be late once more because something had cropped up and priorities had shifted. She hadn't been able to rely on him to be punctual while they were together and had no leverage now that they lived apart. It was hard on her and, she suspected, even harder on the girls. At seven-thirty she began to worry. She still had to drop Junior off at her mother's. When Rowan's car pulled into her drive at seven-thirty-five, she almost cheered.

'Hi,' said Rowan neutrally. He stood in the doorway as if he had no more right to enter than an encyclopaedia salesman.

'Hi. Aren't you going to tell me I look nice?'

'You look nice. Really nice.'

Sandra got the distinct impression he'd rather she didn't.

'Meeting anyone special?'

'I wouldn't dress like this for the postman.'

'Anyone I know?'

'None of your business.'

'I guess it isn't.' What little levity Sandra had managed to inject into the exchange disappeared. 'Girls ready?'

'Rearing to go,' said Sandra. 'Want to come in?'

'Claudine's waiting in the car.'

'Invite her in.'

'Don't think that's a good idea.'

'Who doesn't? You or her?'

'I'd agreed to take her to a party, a Mauritian get-together, before I realised it was my turn for the girls. She's not happy. It's her birthday next weekend so I said we'd do something special to make up.'

Sandra affected sympathy but really wanted to smile. So much for the bachelor life. 'There are just a couple of things. Rocky's fighting off a cold, so make sure she takes her vitamin C tablets and echinacea each night. It helps if Pandy takes them first.'

'No worries.'

'Also, the gutters are full of leaves again. I hate to ask, but is there any chance you could hop up on the roof when you bring the girls back?'

Rowan sighed heavily. 'I suppose so.'

'Daddy!'

Rowan's face lit up instantly as his two daughters hurtled towards him. They threw themselves into his arms and shrieked with delight.

Sandra smiled. This was how it used to be. Daddy comes home and for minutes at a time she ceases to exist. Even now she didn't feel the slightest hint of jealousy. It always buoyed her to see that Rowan had lost none of his attachment to the girls. She believed that if he ever came back home, the girls would be a large part of the reason. 'I'll get their bags,' she said.

'Come and see Juni,' screamed Rochelle. 'He's trying to crawl.'

'Some other time,' said Rowan. 'We're in a bit of a hurry.'

'Please, Daddy!'

'No time. Look, here comes Mummy with your bags.' Rowan stood by while the girls kissed Sandra goodbye. 'Enjoy yourself.'

Sandra smiled. 'But not too much, right?'

'Right.' Rowan smiled back but his smile was unconvincing.

Sandra kept waving until Rowan's car had disappeared from sight, pleased with the effect she'd had on him but disappointed that she was making no progress in reconciling him with Junior. It was always the same. Rowan always had an excuse for not seeing Junior and went out of his way to avoid any contact. On occasions, because of softball commitments, she'd begged him to take Junior as well when he'd picked up the girls. His response had been so immediate, so emphatic and so cold, she'd given up asking. All the same, she felt an opportunity had slipped by. If she'd managed to entice Claudine out of the car and into the house, the young Mauritian would most certainly have fallen in love with Junior. All it would have taken was one of his big smiles. Junior could make them so personal, Claudine would have been smitten instantly. If Rowan wouldn't take Junior for a weekend, maybe Claudine would, and she doubted that Rowan could last a whole weekend without becoming another of Junior's conquests. Sandy believed that, once Rowan became attached or simply accustomed to Junior, it would only be a matter of time before he came home to live, that the pull of her and the two girls would prove irresistible.

There again, she had to accept even that plan was flawed. Claudine was capable of providing Rowan with the kind of permanent relationship she feared. On the occasions Sandra had met Claudine at the agency, she'd been impressed not only with the younger woman's vivacity but also her maturity. She was no flighty one-night stand. In the past they'd always greeted each other with smiles and never missed the opportunity to exchange pleasantries. But the last thing Sandra could afford to do was appear to give their relationship her blessing. In hindsight, she was relieved that Claudine had remained in the car.

The prospect of a cocktail loomed large in her mind. She needed something to lift her spirits and put her back in the mood she was in as she'd showered, dressed and experimented with her make-up. Allowing ten minutes to drive to Marion's and five minutes for chat, she could be at Cremorne just after eight. That would give her twenty-five minutes for a Fluffy Duck or even an Orgasm before the movie started. Maybe some men would try to pick her up. They wouldn't succeed but the attempts always did wonders for her ego. One day, one of them might even hit the button that awakened her libido, like Snow White out of her slumber. Life wasn't perfect, but it was slowly getting better.

'Germaine Greer?' said Sandy. She picked *The Whole Woman* up from Marion's side table and discovered her mother was two-thirds of the way through it. Yet when *The Female Eunuch* had been published, her mother had dismissed it as garbage, the bitter gripes of a troublemaker who needed a husband to sort her out.

'I think she's lost the plot, dear. Not quite up to her earlier work. That had edge. Admire the fact that she has a mind of her own, regret that she doesn't always use it.' Marion took Junior off Sandy and propped him up on the sofa where she'd been sitting reading.

'You didn't like her early work.'

'Whatever gave you that idea?'

Sandra decided to change the subject. 'No Clive?'

'He's having a whisky with some friends at the RSL club. He was in the RAF, you know. Joined after the war because they had jets and the RAAF didn't. Saw active service. Dropped bombs on Suez. Full of surprises is Clive.'

'He surprised me in hospital.'

'I think he said he flew Canberra bombers. One time when he went to an air show in New Zealand he thought he'd caught up with his old bus, as he referred to it. Can you imagine getting sentimental over a bomber, of all things?'

'He said I was my mother's daughter and winked.'

'Did he? How very forward.'

Sandra hesitated. The question had been lurking in the back of her mind since she'd come home from hospital and at last she had the opportunity to ask it. She hesitated because she feared her questions might open doors best left closed. But the fact that her mother appeared to be ducking the issue only made her want to press on. 'Are you going to tell me what that was all about?'

Marion turned and began plumping up cushions. 'I really don't know.'

'It's something I've been meaning to ask you. You were talking about adoption. You said you knew about such things. Clive agreed, as I recall.'

'Really?'

'Really.'

Marion smiled darkly. 'Slip of the tongue. Must have been the shock of seeing Junior. Thought you'd forgotten about it actually.'

'Clive made sure I didn't.'

For a brief moment, Marion seemed to lose her composure. 'Well, it can do no harm telling you now. Family skeleton, for what it's worth. Rattled a few more since so I guess there's no harm dragging it out of the cupboard again.' She looked Sandra squarely in the eyes. 'I'm afraid you weren't an only child, dear.'

'What?' Sandra's jaw dropped.

'No, you've got a brother somewhere. Had a baby boy two days after my sixteenth birthday. They never let me see him, of course. Never told me where he went. Whisked him away the instant he was born. Like it had never happened. For the best, really.'

'You had a baby?'

'Don't be so shocked, dear. You weren't the first to drop your knickers in haste. Of course, there was a scandal. God only knows what would have happened if the baby had been black.'

'Colour makes no difference.'

'Did in my day.'

'Who was the father?'

'You can't guess?'

'Oh God.'

'Of course I was forbidden to see him. We lost touch for years and then he turned up two weeks after I'd married your father.'

'Oh God.' Sandra's head reeled.

Marion looked at her watch. 'Shouldn't you be somewhere else, dear?'

'Oh God,' she said, again. The softball girls would be wondering where she was. 'Didn't you ever try to find him?'

'Clive did. Got nowhere, of course. Confidential meant confidential in those days.'

'Have you tried since?'

'No point. Too much water under the bridge. No good would come of it now.'

'How do you do it, Mum? Every time I talk to you, you find another way to pull the rug out from under my feet.'

'Don't be melodramatic, dear.'

The softball girls were well into their second or third drinks by the time Sandra had parked her car and joined them. Some young guys were hovering hopefully around them, filling their ears with chat. Her evening improved the instant she saw the effect her appearance had on the girls and noticed the guys looking at her with sudden interest. Stuff the Fluffy Duck, she thought, and stuff the Orgasm. She was determined to enjoy herself and before she could do that she had to get Rowan and

Claudine out of her head, plus her maddening mother and the mind-numbing news that somewhere she had an older brother.

'Somebody get me a vodka and tonic,' she said. 'Heavy on the voddy, easy on the tonic.'

'I'll get it,' said one of the guys. He was cool, assured and probably thought Sandra was a definite prospect. He turned to fight his way to the bar.

'Nice botty,' she said. The girls looked at her in astonishment.

Sunday began with a chill that suggested clear skies and the prospect of a perfect, warm winter's day, which, for once, the forecasters could take credit for predicting. Sandra had planned to sleep in until eight before racing off to take the Under-19 reps through their last practice before the State finals in Lismore. For the first time in five years she wouldn't be going with them. Coaching a team through the finals was a full-on job and she couldn't do it while nursing a baby. She was disappointed and so was her team. But she had commitments, one of which had just decided that five-thirty was a fine time to wake up, and there was no Sarah to take him into her bed.

Sandra tried ignoring the tinkling, clicking and tooting of his Fisher-Price activity centre but she couldn't ignore his giggles. They made her smile, despite her determination to keep dozing. As babies, both of the girls had given the activity centre a solid workout, but neither of them giggled and chortled as gleefully as Junior. When Sarah took him into her bed and the girls joined in the giggling, Sandra knew she was listening to the sound of pure happiness and it infected her as well. She was only sorry Rowan wasn't there to hear it.

She gave up trying to sleep and brought Junior back to her bed. She made a little nest for him and stroked his head. The girls loved pulling his hair straight, letting go and watching it spring back into place as if nothing had happened. Junior liked it too. Sometimes the stroking and gentle hair-pulling lulled him back to sleep, and this was one of those times. His eyelids grew heavy and eventually closed. Why wouldn't he sleep? He was surrounded by love and affection, wanted for nothing and lay safe and secure in his mother's bed where nothing could ever harm him. Sandra slipped contentedly back into sleep. Her mistake was in thinking all her dramas with her Fiji baby were far behind her.

Nineteen

The alarm clock woke Rowan at six o'clock. He rolled out of bed grateful that there was nobody sharing it, nobody to complain and suggest that he did his stretches elsewhere. When he'd first resumed his bachelor life, he'd been like an alcoholic let loose in a distillery. He'd been stunned by the number of beautiful, young women who wanted to take Sandra's place. More than anything he'd been stunned by their directness. He guessed that for them he was an easy ticket to a life of luxury, fashionable clothes, expensive restaurants and relative significance among the advertising fraternity. They were eager to stake their claim.

But if the women were easy to pick up, they weren't always so easy to put down. After a series of acrimonious break-ups, some of which resulted in resignations and ugly scenes in the office, he learned to be more selective in whom he invited into his bed. One especially bitter young woman who, after only a week of cohabitation had begun dropping references to engagement rings, showed her fury at being discarded by cutting fifteen centimetres off the left leg of every pair of trousers in his wardrobe. Rowan couldn't even begin to speculate why she only attacked the left legs. The reality was he had to replace thousands of dollars worth of clothing.

Of all his one-night stands and brief relationships, only one meant anything to him. Claudine was keen to move into his townhouse but he hesitated. She was bright, sparkling, lovely and loving, and exquisitely exotic. That was the problem. Her French Legionnaire father had given her the style sense of a Parisienne but she had her Mauritian mother's looks and skin colour. He was happy for them to get serious, even flattered, but what if they had a child? And what if he looked like Junior?

Rowan stretched without enthusiasm, finally deciding to head down to the gym on his way to work in an attempt to get his blood flowing. He slipped his tracksuit on over his gym shorts and singlet, grabbed a clean shirt, tie and suit and left, saying goodbye to no one. He pulled out into a street as devoid of life as the moon. Once he'd lived at Avalon, up on the northern beaches, and by six in the morning the streets would be buzzing with surfers and tradesmen's vehicles. Even the Middle Harbour side of Mosman, where he'd left his family, had early commuter traffic and more than a handful of joggers flattening the pavement. But there were no tradesmen, surfers, joggers or commuter traffic in his little Mosman cul-de-sac.

The gym was bustling with young women hell-bent on taking over the world or, at very least, the company they worked for. They leapt, stretched, bounced and rebounded to techno music, which Rowan suspected hadn't been recorded but cast in a forge. It was music to armourplate by. Rowan hopped onto the treadmill to warm up. Jogging around streets did not interest him. Streets had dogs that bit, gutters that twisted ankles and every intersection had impatient drivers who regarded joggers as little more than speed bumps. The treadmill was merely boring. He thought of joining the aerobics class but it was heading to its climax. Instead, he began a circuit of the Nautilus machines. Gradually his body came to life, responding to the demands he placed upon it. The instructor was waiting for him by the heavy bag.

'Thought you'd come in,' he said.

'Nearly didn't,' said Rowan.

'If you want to come by some evening I've got a young Samoan boxer for you. He'd give you a good workout. He's got great speed, great eyes and a punch – if he ever learns to throw it properly – that could stop a bus. The beauty is, he's only eighteen and keen to learn. What do you reckon?'

'I dunno.'

'What's the matter?'

'Not in the mood.'

'You need one of them new business things.'

'Got one.'

'Then get a new bird. Look at that mob over there.' He pointed to the aerobics class gathering for the next session. 'Get it up, get it on, get it in. There are some real heart-breakers in that lot.'

'Ball-breakers, more like.'

'Find a bus and fall under it,' said the instructor. 'I give up.'

'See you,' said Rowan.

'You come down one evening,' said the instructor, as a parting shot. 'You need to get some sense knocked into yer.'

Rowan strolled into the office with a double espresso he'd bought from the downstairs café and two Granny Smith apples from a street vendor. The door was unlocked, the lights on and nobody in sight. When he wandered around to his office, he found Blake at the fax machine.

'G'day,' said Rowan. 'I'm relieved to see the fax hasn't been nicked.'

'What's your problem?' said Blake.

'What's my problem? The whole place is wide open for anyone to walk in and help themselves and you ask me what my problem is.'

'Give me a break,' said Blake wearily. 'Half the studio's been here since six doing up the ads for the presentation to Daewoo. Mark and Elaine are fluffing about somewhere and so is Claudine.'

'Claudine's in already?'

'Yes. I asked her to come in early to man reception. She's probably just gone for a pee.'

'Oh.'

'Oh – is that all? Sorry too big a word for you?'

Rowan finally cracked a smile. 'Sorry,' he said. 'How's the presentation coming together?'

'Nothing you can fault.'

'But?'

'That's just it. There's nothing wrong with the work but it doesn't give me a hard-on.'

'Can't reinvent the wheel every time.'

'It's the "C" word, Rowan, the word you once professed to loathe more than any other in the English language.'

'Crap.'

'Really? A year ago these ads would never have been comped up. You would have thrown them out the door, along with whoever did them. They're complacent, Rowan, capital C complacent.'

Rowan bowed his head. He couldn't recall exactly how the campaign went, which was never a good sign. 'Ah what the hell, what does it matter? They're going to come here anyway.'

'Jesus Christ, I don't believe I'm hearing this. If this is the agency's new philosophy, then count me out. I'm ringing Nathan Glengarry. Right now their work's shitting on ours. That's the difference between us and them. They're consistent. They've been good for years. We're going to wind up five-minute wonders.'

'Have you finished?'

'For now.'

'Good. You've got to realise we're not going to win awards with every ad we do.'

'Rowan, that's bullshit. The point is, we have to try to win awards with every ad we do. We've got to try to make every ad better than anyone else could have done. These aren't my words, they're yours, only you seem to have forgotten them.'

'I thought you'd finished. By the way, how're you getting on with Tiny?'

'Fine. But that's another thing. The Fiji Tourist Board doesn't want me, they want you. You gave them your personal commitment that you would handle their business. You may have forgotten but they haven't.'

'Times change.'

'And accounts change agencies.'

'They won't move.'

'Don't bet on it. And let me ask you this. Can we afford to lose an account that's generating income? New business is fine but it takes at least six months for earnings to come on-stream. We've put on a lot of new business but it's not yet paying its way.'

'Okay,' said Rowan wearily. 'I'll ring Tiny.'

'Good. There's one more thing I want you to do.'

'What's that?' said Rowan cautiously.

'After we've shown Daewoo their shiny new ads, I want you to tear them up and apologise for the fact that they're not as good as they should be.'

'What!'

'Just to show we're not complacent around here.' Blake turned and disappeared into his office, leaving Rowan holding a coffee gone cold.

'Get you another?'

A wave of perfume engulfed Rowan. 'Morning, Margaret,' he said. 'Thank you, I'd love another coffee.'

'He's right, you know,' she said softly.

'I know,' said Rowan. 'That's the trouble.'

Returning to work after the Christmas break had taken every bit of courage Rowan possessed. On Christmas Eve he'd left the agency on top of the world and in control of his destiny.

He'd returned ten days later a man reduced to ridicule, nerves raw and exposed and singing like toothache. He had no idea how he'd even begin to explain the baby and was overwhelmed to discover he didn't have to. Blake had done the job for him, patiently ringing every member of staff, whether at home or on holiday. He'd also contacted all their clients and Rowan's friends and rivals in other agencies. Instead of encountering embarrassed silences and people shying away from eye contact, Rowan had been engulfed by a wave of solidarity. Staff had slipped unannounced into his office for the sole purpose of giving him a reassuring hug or handshake and offering the advertising equivalent of sincere commiserations.

'Bummer,' they'd said.

Rowan had been staggered by the letters of support that arrived by mail, e-mail and fax, and by the number of phone calls from clients and associates. Maybe everybody really liked and felt for him, or maybe in his fall they had intimations of their own vulnerability. Whatever their motivation, Rowan had drawn strength from their support, but deep inside he resented being the object of other people's compassion. He'd felt a bit like a favourite dog that had narrowly survived being run over and which everyone suddenly wanted to pat. He couldn't forgive Sandra for that.

His instinct had been to bury himself in his work, which he'd done with both vigour and passion. Work was the only constant in the upheaval. He'd become so driven that staff who'd previously found him demanding began yearning for the good old days. He'd pushed everybody to their limits, worked them late and wrung their brains dry, argued, fought and harangued. His agency had continued to grow and prosper as a result. It took four months but eventually he'd worn himself out and taken his foot off the pedal. Ever since, he'd had trouble putting it back on.

'Your coffee.'

Rowan snapped out of his daydream. Margaret placed his coffee on his desk and waited for him to acknowledge her. He'd taken to slumping in his chair and swivelling it so that he gazed up at the sky through his window, lost in thoughts. It had become such an accustomed position that some of the staff had begun calling him ET, and when people asked where he was, they'd reply, 'Phoning home.'

'Blake wants to know when you want to review the work for the presentation and run through a rehearsal. You only have an hour and a half.'

'Let's go in five,' said Rowan.

'I also have a list of people for you to ring before the presentation gets under way. They're all expecting your call.'

'Better make it ten. Oh, and add Tiny to your list, though I can probably ring him this afternoon.'

'One more thing.'

'What?'

Margaret took a deep breath. 'I've made an appointment for you to see your doctor and get a check-up.'

'Why? I'm fine.'

'My late husband used to say that, while cancer was eating his liver. You're not yourself, Rowan. That's apparent to everybody who works here, even if it isn't to you. If the problem's physiological, it's my job to see that you get it fixed. The appointment's at five.'

'Okay,' said Rowan.

'You're going?' Margaret's eyebrows shot up in amazement. The Rowan of old would have thrown her out of his office.

Rowan looked at the little bottle of pills Margaret had bought for him at a health-food shop, trying to decide whether to swallow a couple or slam-dunk the whole lot, bottle and all, into his wastepaper bin. He decided against tossing them away, on the basis that his office practised recycling and the Armenian cleaner would only have to fish the bottle out of the bin later. The pills were not quite black and not quite brown, looking remarkably similar to the pellets rabbits leave behind. Judging by appearance, Rowan suspected they'd taste worse than rabbit pellets. His doctor had given him a clean bill of health and his blood tests had given no indications of abnormality. That, Rowan decided, was good enough for him. Unfortunately, it wasn't good enough for Margaret, who suspected Chronic Fatigue Syndrome which, she said, doctors were reluctant to diagnose. She'd left him a glass of water and dosage instructions, insisting that two capsules four times a day would shake off his lethargy and restore his zest for life. Rowan knew a sales pitch when he heard one but took two capsules anyway. He was right. They tasted like rabbit pellets.

His phone rang and Rowan knew who was calling the instant he heard the booming voice, a blast from a past he was trying to erase. 'Tiny!' he said, hoping his voice conveyed something of the warmth and affection of old. 'Where the hell are you? I've been trying to ring you for a week.'

'Visiting my constituents,' said Tiny. 'Visiting all the major east-coast resorts and showing them what they get for their fees.'

'How have you been keeping?' asked Rowan.

'The same as always. And you?'

'Same.'

'That's not what I hear.'

'Oh, what do you hear?'

'It's what I don't hear. You don't talk to us any more. Once we were your special client, now you don't come to meetings and you hardly ever call.'

'Surely Blake's looking after you?'

'Blake is a very good man, but Blake is not you. Blake is not the man to stand up in front of our many members and tell them what is what, make them forget all their complaints and special considerations and grasp the big picture. Some of our members are beginning to think you have abandoned us.'

'I've been busy, Tiny, very busy.'

'Unfortunately, we have not. Australians are going to Bali, New Zealanders to the Cook Islands, and it seems the Japanese are staying home. Some of our people are getting restless.'

'I'll talk to Blake.'

'I think it would be better if you came to Fiji and talked to us. I will contact all our members. We have problems and need a solution. If I tell them you're coming, they'll all want to be here. We are spending an extra half a million and they want to know why we're not getting results.'

'I'll see what I can do.'

'You have to do better than that.'

'Have to?'

'It will take four weeks to get everyone together. I will fax Margaret the details. Don't let me down.'

'I'll do my best.'

'Aren't you listening to me? I'm ringing as your friend, not just as your client. My constituents are not happy. If I'd said this to you last year, you would have been on the next plane to Nadi. Don't you want our business any more?'

Rowan closed his eyes in self-disgust. The Fijian Tourist Board had been one of his foundation accounts and Tiny was as much a friend as a client. Of course he didn't want to lose them, but how could he explain? How could he confess that he didn't want to fly to Fiji or have anything whatsoever to do with Fiji? Reluctantly he had to accept that Tiny had left him little alternative but to bite the bullet. 'I'll be on the next plane.'

'Next month will do fine!' said Tiny. 'Welcome back!'

Welcome back, thought Rowan. Even as he hung up he was trying to think of ways he could send Blake and still hang on to the account. His options didn't look good. When the phone rang a second time he scowled at Margaret. She shrugged. 'Sandra,' she mouthed. He snatched up the phone angrily.

'I'm busy,' he snapped.

'It's an emergency.'

'What's wrong?' asked Rowan quickly. 'The girls all right?'

'The girls? Yeah, they're fine. No, it's to do with softball.'

'Softball?'

'Sharon, my co-coach, has come down with glandular fever. She was taking the Under-19s up to Lismore for the State champs. Now the team's stuck without a coach unless I go, and I've got the kids.'

Rowan stiffened. He could see where the conversation was headed.

'I hate to ask you, Rowan, but I really owe the team for helping me during the last few months. Could you possibly come home for the weekend and take over?'

'It's Claudine's birthday. I've promised. Besides, I let her down last weekend.'

'I know. I'm sorry.'

'Maybe I could take the girls.'

'There's Junior, as well. And a cat.'

'Oh Christ. Can't Marion help?'

'They're going away for the weekend to the Blue Mountains.'

'Can't someone else help?'

'Who? Who wants three kids and a cat for the weekend?'

'Where did the cat come from?'

'Pet shop. Try walking past a pet shop window with two young girls when it's full of ginger and white kittens.'

'I've got my whole weekend arranged.'

'I can't let the team down. They've trained like demons for the past four months. They're in with a good shot provided they have a coach.'

'I can't let Claudine down. Not after last week. Anyway, it's her birthday, for Christ's sake. Do you think you could find anyone to take Junior?'

'It's all or nothing, Rowan. Junior's part of my family, even if he isn't part of yours.'

'Claudine is going to be so pissed off.'

'If she came with you, I'm hardly in a position to object.'

'I'm not sure I could handle her sleeping in our bed. I'm not sure she could handle it, either.'

Our bed, thought Sandra? Our bed? She had a silly urge to smile. 'But you'll do it anyway? You'll come and stay?'

'You haven't left me much choice. Oh God, Claudine's booking a restaurant for Friday night and we're supposed to have dinner at Blake's on Saturday night.'

'You could take the kids with you on Saturday,' said Sandra. 'Blake and Noelene won't mind.'

'What about Friday night?'

'Rain-check?'

'Damn you, Sandy.'

'You'll do it?'

'Reluctantly.'

'Oh thanks, Rowan! I'll make it up to you somehow.'

Rowan hung up and stared at the little bottle of pills Margaret said would turn his life around. They had. He'd only taken two and already his life had taken a definite turn. For the worse.

Rowan decided to warm up with a light jog on the treadmill before moving on to the step machine for an aerobic charge. He'd gone to the gym to work out the frustrations of a

Thursday afternoon that had got progressively worse. At some stage he knew he'd have to get serious and do some strength-work on the Nautilus, and that wasn't a prospect he looked forward to. He'd taken two more of Margaret's pills before leaving the office but still felt as flat as piss on a plate. He'd only just begun on the step machine when the instructor spotted him and offered an alternative.

'It'll liven you up,' said the instructor. 'Faster than a mud wrestle with Elle Macpherson.'

'Sure,' said Rowan. 'Which one is he, anyway?'

'Blue trunks, blue head-gear.'

Rowan turned his attention to the young Samoan in the ring, winced as the boxer snapped his opponent's head back, then followed up with a right to the body that damn near snapped his spine. His opponent crumpled to the canvas. 'Jesus,' said Rowan. 'You want me to go in with him?'

'If you're scared, I'll give Tiger a call.'

'You reckon Tiger can handle him?'

'Reckon Tiger's wife could. C'mon, we better give the bloke he hit a hand. I want to get him off the canvas before he pukes. Bloke's all heart but he's hopeless.'

Rowan hopped into the ring with the instructor and helped the troubled boxer to his feet. The man was just winded. Rowan took a good look at his opponent. All he saw was a Fijian with a different label and, it slowly occurred to him, a chance to get even. 'Since I'm here, I may as well go a couple of rounds,' he said. He smiled ingratiatingly at the Samoan but his mind was filled with the notion of bloody revenge. 'Want to keep going?'

'Yeah, man,' said the Samoan.

Sucker, thought Rowan.

'I'll get you some gear,' said the instructor.

The Samoan danced around the ring, ducking and weaving and jabbing an imaginary opponent while Rowan laced-up.

'Bloody hell,' said Rowan. 'He's fast.'

'Fast but erratic,' said the instructor. 'He misses too often and sometimes his punches land before he's got himself set. It's like being hit by a fistful of candy floss.'

'Tell that to the last bloke.'

'Lucky punch,' said the instructor. 'Okay, work to the kid's body but try to keep your gloves up this time. All Polynesians are head hunters, it's in their blood.'

Rowan touched gloves with the young Islander and started to move in. The kid danced away, feinted left, right, then skipped away to the left. Rowan could only marvel at his energy. He moved quickly to cut the Samoan off at the corner, fired a jab at his chin to drag his gloves up, then let rip with a thunderous right to the kid's stomach. Rowan never even saw the counter-punch that curled in over his guard, smashed into the side of his jaw, sent his mouthpiece into sub-orbital space and landed him flat on his face. Alarm bells shrilled frantically in his ears, his brain disengaged and slipped into neutral. He was vaguely aware of people splashing water on his face and helping him to his feet, of his knees buckling and his jaw failing to follow instructions.

'What a punch!' said the instructor gleefully. 'What a fuckin' beauty. Told you to keep your hands up.'

In the opposite corner the young Samoan began shadow-boxing, as if Rowan was no more than a minor distraction, long past usefulness. Cold fury settled on Rowan. He had a score to settle and more fuel had just been added to the fire.

Rowan suffered through a dinner consisting of a can of Campbell's garden vegetable soup and a tub of chocolate ice-cream. The scotch fillet he'd planned to sear and eat with potato salad stayed in the fridge. At ten he made the call he could no longer postpone. Right from the start, they had agreed to keep their office and private lives apart. She was his receptionist by day and girlfriend by night, and all their private arrangements were generally made over the phone after hours.

'Where have you been?' said Claudine. 'I've been waiting all night.'

'Gym.'

'I booked The Quay for Friday night. They've given us a window table overlooking the Opera House.'

'Godda problem,' said Rowan.

'You all right? You sound funny.'

'Toothache.'

'Poor baby.' She laughed. Rowan grimaced.

'Have to cancel,' said Rowan, and explained his predicament. He couldn't soften the pill with sweet-talk because his sore and swollen jaw would not allow it. Instead, he kept words and sentences deliberately short so he wouldn't precipitate more swelling. He apologised and promised restitution, a postponement of her birthday dinner until the following week, with a bottle of Dom Perignon to open proceedings. Just pronouncing Dom Perignon was agony. Claudine was unimpressed and let him know by her silences. She said she'd prefer not to spend the weekend in Sandra's house but agreed to meet him at Blake's on Saturday night. As far as Friday night went, she said, she'd make her own arrangements. Rowan heard her disappointment, but what stayed with him after she'd hung up was a sound he was coming to dread.

The sound of a relationship breaking apart.

On Friday afternoon Rowan picked up the girls from ballet and drove home to relieve the girl from next door who was baby-sitting Junior. When his two girls instantly raced away to play with their brother, he felt a twinge of jealously, as though they were being disloyal to him. He let them play together until six, then drove them to McDonald's to burn off another hour. Home again, he bathed and dressed them for bed. It was still only seven-thirty. He left them playing in the lounge while he set about heating his pre-cooked dinner in the microwave — steamed blue-eye cod with mashed potato and peas. The meal did not appeal — it was the kind of meal prepared for invalids, the aged and boxers who neglected to keep their guard up.

He found a bottle of scotch in the cupboard — his scotch — and poured himself a double. Out in the lounge the girls were giggling hysterically, yelling for him to join them. Joining them meant playing with Junior and, once again, Sandy had left him no choice. He found Junior lying belly-down on the carpet, head back and tongue out, a maniacal grin on his face as he watched the kitten chase a piece of cloth on a string that Sarah was jiggling about. Clearly Junior had seen a role model, another creature on all fours, whom he could emulate. He pushed himself up onto his hands, arms rigidly out in front of him, and kicked his legs to propel himself forward. It might have worked for the kitten but it didn't for him. Each time he tried, he toppled over face-first. The girls thought it was hysterical and so did Junior. Even Rowan had to laugh. Black kids were supposed to be great movers, he thought, but they couldn't crawl for nuts.

When the girls calmed down he put on a video for them to watch while he slipped into the kitchen to eat his blue-eye. Sarah settled into a corner of the sofa with Junior snuggled into the crook of her arm. Rochelle lay on a cushion on the floor in front of them, propped up on her elbows. He immediately recognised the theme to *The NeverEnding Story*. Sarah used to play it on the piano.

Later, when Rowan changed Junior's nappy before bed, Sarah insisted on supervising to make sure he did it right. She also insisted on reading Junior a story. In turn, Rowan insisted on reading her and Rochelle a story.

Afterwards, he felt strangely contented as he poured himself a second scotch for company. When the kitten began scratching at the front door, he realised he had another domestic duty to perform. He went out with it in case it decided to run away or was confronted by the big tomcat that lived up the road. He cleared the mailbox while the kitten went about its business. Three letters and junk mail. He looked up at the stars and discovered nothing much had changed since he'd moved out. Down on Middle Harbour a sudden flare of a match identified two fishermen in an aluminium dinghy. In the stillness, their voices carried across the water. The fish weren't biting. Nothing much had changed there, either. The night had the reassuring familiarity of other times, better times. When he called the kitten, it came straightaway and purred when he picked it up. Any moment now, thought Rowan, the mopoke is going to call.

It did.

Rowan heard a bell tinkle and a sound like a stick being run along a picket fence. He waited for a toot to confirm his suspicions before dragging himself out of bed. Junior met him with a smile that could crack granite. Rowan picked him up.

'You little terror,' he said softly. 'It's only five-thirty. We should have wrapped you up in brown paper and sent you back to Fiji the day you were born.' Junior chuckled at the idea. Rowan carried him down to the lounge and laid him down on his lambskin. 'Stay there while I warm you some milk.'

Rowan dragged himself bleary-eyed to the kitchen. He shivered and wondered if he should put a heater on for Junior. He wandered back into the lounge with Junior's bottle and found him propped up and wobbling on hands and knees.

'Good on you!' said Rowan. Junior looked up at him, all eyes and hope, tongue sticking out in concentration. He raised one arm tentatively and advanced it a couple of centimetres. This achievement reduced him to laughter. He began wobbling precariously.

'C'mon, you can do it.' Rowan sat down on the edge of the sofa and held Junior's bottle out towards him. Junior propped and reached out his arm. 'You want it, you come get it,' said

Rowan. For a moment he thought Junior was going to cry. Instead, Junior looked at the bottle of milk and then the distance between it and himself, and set about closing it. His legs skidded out from under him and he landed flat on his tummy.

'C'mon,' said Rowan. 'A real man would get up and go again.'

Junior started laughing and momentarily lost concentration. Eventually he forced himself back onto his knees and inched forward, reached for the bottle and again fell short. Pushing himself back up, he steadied, lifted an arm and placed it in front of him. He dragged his opposite leg forward, moved his other arm forward, wobbled, steadied, then let his opposing leg catch up.

'Atta boy!' said Rowan. He waved the bottle. Junior laughed and collapsed. 'C'mon,' said Rowan. 'C'mon, you little terror!'

Once more Junior pushed himself up onto his knees but the effort was beginning to take its toll. He wobbled and slipped over onto his hip.

'No quitting,' said Rowan. He waved the bottle again, teasingly.

Junior pushed himself up onto his knees, fixed his eyes on the bottle and launched himself. Rowan wasn't sure whether Junior crawled the last thirty centimetres or sailed through the air. It didn't matter.

'Yes!' said Rowan. 'Yes!' He whipped Junior up off the carpet and held him high above his head. 'You little beauty!' He propped Junior up on his knee and slipped the bottle into his mouth. Junior's triumphant laughing gave way instantly to a contented gurgle but his eyes continued to explore Rowan's as he sucked.

'Well done, Dad.'

Rowan spun around, embarrassed. Sarah was standing in the doorway, arms folded with a smirk on her face. She looked a dead ringer for Sandra.

'Did you see what Junior did?' he said.

'I'm proud of you, Dad. We've been trying to get him to crawl for ages.'

'He crawled all the way from his lambskin.'

'Did he?'

'All the way. Little terror crawled all the way.'

Sarah put her arms around his neck and gave him a kiss. 'He likes you, Dad. He crawled for you.'

Rowan winced.

'Want me to take him back to bed with me? That's what usually happens.'

'I guess he'll be warmer in bed.'

'Thanks, Dad.' Sarah picked Junior up off Rowan's lap and carried him off to bed.

'How about that?' said Rowan softly. He felt unaccountably proud of himself.

He decided to make use of the early start by catching up on research reports. As he started to make his way to his study, he checked the distance between the sofa and the lambskin. Marginally over two metres. One small step for mankind but a landmark journey for Junior. Needing a coffee, he ambled back towards the kitchen. Out of habit he picked up the three letters he'd taken out of the letterbox the night before and thrown onto the hall table. When he saw they were all addressed to Sandra, he realised his error. He was about to put them back when one of the stamps caught his eye. The name and address of the sender was printed at the foot of the envelope. Why, he wondered, was Sandra getting letters from R. Satyarnand & Sons, solicitors, of Nadi, Fiji?

Twenty

When Sandra had arrived home at four in the morning, she'd found Rowan fast asleep on the sofa. She'd covered him with a blanket and left him to it. By the time she'd showered and had her Milo it was well after five. Even then, sleep had eluded her. Her team had performed brilliantly, going down in the final by only one run. She believed they would have won if Lucy's troublesome knee hadn't packed up in the semi-final. Her replacement put down a waist-high rocket that Lucy would have swallowed. The excitement of the game, plus the long drive home with her contingent of girls singing every lewd song they knew, kept her staring at the ceiling. Other issues pressed in upon her. How had Rowan reacted to Junior? Had he dared to show himself in public with him? How had Claudine reacted to the postponement of her birthday dinner? She finally dozed off shortly before Rowan awoke and quietly let himself out.

One of the benefits of taking emergency appointments

and seeing people who couldn't get treatment elsewhere was the opportunity to win over new patients. Sandra liked to think she treated all her patients to the best of her ability but in truth she put extra effort into her new ones. Many became regulars, and in this way she built up her business. There were two new patients to see before noon and she had another scheduled first up after her lunch break. She briefly considered putting her head down for twenty minutes to compensate for her lack of sleep, but feared she'd struggle to get going again. After a coffee and peanut butter sandwich she wandered back into her clinic. The name in the book said Jenny Pengelly and the thought crossed her mind that Jenny might be related to Caroline. When she opened the door to her waiting room she froze.

'Can I come in?' said Caroline. 'Please?'

Sandra stepped back to let her through, uncertain whether to feel guilty or angry, pleased or bitter. '*Jenny* Pengelly?'

'That's right, Jenny. Look.' Caroline opened her bag, took out a photograph and passed it to Sandra.

Sandra squealed with delight.

'She's three weeks old and her name's Jeong-Lan. But we've decided we're going to call her Jenny.'

Sandra's eyes began to mist over. 'She's beautiful.'

'The photo arrived in the mail on Friday. Mike and I agreed you had to be the first person we showed it to.'

'Oh Caro, I'm so happy for you!' Sandra threw her arms around Caroline and hugged her. Her eyes flooded with tears when Caroline reciprocated. 'God, I've missed you,' she said.

'And I've missed you,' sobbed Caroline. 'I can't tell you how many times I've picked up the phone to call you and then hung up. I couldn't bear it if you refused to talk to me.'

'Are we a couple of stupid bitches or what?' said Sandra.

It wasn't until the evening of the following day, after the girls had gone to bed, that Sandra finally got around to checking her mail. She threw the letters from Telstra and Sydney Water into a drawer, to lie unopened with the rest of the bills that needed paying. She was about to send the letter from Fiji flying after them when she noticed the small print on the envelope, and hesitated. For no apparent reason she began to feel apprehensive. Why would Fijian solicitors be writing to her? She vaguely remembered Caroline and Mike talking about a letter they'd received from Hawaii after a holiday there. It was from a real estate agent, offering them time-share condominiums on Maui. Shaking off her disquiet, she opened the envelope expecting the contents to be something similar.

She read the letter, then sat stunned, stuck somewhere between horror and disbelief. She read it again and again but the words grew no kinder. Though couched in legal courtesies, the message was plain enough. In panic she snatched up the phone. All she got was Rowan's answering machine.

Twenty-one

Claudine looked stunning, so ravishingly beautiful that Rowan began to question his sanity. She wanted to move in with him, and their relationship had certainly reached the stage where that was the logical next step. Yet he was hesitating, reluctant to make the commitment, even though he knew any normal person would grab the chance with both hands. Despite the fact that The Quay was one of the most chic restaurants in town, Claudine had left her jewellery at home and elected to wear a simple white shift, which had the effect of making her skin appear darker and more vibrant. She looked fresher than dew on a rose. He noted the covert glances from other men in the restaurant who would gladly swap places with him, and the not so admiring looks from women who'd dressed more elaborately yet found themselves upstaged. Even the waiters, who normally set a high standard, were more attentive than usual.

Rowan was ambivalent about champagne, even champagne as prized as Dom Perignon, but not so Claudine. She adored it, and it seemed to fuel the French side of her character. They slipped into the easy conversation that had characterised the best moments of their relationship. They ordered different entrées and main courses so that they could share and enjoy more of the chef's undoubted skill. They teased and flirted with each other as only two people confident of their relationship can. Yet Rowan was aware that he was holding back. Sooner or later she'd put him in a position where he'd have to say the three words that never failed to get him into trouble. Not 'I love you' but 'I don't know'.

Rowan wasn't sure when the questions would come. The longer the evening lasted, the more confident he became that she wouldn't risk spoiling it. Maybe she'd wait until he took her home to his townhouse, maybe she'd wait until they were in bed and his passions aroused, or maybe she'd hold off for another day entirely. But the questions would come. He smiled at her across the table for no apparent reason and she responded with a smile so loaded with sexual innuendo that he blushed. How many more times, he wondered, would he take her in his arms and make love until the kookaburras laughed?

He knew the pattern of her questions because they'd been through it all before, but this time she'd up the ante, demand commitments he wasn't ready to make. She'd fix him with her big eyes but it wouldn't do her any good. She wanted more than he was ready to give and wasn't the type to accept equivocation. He needed time and patience. She wanted certainties, not possibilities, possession not time-share. When could she move in with him? Why couldn't they go out together more?

When would he divorce Sandra? Questions, questions. All he could give her in return were the three words of a man adrift, a man afraid of losing something he hesitated to possess.

'I don't know,' he'd say. He might just as well say goodbye.

But the evening, the food and his role-playing worked their charm. Her body language became more suggestive, her smiles more blatantly erotic. When their passionfruit soufflés arrived, she insisted on reaching across the table and spoon-feeding him. He had no option but to reciprocate. She put her mouth around his spoon and slowly eased the contents onto her tongue, never taking her eyes off his, her intentions both obvious and shameless. She made him feel like an out-of-town businessman with an overly willing escort. He frowned, made stage glances around him in an effort to dissuade her, but she was emboldened by the wine and was enjoying his discomfort. Their waiter smirked as he passed by. Rowan was wondering how he could conceal his embarrassment and the determined stirrings in his trousers when Claudine gave him a reprieve.

'Let's go,' she said.

'Now?' said Rowan. His spoon was poised ready to deliver another mouthful.

'Now!' she said, leant back and slipped her foot up between his thighs. Rowan jumped as though hit by an electric charge. She laughed.

'I'll call for the bill,' he said.

'Pay at the desk,' she said. 'I'll get my coat. Hurry!'

Rowan caught the waiter's eye so easily he suspected he was awaiting his cue. When Rowan discovered his account was already made up, he knew his suspicions were well founded.

'Something the matter with the desserts?' said the waiter. 'Or will Sir be having something at home?'

By the time Rowan had paid, Claudine was waiting for him at the door, hopping from one leg to the other. The phrase 'hot to trot' sprung to his mind, but he'd never seen anyone quite so hot or so eager to trot. On the way home she unzipped him, slid her hand inside his trousers.

'Give me a break,' said Rowan.

'He likes being stroked. See? Like a big fat cat.'

'He'll need his own seatbelt if you don't stop.'

Claudine just laughed. As soon as they were inside his garage she started to pull her dress up.

'Not in the car,' said Rowan. 'Please. Inside.' As he opened the front door his phone began ringing. He reached for it automatically.

'Leave it!' said Claudine. 'Let your machine answer!' She pulled her dress up over her head and kicked off her shoes. Not only was she not wearing a bra, she wasn't wearing panties. Rowan's jaw dropped. He'd spent the entire evening sitting in a plush restaurant with a woman who was naked but for a simple shift. Claudine stuck out her hips and cupped her breasts. Once she'd got his attention, she licked her fingers and let them slip down to her delta. Any reasonable man would have swept her up in his arms and thrown her on the bed, leapt on top of her and remained there until exhaustion or death. But Rowan could not leave a ringing phone unanswered.

'You go ahead,' said Rowan. 'Warm up the bed.'

'Come with me!' said Claudine indignantly.

Rowan picked up the phone.

'Rowan?' said Sandra. 'Oh, thank God! I've been trying to reach you all night.'

'What's the problem?'

'They're trying to take Junior off me!'

'Who is?' He covered the mouthpiece and whispered to Claudine, 'It's Sandra. This'll take a minute or two. You go on ahead, but don't start without me.' His attempt at humour failed. Claudine stepped back from him, hurt and accusing, all her spark and vibrance gone. She turned and stamped off to the bedroom, slamming the door behind her.

'Say again,' said Rowan.

'I've got a letter from solicitors in Fiji who say they represent Junior's natural father. Rowan, they're asking for custody! They want to take Junior away from me. What am I going to do?'

Rowan immediately thought of the letter on the hall stand. 'For the moment do nothing. Just ignore it. They're in Fiji, you're here and they have no claim to custody unless they can prove paternity. So just ignore it.'

'What if they can prove paternity?'

'That'll take months. Sandra, nothing is going to happen for a very long time. You've got between now and then to contact a lawyer and get yourself organised. No court is going to sanction the removal of a child from his natural mother, especially when the father lives in a mud hut on a remote island in Fiji. Use your brain. Family law courts always do what's best for the child.'

'Are you sure?'

'Yes. Absolutely. Now stop worrying, go to bed and we'll talk about it in the morning.'

'You're that sure?'

'Absolutely. Now, goodnight.' He hung up and stared at the phone. He could picture Siti on the beach at Coralhaven tending the boats, as relaxed and carefree as any man could be. He couldn't begin to imagine why Siti would want the burden of another child to raise or even guess at why he was seeking custody. He felt sorry for Sandra, but in a way also felt that what was happening was justice. At the end of the day Junior was half-Fijian and looked full-blooded Fijian. Fiji was probably where he belonged. Despite the reassurances he'd just given Sandra, part of him welcomed the idea that Junior might be removed from his life.

He was still preoccupied with the consequences and possibilities when he opened the bedroom door. For a second he seemed surprised to find Claudine posed naked on his bed, waiting for him, watching for his reaction. He tried to change gear, remember where they were the instant before the phone rang and what was required of him. In that hesitation, Claudine realised all her fears.

She flew at him, scratching and clawing. Tears streaked her cheeks. 'You bastard!' she screamed. 'You bastard! You go back to her! Go on! You don't want me, you want her!' She threw herself face down on the bed sobbing. 'You bastard! That's what you want, isn't it? You want her!'

'I don't know,' said Rowan.

'She's resigned.' Margaret stood to the side of Rowan's desk, hands by her side, face stern.

'Better get a temp.'

'What? She's upset. I thought maybe if you spoke to her ...'

'Margaret, do you want to man reception?'

'No.'

'Neither do I. So please do your job and get a temp while we look for someone permanent.'

'That's it? That's all you've got to say? God help me when I resign!' Margaret spun on her heel and marched angrily out of his office.

Rowan returned to catching up on the latest research for Lavalle but struggled to regain concentration. Folders stacked up in his in-tray like a Hong Kong tower apartment block.

Claudine had ignored all his pleas and protestations, dressed and called a cab. Along the way she'd thrown shoes at him, both bedside lamps, managed to sweep everything off the bathroom shelf onto the floor, rip the phone cord out from the hall wall and abuse him in French, Mauritian and English. She'd broken the glass panel in the door by slamming it. Rowan had spent almost an hour cleaning up the breakages. Yet even then he knew the relationship could be salvaged, provided he made the necessary concessions. But he baulked at them. The past was too immediate and he wasn't ready to close the door on it. Rather than face Claudine with more equivocation, he decided not to face her at all. He didn't know whether he was motivated by kindness or cowardice.

The phone rang and Blake called him into the boardroom

to give final approval on some ads prior to presentation to Lavalle. Rowan couldn't put the research report down fast enough. Blake recapped the brief and ran quickly through the thinking and advertising strategy. The creative team proudly showed their ads, a TV storyboard and four derivative posters.

'That the best we can do?' said Rowan.

'What?' said Blake.

'Have we lowered the bar or something?'

'What's your problem?' said Blake angrily. 'You've already approved every idea here. The work's terrific.'

'So that's what terrific looks like now? I used to call that complacent.'

Blake turned to the creative team, who sat stunned, mouths open. 'Guys, go find something else to do. I'll see you in five.' He waited until both writer and art director had left and delicately closed the door behind them. He returned to his seat and swung around to face Rowan. 'What the fuck is going on?'

'I was about to ask you the same fucking question.' Rowan stood so that he towered over Blake. 'When did crap become the gold standard around here?'

Blake leapt to his feet, reversing the advantage. 'Are you suggesting that work is crap? You approved it all along the line. You laughed and told the guys they were geniuses. That's good work, I know it and you know it, and it'll work its tits off.'

'It won't because it won't run.'

'The fuck it won't!'

'It isn't just crap, it's complacent crap! And so long as this is my agency, we don't run crap.'

'Your agency? That's rich. You haven't been part of this agency for the last three months. You've been as useless as a spare prick at a wedding.'

'Maybe. But you better get used to the fact that I'm back!'

'Too fucking late. I'm presenting this to Lavalle at two o'clock this afternoon.'

'Over my dead body.'

'No Rowan, over my resignation.'

Rowan paused to give himself time to rein in his temper. He picked up the storyboard and poster roughs. 'You'd resign over this?'

'Believe it, Rowan.'

'You have that much faith in it?'

'Absolutely.'

'Then let's see who's right. If they reject it I want your resignation on my table!' Rowan turned and stormed back to his office. Once he'd been in absolute control and his judgement final. Now it seemed nobody quite trusted him any more. Worse, he didn't trust himself.

'Don't blow it,' said Margaret as he passed her.

Rowan spun around. 'What did you say?'

'Rowan, if you're going to yell at me, I'm going to walk right now. Can we go into your office and talk?'

Rowan turned and strode into his office, leaving Margaret the option of following him. He hadn't even reached his chair before she slammed the door behind him.

'Was that necessary?' he snapped.

'How many staff do you want to lose today, Rowan?'

'How many do you propose?'

'Apart from Claudine and me? Blake for a start, and any of the creatives who want to follow him.'

'What are you saying?'

'C'mon, Rowan. Surely you know he's talking to Nathan Glengarry?'

'What?' The fire went out of Rowan and his shoulders slumped.

'What did you expect him to do? Sit around while you commit harikari and take the agency down with you?'

'How do you know he's talking to Nathan Glengarry?'

'Barth told me. They've had lunch together on at least two occasions that he knows of. The fact that Blake hasn't jumped ship yet means he's giving you the benefit of the doubt, which, to be brutally honest, you don't deserve. Individually you're both clever but together you're dynamite. You bring out the best in Blake, and maybe he doesn't want to lose that. Nobody wants to see you two split up. That's why Barth was indiscreet. That's why I'm being indiscreet.'

'Oh Christ, Margaret. What can I do?'

'What you do is entirely up to you.' Margaret turned and left his office, closing the door behind her.

Rowan swivelled his chair to face the window and stared into space as he tried to gather his thoughts. He didn't want to lose Blake, Margaret or anyone. In truth he didn't even want to lose Claudine. He realised his life, both professional and private, had lost focus and he needed to face up to issues instead of ducking them. But how? When the phone rang he snatched it off the cradle. 'Yes?'

'You were supposed to ring me.'

Sandra. On top of everything else.

'Or you ring me, which you've done.'

'Can we talk about this custody business now?'

'What's there to talk about? What more can I say? Nothing has changed since we spoke. What you need is a lawyer, not an advertising man.'

'But you said you'd help.'

'Ring Ryan Scott,' said Rowan. Ryan Scott was both his and the company's lawyer. 'Make it his problem, just don't make it mine.'

'You said you'd help me. You promised.'

Rowan heard the little choke in her voice. 'Okay! I'll ring Ryan. Anything else you'd like me to do? How are you off for milk and bread?' He slammed the phone down. Margaret's naturopathic pills toppled over on the desk in front of him. He threw them so hard against the wall, the bottle broke. Nothing was as it should be any more. Someone or something had to bear the blame.

At two that afternoon Rowan joined Blake to present the new round of creative to Lavalle. Rowan dominated the meeting. He strode his platform like a man possessed, selling every idea as though it was his brainchild and his alone, as though his earlier argument with Blake had not taken place. He dazzled with insights, argued with passion, and such was his conviction that nobody dared utter a word for the entire duration of his presentation. Lavalle saw enthusiasm in combination with brilliance, and lapped it up. But Blake saw through to the truth. He saw a desperate man with nothing left in his life but his work, desperate to prove he still had the gift. Through the torrent of words Blake heard the fear in his voice, the bitterness and anguish in his cry.

Rowan rang Ryan Scott the moment the presentation concluded. He hoped Ryan would substantiate his advice and tell him the Fijian solicitor was pissing in the wind and that the problem would just go away. Ryan's words weren't entirely encouraging.

'Interesting,' he said. 'On the surface, Sandra should have nothing to worry about. Inter-country residency applications are seldom granted. However, it may prove hard to deny contact.'

'What's contact?'

'It used to be called access. Visiting rights. With the father in Fiji, that could prove interesting. The question is, who would visit whom?'

'You're joking.'

'It's a possibility.'

'Okay, I'll warn Sandy. When can you see her?'

Ryan made an appointment for four the following afternoon.

Rowan hit speed dial and called Sandy. 'They can't take Junior away from you,' he told her. 'Worst case, and things would have to go very badly for this to happen, you may have to let Siti have Junior for a couple of weeks a year.'

'I won't let Junior go,' said Sandra. 'Siti can't have him, not for a second. I won't let anybody take him away from me.'

'Tell that to the judge,' said Rowan wearily.

Rowan was staring out the window, lost in thought, when Blake slipped into his office.

'I've booked the Flower Drum,' said Blake. 'Drinks first in the boardroom.'

'What's the occasion? We win Daewoo?'

'Daewoo rang while we were in with Lavalle. We came second.'

'Second? Who got it?'

'Nathan Glengarry.'

'Fuck! I thought we were supposed to be certainties!'

'We were, but failed to deliver. We gave them little original thought and indifferent creative. How much time did you give the pitch? Five minutes? Less? We got what we deserved, Rowan, and the sooner we face up to that, the better.'

'I can't do everything.'

'That doesn't excuse you for doing nothing.'

'Fuck it! Why does it have to be that smarmy prick, Glengarry? I bet he's loving this.'

'Everyone likes to win, Rowan. And so do I.'

'Is that what Glengarry offered you? Has Nathan promised to make you Account Director on Daewoo?'

'Head of Account Service, actually, and full director with shareholding.'

Rowan slumped back in his chair, suddenly tired. He wanted to fight Glengarry but was beginning to suspect the battle was already lost. 'Good offer. Bloody good. Why the hell didn't you take it?'

'Offer's still open.'

'Did he promise you'd work with someone like me,

307

who thinks the sun shines out of your arse?'

'Not in so many words.'

'Did he give you any indication of how devastated I'd be if you left?'

'He didn't have to.'

'Did he tell you I'm the biggest prat that ever walked the planet?'

'I knew that already.'

'Did he tell you I'd go down on my knees to keep you?'

'That may not be necessary.'

'Jesus, Blake, what do I have to do to keep you?'

'Turn back the clock, Rowan. All we have to do is go back to the way things were. Set the highest standards and stick to them. Insist on the best and accept nothing less. Think hard, work hard and grab this damn industry by the scruff of its neck and wring the living shit out of it. I want to enjoy work again and that means being good enough to win. Awards, new business, client presentations. We can't win if we don't behave like winners.'

Rowan closed his eyes. The words were so familiar, it could have been him speaking. Probably once were his words. He wondered, if the circumstances were reversed, whether he'd have been so loyal. 'It's a deal,' he said. 'Give me another chance and I won't let you down. I mean it.'

'Enough said. Now, are you coming to the Flower Drum?'

'If we didn't get Daewoo, what are we celebrating?'

'I thought we should reward everyone who worked on Lavalle.'

'Does that include me?'

'You're a fringe candidate, but yeah.'

'Thanks,' said Rowan. 'Better a celebration than a wake.'

Blake smiled. He ducked back into his office and rang his wife to warn her not to expect him home until the small hours of morning. He also warned her to expect company and to make up the spare bed. Blake was using the success of the presentation as an excuse to get Rowan out and fill him full of booze. It was the industry therapy and its benefits, at best, only temporary. But even Prozac only promised temporary relief. By the end of the night, he didn't expect Rowan to know his own name, let alone the way home.

Twenty-two

Sandra rang Caroline and tearfully told her about the letter and her solicitor's response. Caroline was at first aghast and then outraged. She told Sandra not to worry, told her that nobody could take Junior off her, insisted that no court would ever allow it. These were exactly the words Sandra wanted to hear. She just wished she'd hear them from Rowan.

'Will you come with me to the solicitors?' she asked.

'Oh Sandy, I'd love to,' said Caroline. 'But have you forgotten? Mike and I fly out to Seoul tomorrow morning, to pick up Jenny.'

'Of course,' said Sandra. She'd only just got her friend back and, in embracing the comfort and support she provided, had really come to dread the nothingness of the void in which she'd been drifting. She feared the prospect of again having no one to turn to, no one to offer a hand or a shoulder to cry on. Yet just when she needed Caroline most, her friend was going away, leaving her once more isolated and vulnerable.

'You'll be all right,' said Caroline.

'You're right.'

'Nothing's going to happen before we get back.'

'I guess not.' Sandra tried to put on a brave face. 'Whenever I feel down, I'll think of you and Jenny.'

'Oh God, Sandy, Mike and I are so excited.'

'I envy you,' said Sandra.

'The first issue we need to address is the identity of Junior's father. Is this Sitiveni Kefu the father?'

Sandra was thoroughly intimidated by her surroundings. Rowan had often joked to her that lawyers, not the meek, would inherit the earth and now she could see what he meant. From her chair, she could look out through the floor-to-ceiling window of Ryan Scott's forty-second-floor office and see ferries pulling out from Circular Quay, see right down the harbour and Taronga Park Zoo to North Head and beyond, to an expanse of ocean. His desk looked like it had been designed and built in an Italian studio. An intricate and probably antique hand-woven rug covered most of the polished timber floor. A Brett Whiteley cockatoo occupied the wall opposite his desk. She sat on a chrome chair around a chrome table with a glass top that seemed to float centimetres above its frame. Ryan and a colleague who specialised in family law sat opposite her. His colleague's name was Meagan, which suggested homely Irish ancestry, but she looked sculpted and cold as marble, as though she'd been designed in the same studio that had produced the desk. Sandra thought Meagan could walk through a tornado and emerge on the other side without a hair out of place. She could not imagine her ever standing at a kitchen sink, ever nursing a child.

'Yes,' said Sandra. 'Sitiveni Kefu is the father.'

'I see,' said Ryan. 'Could you please explain the circumstances.'

'Beg your pardon?' said Sandra.

Meagan reached over and put her hand on top of Sandra's. It was a gesture intended to provide reassurance. Sandra flinched involuntarily at the coldness of her touch.

'We need to know the full details.'

'Is this really necessary?' said Sandra in dismay. She looked to Ryan for support but received none. It was one thing to tell Caroline and the softball girls what had happened, another to bare her moment of madness to people she hardly knew.

'I'm afraid so,' said Ryan. 'Unfortunately, you're going to have to get used to telling your story if this ever gets to court. The nature of your relationship with this man could impact on the decision. For example, were you a willing party to the ... uh ... encounter? Did he force himself upon you? Did he rape you?'

'It wasn't rape,' said Sandra quickly. 'It wasn't anything like that. It seems this man, Sitiveni, has made something of a career out of seducing bored and foolish female guests, but in all honesty, I was equally to blame. I don't know, it was just a whim, a get-square with Rowan that went wrong.' Sandra felt her blood rising and her face flush with embarrassment. She told her story, omitting nothing, not looking at either of the two lawyers. She spoke, instead, to the ferries moving silently in and out of the quay hundreds of metres below her.

'There is no possibility of anyone else being the father?' asked Meagan when she'd finished.

Sandra nearly choked in outrage. 'What? What are you suggesting?'

'I'm sorry,' said Meagan. 'There are questions I have to ask. I'll take that as a no.'

'How did Sitiveni discover you'd had a child? Did you go back to Coralhaven?' asked Ryan.

Sandra explained about meeting Finau in hospital. She supposed it must be her who'd spread the word.

'And there has been no contact between you and the father, or you and Finau, until this letter?' continued Ryan.

'None at all.'

'Tell me about the father, what he does, where he lives, marital status, family, et cetera. Is he violent? Does he drink, do drugs, beat his wife or abuse his mother? Tell me everything you know. Is there anything about him that would make him unfit as a father?'

Sandra did her best to recall as much detail as she could and relayed what Finau had told her. She paused occasionally so the two lawyers could keep up with their note-taking. Their thoroughness concerned her. Surely they didn't think there was even a remote chance that Sitiveni could take Junior off her? 'What happens next?' she asked.

'We'll need to respond,' said Ryan. 'The tone of the letter suggests we're unlikely to reach agreement without going to court. If they'd simply asked for contact, we could negotiate something. However, they've quite deliberately raised the possibility of full custody. They must surely know the court would never agree to that. My suggestion is that we write to them and inform them in no uncertain terms that, if they choose to proceed, we will contest their application most vigorously.'

'Rowan said we should just ignore the letter and stall for time.'

'That's one option,' said Ryan.

'Don't they have to prove paternity before they can do anything?'

'I imagine Satyarnand & Sons will have a statement from this woman, Finau, in which you admitted to her that Sitiveni is the father. I doubt they would have proceeded without it.'

'Can't we deny it?' asked Sandra.

'Yes, we can force them to do DNA tests. There are only a couple of labs that I know of who do these sorts of tests and they're usually pretty busy. It would certainly buy us some time but I'm not sure what the benefit would be. We already know the result and, in light of your story, it won't look particularly good for us in court. At best, it will be seen as deliberate stalling, at worst suggest that Siti was not your only Fijian lover. It won't help if we call your morality into question.'

'But what about the cost? Sitiveni doesn't have much money. I thought that if we dragged things out, maybe the cost would put him off.'

'From what you've told me of Siti's circumstances, I'm surprised he's gone this far. It leads me to believe that somewhere along the line his costs must be covered. Maybe the Fijian equivalent of the Department of Community Affairs is involved. The boy is half-Fijian.'

'What are we going to do?'

'That depends on how long you want this hanging over your head. I would have thought a speedy resolution was in your best interests.'

'He can't win, can he?'

'Residency, no,' said Meagan. 'Contact may be another matter. Contact would give the father the right to see the child and take him out for the day, weekends even.'

'But he couldn't take him back to Fiji?'

'We'll contest that, naturally,' said Meagan.

'He can't afford it,' said Sandra. 'He lives in a grass hut, for heaven's sake.'

'Millions do,' said Meagan calmly. 'And do so happily. I expect Siti's lawyer will apply for a specific issues order.'

'What would that do?' asked Sandra. Her hopes peaked and dipped.

'A specific issues order may require that the child spend a set number of weeks a year with the father.'

'No way!' said Sandra. She was beginning to wonder whose side Meagan was on.

'Calm down, Sandra.' Ryan reached across the table and took Sandra's hands in his. 'Naturally we will vigorously contest any application they make. We'll argue strongly against any specific issues order. We have a lot of very good arguments in our favour. The best interests of Junior, for example. He has a family here, two half-sisters and a loving, caring mother. He has a good home and you have a good income and solid support from Rowan. You are providing Junior with a good, stable environment, and that's very important. As he gets older there will be his schooling to consider, and nobody would want to see that interrupted. All these things will be taken into consideration.'

'Then I've nothing to worry about.'

'I wouldn't quite go that far, Sandra. But I am confident we can show that even temporary residency, no matter how brief, would prove disruptive, destabilising, injurious and not in Junior's best interests. Furthermore, the father has provided no financial support for the child, nor is there any offer of support in the letter from his solicitor. Probably the strongest influence in our favour is the court itself. The Family Court is reluctant to separate mothers from young children unless it is in the child's best interests. In your case, that is clearly not so. Secondly, the Court is generally wary of allowing a child to be taken out of the country, in case they are not returned. The problem is, once they leave the country, they also leave the Court's jurisdiction. You can understand their reluctance.'

'So common sense will prevail,' said Sandra. 'What you're saying is they can't win.'

'There is a cultural issue to consider,' said Meagan. 'You are providing the child with an exclusively Anglo upbringing yet he is, by blood, half-Fijian. The court may well be sympathetic to an argument that the child is entitled to know and be familiar with the culture of his father.'

'I can take him to Fiji on holidays,' said Sandra desperately.

Meagan smiled thinly. 'They may not regard that as enough. I can see a court granting the father an order requiring the child to live with him for a specified period of weeks each year. To holiday with him, if you like, but without you.'

Sandra turned to Ryan. 'Is that likely?'

'No, but it's a possibility. The cultural argument is their strongest argument and they've signalled their intention to use it by raising it in their letter. This is what I meant when I said things could get tricky. Polynesian Fijians have become particularly nationalistic as you know and the danger is that we may appear racist, especially if the governments become involved. They will argue that a good home in Fiji is the equal of a good home in Australia, and that is hard to argue against without appearing racist.'

'I won't let Junior go. Not for a day or a week. I'll never let him go. If they take him to Fiji, he might never come back. I might never see him again.'

'I don't think it'll come to that,' said Ryan. He stood and gave Sandra his most engaging smile. Clearly her time was up. 'I'll write to them. Make them think twice before proceeding.'

'I think a specific issues order is entirely possible,' said Meagan. 'There are a number of precedents in circumstances not too far removed from these. Some judges are quite sensitive to accusations of racism.' She also stood and fixed her pale-blue eyes on Sandra. 'You would do well not to lose sight of the fact that the child has two parents, and both parents have rights. They have rights in law. The child also has the right, in law, to know the father.'

Sandra's anger and frustrations boiled over. 'Would you stop calling my baby "the child"! He's not "the child". His name's Junior and he's my child. And as for his father, he has no rights, none at all! Dear God, he's only the father because a condom broke!'

'Pardon me,' said Meagan. 'But isn't that also how you came to be the mother?'

Ryan had a hand held out as if he intended to escort Sandra back to reception. Sandra ignored it. She grabbed her handbag and all but ran towards the lift, past secretaries who looked at her as though she was desecrating something sacred. She'd had enough of lawyers but more than anything didn't want to put herself in a position of having to shake hands with Meagan. Meagan's hands were the cold, dispassionate hands of the law, and one day the law might take her baby away.

Two weeks after her meeting with Ryan Scott, Sandra understood why he'd recommended a speedy resolution. In the middle of treating her patients, she'd find her concentration wavering and her mind drifting away down joyless roads. What if she failed in her bid to block Siti's applications? What if the court let him take Junior back to Fiji? What if he packed up his family and left Coralhaven? How would she ever find him among the hundreds of islands and thousands of villages? What if she never saw Junior again? Sometimes her fears would numb her brain and she'd freeze in the middle of treatment, her patients having to drag her out of her reverie. She wanted news but dreaded it. Every journey to her letterbox was filled with trepidation, every incoming phone call with apprehension.

When she took Junior and the girls down to Balmoral Beach, to play on the swings or on the beach, she was scared to let them out of her sight in case someone snatched him away. She told herself it wasn't just paranoia but common sense, following the much-publicised abduction of two Melbourne children by their Malaysian father. Once they were in Malaysia, the Family Court was powerless to recover and return them to their distraught mother. It would be the same if Junior was whisked away to Fiji.

As she sat at one of the picnic tables with Junior on her knee, a young woman approached her and began chatting. She appeared to be fascinated by Junior. Sandra was happy to oblige when the young woman asked if she could take a mother-and-son photo. Sandra thought she'd take one shot and that would be that. She became alarmed when the young woman began issuing instructions, posing them, telling them where to look and how to look, her film speeding through her camera in a constant whir of electric motors. 'Beautiful,' she said. 'Terrific, nice, very cute, yes, yes, chin up! Look at me!'

Her demeanour was altogether too professional for Sandra's liking. 'That's enough!' Sandra said, her alarm growing. 'Who are you?'

The young woman took no notice and kept shooting. Then, when she'd finished the roll of film, she simply turned, shouted a thankyou, walked briskly to her car and drove away, leaving Sandra upset and fearful but not knowing precisely why. Later, when Rowan came to collect the girls for the weekend, she voiced her concerns about the photographer. He told her she was imagining things.

Sandra desperately wanted to pour her heart out to Caroline but she wasn't due back from Seoul for another two days. When she turned to her mother for sympathy, she came away empty handed, as usual.

On Monday morning Caroline rang to say they were back from Korea. Sandy had to fight the urge to drop everything, cancel her appointments and rush around to their house. She wanted to see their new daughter and introduce her to Junior, but more than anything else, she was desperate for the understanding, support and guidance she needed to sustain her until the court hearing. But her patients needed help and she needed their money. Cancellation was never an option.

As soon as her last patient left, she threw the kids into her car and raced over to Caroline's without even bothering to change. She cautioned the girls to be quiet and on their best behaviour, fearing that Jenny would be worn out by the long flight back to Australia and fast asleep. However, when Caroline opened the door, Sandra discovered it was Mike who was asleep, that Caroline was exhausted and desperate to join him, and that Jenny had slept for the entire flight and now wanted to party. Sandra immediately assumed the roles of babysitter and cook, and sent Caroline off to bed with a promise to wake her and Mike for dinner. There'd be time afterwards for them to hear her problems, if not later that night then the following day. Suddenly the need for support had lost its pressing urgency. It was enough to share in their joy and know that at last her friends were home and that help was once more at hand.

Sounds of laughter drew her into the lounge where she found Sarah nursing a chubby Jenny, who was plainly delighted with her new playmates. Junior was trying to crawl to Sarah and Jenny but every time he got close, Rochelle snatched him up and took him back to the opposite side of the room where she again released him. Two Aussies, one half-Fijian and a Korean all killing themselves laughing. Sandra smiled but it saddened her to realise that even if the judge of the Family Court entered the room right at that moment and saw how happy the kids were together, it wouldn't make a blind bit of difference to the outcome.

She realised Mike was up and about when the doorbell rang and heard him respond to it. She helped Sarah put Jenny back into her crib and went to fill her bottle with warm milk.

'Daddy!'

Sandra peeked through the doorway to the lounge. She couldn't see Rowan but heard his voice.

Mike slipped into the kitchen and put a hand on her shoulder. 'You don't mind, do you?' he asked. 'Big occasion. It's hard when we're close to both of you.'

'Not at all,' said Sandra. 'It's his lucky day. This is his favourite pasta.'

Over dinner, Mike and Caroline told all about their experiences in Seoul, how the road outside their hotel could be converted to an airstrip for fighter bombers if the North invaded, of the underground shopping malls that doubled as ordnance depots storing jet fuel, rockets and high-explosives. Of lying awake at night in their bed, just waiting for someone to drop the match that would launch them and their hotel into the stratosphere. They described their visit to the child welfare centre where they were ushered into a crowded office filled with half a dozen employees busily belting away on old typewriters. Jammed between desks was an old sofa and coffee table, which was where adoptive parents received their child.

They told how they felt, just sitting there waiting, surrounded but unable to converse with anyone, and the unreal moment when the centre's doctor had brought their daughter into the room and they'd seen her for the first time.

'They warned us that Jenny would probably be frightened,' said Mike. 'They had us terrified of touching her and all the while we had this audience of clerks around us, waiting to see what would happen.'

'What did happen?' asked Sandra, as engrossed as if watching a movie.

'Nothing,' said Mike, and laughed.

'Poor Jenny had had a going-over from the doctor before they brought her to us,' said Caroline. 'It probably hadn't been the gentlest examination any kid ever had. She was frowning and ready to burst into tears. They handed her to me and her face just burst into a smile.'

'It's like she knew who we were and had been waiting for us,' said Mike. 'It was really weird. Wonderful but weird.'

'We saw her for an hour a day every day after that,' said Caroline. 'The idea was to give Jenny time to become accustomed to us. We didn't pick her up until the sixth day, and then drove straight to the airport. One moment we had no child, the next we had a daughter and were heading home. I guess it's no different to going into hospital with a big belly and leaving a few days later with a baby. The sense of awe and shock that a little human being is suddenly your responsibility is probably the same.'

'Sounds the same to me,' said Sandra.

'The flight home took eleven and half hours,' said Caroline. 'But we're home and we've got the baby we've always wanted. She's ours and nobody can take her away from us.'

'Lucky you,' said Sandra.

Mike looked away. Caroline sat stunned, a look of horror frozen on her face.

'Oh jeez, Sandy, I'm sorry! I can't believe I said that!'

'Don't worry about it,' said Sandra. 'I know exactly what you meant.'

'How are you going with Junior?' Mike asked cautiously.

'If I told you, you wouldn't believe me,' said Sandra. 'And I'm not going to take the gloss off your first night home with your daughter by telling you.' She laughed. 'But watch out tomorrow.'

'Has Ryan been in contact with you at all?' cut in Rowan.

'I've had no word since our meeting. I don't know if that's good or bad.'

'I have to go to Fiji next week. Do you want me to sniff around for you?'

'Would you?'

'May not do any good, but we won't know if I don't try.'

'I'd really appreciate that, Rowan.'

'No worries. Now, let me have a look at this little girl.' He pushed his chair back and wandered over to the crib, which Caroline had wheeled into the dining room. Jenny was fast asleep. He pushed the blankets away from her face with a finger to get a better look. 'She's gorgeous.' He turned to Sandy and smiled. 'Maybe we should have adopted a kid.'

'You still can,' said Sandra. Junior's laughter carried through from the lounge.

Over the following days Sandra drew comfort from Rowan's offer of help, but it still didn't allay all her fears. The letterbox was still a forbidding presence at the foot of her pathway. She could no longer bear to empty it, and gave the job to Sarah. With the letters spread out on the hallstand, she could see instantly if there was anything from R. Satyarnand & Sons or not.

Another thought troubled her and kept her lying awake at night, staring at the ceiling. Somewhere in Korea there was a young mother who'd lost her baby forever, lost her to strange people in a faraway country. Sandra couldn't help identifying with her. Jenny was only six weeks old, but still not much younger than Junior. Sandra could well imagine the mother's heartache. When Sandra woke up in the morning her pillow was always damp.

Twenty-three

Work once more became the one stable element in Rowan's life and he attacked it voraciously. He put in sixteen-hour days, enthused, inspired and charged the agency with ideas and energy. Blake had seen it all before and recognised the symptoms. Sooner or later Rowan would work himself out and fade back into dreamland. In the meantime he fed the bear, slipping Rowan endless data – research reports, international travel analyses, hotel occupancy rates – encouraging him as they hatched long-term and tactical strategies in preparation for the presentation to the Fiji Tourist Board. When Rowan boarded the Air Pacific 767, he was better prepared for his meeting than he'd ever been. They'd put together a document which weighed almost a kilogram and provided a detailed marketing program that would see the Fiji Tourist Board through the following five years. As an added precaution, Rowan had sent an advance copy to Tiny for his comments. Tiny had been bowled over.

When the flight attendant offered Rowan refreshments, he broke from his usual pattern and ordered a scotch. He knew he'd have a few more with Tiny as they ran through a rehearsal of the presentation, and he'd have a few more with him over dinner. The scotch would help him relax. He'd overcome his reluctance to return to Fiji by persuading himself that Fiji was not a place but a product, not a culture but a unique selling proposition. Not a home for hundreds of thousands of Fijians but a holiday destination for Australians, New Zealanders, Asians, Europeans, and a handful of adventurous Americans. Fiji, he reasoned, was just another product that answered to conventional marketing and advertising disciplines, none of which held any fear for him.

Tiny met him as he stepped off the plane, dispatched assistants to collect his bags and escorted him through immigration. Everywhere Rowan went, familiar faces beamed a welcome. He began to wonder at his stupidity in trying to hand Fiji over to Blake.

'Quite a homecoming,' said Rowan with a grin.

'Homecoming!' Tiny seized on the word. 'I'm glad you think of Fiji as your home, Rowan. You've done so much for us, we like to think of you as one of our own. I will repeat your words tomorrow to the delegates. That is how we will start the presentation.'

'Whatever you say,' said Rowan.

The schedule was much as Rowan had anticipated. The rehearsal took little time as Rowan quickly discovered that, apart from the usual introduction and welcome, he *was* the presentation. All he had to do was cue the slide and video projectors and ensure they were working. Afterwards they met up with Maurice, the manager of Coralhaven, the representative from Air Pacific and a couple of other delegates for a curry at Tiny's favourite Indian restaurant. Rowan kept a careful eye on the number of scotches he consumed. After all, he'd come to Fiji to do a presentation and secure the business into the foreseeable future. The last thing he needed was the handicap of a hangover. If Maurice was aware that one of his employees was trying to gain custody of Junior, he gave no indication. Rowan didn't think it appropriate to mention anything, either. He didn't want to spoil an evening that felt just like the good old days.

Rowan used his alarm clock to awaken him in the morning. Even though Fiji was two hours ahead of Sydney, he was up and about at five-thirty. He hit the gym and thrashed its machines before waking everyone within earshot of the pool by doing laps. By seven-fifteen he was showered, dressed and ready to take on Mike Tyson. He picked up his copy of the *Fiji Times*, which had just been left at his door, and took it with him to the restaurant. As he tucked into a simple breakfast of papaya, passionfruit, bananas and cereal, he set about reading the newspaper from cover to cover. He always liked to know what was going on and occupying the minds of the delegates. Sometimes he liked to drop little snippets of local news into his presentation, a technique that made him appear better informed than he actually was.

The lead story on the front page told of how overseas demand for kava root by pharmaceutical companies had pushed the price of kava almost beyond the reach of Fijian villagers, to whom kava drinking was an integral part of both their culture and recreation. The paper foreshadowed a revolt unless the government intervened to ensure supplies for the local market, something Rowan had no difficulty in believing. It would be like Australia selling all of its beer overseas, or France all of its wine. He finished his papaya and was considering seconds as he turned the front page, a man in control and, for the first time in a long while, totally at peace with the world. He saw the photograph immediately. It seemed to leap off the page at him and suck the air out of his lungs. He sat stunned and disbelieving. The headline above the picture read, 'Fiji Man Denied Access To Son'. The picture showed a beaming Junior and an angry Sandra pointing an accusing finger at the photographer.

'For Christ's sake, Tiny, what's going on?' Rowan stood over the desk in his hotel room, the newspaper spread open in front of him, too agitated to sit and unable to pace, frustrated by the short cord on his telephone.

'I was just about to ring you.'

'Who's out to get me, Tiny? Who's the underhanded bastard that pulled this stunt?'

'Whoa! I thought this was about your wife. Why do you ask me who's out to get you?'

'Look at the timing.' Rowan hopped from foot to foot in agitation. 'Do you think it's pure coincidence that this story runs the morning of the presentation? Who wants to shaft me, Tiny?'

'Some of the delegates have not been happy with your performance these past few months but I don't think any are so unhappy that they'd stoop to something like this.'

'Come on, Tiny, give me names.'

'If you promise to calm down. I've told you already that delegates from the north-east, Vanua Levu and Taveuni, are most unhappy. They have strong nationalistic feelings and believe we would do better with a Fijian agency.'

'Sure, why not? Fiji is the epicentre of cutting-edge advertising.'

'Calm down, Rowan. They are entitled to their opinion and it is not a majority opinion. They would not stoop to the lengths you are suggesting simply to have a Fijian agency.'

'Well, whoever planted the story sure hasn't done me any favours.'

'No, they haven't. And our limited time is best spent working out how to deal with it. There are two questions we must address before the conference gets under way.'

'Shoot,' said Rowan.

'Is there any truth in the story?'

'No. Sandy doesn't have a racist bone in her body.' Rowan told him about the letter from R. Satyarnand & Sons and about her visit to see Ryan Scott. 'I can't be certain there isn't an unintended remark in Ryan Scott's letter. I never saw it. It's Sandy's problem, not mine.'

'Where did the photo come from?'

'I guess someone contacted a freelance photographer. Sandy told me about it but I thought nothing of it.'

'The paper also said you left your wife because she gave

birth to a half-Fijian baby and you didn't want him.'

'I left my wife because she was unfaithful. The fact that the child is Fijian is incidental.'

'In Fiji, the husband and wife would fight, then get on with life. The father would accept the son as his own.'

'I'm not Fijian.'

'Not a good answer to give at the conference. You can expect the delegates to question you.'

'I'd be more worried if they didn't.' Rowan made arrangements to rendezvous with Tiny and hung up. He called Ryan Scott immediately, brought him up to speed and asked him to read a copy of the letter he'd sent to Satyarnand. There was nothing in the letter to justify the story in the newspaper. He read the article back to Ryan.

'Who do you think is behind it?' Ryan asked.

Rowan told him his suspicions.

'I'm not sure you're right,' said Ryan. 'I think I've underestimated Satyarnand. My money is on a follow-up story tomorrow. My guess is that they're trying to get the Fijian government to intercede for some reason. Maybe to get someone to pick up their fees. Pretty clever, when you think about it. However, there appears to be something going on that I don't understand. Why does the father want the kid back when he's got six already? Is it because they're all girls? I don't think so. He's young enough to have half a dozen more kids and he's bound to get lucky sooner or later. I suspect there's another agenda running here.'

'It doesn't make sense unless someone is trying to shaft me,' said Rowan angrily. 'A bottle of Grange says this isn't about Sandy and Junior. I say there won't be any follow-up story because the damage has already been done.'

'You're on,' said Ryan. 'You may find this hard to believe, Rowan, but this business may have nothing to do with you at all.'

Rowan attacked his presentation, detailing strategies and solutions to the delegates as though the future of his agency depended on his success. He didn't make his pitch a monologue, but worked hard to elicit responses from his audience. Most were with him, he could tell by the immediacy of their laughter, and by their silence when he was driving home the points of the hard marketing information. Tiny had warned him that there'd be dissenters but he'd seen no sign of them. He assumed they'd reveal themselves at question time and, maybe, by the nature of their questions reveal who was behind the story in the morning's paper. In the meantime, he argued, harangued, pleaded, urged, energised, enthused and didn't let up for two and half hours. He gave what he believed was the performance of his life, one to silence any critics. But when Tiny asked for questions, the opposition wasted no time revealing themselves.

'Mika Nawalowalo from Deep Diver Resort, Taveuni.' The man stood and drew himself up to his full height. He held up a copy of the *Fiji Times*, opened on the page with Sandra's photo. 'Has anybody not read this story?' he asked to a room fallen silent. 'How do you explain this, Mr Rowan?'

'Call me Rowan. Just Rowan. First names have always been enough and we have no reason to change now. Tell me, Mika, why do I have to explain anything?'

'Sandra Madison is your wife.'

'Ex-wife.'

'This claim of racism is most upsetting.'

'All claims of racism are upsetting.'

'Is your wife a racist?'

'Not on the evidence in the paper you're holding.'

'What do you mean?'

'Well, it's hardly likely, is it? If my ex-wife is prejudiced against black people, Fijians in particular, why did she crawl into bed with one?'

Somebody started laughing and others quickly joined in. The representative from Taveuni sat down. Another man stood.

'Ian Rushmore, Rowan. As you know, I'm a New Zealander who came to Fiji twenty-three years ago. I married a Fijian and we have four children. Your ex-wife suggests Fiji is not a fit place to raise children and I resent that.'

Rowan pulled the faxed copy of Ryan's letter from his briefcase and read it aloud. 'All I get from this,' he said, 'is a declaration of love from a mother who is determined to hang on to her child at all costs. She's offering her son opportunities denied most Fijian children. Heavens above, private schools and private health cover are denied most Australian children. But once again, I have to ask you, what is this to do with me? What has this to do with the advertising proposals?'

Rowan fielded two more questions along the same lines before Tiny stood and called the meeting to order. 'I think we have had enough of the personal nature of these questions. They have nothing to do with advertising or marketing and

Rowan is correct in pointing out that this issue has nothing to do with him. Are there any questions on marketing?' He scanned the room but no one moved. 'In that case, I think we should conclude the business at hand. I move that we unanimously approve the marketing and advertising plan presented by Rowan today.'

'Objection!' Mika Nawalowalo once more stood. 'I suggest we defer a vote until we have all had an opportunity to digest and discuss Rowan's recommendations.'

'I agree,' said Ian Rushmore. 'I have no questions now but that is not to say I won't later.'

'Let's put it to the vote,' said Tiny.

'No,' cut in Mika. 'Approval is traditionally granted unanimously. Right now a vote would not get unanimous approval. I suggest we all get the chance to read the report before we decide so that we can consider our best interests.'

'That's fine by me,' said Rowan. 'My proposals look even better the second time around.'

'I would be surprised if any of our members were behind the newspaper story,' insisted Tiny during the lunch break. 'That has never been our way. If someone is upset, I am their punching bag.' They sat in the open dining area around the pool, in the shade of leafy palms, speaking softly so that they wouldn't be overheard by delegates at the surrounding tables. When Tiny had arranged to have lunch served by the pool, he thought they'd be celebrating the acceptance of Rowan's plan.

'The evidence suggests otherwise,' said Rowan. 'Frankly, I am a bit surprised. I didn't think they were bright enough.'

'They're not,' said Tiny emphatically.

'Mr Madison?'

Rowan turned around to find a young lady in hotel livery carrying a sign with his name on it.

'There is a reporter and photographer in reception asking to see you. They have refused to leave without first speaking to you. The manager wonders if –'

'Of course,' Rowan cut in. 'We can't have reporters cluttering up reception.' He smiled grimly at Tiny. 'Come and get me if I'm not back in ten.'

Rowan stuck closely to the answers he'd prepared for question time. The story had nothing to do with him, he was separated from his wife and, no, he didn't think she was racially prejudiced. He added nothing to the story but knew with certainty another story would run. His interview would be used to fan the flames. What disturbed him more was the reporter's name. He'd seen it often in the *Fiji Times*, usually reporting on politics. What was a political reporter doing engaging in tabloid muck-raking?

Rowan rejoined Tiny and waited until Maurice had finished his conversation with other delegates before pouncing.

'What's going on with Siti?' he asked.

'Wondered when you'd ask. Unfortunately I can't help you. I had no idea what he was up to until I saw the morning paper. All a bit strange, really. Don't take offence at this, Rowan, but Sandra's hardly the first guest Siti's climbed into bed with. He's got more notches on his gun than Billy the Kid. His exploits have made him a legend on the island.'

'Thanks for telling me now.'

'It happens on all the islands, Rowan. Some women come looking for it, others just fall victim. By all accounts Siti's got a good line of chat. Tell me, do you know if he gave Sandy his *lawedua* story?'

'His what?'

'*Lawedua*. You know, the seabird. He's made up this story and the women drop their knickers for it every time.'

'I wouldn't know. He could have told her the story of Goldilocks and the three bears for all I care. All I want to know is why he's so hot to have the kid.'

'Can't help you there,' said Maurice. 'He doesn't have much time for his extra-marital daughters on the island, I know that much. Don't know what he wants with another kid. Want me to have a word with him?'

'Thanks, but I don't think you should get involved. Someone's trying to beat this up and you're better off keeping out of it.'

'Tell you what,' said Maurice. 'I've got an acquaintance at the Australian High Commission. Bagetta Friel's her name. I know she's in Nadi because I spoke to her this morning. Give her a call, say you're a friend of mine and see what she has to say.' He wrote down her contact number on the back of his business card.

'How could she help?' said Rowan.

'She plays by the book but she might know what's going on. Always surprises me how much she does know.'

'You go see her,' said Tiny. 'Clearly there is going to be some hard talking this afternoon and it would be better if you were somewhere else. Heads will be banged. I just hope one of them isn't mine.'

'I'm not sure your theory's right,' said Bagetta Friel briskly. She'd agreed to meet Rowan for a coffee and listened to him without interruption. She wore a navy and white suit, sprayed her hair to immobility, and appeared fit enough to lead aerobics. She looked no more than thirty, had eyes that glowed with intelligence and Rowan couldn't help wondering who she'd upset to be posted to Fiji. 'I don't think any of this is about you. Your presence here in Fiji is fortuitous because it gives more legs to the story. I think you should be directing your attention to the solicitors, Satyarnand & Sons.'

'Go on,' said Rowan.

'It's rather unusual for Rajiv Satyarnand to become involved in a custody case such as this. In fact the whole affair is unusual. This Sitiveni probably couldn't afford the postage stamps Satyarnand & Sons use in a day. My guess is that this is all being orchestrated so that the Fijian Government can step in and take up the case. It would give them a chance to beat the nationalist drum, which would be a good move with the elections coming up. As for Satyarnand & Sons, I'm not so sure about their involvement. Perhaps it's payback time. Rumours abound, linking Mr Satyarnand with elements in the government.'

'This is all about votes?'

'Perhaps. Votes and payback.'

'Can I ask one more thing?' said Rowan. 'In custody cases

like this, what are the chances of the father being awarded contact rights?'

'No idea. I can't think of another case like this.'

'Well, what's your best guess? Would Siti have to visit the kid in Australia or would the kid be sent here?'

'Siti would have difficulty gaining a visa to Australia. We have a lot of problems with over-stayers. Special cases are passed on to the Minister and are not generally viewed favourably.'

'So the kid would have to come here, to Fiji?'

'Who can say? That depends on what the court rules. I don't know of any precedents. If what you've told me is true, I can't even begin to imagine why Siti is bothering about your wife's son in the first place. As I said earlier, this is all very strange.' Bagetta Friel stood. 'I wish I could have been of more help to you.'

Rowan stood and shook hands. 'You've been more helpful than you think.' She flashed him a smile that had Rowan instantly wondering whether he should invite her to dinner, or maybe even open a Fijian office.

Instead of returning to his hotel, he caught a taxi and instructed the driver to find a parking spot as close as possible to the entrance to R. Satyarnand & Sons. The law firm occupied the first floor of a building on the fringe of the commercial centre. Their nameplate was too obvious, and R. Satyarnand & Sons, Solicitors and their phone number were repeated in white paint on all the exterior windows. Rowan saw a company that would never be establishment, one that probably worked the fringe of legality and morality. He thought briefly about wandering in and introducing himself but dismissed the idea immediately. They had no reason to even talk to him, let alone disclose confidential client information.

As he watched, a white sedan pulled up in the No Standing Zone in front of the building. It sat there, motor idling for a good five minutes, before a balding, corpulent Indo-Fijian descended the stairs. He was accompanied by a nervous young man who first held the office door open for him, then raced around to open the car door. Rowan wouldn't have been surprised if the young man had licked the pavement so that his boss could walk to the car without dirtying the soles of his shoes. Rowan smiled grimly and asked his driver to take him back to his hotel. He'd seen the enemy and recognised him for his kind. R. Satyarnand was pompous, arrogant and a bully, a man with little regard for others. He was also something more dangerous. Rowan knew an operator when he saw one.

As he collected his room key, the receptionist handed him a note saying that Tiny was waiting for him in the hotel bar. He was tempted to make Tiny wait while he dashed up to his room for a shower but thought better of it. He found Tiny sitting alone, nursing a beer.

'Hello Rowan,' said Tiny. 'How did you get on?'

'Fine. How about you?'

'Perhaps not so well.'

'Let me order a beer and then tell me.' He caught the barman's eye, pointed to Tiny's beer and indicated two more. 'Okay, fire away.'

'The opposition are outnumbered but refuse to budge.

The fact that other delegates still blame you for the drop-off in tourists meant they had an audience.'

'So what's the decision?'

'They want to give an agency in Suva the chance to pitch for the business.'

'They *what*?'

'Some members agreed, just so that the issue can be resolved and put behind us.'

'Where are the three copies of my report?'

'In my office.'

'Make sure they stay there under lock and key until the other agency has pitched. Okay? Damned if I'll do their work for them.'

'I think that is a wise move.'

'One more thing. I have been your agency for five years. Your business has grown enormously in that time. Don't you think the encumbent agency deserves the opportunity to re-pitch after the Suva agency has had its go?'

'It's not easy to get all the delegates together. They might think that today was your presentation.'

'It was a presentation, not a pitch. I just want a fair deal out of this. Use your influence.'

'I have used my influence, yet we are still having this conversation.'

'I'm not going to roll over, Tiny. I'll fight those bastards with whatever it takes.'

'I'll do what I can.'

'Good man. Now, tell me, what do you know about Rajiv Satyarnand?'

'Watch out for him, Rowan, the man is a rogue but he does have influence.' He made a sound like spitting. 'Bloody Indians, they're the curse of Fiji!'

So much for racial tolerance, thought Rowan.

Rowan's second morning in Fiji followed the same pattern as his first. He trained hard in the hotel gym to work off some of the excesses of the previous night, when he and Tiny had drowned their disappointment. He did laps of the pool until his headache gave up and went off to bother someone else. As he rolled over for a final lap of backstroke, he had to fight back a surge of anger at himself for allowing his commitment to the Fiji Tourist Board to even be questioned, and at Sandy for exacerbating the problem. Above him, the palms and hibiscus surrounding the pool framed a faultlessly blue sky, as though teasing him with a preview of his life after retirement, provided all went well. Just add a boat and a few hungry yellowfin tuna and the fantasy would be complete.

He took the same seat for breakfast and helped himself to the same assortment of fresh fruit and cereal. The same waitress brought him coffee. He unfolded the *Fiji Times* to see how the kava crisis was developing and startled a Japanese businessman by thumping his fist onto the table. The kava crisis had been bumped off the front page. Instead, the Fijian Prime Minister announced he was taking a personal interest in ensuring that Junior Madison was reunited with his biological father. It had become, he said, a matter of national integrity and pride.

Rowan raced back to his room, rang Air Pacific and put his flight back twenty-four hours, rang Sunbird Airline and booked a flight to Coralhaven, rang Maurice and discovered he should have made the calls in reverse order. It was Sitiveni's day off and he'd paddled away to an outlying island to do some fishing.

'He'll be back tonight some time,' said Maurice. 'Stay overnight and talk to him in the morning.'

'Bloody hell!' said Rowan. 'If I stay overnight I'll miss my flight home, and I can't be away another day. Can you fix me up with a boat so I can go find him?'

'Sorry,' said Maurice. 'Can't help you. All the boats are booked. Picnic day.'

'For Christ's sake, Maurice, help me out!'

'You could try your fishing boat mate, Dean, over on Koru. Maybe he can come and pick you up.'

Rowan took down Dean's number and dialled. His wife, Vanessa, answered.

'Dean's out on a charter,' she said. 'Maybe Dilip could pick you up in the reef boat. It'll be a bit wet though. The reef boat's just an open boat with an outboard. Dean uses it to fish the narrow channels for Spanish mackerel.'

Rowan pictured the long, narrow-gutted Fijian reef boat with its centre console and rear-facing game chair, and tried to imagine it in open water with a steep chop running. 'Who's Dilip?' he said.

'One of Dean's deckies. He's a good lad, Indian and ambitious.'

'I'll take it,' said Rowan. 'I should be on Coralhaven by twelve. Get Dilip to talk to Maurice and find out where Sitiveni is most likely to have gone.' Rowan hung up and made one final call to Ryan Scott. He told him about the press coverage, his conversation with Bagetta Friel and his intention to confront Siti. Ryan Scott listened attentively, thanked him and then hit him with a question.

'Why are you bothering?' he said. 'Is it business or personal?'

Rowan had no answer for him, or for himself.

Coralhaven did not sit alone in the indigo sea. It was an island among many, some no more than rocks with green tops, and Rowan was beginning to think he'd have to search all of them to find Siti. They had to check every island and every inlet, in case Siti had pulled his canoe up onto the shore, but many were protected by reefs too shallow to allow their long boat to cross.

Rowan was on the verge of giving up when Dilip called out, 'There he is.'

'Where?' said Rowan. He shielded his eyes against the glare but all he could see was an ocean turned molten silver by the sun.

'Heading for Rakitu Island.'

'What island? Where?'

'Straight ahead, Mr Rowan.'

Straight ahead was like looking into a blast furnace. If he couldn't see an island, how the hell could he pick out a canoe? He covered his eyes with his hands and peeked through the narrowest slip in his fingers. By sheer chance he glimpsed a dark sliver of silhouette and caught a flash of sun glinting on a paddle. 'How the hell do you know that's Siti?' he said. 'He's got to be a mile away, at least.'

'That is his canoe, Mr Rowan, his *waqavoce*.'

Rowan shook his head. He only saw a paddle. Dilip not only saw a canoe but recognised the make and model. Maybe Fijians recognised canoes the same way he recognised friends' cars. He didn't know and didn't care. The sun had blasted his skin because he'd been in too much of a hurry to apply sunscreen, and the spray had not only soaked him to the bone but coated him in salt. He glanced impatiently at his watch. Just after three. That barely left two hours for the return trip, shower and change before he caught the seaplane. How long would it take to make Siti see reason?

'Try and cut him off,' said Rowan.

'He is going in over the reef, Mr Rowan. We must go in through the channel on the other side of the island.'

'Does the channel go around to where he's going?'

'No, Mr Rowan. You must walk.'

Rowan sighed impatiently. He squinted again through his fingers and found the island further to the left than he'd looked earlier. Once he knew where it was he wondered how he'd missed it the first time. The island would struggle for recognition on any map. The fact that someone had even bothered to give it a name flattered it. The island was barely two hundred metres long and no more than a hundred metres wide, rising steeply to a height of around thirty metres. As they negotiated their way through what Dilip had called a channel but Rowan struggled to regard as more than a crack in the coral – and a shallow one at that – Rowan became aware that his walk would not be easy. Beneath the inevitable coconut palms, the undergrowth looked impenetrable.

'Is there a track through to the other side?'

'I don't know of one.'

'How do I get across?'

'Walk around the shore, Mr Rowan.'

Rowan sighed grimly. Everything in Fiji took longer to do than it did anywhere else. Dilip gently nudged the long boat up onto the coral sand. 'I wait here.'

'Thought you might.' Rowan made his way up to the bow before leaping ashore. His feet were already wet but he couldn't see the point in getting them any wetter. He sunk up to his ankles in sand. 'Bugger it!' Sand adhered immediately to his feet and the insides of his sandals. He had the choice of taking his sandals off and having his feet minced on the coral, or leaving them on and copping blisters. Blisters seemed the less painful option.

He scanned the bush at the fringe of the shore, hoping to find a nice grassy trail. There was no grass and no trail. With no choice and no time to waste, he set off around the shore, clambering over rocks, edging across ledges and trying not to step on the black and white sea snakes nestling among the crevices in the rocks. The island might only have been two hundred metres long but it was a darn sight longer when he had to zigzag around every gutter and rock.

He came across Siti without warning as he rounded an outcrop. There was, not twenty metres from him, hauling his canoe up onto the sand. Rowan's impatience spilled over. He was hot, tired, exasperated, and beyond any pretext of courtesies. In front of him was the cause of all his trouble, the man who had planted his foul seed in his wife's womb and stuffed his marriage.

'Hey!' said Rowan. 'I want a word with you.'

Siti turned slowly towards him, showing none of the surprise that Rowan might have expected. He appeared stooped when Rowan remembered him as standing so upright that he seemed to lean backwards. The warning signs were there but Rowan was too steamed-up to notice them. He jumped down onto the beach and strode straight up to Siti.

'Who the hell do you think you are?' demanded Rowan. 'If you want to cause trouble, I'll give you fucking trouble.'

Siti seemed to have difficulty comprehending.

'What's the matter with you?' Rowan realised what the matter was almost as soon as he asked. The bottom of Siti's canoe was covered in empty Fiji Bitter cans. 'Oh shit!' said Rowan softly. Forbidden to drink on Coralhaven, Siti had made the most of his day off.

Rowan saw the punch coming. It started its journey at the Fijian's hip, came arcing at him rather than straight from the shoulder. Rowan had ducked under or away from dozens of similar punches while sparring down at the gym, but this one was unexpected. Even so, it was an easy punch to slip. He transferred his weight to his toes to push away. But there wasn't a hard canvas floor beneath his feet to springboard off. In fact, nothing hard at all. In the instant that the sand absorbed the push of his feet, Rowan realised he was in trouble. He tried to get his guard up but he was too late. Siti's fist exploded against the side of his face. Rowan had been hit hard by the young Samoan boxer but at least he'd been wearing a head protector. Siti's punch hit him with the force of a runaway bus and he had no protection at all. Rowan was out cold before his head hit the sand.

When he came to, his befuddled brain had a hard time working out exactly where he was, why he'd been sleeping in the middle of the day, and what the hell had happened to him. His tongue felt swollen and he could taste blood. Things were loose in his mouth. He could only assume they were teeth. There were no cold sponges to wipe his brow, no salts being waved under his nose, no sympathetic hands to help him to his feet. Nobody to tell him to keep his guard up. He moved his jaw gingerly from side to side. It hurt like hell but there was no grating that would indicate a break. He ran his fingers over his cheekbone. The flesh stung and felt puffy.

His vision began to clear. He spotted a silhouette making its way out to sea over the reef. For whatever reason, Siti had not gone on with the job, and Rowan was grateful for that. Maybe, even in his drunken state, the Fijian had realised that knocking out a paying guest and friend of his boss was not a good career move.

Rowan staggered to his feet. The movement caused a thousand barracuda to sink their teeth into his brain. Pain nearly drove him back onto the sand. He staggered, legs undecided about their function, their movements unpredictable. His hands shook like a cocktail barman's. Nausea rose up from the pit of his stomach, a willy-willy bent on destruction, and he vomited. Big brown seabirds wheeled above his head, shrieking their claim to their preferred parts of his body in the event that he succumbed. All Rowan had to do now was retrace his steps around the shoreline to his boat. The mere thought of it brought a sob to his throat.

Dilip met him before he'd even reached the halfway point and helped him back to the boat. He'd spotted Siti's canoe making out to sea and had become concerned. 'Bloody Fijians,' he said darkly, as he helped Rowan back into the long boat. 'They're not civilised people like us, Mr Rowan. You can't talk to them. They belong back in the trees.'

'They speak nicely of you,' said Rowan wearily.

Margaret managed to get Rowan a private room in Bay View Hospital, overlooking Middle Harbour. He'd spent the flight home holding an icepack to the side of his head, which had blown up and turned purple overnight. His left eye had closed over completely. He'd needed surgery to repair a fractured cheekbone and packing in his left eye socket to prevent his eye from sinking backwards into his skull. The doctor told him he'd been lucky. Rowan knew he'd been foolish. He couldn't for the life of him imagine what had possessed him to go chasing after Siti. He lay in bed, staring at the ceiling and trying to come to terms with his actions. Personal or business? Ryan had asked. Both motives seemed ridiculous. Even if he'd managed to thump the daylights out of Siti, that wouldn't have solved any business problems. If it was personal, it wasn't his problem. Why did he care? Because Sandy was upset? Because Junior had decided to crawl on the one weekend he was looking after him?

He tossed and turned, angry and frustrated by inactivity. Sandy wanted to visit but he'd discouraged her. Both Margaret and Blake flatly refused to bring him work to occupy his mind. They told him to make the most of the break, have a rest and then tackle the re-pitch to the Fiji Tourist Board. When his mobile rang, he thought it was the office with a query and was surprised to hear Ryan Scott's voice.

'Sandra told me what happened,' said Ryan. 'We can charge Sitiveni with assault. That'll look good in court when they push for contact.'

'No witnesses,' said Rowan. 'I could have sustained these injuries falling over. God almighty, by the time the boat skipper found me, I'd fallen over half a dozen times. I spent all night scraping coral out of cuts.'

'It'll help even if he's charged.'

'For Christ's sake, Ryan! If I go to court in Fiji and tell them I sustained these injuries by walking up to a drunken Fijian and accusing him of screwing my wife, for one I'd look stupid, and two, they'd say I got what I deserved.'

'Did you make a complaint to the manager of the resort?'

'It's private business, not resort business. That wouldn't have been fair.'

'Rowan, I wish you'd spoken to me. You've wasted a good opportunity for us. I don't mind you doing the decent thing and playing fair, so long as both sides play fair. And they certainly aren't playing fair.'

'What's the latest?'

'I've had a letter from our Foreign Minister, requesting copies of all documents relating to the case. I've had a phone call from the Department of Community Services with a similar request.'

'You've got to be joking!'

'Wait, there's more. I've heard from a friendly judge of the Family Court that a request has come from high up to expedite a hearing. I find it hard to believe all this crap is coming down, but it is. Someone in Fiji is shaking the tree pretty bloody hard.'

'It's madness! Why would our government get involved? Why should they give a damn? They must know this is all just a political stunt.'

'Of course they do, but it's a question of trade. You may not know it, Rowan, but Australia has a massive trade imbalance with Fiji heavily weighted in our favour. Around fifty per cent of Fiji's imports come from Australia. Our pollies don't give a toss about Junior but they do care about trade. Any hint of an embargo and our blokes turn to water.'

'An embargo over Junior?'

'No, an embargo over racism.'

'I don't believe this. Sandy spreads them for a boat boy and suddenly we have an international incident?'

'I'd start believing if I were you.'

Rowan groaned. His head hurt and his jaw ached. He didn't need any more bad news. 'Did you run a check on Satyarnand?'

'You picked him in one. He's a political adviser to the ruling party, one of their principal fundraisers and back-room boys. Chances are, your Bagetta Friel was right about it being payback time. The government can legitimately use this case to sling their loyal party man a bundle of taxpayers' dollars. Governments around the world do this sort of thing all the time. I suspect Sitiveni Kefu is just a pawn in all this, an innocent who walked off the street and into the wrong office at a timely moment.'

'Or the right office. The thing you have to remember is that he went looking for a solicitor in the first place. Satyarnand didn't go looking for him. Why is he doing this? What's in it for him?'

'Damned if I know,' said Ryan.

'Have you told Sandra what's going on?'

'No. I thought I might wait until you were back on your feet. She's tending to get a bit emotional. I thought we might do this together.'

'Oh no,' said Rowan. 'I've done my bit for Sandy. This is where you earn your fee. So far this nonsense has cost me my wife, my family, my fucking home and maybe one of my biggest accounts. I've done enough. I said I'd look around and I did. That's it. She's on her own. From now on, I'm taking care of my business. I haven't got time to look after hers as well.'

Twenty-four

Sandra lay in bed feeling dispossessed and cast adrift. She'd always believed and trusted in a legal system that claimed to protect the law-abiding and punish transgressors, and a government that protected the rights of its citizens. Yet both, apparently, had abandoned her. She desperately needed someone to stand by her, someone strong who could help her cope with her feeling of utter powerlessness. The move to grant contact to Siti and take away her son seemed not just unstoppable but to be gathering momentum. She'd wake determined to fight to protect her child, as any mother would, but the law gave her nothing to fight against. It named the date of a hearing she was powerless to prevent. It prescribed rules by which the battle would be engaged, not by her but by lawyers, and she was powerless to do anything about them. The government had taken over the agenda and she was powerless to stop them.

Even worse, Junior's plight had aroused the interest of the

Australian media and they'd hijacked her private battle and tossed it into the public arena. She refused interviews and denied requests for photographs but to no effect. The stories still ran, with telephoto shots and footage of her and Junior taken while they were shopping or playing in the park at Balmoral Beach. She feared leaving the house. Even more disconcerting was the photo of Siti that accompanied the stories. She couldn't imagine where he'd got hold of the suit, white shirt and tie. He didn't look a bit like the conman who'd come to fix her spa pump. 'Tug of Love', said one newspaper headline. 'Is He an Aussie, Is He?' said another. The Minister of Foreign Affairs popped up on the TV news to deny accusations of racism and state that the case had become a matter of priority for the Family Court. For the life of her, she couldn't understand why her own government appeared so anxious to give away her child, or why the law was so accommodating to a father who'd never bothered to enquire about his son's health or even ask his name.

Sandra refused to speak to Meagan and had learned not to call on Ryan. He positioned himself as her friend and adviser but charged outrageously for every minute of his time. She had hoped Rowan would assist with the bills, maybe even absorb them into his company's accounts, but no offer had been forthcoming. Her savings were haemorrhaging and she had yet to attend court. Necessity forced her to extend her clinic hours to keep her mind occupied and earn more money, but that also made her tired and cranky. Junior and the girls had done nothing to deserve that.

Sandra desperately needed the Caroline of old for comfort

and understanding, but the new Caroline was totally engrossed in the novelty of being a full-time mum. When she managed to catch her while Jenny was having a nap, Sandra told her all about the government involvement and the hastily scheduled hearing. The more she said, the more depressed she became. Caroline listened aghast, and her interjections only made matters worse.

'Surely they can't do that?' Caroline kept saying, and Sandra found herself explaining how they could, how if the court denied the father access it would leave itself open to accusations of racism. The more she explained why things could happen, why Junior could be taken away from her for weeks at a time, the more she understood Ryan Scott's concern. Worse, she even began to understand Meagan's point of view. The dead weight of despair settled on her and she had to struggle to keep her voice from breaking.

'The trouble is, Caro,' she said, 'if Siti does succeed in getting a court order allowing him to take Junior to Fiji, I'm scared he won't bring him back. What if he leaves Coralhaven and goes back to his village or to his wife's village? What if he goes to his brother-in-law's village or his second cousin's? If he takes Junior with him, we might never see him again. Nobody will ever be able to find him.'

In the playpen tucked away in the corner of the clinic, Junior began tinkling with a toy fire engine that played manic sound effects depending upon which button was pushed. A dog barked, a bird chirped and the fire engine's siren wailed. Junior laughed as if he didn't have a care in the world. The tears Sandra had been suppressing began to well up. She desperately wanted someone to take charge and make sure that nothing bad happened.

'Ooops,' said Caroline. 'Sorry. Gotta go. Jenny's just woken up. By the way, we're thinking of christening her Jennifer Sandra after her soon-to-be godmother. What do you think?'

The sudden change of subject caught Sandra by surprise. Where were the words of comfort, the shared concern, the reassurance that everything would work out? She'd expected Caroline's priorities to shift, but never so far, never so abruptly. 'I'm honoured,' she said quietly. 'Thank you.'

She murmured her farewells and sat staring at the phone, wondering what was going to happen and how she was going to cope. The tears that had welled up dissipated without ever spilling over onto her cheeks. She began to doubt that she even had the strength left to cry, and almost yelped in fright when the phone rang.

'Hi,' said Ryan. 'Can you talk?'

'Yes,' said Sandra weakly. She'd learned not to expect good news.

'We're planning strategies,' said Ryan. 'We have to cover all possibilities. Is there any chance of a reconciliation between you and Rowan before the hearing?'

'Why?' said Sandra, suddenly hopeful, despite the fact she'd hardly seen him since his return from Fiji. 'Has he said something?'

'Not that I know of. I'm ringing him next.'

Sandra's shoulders slumped. If a reconciliation was her best chance, then she didn't have much cause for hope. 'I doubt it,' she said. 'I doubt it very much.'

Rowan arrived promptly at six-thirty to pick up the girls for the weekend. Bloody typical, Sandra thought. The one Friday night she'd made no plans to go out, he turns up on time. He reverted to his old habit of waiting for the girls on the doorstep, as if reluctant to step inside.

'How's it going?' he asked.

'If you'd answered my calls, you'd know,' said Sandra.

'I have a business to run. I'm flat out doing the re-pitch for the Fiji Tourist Board.'

'What's new?'

'I have a life, too,' he said.

Sandra caught a glimpse of movement from the front passenger seat of Rowan's car. She squinted over Rowan's shoulder to confirm her suspicions. 'So I see,' she said.

'Man is not a camel,' said Rowan. 'It's nearly two months since I split with Claudine and that's a long time to go without.'

'You should try nine months.'

Rowan turned away from her, shaking his head. 'Don't do this, Sandy.'

'Fuck you, Rowan,' she said bitterly. 'What does one phone call take? I need someone to talk to and you won't even return one call.'

'It's not just a phone call, is it?' he said. 'It's what the one phone call leads to. I'm already up to my arse in alligators with the pitch. I don't need your problems on top of my own.'

'You once promised me you'd never put the agency ahead of me or the girls.'

'When?'

'Before Coralhaven.'

'Right. Before you fell for Siti's bullshit *lawedua* story. That kind of changed things.'

'What?' Sandra froze. She'd never expected to hear the word *lawedua* again in her life, certainly not from Rowan's lips. She stared at him in horror. Even he seemed surprised and embarrassed by the strength of her reaction.

'Maurice told me,' he said apologetically. 'Apparently Siti tells that story to all the girls.'

'You bastard!'

'I'm sorry.'

'I hate you sometimes.'

'I'm sorry! But don't go blaming me for your problems.'

'I'm not blaming you,' said Sandra fiercely. 'I accept all the blame but there's a lot happening and I'm scared. I need help, someone I can talk to.'

'Talk to Ryan,' said Rowan. 'He's getting paid to listen.'

The girls came up the hall, arms filled with bags and toys, not rushing as they usually did to jump into their daddy's arms, but continuing a squabble that had flared intermittently since they'd got home from school. Behind them, Junior chased along on all fours, crying over the loss of his playmates, eyes and nose streaming. Sandra hugged the girls and kissed them goodbye. She scooped Junior up into her arms and looked Rowan squarely in the eye.

'Have fun,' she said.

'I intend to.'

Sandra waved to the girls until Rowan's car had disappeared from sight, then closed the door and slumped down onto the floor. She needed help and had been rebuffed. She needed reassuring and had been humiliated instead. She became aware of Junior staring at the bitter tears rolling down her cheeks and brushed them away. At least she'd learned something. At least she knew how he'd responded to Ryan's query about reconciliation.

She carried Junior back into the lounge and rolled his big furry ball along the carpet for him to chase. He ignored it, which was unusual because he loved nothing better than to use his new-found mobility. He snuggled into her shoulder instead, sniffling and unhappy. What would he be like, wondered Sandra, if he was taken away from the girls for a week? What would the girls be like? What would she be like! Dread enveloped her and settled in the pit of her stomach. The hearing was just two weeks away and she couldn't face it with any sense of optimism. She placated Junior and finally made him laugh by pulling a ribbon along the floor for the kitten to chase. Before long he was his usual happy self, but that was a state beyond Sandra. Something else troubled her. There was something oddly familiar about the silhouette in the passenger seat of Rowan's car.

Ryan maintained it was the short deadline for the hearing that caused the problem, but Sandra suspected it wouldn't have mattered if the hearing was set down for a Friday a year away. Solicitors did nothing until they absolutely had to. Ryan kept her busy right up until the last minute hunting down statutory declarations and documents. Ryan wanted letters proving Junior was enrolled at SCECGS Redlands and waitlisted at Shore, that he was covered by private health insurance and vaccinated and inoculated against every known childhood disease. He wanted her tax returns, bank statements, financial statements, and a letter from Rowan guaranteeing continuing support. He wanted statements from Sarah's school teacher, Rochelle's kindy teacher, their doctor and dentist, and statements from Mike and Caroline, all to prove that she was a good and capable mother. Though nobody hesitated to oblige her, Sandra felt demeaned by the necessity of having to make the requests.

The night before the hearing, the softball girls turned up to wish her well and lend their support. With the exception of Sharon, the assistant coach, they were all under nineteen and incapable of offering much in the way of advice. But they brought with them the irreverence of the young, the latest scandal and gossip, and several bottles of pre-mixed vodkas and coffee liqueurs. They claimed they were all going to turn up in court to see the man who'd impregnated their coach so comprehensively. Up until then, it hadn't even occurred to Sandra that Sitiveni would be in court. She'd imagined it would all be handled by solicitors. The girls were lewd, crude and outrageous about what they intended to do to Sitiveni but Sandra hardly heard a word.

How could she face him? How would she feel? What would she say if she had to speak to him? The prospect sickened and horrified her. Would she be able to contain her anger? The girls' laughter dragged her away from her thoughts.

'Get this into you,' said Sharon, her co-coach. The vodka and tonic had enough alcohol in it to stun a division of Cossacks.

Caroline arrived without baby attached, believing she was on a mission of mercy to comfort her troubled friend in her hour of need, and walked into a party in full swing. She put away the tissues and made cocktails.

Midway through the evening Rowan rang. Sandra had just downed her third Screaming Orgasm when she picked up the phone.

'You okay?' said Rowan.

'I thought we weren't speaking.'

'I just rang to wish you good luck tomorrow.'

'Thank you.'

'What's going on there? It sounds like you're having a party.'

'That's what it sounds like, all right.'

'Who's there?'

'None of your business.'

'Sounds like a hens' night.'

'You wish. I'll pass on your thoughts to the roosters. No one's telling *lawedua* stories yet, but the night's still young.'

'Ouch. Well, I hope you come out in front tomorrow.'

'Thank you.'

'And have a good night.'

'I intend to.' Hanging up, she felt unreasonably pleased with herself. She'd got the distinct impression that Rowan wasn't thrilled at the prospect of her having parties. She grabbed another cocktail just as the phone rang again. It was Ryan. He rang to reassure her and say that he couldn't be better prepared for the hearing. Sandra swallowed a mouthful of cocktail and announced she couldn't be better prepared either.

But once everybody had gone home, she found herself alone in her bed and all her brave front counted for nothing. They'd partied like it was the end of the world. But it was only the end of her world that threatened, not theirs.

Twenty-five

Sandra awoke feeling detached from her body, as though she existed somewhere outside it like a mildly interested observer. She performed the morning rituals on remote, driving the girls to school before returning home to fret until it was time to leave for the hearing. At twelve-thirty she called a taxi to take her and Junior to Ryan Scott's office. She no longer trusted herself to drive.

Sandra had expected the hearing to take place in a courtroom that bore at least a passing resemblance to the courtrooms she'd seen on TV, but instead they were ushered into a windowless shoebox in the middle of a high-rise building, where participants and spectators alike sat in rows as though they were in a cinema. When Siti arrived with the counsel appointed by Rajiv Satyarnand, Sandra hardly recognised him in his dark-blue suit, white shirt that still bore the creases from the box it had come in, maroon tie and squeaky new shoes. He seemed timid and uncertain, nothing like the confident predator she remembered, the man who'd conned his way into her bed.

She'd expected to feel intimidated by him but instead felt nothing but loathing and disgust. What shocked and surprised her most was that his wife accompanied him. Sandra remembered her as the shy, smiling housemaid who'd cleaned their *bure* and made their bed. She wore an ill-fitting, funereal navy suit and an expression that combined fear and sadness in equal measure. Sandra turned away in shame when she unexpectedly glanced up in her direction.

Sandra's feelings of apprehension grew. Could anything good come from such a cold and heartless place? Ryan seemed fully engaged in explaining details of the case to her barrister. She couldn't understand why, with so much at stake for her, they hadn't fully prepared earlier. She wanted to scream at them. Her dismay increased when the judge entered and they were all required to stand. The judge was a man – she'd fully expected a woman, a mother, someone who could sympathise with her plight.

Her sense of unreality heightened as both counsels made their submission. She heard Sitiveni described as a model husband, model father and model worker who'd never been unemployed since leaving school and had worked the previous twelve years at Coralhaven. A statutory declaration from Maurice described him as a model employee who regularly attended the Methodist church services on the island. There was no mention of his extra-marital activities. The description bore no relationship to the calculating seducer she'd encountered on Coralhaven. Then she heard a person who shared her name described in similarly glowing terms but found it no easier to equate that person to herself.

Nothing she heard seemed remotely connected with the events that had led to Junior's conception. When her counsel challenged Sitiveni for waiting eight months before making any effort to contact the mother of his child, she heard the charge rebuffed on the grounds that Siti had no telephone and no way of contacting her until he'd found a solicitor willing to take on his case. R. Satyarnand & Sons were portrayed as generous, warm-spirited benefactors. When her counsel accused Sitiveni of fathering two children in the village by women other than his wife, they simply denied the charge. Siti's wife supported the denial. When her counsel accused Sitiveni of preying on the female guests of the resort, the description seemed ill-fitting and far-fetched, desperate allegations made by a desperate counsel. The charges were easily denied. Siti was sober and spoke with a soft, child-like innocence. Even Sandra had trouble not believing him. She sat through proceedings that seemingly had nothing to do with her, as though the hearing had no more grasp on reality than a play, a play in which everyone except her knew the outcome.

The judge congratulated both parties on the way they had conducted their arguments. He complimented Sandra on the way she was raising her three children and providing for them. He stated that he had no doubts whatsoever that Junior's best interests would be served by leaving him in the care of his mother, and he ruled that way. The judge smiled at Sandra, a momentary and unexpected flash of humanity, and for a brief instant she thought her trial was over and that, despite all, sanity would prevail. She bent forward to kiss Junior, asleep in her arms. Then she heard the word that sent a chill racing down her spine.

'However,' said the judge.

One of the lifts was out of operation when Sandra was ushered from the court. She barely registered the fact, just as the judge's justification for his specific issues order had reached her ears but not penetrated her brain. She'd ceased hearing and feeling the instant he'd read out the bare detail of his order. The significance of the lift being under maintenance became apparent when Sitiveni, his wife and counsel joined the queue for the one lift that remained operational. When they followed her into the lift, she felt insult had been added to injustice, wanted to scream, accuse and abuse, leave nobody in any doubt about the true nature of the man who'd fathered Junior. She could scarcely believe her ears when Ryan began joking with the opposing legal team, was stunned to realise they were good friends, defeated when they began discussing golf. Her feelings of powerlessness and isolation intensified. She stood clutching Junior to her breast, staring at the broad shoulders of Siti in front of her.

When the lift doors opened she was swept out with the tide, friendless and abandoned. A hand touched her arm timidly, ran briefly and lightly across Junior's forehead. She turned in surprise and found herself looking into the big, sad eyes of the woman who'd been their housemaid on Coralhaven.

'Sorry, Mrs Sandra. So sorry,' she said. Her voice was so

soft, so shy, so filled with remorse that Sandra barely heard her. She was gone before Sandra could react.

Sandra stood by the kerb waiting for the car to arrive that would take them all back to Ryan's office. Ryan was still chatting animatedly to his colleague from the opposing side. She felt bitter and betrayed.

'It was a good win,' said Meagan. Sandra hadn't even been aware that Meagan had ghosted up alongside her.

'What the hell do you mean?' said Sandra through gritted teeth. A car pulled up in front of them.

'Get in,' said Meagan, 'and I'll explain.'

Sandra climbed in. There was no child safety capsule or child car seat for Junior, and she fussed around, shortening the middle seatbelt for him, refusing to allow the driver to move off before she had Junior safely secured. Behind them car horns blared angrily.

'I think we did rather well,' said Ryan. He'd taken the front passenger seat and turned around to address her. 'We certainly did as well as we could possibly expect. I think we must have got old Moncrief on a good day.' Moncrief was the judge.

'I suspect the decision was made before the hearing,' said Meagan. 'Clearly he'd thought it through. It favours us but nobody could argue that it isn't a fair decision.'

'Stop it! It isn't fair!' shrieked Sandra. 'Stop pretending we won! We lost. The judge gave that man permission to take my child back to Fiji with him. You let him do that!'

'Under the circumstances, there was no way of preventing that,' said Meagan calmly. 'The judge has made contact possible but unlikely. He made the best of a difficult situation.'

'Calm down and listen,' said Ryan. 'All Sitiveni Kefu won is the right to have Junior stay with him for one week a year from the age of one to the age of five, and five weeks a year thereafter.'

'I won't let Junior go!' said Sandra. 'Didn't you take any notice of Siti? He didn't even look at Junior in court. He didn't even look at him in the lift, for heaven's sake. Didn't touch him, didn't say hello, didn't want to know him. And you expect me to give that bastard my child!'

'I don't expect it'll ever come to that,' said Ryan calmly. 'The judge specifically stated that Sitiveni must take full responsibility for Junior while in his custody, and those responsibilities include collecting Junior and bringing him back to you on each occasion he has contact. Now, where do you think he's going to find the money for that?'

The impact of the ruling slowly dawned on Sandra.

'What this means is that Sitiveni and no one else can collect and bring Junior back. He can't delegate the responsibility to one of his relatives, say, who travels back and forth between Australia and Fiji on a regular basis. He can't just put him in the care of Air Pacific. Now, everything you've said to me previously suggests that sort of money is way beyond his means. I feel the judge acted upon that certainty.'

'It's a good ruling,' said Meagan. 'On the face of it, everybody comes out of it well. Sitiveni gets time with his son. The Fijian government has a public relations boost in the run-up to their elections. Their tame solicitor has his payday. Neither our politicians nor our courts can be accused of racism. The fact that Siti can't afford to see his son is irrelevant to the decision.'

'This has been an extraordinary case and, for you, a most unfortunate one,' chipped in Ryan. 'Governments got involved, our friends R. Satyarnand & Sons dipped their grubby hands in, and it seems everybody has had their own agenda that has had little to do with the main issue. But the thing is, Sandra, to all intents and purposes, it's over. The race is run.'

'That's it?' said Sandra incredulously. 'Just like that?'

'I was concerned that they may appeal the order on the grounds of the cost burden and had a quick chat with my counterpart,' said Meagan. 'He suggested that would be very unlikely.'

'But Siti could still come and take him away?'

'Yes, if somebody advances him the money, but why would anyone do that? Neither the Fijian government or R. Satyarnand & Sons have any reason to continue funding him. They don't need him any more. He's served his purpose and that's it.'

'I still can't believe it's over,' said Sandra. For a brief moment she wanted to kiss Ryan and even hug Meagan.

'Take my word for it,' said Ryan Scott smugly. 'You'll never hear from Sitiveni Kefu again.'

Twenty-six

Blake needed a good reason to drag Rowan away from his desk, and Margaret's birthday provided it. Rowan had slipped into the habit of refusing all lunchtime invitations and either grabbing a quick sandwich or going without. The re-pitch had become an obsession and working through lunch had become part of his routine, guaranteeing him his fix of work before he left each evening for the gym and then home. Work, gym, home. That was his life but it seemed to bring him little joy. At Blake's urging he booked a table for four and ordered a birthday cake to be delivered to the agency mid-morning so the staff could share in the celebrations. As it happened, the creative department had already decided to celebrate Margaret's birthday and contributed with a card depicting her as a lion tamer, complete with whip and chair, advancing into what could only be his office. They'd used the Cola Frisks line 'Just like the real thing'.

Rowan and Margaret arrived first at The Quay and were

given the table he'd shared with Claudine the night she'd worn nothing but her little white number and a smile. The thought depressed him. She'd gone but nothing had changed. The previous ten months had been a series of different faces and bodies just passing through, slipping through his fingers as inevitably as sand. Mike envied him, most men envied him, but outside of his work life and daughters he found little worthy of envy. Sex was only wonderful when you couldn't get enough of it, and quickly lost its gloss when you could. He couldn't help recalling the time so recently when the world had been his for the taking, when the ultrasound image framed on his desk had been of his son and Sandy had been his partner for life.

'How's Sandy?' asked Margaret, as if reading her boss's thoughts, something she claimed all good secretaries could do.

'She hasn't stopped smiling,' said Rowan. 'When I called around to pick up the girls last Friday, she was right back to her best, dressed to kill, confident and utterly gorgeous. I hadn't seen her so happy since ... well ... we won't go into that.'

'Do you ever wish you could go back in time?'

'Sometimes,' admitted Rowan.

'Only sometimes?'

'Maybe a bit more often.'

'I think about that every morning,' said Margaret. 'If I could, I'd make sure my husband ate more vegetables and less red meat. I'd make sure he wore gloves and a face mask when he sprayed the garden. I wouldn't let him smoke and I'd count his drinks. I'd make him exercise, and I'd buy a dog so he had to go for a walk every morning. I'd have done a thousand things, if only it could have held the cancer back for another twelve months.'

'You didn't give your husband cancer, Margaret.'

'No, of course I didn't. But I can't help wishing I'd done something to turn back the tide or at least delay it. We'd been through the hard years and were due our time in the sun.'

'We can't go back,' said Rowan. 'None of us can.'

'I can't. Most of us can't, but some of us can. Those of us who can't look at those who can and wonder what on earth they're waiting for.' She raised her eyes, locked onto Rowan's and held them until he weakened and looked away.

'You're kidding yourself,' he said.

'Am I?'

Blake and Barth's arrival prevented the conversation from developing any further.

Rowan back-pedalled, ducking, evading and parrying the barrage of punches and combinations the instructor threw at him. The punches weren't intended to hurt, simply to penetrate Rowan's defences.

'Good, good,' said the instructor. 'At last you seem to have got the feel for where your hands ought to be.' He backed off as if the session was over, then fired a lightning right hand. Rowan's glove was there to deflect it. 'Good, you're done.'

Rowan dropped his gloves. 'It's weird,' he said. 'Now that I know where my hands are supposed to be, I can't imagine why I ever held them anywhere else.' He climbed out of the ring. 'A cyclone couldn't get through these.'

'A good boxer will,' said the instructor. 'But there's no reason why one should ever be given the chance.'

'So, have you got anyone mediocre for me to spar with?' asked Rowan acidly.

'Heaps, but you're not sparring with anyone. Not for twelve months. You want your cheek broken again, the packing knocked out of your eye socket, go to some other gym. Claim on their insurance.'

'Twelve months?'

'We can still work on your defence. It should be good by then. Want me to hold the heavy bag?'

'Yeah,' said Rowan. 'Stand in front of it.'

The instructor laughed. Rowan worked on the heavy bag, then slowly warmed down. The evening aerobics session, an advanced class, was under way. It was filled with young women fresh from corporate battlefields, who put a greater store by washboard stomachs than ample breasts, well-muscled thighs than nicely turned ankles, who liked looking at their trim bodies in mirrors. Rowan couldn't blame them. He liked looking at them, too.

When he arrived home, the lights of his townhouse were already on and another car in his garage. A warm north-wester was blowing in off the outback deserts, which meant dinner on the terrace overlooking the harbour, watching jet cats and ferries parade by. The only negative about dinner would be the dinner itself, fresh from freezer to table. He let himself in and headed straight for his kitchen, following the smell of something Italian being resurrected.

She was wearing an apron over a string bikini and was

doubled over taking a tray out of the oven. Rowan's eyes fixed on her perfect bottom and he sucked in his breath.

'Hi!' he said. 'What have we got?'

'Lasagne and garlic bread from Lucio's. It's just about warmed through.' Glynis put down the bottle of red she was opening, threw her arms around his neck and kissed him. Glynis had also got what she wanted.

As Rowan suspected, Glynis had set the table outside and surrounded it with citronella candles to keep the mosquitoes at bay. He took his glass of wine and slumped down in one of the chairs facing the harbour. Glynis had covered the table with a white tablecloth, placed candelabra at each end and made little Opera Houses out of the table napkins. She thought that was a cute thing to do but Rowan had dined at too many pretentious bad restaurants and thought otherwise. Fancy napkins usually meant bad food and Rowan smiled ruefully at the realisation that tonight would not be an exception. After her bitter exit from the agency, Glynis had spent eighteen months touring Europe. She'd come back into his life simply by ringing him.

'Are we still friends?' she'd asked.

Perhaps because of his recent abstinence his thoughts had flashed immediately to images of her naked on his sofa and the things she'd done to him. Maybe his depression had caused him to lower his guard. Not for a second did he consider the rest of the package.

'Sure,' he'd answered, and that was all the encouragement Glynis had needed. Within a fortnight she was spending more nights at his place than at her own. Blake thought Rowan was off his head and told him so. Rowan half agreed, but Glynis had a fabulous body, custom-made for love-making, and few inhibitions, which, he felt, was exactly what he needed. When they had sex she had a way of concentrating so intensely on the sensations it aroused in her that sometimes Rowan felt excluded, little more than a provider of body parts. Sometimes she wanted more than he could give, even when he'd given plenty, and he'd doze off knowing that alongside him she was still touching herself to keep the buzz going. He could only wonder at her appetite.

Glynis brought out their lasagnes, placed a bowl of Woolworths salad mix and a bottle of Paul Newman's ranch dressing in the middle of the table, untied her apron and slipped off her bikini top. She sat on the opposite side of the table between him and the view. She smiled, waiting to be complimented.

'Well done,' said Rowan. She'd warmed the lasagne, opened the foil around their garlic bread, tipped the salad out of its plastic container into a bowl and opened a bottle of wine. Her breasts sat up proudly and eyeballed him. How many men would die for this? Rowan wondered. Only one thing could spoil it. Like Claudine and all her predecessors, she wanted to move in with him, and he knew from bitter experience that it was only a matter of time before he once more had to make a decision.

'Have a good day?' she said.

'Good,' said Rowan noncommittally. She was the receptionist for a competing advertising agency so he had to be careful what he told her. 'Interviewed a young creative team today, wasted in a crap agency. They're hugely talented but still don't know shine from shit and their creative director is too thick to explain the difference. They're angry, full of naked aggression. I got a commitment from them and left Blake to sort out the details. They're exactly what we need.'

'Who are they?' asked Glynis.

'You've got to be kidding.'

'Where are they from?'

'Not saying. Not until they've resigned. I don't want counter offers.'

Glynis laughed. 'I told them to ring you. Have you heard from Tiny?'

A shadow crossed Rowan's face. 'The Suva agency pitches tomorrow.'

'Then worry about it tomorrow. How's the lasagne?'

'Exactly like Lucio's except not as warm in the middle.'

'Good cooks give bad sex,' said Glynis.

Rowan smiled. Conversation with Glynis never plumbed depths but she could make him laugh. 'What are we listening to?'

'A new CD I bought today. *Romanza*, by Andrea Bocelli. What do you think?'

Rowan smiled. Glynis hadn't missed a trick. He wondered how much of her day had been spent planning dinner. What do you have with an Italian dinner? Italian love songs. 'Very nice,' he said.

'I thought it would get you in the mood,' said Glynis.

'You don't need any help to do that.'

'Why, thank you!' she said. She prattled on for another ten

minutes, telling him all about her day before gathering the dirty dishes and taking them into the kitchen. Rowan settled back to absorb the view. He smiled when he heard one of Taronga Park Zoo's lions roar. He figured he was about to roar himself.

'Guess what's for dessert?' said Glynis.

'Are we having dessert?'

'You are.' Glynis had divested herself of her bikini pants. She sat down on his lap, facing him, and began to pull his T-shirt over his head.

'Whoa,' said Rowan.

'What's the problem? You said you liked naked aggression.'

'Not out here.'

'Why not? No one can see us.' She removed his shirt and turned her attention to his trousers.

Rowan didn't need to look around to know there'd be no prying eyes. Despite the fact that his terrace looked out on the world, it was quite private. Why not? he thought. The important parts were springing into readiness. He leant back in his chair, cupping her perfect bottom in his hands as she gently lowered herself onto him, eyes closed. Rowan felt a mild wave of relief in addition to the other sensations. Glynis didn't talk while she screwed.

Twenty-seven

In the days following the hearing, Sandra's world took on a whole new hue. The shadow had gone and in its place there were colour, life and laughter. Mike and Caroline invited her over for a celebratory dinner and filled her full of Bollinger. She let Junior and the girls stay up past their bedtime watching videos, gave them more ice-cream, played with them, listened and laughed with them and made up for the past dark days when she'd been too exhausted and distracted to be much of a mother at all. She took Junior to the ballet school's annual performance, smiled as Junior won the hearts of all around her, including many who couldn't understand her determination to hang onto him. Sarah danced like an angel and Rochelle like an elephant on ice, but it didn't matter. The girls had a ball, Junior had a ball and so did Sandra. It felt good just getting out and doing things.

In the quiet of the evenings she made a list of exhibitions she wanted to see. There was a Jeffrey Smart retrospective at the New South Wales Art Gallery, which she put at the top of her list, and Hockney's 'Grand Canyon' to see down in Canberra. Canberra seemed a long shot with three children, but why should it? Her mother had set the example. When Marion wanted to do something, she just went ahead and did it, and Sandra thought she should do the same. For the first time in ages she felt free to get on with her life and couldn't see any point in putting limitations on it. Canberra was just a four-hour drive and a night away from home. Where was the problem in that? She decided to go the next time Rowan had the girls for the weekend.

She also made a list of movies she wanted to see, determined to get a few under her belt before the school holidays and the raft of kiddie movies that were released simultaneously. The girls loved being taken to the movies and Sandra was interested to see what Junior would make of the experience. She gathered together restaurant reviews to check out with Caroline. Her softball girls wanted to celebrate her stunning victory in court and Sandra had convinced them to make a special night of it in a good restaurant, instead of just drinking too much in a pub somewhere and getting silly. Sandra made plans and plotted activities weeks in advance, like someone who'd just been released from incarceration. She felt liberated.

Her freedom also gave her the opportunity to turn her attention back to the main game, which was winning back Rowan and reuniting the family. It was here that she found her only cause for concern and the only cloud in her otherwise glorious sky. The cloud had a name, and its name was Glynis.

Sandra resolved to keep her weather eye on her.

Caroline arrived mid-morning to have her back treated, bringing with her not just Jenny but the latest bulletin on Glynis. Once she'd parked Jenny in her bouncer, where she could watch Junior at play, she told Sandra all about their dinner with Rowan and two other couples out on the terrace of his townhouse.

'We met his new girlfriend,' said Caroline. 'Honestly, I thought Mike's eyes were going to pop out of his head. She can't be more than nineteen.'

'She's twenty-three,' said Sandra. 'She's the one Rowan was having a fling with before we went to Coralhaven. I made Rowan fire her.'

'Well, she's back and wants everyone to know it. She was wearing this handkerchief-sized black shift that was too short and cut too low. The men didn't know whether they were going to get a tit in their face or have their photo taken every time she bent over.'

'Photo taken?'

'A flash, Sandy. She's got the cutest little bum, too. It's just not fair.'

'Did she give the boys what they wanted?' asked Sandra, intrigued.

'I'll give the little trollop credit. She'd judged both the neckline and hemline to millimetre perfection. We'll never know if she was wearing knickers or not. When she took some plates inside, Mike turned to Rowan and said, "Jesus, Rowan, what are you doing to us?" Do you know what Rowan said?'

'Tell me!'

'I shouldn't.'

'Caroline!'

'He said, "Glynis is a woman of few mysteries."'

Sandra exploded into laughter. 'That,' she said, 'is Glynis to a T.'

'Women like us have to worry about girls like that,' said Carolyn.

'Not necessarily. Men have sex with them, not relationships. They're just trophies, means to indulge the male ego.'

'Are you sure about that?'

'I wish.' Sandy pushed hard to loosen up the muscles in Caroline's lower back. 'This is like rope. What have you been doing?'

'Blame little madam,' said Caroline. 'The problem with adopting a Korean baby is that they expect to be carried around all the time. You know how you never see Swedish hikers without a backpack? That's me, from morning till night, every bloody day.'

'You love it.'

'Yes, I love it.'

When Caroline left she took Junior with her, to give Sandra a break and as a means of keeping her daughter off her back. Jenny and Junior could entertain each other. Throughout the rest of the day Sandra found her thoughts wandering inescapably back to the story Caroline had told her and felt uneasy. She remembered how Rowan liked to talk and how they'd sometimes finish dinner but not leave the table until well after midnight. Sometimes they talked about work, his and hers, sometimes politics, sport or religion, sometimes their plans for the future and Rowan's dream of owning a game-fishing charter boat. She couldn't help wondering what he talked about with Glynis, or if they talked at all. She suspected she knew what Rowan wanted from Glynis, and was absolutely sure she knew what Glynis wanted from Rowan. He wanted sex and to some extent company, but Sandra was certain Glynis's ambitions stretched way beyond that. She recalled seeing her in the studio at the agency bouncing Rochelle on her knees, sampling the role of wife to Rowan and stepmother to his kids. She wanted Rowan, lock, stock and barrel. Maybe Glynis was different to all of Rowan's other conquests. People tended to underestimate Glynis because of her looks but Sandra saw a tenacious young woman who knew exactly what she wanted and was determined to get it. She only hoped Rowan screwed the little trollop with his eyes wide open.

'Imagine if children got gout, dear,' said Marion. 'Infanticide would probably become legal.'

'That bad?' said Sandra, phone jammed between her head and shoulder as she made spaghetti bolognaise. She tried to sound sympathetic and was glad Marion couldn't see the smirk on her face.

'Worse. I've filled him full of Indocid and made him put his foot up but he's quite impossible. Know what he's asking for now?'

'What?'

'Junior. He wants to know if we can borrow Junior for the day.'

'Clive wants Junior for the day?'

'Yes, dear. I rather think he regrets never having had children of his own.'

Sandra bit her tongue. 'Tell Clive that Junior would love to spend the day with him. How do you feel about having Junior?'

'I'll manage. Actually, be nice to see a happy face around here for a change.'

Sandra smiled. Junior had struck again. Not even Marion was immune to his charm.

When the phone rang just after three the following afternoon, Sandra assumed it was Marion, ringing to arrange a time to come and collect Junior. She was sipping a coffee while her patient lay waiting for the interferential to stop sending electric currents deep into the muscles of his lower back. Sandra had just received something of a shock herself, but of a very pleasant kind. The mailman had dropped off a letter from Ryan Scott and a cheque refunding all her legal fees. The letter said Rowan had instructed Ryan to bill the charges to the agency as consulting fees. She thought nothing short of an earthquake could knock the smile off her face, but she was wrong. Her world began to topple off its axis the instant she heard Meagan's voice.

'We've had a letter from Fiji,' said Meagan, without preamble. 'It requires you to deliver Junior to his father at the airport motel in Kogarah before noon on Tuesday, December twenty-ninth. It appears we've all misjudged his ability to pay. I'm sorry, but there is nothing we can do legally to prevent this.'

Sandra hung up, gasping for breath, groping for understanding, too stunned to react. The phone rang again almost immediately. She grabbed it, hoping it was Meagan saying it was all a terrible joke. It wasn't. Meagan wasn't the kind who made jokes. It was her three o'clock patient, cancelling because her daughter's cat had just been run over. She couldn't understand why Sandra suddenly burst into tears.

Twenty-eight

Rowan was doing his ET impression when Blake burst into his office. 'Margaret told me Tiny rang. How'd the other agency go?'

'Better than expected. Tiny thinks someone's been feeding them information and our documents for some time. Bit of a problem.'

'Oh Jesus.'

'It's not over, Blake, not by a long shot. Truth is, we can't afford to lose the account right now. We need their revenue. They pay a lot of salaries and leases.'

'Did the Suva agency have our latest document?'

'No. Tiny did a good job of keeping them locked away.'

'Did he say what their ads were like?'

'Most of the delegates wouldn't know a good ad if they tripped over it. They just want to see the name of their resort in big type. Clients like these buy confidence, you know that.'

'So when do we pitch?'

'The delegates have yet to sit down and decide whether our pitch is necessary. They could reject the Suva agency or even reject us. Apparently quite a few of the delegates aren't too thrilled by the prospect of more meetings. They feel they're neglecting their own businesses.'

'So where do we stand?'

'Somewhere between success and failure. Somewhere between hiring the new creative team or letting them slip away. Somewhere between reducing our overheads and leasing a new Mac for the studio. In short, I don't bloody know.'

'Anything I can do?'

'Yeah. Next time I look like goofing off on a piece of business, come and kick my arse real hard.'

'I did, remember?'

'Thanks, Blake, you're a real pal.'

Rowan unravelled Glynis's arm from around his neck and claimed time-out for a coffee. He'd planned a quiet night catching up on the shows that ran his ads so he could assess their suitability and effectiveness of his commercials. She regarded a night in front of the TV as an opportunity for extended foreplay. Rowan suggested they take the coffee to bed before they began the final round. He was carrying both cups into the bedroom when the phone rang.

'Let your answering machine get it,' said Glynis. She lay stretched out on the bed, kittenish, impatient to resume engagement. Rowan had visions of Claudine posed similarly, before exploding into jealous rage and storming out of his life, yet he still put the cups down and lifted the handset.

'Rowan? It's Caroline.'

'Hi,' said Rowan. 'How are you?' He immediately wished he'd taken Glynis's advice.

'Is it okay to talk?'

'If you're quick.'

'Have you heard the news?'

'What news?' said Rowan reluctantly. His dismay grew as Caroline told him.

'Is there any chance you could whiz around and see Sandy? She sounds a total mess. Mike's out and I'm stuck here with Jenny.'

'I'll give her a ring.'

'Be better if you called around.'

Rowan looked up at Glynis, wondering how much of the conversation she'd heard, wondering if fate could be so fickle that it indulged in replays. The look on Glynis's face was worryingly similar to Claudine's. 'Unfortunately, not better for everyone.'

'Rowan, I wouldn't ask if it wasn't an emergency.'

'I wouldn't hesitate if I didn't have problems. Tell you what, I'll call her and play it from there. That's the best I can do.'

'Thanks, Rowan,' said Caroline.

Rowan put the receiver down. 'Fuck!'

'What's up?' said Glynis.

'Trouble. I have to call Sandy. I'll use the hall phone.'

'No!' said Glynis sharply, sounding exactly like Claudine. 'Not now! Make her wait. You're not her property any more.'

Not her property any more, thought Rowan. So why did he feel duty-bound? 'Watch TV,' he said.

Glynis angrily grabbed a corner of her sheet and jerked it up over her head, turning her back on him. Rowan closed his eyes and counted to ten. He counted slowly but it didn't help. The rubber band had been wound too tightly.

'Listen, Glynis,' he said icily. 'I've got a lifetime behind me that I can't ignore and can't change. God knows, there are times I wish I could. If you want to spit your dummy out, that's fine. Just do me a favour. Go somewhere else to do it. I come with baggage and either you accept that or you can fuck off. Fuck off now! Do you hear me?'

Glynis lowered the sheet and turned around to face him, shocked and fearful, as if suddenly realising she'd overplayed her hand and put her ambitions at risk. She nodded contritely, was wise enough not to speak.

Rowan closed the door behind him, and in the hall dialled Sandra's number. 'I just heard,' he said as soon as she answered. 'You okay?'

'What do you think! Oh God, Rowan, it's not fair! They told me I had nothing to worry about.'

'I got a message to ring Ryan at the office but other things took precedence. For what it's worth, I think you're worrying unnecessarily. I take both girls off you and I've always brought them back no worse for the experience. I'm sure Junior will survive a week in Fiji and probably forget all about it within a couple of days.'

'Siti isn't you and I can't count on him bringing Junior back.'

'I'll get Ryan to speak to the solicitors in Fiji. There may be some way we can put pressure on them. Junior doesn't turn one till Christmas and that's almost two months away. There's plenty of time to sort something out.'

'I don't want Junior to go anywhere.' Sandra was once more on the verge of tears.

'Trust me,' said Rowan. 'The law says Siti can take Junior anywhere in Fiji he likes, but just remember this. The easiest place to hide is in a big city, the hardest is in a small village. Fiji is just a bundle of small villages. In remote areas the police know everything that's going on, they know everybody by their first names. Siti can run, if he's foolish enough, but he can't hide. So relax and go to bed. I'll talk to you in the morning.'

Rather than go straight back into the bedroom, he wandered through to the kitchen and poured himself the dregs of the red wine. He wished he'd poured himself a scotch instead, because that was what he really needed. Sandra did have reasonable cause for concern, given that nothing else about this case made sense. Despite his assurances, he was beginning to swing around to her point of view. Siti only needed to take Junior to Fiji once, if his intention was to abscond with him. Maybe Siti wanted a son as badly as he did, badly enough to steal one. In the absence of any other explanation, the circumstances seemed to point that way. But if so, why had he turned his back on Junior in the lift? Why hadn't he seized the opportunity to at least touch his son? Nothing made sense and thinking about it only made his head ache. He groaned aloud. It wasn't his problem. Why did people keep insisting it was?

'Are you coming back to bed?'

Rowan started. Incredibly, he'd forgotten all about Glynis

and his other duties. 'Eventually,' he called back. He heard a rustle of sheets and soft footsteps in the hallway. Glynis wandered naked into the kitchen, carrying his coffee. 'It's gone cold. I'll just put it in the microwave for you.'

'Thanks.'

She selected thirty seconds and hit start, turned and hoisted herself up onto the edge of the kitchen bench in front of him, her legs slightly apart. Rowan sighed. Glynis wasn't the sort of girl who took eventually for an answer.

Sandra always read the newspapers and watched the evening news on TV. Sometimes during the day she turned her radio on for patients to listen to while they received ice, heat or mechanical treatment. Whenever she listened to the hourly news updates, her brain simply filtered out items that had no relevance to her, among them stories relating to the Family Court. Until R. Satyarnand & Sons had sent their letter, Sandra had never thought that the Family Court would figure in her life. Now she was stunned by the number of times it was mentioned in the news.

One woman had been shot and another stabbed to death by their estranged husbands, right outside the Family Court. In America, a woman was reunited with her grown-up daughter who'd been abducted by her ex-husband some twenty years earlier. News of another tragedy nearly brought her to tears. In South Australia a man had collected his four youngsters from his ex-wife and driven off into the bush. They were supposed to be going on a picnic for the day. The man had connected a rubber hose to his car's exhaust pipe and gassed himself and all four children in an apparent murder-suicide. The radio suggested it was another custody battle that had ended in tragedy, and listed five similar cases that had occurred over the previous two years.

An eminent judge called for a complete overhaul of the family law courts, claiming that there was nothing to prevent similar tragedies happening. Sandra heard his warning with horror. This was the same court that had instructed her to hand over her son to a stranger who was going to take him out of the country. She couldn't help thinking of Marion and the child her mother had lost forever, the brother she'd never known and would never know. She thought of Clive and the delight he took in Junior's visits, as if trying to understand and make up for what had been denied him so many years earlier.

Sandra knew with absolute certainty that she was right to hang onto Junior and knew with equal certainty that she could not allow history to repeat. She would not give her son away to anyone, not for a minute, not for a day, not ever. But whenever she rang Ryan or Rowan to insist that they do something, they simply reminded her of the judge's decision and her lack of options. As the days passed, her apprehension did not diminish but increased. Every day brought her nearer to Junior's first birthday.

Twenty-nine

Rowan had just come from looking at the first cut of the agency's new commercial for Cola Frisks, in which a guy puts on a virtual reality headset and thinks he's John Travolta dancing with Olivia Newton-John. As far as he's concerned, he's right there in the movie. As far as everyone else in the entertainment centre is concerned, there's a dork making a total prat of himself mincing up and down the floor. Yet the film was shot sympathetically and had everyone laughing, even the clients. It wasn't a put-down of a kid who couldn't dance, it was just that he was lost in his fantasy world. Half of the humour came from the reactions of the people watching.

Margaret was waiting to intercept him as he strode towards his office. 'Phone Caroline,' she said. 'It's the most urgent. Your other messages are on your pad. How was the commercial?'

'Fantastic.'

'When can I see it?'

'Just go into the boardroom and demand they play it again. The client's still there talking to Blake, but he won't mind. Clients like to see people excited over their commercials.'

'Me too?' asked Barth.

'Hell, take the whole bloody agency,' said Rowan. 'Give everyone a laugh.' He carried on into his office. Through the glass partitions he could see secretaries abandoning their posts and heading for the boardroom, where he knew they'd be joined by people from the studio and accounts. He felt a surge of pride as he reached for the phone. Something was functioning as it should. Billings had more than doubled in less than two years yet everybody still got excited about what they did and wanted to be involved. Only the Fiji Tourist Board cast a shadow over his business. The phone rang as his hand closed around the handset.

'Hello?'

'Mr Nadruku from Fiji,' announced the receptionist.

'Hello, Tiny?'

'Hello, Rowan. Are you sitting down?'

'Should I?' The elation Rowan had been feeling began to dissipate.

'I think so.'

'Okay, I'm sitting. What's up?'

'I'm afraid you're going to have to come up with something special for the re-pitch.'

'Why? What's happened?' Rowan could hear laughter coming from the boardroom. He smiled bitterly. It was always the same story. One step forward, one step back.

'The majority of delegates want you retained but the opposition have become more vocal and demanding. A government minister has joined the fray by declaring that Fijian tourism should be promoted by a Fijian agency. The opposition is demanding I release your last report to them.'

'Don't do that, for Christ's sake.'

'I may not have the choice. It's theirs. It belongs to them. The delegates have paid for it and are entitled to it. At the end of the day, I am employed by them.'

Rowan took a deep breath and put himself in Tiny's place. He realised he had no choice but to concede. 'Okay, Tiny, let them have it. I'm the fool who put the account in jeopardy in the first place and I'd hate to see you get fired over it.' Rowan could almost hear the big man's relief over the phone. 'Let them have it, Tiny. And when I next see the delegates, God as my witness, I'm going to let them have it, too. Right between their eyes.'

'I'll be in your corner, Rowan.'

'I'd never doubt that. Go and appease the pricks. Those arseholes are kidding themselves if they think they can roll me so easily. How long have we got?'

'Two weeks.'

'We'll be there.' Rowan hung up and stared at the phone. Tiny had asked for something special and he'd promised him he'd dish it up to the opposition. Dish what up? How? And how was Tiny going to gather all the delegates together with Christmas right on top of them? He wished Blake had finished with Lavalle so that they could put their heads together, thought briefly about calling him out of the meeting, then decided to be patient. Blake had earned his moment of glory. In the weeks ahead there'd be little peace for either of them. He decided to fill in the time until Blake was free by ringing Caroline.

'Hello, Caro?'

'Rowan, thanks for calling back.'

'What's the problem?'

'I have to ask a big favour. Promise you won't snap my head off?'

'I'm having a bad day, Caro. Tell me you're not going to make it worse.'

'I was thinking more about spoiling your weekend.'

Rowan sighed. 'What does Sandy want this time?'

'It's not Sandy, it's me. We're going up the coast on Friday for the weekend and want to take Sandy with us, to give her a break. Try to take her mind off things. Problem is, we're taking Jenny and I'm not sure the people we're staying with could cope with two small children.'

'You want me to take Junior, is that it?'

'The way Sandy is right now, you're the only person she'd trust. She's accepted she needs a break to keep her sanity but won't leave Junior with anyone but you.'

'How is she?'

'I'm disappointed that you have to ask. She's a bloody mess. That's why we want to take her with us. Have the solicitors in Fiji responded at all to Ryan Scott's letter?'

'No. And they didn't respond to the follow-up, either. I thought about hiring a private detective to keep an eye on

Junior while he's in Fiji but Ryan won't have a bar of it.'

'Why not?'

'Because, according to my friend on Coralhaven, Siti has applied for leave over Christmas and New Year and he's taking his family back to his village. His village is up in the hills on the north coast. Anyone following them would stick out like the proverbials. Satyarnand & Sons have shown themselves to be sharp operators. They would seize on that as being against the spirit of the specific issues order and God only knows where that could end up.'

'Poor Sandy,' said Caroline with feeling. 'Have you told her?'

'She knows.'

'No wonder she's depressed. Now, what about the weekend?'

'Now I'm depressed,' said Rowan.

'I wouldn't ask if it wasn't important.'

'Here we go again,' said Rowan reluctantly.

'You'll do it?'

'You don't leave me a lot of choice.'

'Thanks, Rowan. It'll do Sandy the world of good.'

'I'm glad someone's coming out in front. I'll move back to the house for the weekend.'

'Oops,' said Caroline. 'I'm not sure how Sandy would feel about having Glynis sleep in her bed. She's got a thing about Glynis.'

'Oh Jesus!'

'Sorry.'

'Maybe one day you and Sandy will wake up and discover

I'm entitled to a life as well. Ah, stuff it! I guess I can always give Glynis the weekend off.'

'The way I hear it, you'd be the one having the weekend off.'

'Don't push it, Caro.'

Caroline laughed. 'You know Mike's jealous as all hell, don't you? If you ever get tired of being you, he'll step into your shoes. Will you tell Sandy or will I?'

'I'll leave it to you. I dare say she'll call me afterwards to make final arrangements.' Rowan hung up, wondering how Glynis would react to being relegated to the benches. Probably not well, but she had two days to get used to the idea. Two days of petulance and frosty looks. At least Claudine had moved back to her place when she was pissed off, instead of hanging around and making his life miserable as well.

'There are two halves to the Tourist Board account,' said Rowan. 'One half is about impressing the people we're trying to entice to Fiji, the paying prospect, and the other half is impressing the delegates.'

'What do you propose doing?' asked Blake.

'Tiny said we have to come up with something special, and by that he means whistles and bells. Hell, they've got the document and that's pretty special.'

'Was special. Handing the document over has kind of levelled the playing field.'

'Exactly. Tell me, Blake, in your experience what's the one thing that gets a diverse client singing the same tune?'

'Oh God, no. Not a jingle!'

'Jingle? What do you think I am? I'm talking about a symphony of sound and sentiment. Something grand and soaring. Something anthemic that'll tap into all this Fijian nationalism and pride. Something that'd bring a tear to a glass eye. Probably cost us twenty to thirty grand to do it properly and there's no point doing it any other way.'

'Still sounds like a jingle to me.'

'Just imagine if we could get somebody to give us a contemporary equivalent of "Time For A Cool Change". Maybe drag Glenn Shorrock out of retirement. He spends a lot of time in Fiji, maybe he'd be sympathetic.'

'Rowan . . .'

'What?'

'Don't you think we should leave something to the creative department?'

For the next two days Rowan spent most of his time working late as he tried to reduce the tower of paper in his in-tray. This only pissed Glynis off more. He left for the gym each morning before she woke and returned long after whatever she'd reheated for dinner had congealed on its plate. He went to bed without eating and dessert was never in the offering. He began to look forward to his weekend back home.

Thirty

Junior woke around one o'clock in the morning, just as Rowan was heading to bed. Rowan changed his nappy, washed and powdered him, but still Junior grizzled and wouldn't go back into his cot.

'Your mum's gone, mate, so you're just going to have to put up with me.' Rowan carried Junior through to the lounge, flicked the TV back on and settled into a corner of the sofa. Junior took his cue from Rowan and nestled into the crook of his arm, resting his head on Rowan's shoulder and straddling his chest with one arm.

'Hope you like tennis,' said Rowan. Channel Seven was showing an indoor tournament, a preliminary to the Australian Open. 'The bloke in the black shorts is Todd Woodbridge, an Aussie. The other one's a Frog. Just so's you know, we hate the French. If you want to cheer for the Frog, you're going to have to find your own sofa.'

Junior took it all in. Todd Woodbridge executed a perfect

drop volley to break service.

'Uh!' said Junior.

'Damn right, uh!' said Rowan. 'You don't have to be a big, boofy bloke to win at tennis. It's not just a power game. Craft and guile have their place, too.' Junior took that in as well. Todd Woodbridge began to serve at 5–3.

Rowan awoke as Todd Woodbridge took the match in three sets. At first he couldn't work out where he was, what he was doing or why he couldn't move his right arm. It felt trapped under a dead weight and buzzed with pins and needles. When he realised the weight was Junior, he couldn't prevent a slow smile from spreading across his face. How many times had he woken in front of the TV in the wee hours of morning with an unconscious Sarah or Rocky in his arms? The whole thing had the warm, familiar feel of better times, of times past, when his home life had both content and substance. He rose as gently as he could, tip-toed back to Junior's bedroom and tucked him up in his cot. Junior didn't stir. He tip-toed into Sarah and Rochelle's room and found they'd both kicked off their blanket and sheet. Rowan covered them and kissed each of them lightly on the forehead. He tip-toed back into the hall and down to his bedroom where he climbed immediately into bed.

As he waited for sleep, he listened to the familiar creaking of the house that was once his home and the surrounding night noises. He knew that if he listened really carefully he might hear the gentle plop of mullet jumping in the bay below. The sounds didn't soothe so much as make him feel he'd walked out on something precious.

The following day he bundled the kids into the car and drove to the Flower Drum for yum cha. The Flower Drum didn't like taking bookings for Saturday yum cha because it was their biggest day, when Chinese from all over Sydney flocked into the city for their tasty little dishes. But the restaurant obliged because they liked the idea of losing Rowan's custom even less. The girls had mumbled about McDonald's but Rowan wanted the anonymity of the hectic, noisy, bustling Chinese restaurant where nobody would notice – or even care – that one of his kids was a ring-in. He couldn't think of a better place to hide the cuckoo in his nest. They put Junior in a highchair, which gave him a clear view of the goings on. He loved the noise and the shouting waiters, the women hawking dishes from trolleys.

'Wo!' shouted Junior, pointing at the gai lan.

'Bah!' he shouted to the dumplings.

'Wey!' he yelled to the prawns in rice paper.

Every time he called out, the girls broke into hysterics. Sarah gave him a chopstick, which he waved with the elan of a conductor, as if orchestrating the activities. Waiters and waitresses tousled his hair, people at surrounding tables turned to watch the performance, nodding and smiling. Rowan gave up trying to quieten Junior. If he'd stuck a flashing blue police light on Junior's head, he wouldn't have attracted more attention.

'Wo! Bah! Wey!' shouted Junior.

'He's speaking Chinese,' said Sarah.

'Just concentrate on your food,' snapped Rowan. But he was wasting his breath.

They went home via the recording studio so Rowan could hear a rough of the proposed Tourist Board sound track. What the creative team played him was nothing like Little River Band but sounded fantastic nonetheless. His nipples went hard and the hair on the back of his head stood on end. Even more importantly, the melody stuck on just one hearing. 'Bloody hell,' he said. 'How smart was I, hiring you? It wouldn't surprise me if the Fijians made this their national anthem.'

Sunday dawned hot and sticky. The girls wanted to go down to Balmoral Beach but he drove them around to Mike and Caroline's instead – he didn't think they'd mind if he used their pool in their absence. He took an esky filled with cold drinks, a large combo pack of crisps, and promised ice-creams on the way home. His strategy was to convince the girls they'd have a better time with a swimming pool all to themselves. The reality was that he couldn't face the crowds at the beach after the embarrassment at the restaurant.

Later, when they stopped for ice-creams, the girls conned Rowan into buying a Christmas tree. They spent all afternoon and evening decorating it, only breaking to make the run to McDonald's for takeaways. It reminded Rowan of the Christmas Eves when he and Sandra used to sit on their bed wrapping presents to put under the tree, a pleasure which this year would be denied him. He could no longer look at Junior and blame him – he was long past feeling any resentment towards him. It was hard to hate a kid whose idea of bliss was to perch on Rowan's knee and give him hugs for no better reason than because he felt like it. Nevertheless, Junior was the cause of the disruption in his life. When he remembered how he'd lain awake listening for the plop of the mullet jumping, he couldn't help speculating on whether things would work out for the best if Siti did abscond with Junior. Maybe he could pick up where he'd left off twelve months earlier.

'Ready,' said Sarah. 'Everybody watch.'

Junior seemed to sense something momentous was about to occur and shuffled upright on Rowan's knee. Sarah turned on the Christmas-tree lights.

'Ayyy!' said Junior. He turned around to Rowan, eyes as big as saucers, and pointed to the tree. 'Uhhh!' he said. It was the most stupendous and marvellous thing he'd ever seen and he wanted to make sure Rowan didn't miss it.

'Way to go,' said Rowan. He hugged Junior automatically.

Mike and Caroline dropped Sandra off shortly after eleven, long after the kids had collapsed into their beds. She had to wake Rowan, who'd fallen asleep on the sofa.

'Hi,' he said sleepily.

'I see the girls talked you into buying a Christmas tree,' she said. 'Didn't they tell you I'd decided to make do with a small artificial tree that I could keep on the table out of Junior's reach?'

'No,' said Rowan. 'Does it really matter?'

'I don't suppose so. I'll make a barricade.'

'They had fun doing it.'

'I bet,' said Sandra.

'Did you have a good time?'

'Yes, and much needed. I really appreciate what you did.'

'No trouble.' Rowan stretched and yawned. 'I'd better head off.'

'You can stay here if you like.'

'No, I'd better get my things.'

'Before you go, what about Christmas?'

'What about Christmas?'

'Are you coming here Christmas Day? The girls will be upset if you don't.'

'I haven't thought about it.'

'Could you ring me tomorrow?'

'Sure.'

'Okay.' Sandra noticed that Rowan still hadn't moved towards the door. 'Thanks again.'

'Right, see you,' said Rowan. 'Oh, you better check Junior's nappy. We spent half the day in Caroline's pool. He tried to drink the contents.'

'Okay.' Sandra followed him as he finally headed to the door.

'I see he's walking now,' said Rowan.

'Yeah. Slow to crawl, quick to walk.'

'Bye,' said Rowan.

'Bye,' said Sandra.

Rowan wandered down the pathway to the drive and climbed into his car. When he looked back, Sandra was still framed in the doorway. He waved, she waved back. He reversed down the drive and swung around so that his car faced home. He had the damnedest feeling he was heading the wrong way.

'Hi!' Glynis opened the front door for him before he had a chance to insert his key in the lock. She was half asleep, and naked but for a sheer nightie that made no concession at all to modesty. Rowan had expected to arrive home to an empty house and couldn't for the life of him imagine what Glynis was doing there. She propped, waiting to be kissed, so he kissed her. She draped her arms around his neck and pressed herself against him. Clearly she had plans for the evening that Sandra's late arrival home had only delayed.

'I see you've been busy,' said Rowan.

'I spent all afternoon decorating it,' Glynis said proudly. 'I brought the lights from my flat. Like it?'

'Yeah,' said Rowan. 'The girls just spent the afternoon decorating one at home.'

Glynis flinched. 'I thought this was your home.'

'Spare me,' said Rowan wearily.

Glynis decided to let the matter drop. 'Coffee?'

'No thanks,' said Rowan. 'All I want is bed.'

'Good idea,' said Glynis.

Rowan had the sinking feeling it wasn't.

Because of his preoccupation with the Fiji pitch, Rowan forgot to ring Sandra until Wednesday, when Glynis prompted him. She rang him on his private line.

'What do you want to do Christmas Day?' Glynis asked. 'Do you want me to book a restaurant or order some seafood? Do you want me to get a ham?'

Rowan slumped. Why hadn't he pre-empted her? Why hadn't he realised she'd naturally assume they'd be spending

Christmas Day together? He tried to think of some way of softening the blow but knew there was nothing he could say. 'I'm spending Christmas Day at home,' he said. 'With the girls.'

The line went silent. 'Hello?' he said eventually. 'Still there?'

'What about me?' said Glynis.

'I don't know,' said Rowan. More silence followed.

'Are we still going to the film studio party tonight?'

'Sure,' said Rowan.

'We can discuss it then,' said Glynis, and hung up.

'Fuck!' said Rowan. Margaret overheard but ignored him. He dialled Sandra's number. 'Can you talk?' he asked.

'I'm in the middle of treating someone,' she said. 'I'll call you back when I'm free.' She hung up.

'Fuck!' said Rowan, this time louder. Margaret stood, picked up her coffee cup and began to walk away towards the kitchen.

'Margaret!' he bellowed. She ignored him. He rose from his chair and ran to the door. 'Please,' he added. She stopped and turned back, stony-faced.

'You called?' she said.

Rowan became aware of all the eyes watching him, secretaries and passers-by, waiting to see what happened. Barth shook his head in admonition. 'Come into my office,' said Rowan. 'Please.' She followed him and sat down opposite him.

'My apologies,' said Rowan. 'These are trying times and I'm going to lose it occasionally. When I do, could you please ignore me? Just block your ears or something. The thing is, I get enough aggravation from other women in my life. I don't want to get it from you as well. If I make you cranky, do me a favour, just be up-front and tell me.'

'I've told you,' said Margaret. 'And I've told you what the cure is. You've just got to unblock your ears and hear me. Now, can I get you a coffee?'

'Why not?' said Rowan helplessly. He turned back to his work, signed a few letters and a pile of client Christmas cards, smiled ingratiatingly when Margaret returned with his coffee. The phone rang, Sandra returning his call.

'Hi,' he said, doing his best to make his voice upbeat. 'Sorry I didn't ring earlier. I forgot. But count me in for Christmas Day.'

'Oh Rowan,' said Sandra. 'I've just realised it's less than two weeks away. Just thirteen days.'

'Nine days,' said Rowan. 'Christmas Day is Saturday week, nine days away.'

'That bastard takes Junior away from me in thirteen days. You have to do something!'

'There's nothing more I can do,' said Rowan quietly. 'There's nothing anyone can do.'

'There must be!' said Sandra.

'What does Ryan say?'

'Same as you. He's useless!'

'Sandy, there's nothing anyone can do. You just have to accept that. Siti will bring Junior back. He has no choice. Can you imagine how our government would climb into the Fijian government after the fuss they made earlier? If Siti tries anything, don't you think the Fijian government would crack down on him?'

Sandra listened but all she could think about was the murder-suicide of the father and four kids in South Australia; the mother in America who spent twenty years tracking down her daughter. 'Would you let a stranger take him away if he was your son?' she said accusingly.

'If he was my son, nobody would be asking the question.'

Sandra began to sob.

'For Christ's sake, Sandy,' said Rowan angrily. 'Nothing is going to happen. Junior's just going to have a week in Fiji with his dad. That's it.'

'Sometimes I hate you,' said Sandra bitterly.

'So you keep saying. See you Christmas Day.' Rowan hung up and dialled Caroline.

'Hello, Caro?'

'Hi Rowan. What's up?'

'I have to go to Fiji on business for a couple of days. Can you keep an eye on Sandy?'

'You bet.'

'Are you having Christmas Day with us?'

'Absolutely,' said Caroline.

'Great. I'll see you there.'

'Don't forget my present,' said Caroline. 'Something tight in cling wrap.'

'What?'

'Forget it.'

'Hey, Caro?'

'What?'

'When you take Jenny out, what do you do when people stare at you?'

'I'm not aware that people stare at us.'

'You must be.'

'No, not unless Jenny starts kicking up a fuss or something. Why?'

'What about when you and Mike are out together with her? What do people think then?'

'What do they think? They think we've adopted a baby girl from Korea. What else would they think? There's no novelty any more in inter-country adoptions. You can walk through Mosman any day of the week and see parents with kids from Colombia, Sri Lanka, Korea, Taiwan and God only knows where else. What are you getting at?'

'Nothing,' said Rowan. 'See you at Christmas.'

'I thought we'd at least spend Christmas Day together,' said Glynis. She'd waited until they were in his car and heading home from the party before raising the issue. Rowan had made it through the night on just three beers. Glynis had added orange juice to her champagne but still managed to drink more than half a dozen.

'Christmas is family time,' said Rowan. 'That's all there is to it. You spend Christmas with family whether you like it or not.'

'My family lives way out in Dubbo.'

'So surprise them. Go home to Dubbo.'

'Stuff you! I will.' Glynis started crying.

'Bloody hell!' said Rowan, which only made Glynis cry harder.

Rowan sat in his office with Margaret, trying to reschedule his week's appointments and meetings around his trip to Fiji. He'd rung Tiny days earlier to change the conference centre to one with a better sound system. The track had cost thirty grand of his agency's money and he wanted the delegates to hear every note.

When his direct phone rang he rolled his eyes, expecting another harangue from Sandra or tears from Glynis. Tiny's voice caught him by surprise.

'What's up, Tiny?' said Rowan.

'How are you going with your big surprise for me?'

'It's finished. It's wonderful. And I've told you that already.'

'Okay. Now ask me how I'm going with my big surprise for you.'

'What surprise?'

'The meeting has been called off.'

'You're kidding!'

'Once I'd copied and mailed out your report, it quickly became apparent to most delegates that your agency has far more depth than the Suva agency. It confirmed what they already knew. The phones have been running hot, Rowan, with various parties trying to get unanimity. As of this morning we have it. Congratulations on your reappointment.'

'We've won?'

'You've won.'

'You mean I don't get to fly over and play my thirty thousand dollar anthem? Fuck you! I'm still coming.'

'Send it to me for Christmas, Rowan.' Tiny started laughing. 'You owe me a present.'

Margaret rose and planted a kiss on Rowan's cheek. Her smile was exceeded only by his.

Thirty-one

The phone awoke Rowan at seven on Christmas morning. He knew immediately who was ringing and fought back his natural instincts to answer it. After five rings his answering machine intercepted the call. He relaxed. The phone rang again. Glynis was nothing if not persistent. Rowan rose wearily and locked himself in the toilet, realising that if he spoke to her, there was a danger she'd want commitments he had no desire to give, and he'd end up suggesting she find someone else. Glynis didn't deserve to hear that on Christmas Day and certainly not over the phone.

He turned his car into Sandra's driveway just before nine on a perfect Christmas morning. A blue sky towered above him, dry and clear. Middle Harbour had shaken off the algal bloom that had turned it garish green, and it sparkled in the early light. Nature was doing its best to lighten his load but Rowan harboured no illusions about the ordeal ahead of him. He'd arrived early, not just because the girls would be impatient for their presents but as a gesture of support. Sarah and Rochelle raced out to meet him, wearing new swimming costumes and sandals, totally committed to the spirit of Christmas. Rowan envied them. Sandra met him in the hallway with a kiss.

'Merry Christmas,' said Rowan. 'You look terrific,' he added, even though she didn't. Sandra had made a special effort but her concern for Junior had marked her indelibly. Rowan had never seen her so drawn or tense. 'Enjoy today,' he said gently. 'We'll take care of tomorrow as it happens.' Sandra smiled but her smile was thin-lipped. Rowan made a mental note to avoid all mention of the forthcoming days.

'I see you remembered the presents,' she said.

'I got the girls exactly what you said. I'd better let them open them so I've got time to put up Sarah's netball hoop before Mike and Caro arrive. Where's Junior?'

'He's discovered wrapping paper. Follow me.' They wandered into the lounge where Junior sat surrounded by wrapping paper, fascinated by the bright colours and intrigued by the rustling it made.

'Can we open our presents, Daddy?' begged Sarah.

'Can we?' asked Rochelle.

'Go ahead,' said Rowan. 'And while you're at it, you might pass that big one to your mother.'

'For me?' Sandra smiled instinctively and Rowan caught a glimpse of her normal self.

'Can't have a new car every year,' said Rowan. 'I rang Caro and she suggested I got this. It's not what I would have chosen.'

Sandra unwrapped her present with the eagerness of a child. 'A rice steamer,' she said. 'Not like you at all but I've wanted one for ages. Thank you.' She kissed Rowan again.

'I would have gone for the frilly lingerie myself,' said Rowan. 'There's some stuff for Junior, too. Maybe you should throw away the presents and just give him the paper.'

'You brought a present for Junior?'

'There are some things a boy should have.'

'Girls,' said Sandra eagerly. 'Help Junior with his presents.'

Sarah and Rochelle put aside their treasures to help Junior. 'Best part of Christmas,' said Rowan. 'Watching the kids open presents.'

'Look,' said Sarah. 'A cricket set.' She held up a miniature bat and stumps and a soft, furry ball.

'He's too young for that,' said Sandra, laughing.

'Never too young,' said Rowan.

'And a football,' said Rochelle.

'God, you're an optimist,' said Sandra.

'If he can walk, he can kick,' said Rowan defensively.

'What's this?' said Sarah.

'What's it look like?' said Rowan.

'A steering wheel.'

'And?'

'All the stuff you get in cars.'

'It's a play bus console, actually,' said Rowan.

'It's fabulous,' said Sandra. 'Is it Fisher Price?'

'I don't know. I saw it and couldn't resist it. It's got a steering wheel, horn, flashing lights, switches, dials, and a voice that says "mind the step". Everything a boy could want. It's for his birthday.'

'His birthday?' Sandra's eyes widened. 'You bought him this for his birthday?' She looked at him in wonder and turned to the girls. 'Let Junior play with it.'

Junior stopped scrunching the wrapping paper and stared at his new toy with genuine awe, too overwhelmed to touch it. Rowan crouched down alongside him, turned the steering wheel for him and tooted the horn. Junior clapped his hands together. When Rowan flashed the lights, Junior couldn't take his eyes off them.

'Here you go,' said Rowan. 'You do it.'

But Junior still didn't dare touch it. Just sitting in front of it, knowing it existed, was enough for the time being.

'I never thought his birth was something you'd want to commemorate,' said Sandra cautiously.

Rowan stood and shifted uncomfortably. 'I have always sympathised with people whose birthday falls on Christmas Day. Look at him. First wrapping paper, now his very own steering wheel. Boy's having a big day.' He smiled. Sandra had brightened up two hundred per cent since he'd arrived. Now he just had to keep her going all day. 'How about you make me coffee?' he said.

'Okay. You stay here and open your presents.'

The girls gave him new photos of themselves, set in matching silver frames, to accompany the pictures he already had on his desk at the office. Sandra gave him new board-shorts, two short-sleeved Mambo shirts, three pairs of socks and three pairs of Calvin Klein undershorts. Rowan had to smile. Sandra couldn't stop thinking like his wife, even when she wasn't.

Marion and Clive arrived just as Rowan finally succeeded in fixing the netball hoop to the back of the garage. They made a rather pointed fuss over how pleased they were to see him. Mike and Caroline arrived with Jenny half an hour later. Rowan handed over the presents he'd brought and warned them not to open them in front of the kids.

'Come into the bedroom,' said Sandra. She was as eager as Mike and Caroline to see what he'd given them. Rowan held his breath. If he'd calculated correctly, his gifts would keep the company bubbling all day. He hoped Sandra wasn't too strung out to see the funny side. He poured himself a whisky and waited. Suddenly gales of laughter burst from the bedroom, followed by a second round.

'You're evil!' said Caroline, as she burst out of the bedroom. She was laughing so much she had tears in her eyes. Rowan had given her a big, black vibrator in the shape of a penis and taped it to two rockmelons in cling wrap. She threw her arms around his neck and kissed him. 'Every time I use it, I'll think of you,' she said.

'Don't sell me short,' said Rowan.

'You're a total bastard,' said Mike. 'You don't have a conscience.'

Rowan had given him a blow-up sex doll with a little handmade card that introduced her as Glynis. 'It's what you both wanted,' he said innocently.

'I don't know how you had the nerve to buy them,' said Sandra.

'Nothing to it,' said Rowan. 'I sent Barth.'

Marion and Clive wandered over to make their contribution. 'Look what he gave us,' said Clive.

'What is it?' said Sandra.

'A packet of Viagra for Clive and naughty knickers for me,' said Marion. 'Just this once I think I would have been grateful for a scarf.'

Christmas Day passed without drama, feeding off the momentum generated by Rowan's presents. Occasionally he or Caroline spotted Sandra looking wistfully at Junior and engineered a diversion. Sandra never stayed down for long. She played her part bravely, but it was clear to everyone that her fears hadn't gone away. She'd just put them on hold.

Sandra awoke on Boxing Day with a sense of dread that nothing would dispel. She could hear Junior driving his bus console in the girls' room, and hear their muffled laughter. It only made her heartache worse. She stayed in bed, not to sleep, for there was no possibility of that, but to shorten a day that promised to be too long. There was no one to help her get through it. Rowan was going sailing with Blake, to watch the start of the Sydney to Hobart yacht race. Mike and Caroline had other commitments, as did Marion and Clive. What was she going to do? she wondered. How would she cope? Treat it as a normal day, make breakfast as normal, take Junior and the girls to the beach, laugh and have fun just like normal?

How could she be normal, when in just two and a half days' time she had to hand Junior over to a man she didn't trust? Her fears settled on her like a hangover and she began to weep into her pillow. How was little Jenny's mother in Korea feeling? she wondered. Was she enjoying Christmas? Or was she pining for her lost daughter?

Eventually she dragged herself out of bed to make breakfast. Scrambled eggs for Junior and Rochelle, toast and Vegemite for Sarah, who'd decided all of a sudden that she didn't like eggs, and toast and honey for herself. Junior clattered into the kitchen, dragging his bus console behind him.

'Ugh!' he said. 'Ahhh.' He held his arms out.

Sandra picked him up and hugged him as tightly as she could. Sarah followed Junior into the kitchen, tripped on the toy and crashed to the floor.

'For goodness' sake, Sarah, watch where you're going!' Sandra glared down at her prostrate daughter. Sarah burst into tears.

'Oh darling, I'm sorry!'

'It wasn't my fault,' sobbed Sarah.

'I know.' Sandra knelt down alongside her. 'I shouldn't have shouted.'

Sarah put her arms around Sandra and Junior and buried her face to hide her tears.

'You okay?' asked Sandra. 'Didn't bump your head?'

'No,' said Sarah. She paused momentarily, then lifted her head up so she could look at her mother. 'When does the man come to take Junior away?' she asked.

'Tuesday. The day after tomorrow.'

Sarah bit her lip and hugged her mother more tightly. 'He will bring him back, won't he, Mummy?'

'Of course,' said Sandra. 'Of course he will.' It suddenly

dawned on her that her assurances sounded like Rowan's, and that he had no more valid reason to give reassurance than she had. In the dark hours of night, as she'd lain awake worrying, Rowan's assurances were all she'd had to cling to. She'd always relied on him, trusted him. He was the rock that stood firm against all adversity, his was the anger that defied all challenges. It shook her to her boots to think she'd been clinging to nothing. She held on to Junior and Sarah fiercely.

'Nothing has changed,' said Rowan evenly. 'The Fijian government would be seriously embarrassed if Siti tries to run off with Junior. Every policeman would be on the case. At worst, at very worst, Junior would arrive home a day late.' He smiled, did everything he could to trivialise Sandra's fears, but she remained unconvinced.

When Sandra had come back from the beach, she'd found Rowan sitting on the front doorstep, not entirely sober from seeing off the Sydney-to-Hobart fleet. He'd offered to barbecue some steak and sausages Sandra had in the fridge and she'd accepted. They'd managed not to discuss Junior until later that night, when the girls had gone to bed.

'You can't be sure,' said Sandra. 'Nobody can be.'

'Life's full of uncertainties,' said Rowan amiably. 'However, in degrees of certainty, I'd say Junior's return ranks up there with death and taxation.'

'What do you mean?' said Sandra.

'Death and taxation are the only two certainties in this world,' said Rowan. 'Now, how about we change the subject?'

'That's all this is to you, a subject for conversation?'

'Now you're being silly.'

'You're going to have to do something, Rowan. Everything you say sounds reasonable, except it flies in the face of everything we know. Once Siti gets Junior over to Fiji, he's going to keep him there. Nothing else fits!'

'We've been over this a thousand times,' said Rowan evenly. He finished off the wine in his glass.

Sandra's lips retreated to thin red lines and she turned away from him.

'Take a couple of Mogadons,' said Rowan. 'Things will look better after a good night's sleep.'

'I wish you'd listen to me,' said Sandra fiercely. 'Does it occur to you that just once, just this once, I might be right and you might be wrong?'

'I'm going to get your Mogadons now,' said Rowan, rising from his chair.

'Sure! Take two Mogadons and when I wake up, everything will be better. But it won't be better, will it, Rowan? It won't be better. Why won't you listen to me?'

'Sandy, the whole damn street is listening to you.' Rowan tried to suppress a yawn. 'I assume you still keep them in the bathroom cupboard?'

Sandra turned her back on him, in no way appeased but surrendering to the inevitable. Mogadons had replaced Milo as her bedtime staple.

'I'm staying here until you've taken them,' said Rowan.

When Rowan rang Sandra the following morning, Caroline answered the phone.

'Where's Sandra?' he asked.

'Seeing the girls off. The mother of one of Sarah's girlfriends is taking them both out on a boat for the day. Up in Pittwater. Seems Sandra has served her penance.'

'How is she?'

'Don't ask. I'm helping her pack Junior's bags. She's packed a whole shop.'

'What do you mean?'

'Well, she's worried about the drinking water so she's packed some chlorine water-purifying tablets. She's worried about what they'll give him to eat so she's packed enough cans of baby food to last until next Christmas. She's worried about the milk so she's packed two cans of formula. Add in the Lomotil in case he gets diarrhoea, the Baby Panadol in case he gets a headache or runs a temperature, his cough medicine, rash cream, sunscreen, blockout, aftersun, baby oil and enough nappies for ten kids. That's just one bag. The other's full of clothes and his favourite treats. I think Uncle Toby's have just met their sales target for next year.'

'Sounds like you have everything under control,' said Rowan.

'Everything except Sandra. She's made me check every item off against her list three times now.'

'Tears?'

'I think she's holding off until the girls have gone. It's the uncertainty, Rowan, the not knowing what's going to happen. I'd be the same.'

'Ring me if there are any problems. I'm at the office.'

'Okay,' said Caroline. 'I'll tell her you called.'

As soon as Rowan hung up, Margaret came into his office and handed him a note. Glynis had rung again from Dubbo and wanted him to ring back. He picked up his phone and checked his watch.

'Margaret, I'd be grateful if you could find some reason to interrupt me in exactly ten minutes. If I start rolling my eyes, make it five.'

'My pleasure,' said Margaret.

Caroline rang around six in the evening. 'Everything Sandy said is true. You are a workaholic.'

'We've two teams working through the break on new campaigns. Blake flew out to the States this morning to go skiing in Colorado. Balance left to do the work, yours truly. Now what can I do for you?'

'I've made Sandy lie down for a while. She's really upset. Every time she looks at Junior, which is most of the time, she bursts into tears.'

'What can I do?' asked Rowan.

'I'm just ringing to say I've decided to spend the night here and drive her to the Airport Motel tomorrow.'

'What would Sandy do without you?'

'It may not be enough.'

'What do you mean?' said Rowan.

'It's you she needs, Rowan. I'm worried about her now. I can't imagine how she'll be while Junior's away.'

'Maybe I should take the girls off her hands.'

'God, don't do that! They're all she's got to hang onto. Thing is, I can't stay here all week.'

420

'Don't say it, Caro.'

'You could have Junior's room.'

'Gee, thanks.'

'If you won't do it for Sandy, do it for the girls. Sarah keeps bursting into tears for no apparent reason, and Rocky's due to come out in sympathy any moment. Tell me, Rowan, what's so great about your life right now that you can't put yourself out for just one week? What's so precious about it? What have you got to lose? Tell me, because whatever it is, I can't see it.'

'Caro, quit while you're ahead.'

'No! You could have prevented all this, you know?'

'How, for Christ's sake?'

'You could have done more.'

'What more could I have done?'

'You could have done something. You could have stopped it, if you'd wanted to. I think deep down you want Siti to run off with Junior, get him out of your life.'

'Now you're being foolish. I like the kid and he likes me. I don't want Siti to take Junior to Fiji any more than Sandy does.'

'Really? You sure kept that a secret!' Caroline slammed the phone down.

Rowan slumped back in his chair and closed his eyes. He should have been angry but merely felt weary and frustrated. He'd made a career out of solving problems for his clients, why couldn't he solve the problems in his private life? Sure, there'd been a time when he'd wished Siti would just remove Junior from their lives but that time had long passed. Nevertheless, Caroline's accusations had stung him. Could he have done more? He sighed and picked up the phone, silently ruing his resolution to tackle problems head on, rather than let them drift and hang over his head. He was pleasantly surprised when Tiny answered his call.

'What are you doing at work?' said Rowan.

'It's our peak season,' said Tiny. 'You, of all people, should know that. What can I do for you?'

Rowan told him.

'I can tell you something that might interest you,' said Tiny. 'I bumped into Rajiv Satyarnand at a pre-Christmas party. He told me he no longer represented Sitiveni and refused to discuss the case.'

'What?' Once again Rowan got the gnawing feeling that there was another game being played that he didn't know about. He thanked Tiny and hung up. He sat at his desk while his mind tracked back and forth over familiar ground. As the minutes ticked by, he became more and more convinced that he'd missed something, that he had the answer to the puzzle but couldn't recognise it. His search was fruitless and dispiriting. At eight he took Margaret and the creatives to the Flower Drum as compensation for working through a public holiday. At eleven he paid the bill and went home to his townhouse. Glynis had left five more messages on his answering machine. She was hurt and tearful and desperate for him to call. Instead he went straight to bed. At two o'clock he was still searching the ceiling for answers. At three he came up with an idea.

Thirty-two

Rowan awoke at six, ready for action yet knowing there could be none for at least four hours. He rose, stretched, slipped into his exercise gear and drove to the gym. It was empty but for the diehards who'd show even in the middle of a nuclear holocaust. He worked through his normal routine, lifted weights, pummelled the heavy bag, sharpened his reflexes on the speed ball and warmed down on the treadmill. His workout took a full hour but he was still fidgety at its conclusion. He drove home, showered and went straight to the office. For breakfast he bought his apples from a street vendor as usual and a cappuccino from a nearby café. As first in, he unlocked the agency doors, disarmed the burglar alarm and turned on the lights. The clock above reception ticked over to eight. Rowan still had two hours to kill. At least two hours.

He rang Ryan Scott at home and got his answering machine. Rang his mobile and discovered Ryan was three thousand kilometres away, at Port Douglas, and really pissed off at being woken up. Ryan thought Rowan's idea was ridiculous, told him to forget about it, and hung up. Rowan thought of ringing Sandra but had nothing to give her except hope springing from an idea that could easily founder, an idea her solicitor thought sucked. He buried himself in work instead.

When Margaret arrived, she found him immersed in writing the document to back up their new business presentation. The coffee in the polystyrene cup alongside him was clearly cold and untouched. She took it away, microwaved it, poured it into a proper cup and returned it.

'Thanks,' he said, without looking up. He wrote urgently, pounding the keys on his keyboard as if he was hacking away on an old manual typewriter. His coffee remained untouched. At exactly ten o'clock he saved the document and pushed his keyboard away. It was time. Opening his desk drawer, he removed the file containing copies of the letters R. Satyarnand & Sons had sent to Sandra and dialled their number. The phone rang four times, five times, six times. He closed his eyes in frustration. Did they start at eight like other businesses in Fiji or were they closed for Christmas? Rowan was gambling on the fact that his glimpse of Rajiv Satyarnand had shown him a man who'd boogie barefoot on bindii if there was a buck in it.

'R. Satyarnand & Sons. How can I help you?' The voice was female and its owner seemed short of breath, as if she'd had to run.

'I'd like to speak to Mr Rajiv Satyarnand, please,' said Rowan. 'I'm calling from Australia,' he added, in the hope of communicating a sense of both urgency and importance.

'May I say who's calling?'

'Rowan Madison.'

'One moment please.' She put Rowan on hold and forced him to listen to Enya.

'Rajiv Satyarnand.' The voice was cold, deep and austere. Rowan had been expecting an Indian accent, but Satyarnand sounded typically Eton and Oxford.

'Mr Satyarnand, I have a proposition to put to you. Firstly, are you aware of who I am?'

'Of course.'

'I have a problem, Mr Satyarnand, and it occurs to me that no one is better placed to solve it than you.'

'I assume it has to do with the Sitiveni Kefu case?'

'Correct.'

'In which case, I am hardly placed to do anything for you.'

Rowan gritted his teeth, forced himself to keep his voice pleasant. 'Please hear me out. My understanding is that you no longer represent Sitiveni Kefu. This case has had an unfortunate consequence in that it has caused my wife considerable distress. She is convinced that Sitiveni Kefu will not return her child to her.'

'Why would she think that?'

'Why does a village Fijian employ an eminent and doubtless expensive solicitor to represent him in a custody case? Why does he express satisfaction with a ruling that allows him to see his child for only one week a year? Why does he agree to a ruling that requires him to fly to and from Australia twice each contact visit, which both of us know he can't afford?'

'It is not for me to question my client's motives.'

'If his intention is to abscond with the child, he only has to fly to Australia once. This is my wife's concern. My point in calling you is to put her mind at ease.' Rowan took a deep breath. Ryan had warned him his idea was foolish and the longer the conversation went, the more foolish it seemed. 'I would like to retain the services of your company for the period that the child is in Fiji, Mr Satyarnand, to ensure that he is returned to Australia in accordance with the ruling.'

'That is out of the question.'

'Name your price,' said Rowan bluntly.

'It is not a question of money but ethics.'

Ethics? The shyster was talking ethics. An edge crept into Rowan's voice. 'How does ensuring a judge's instructions are carried out impinge on your ethics?'

'Your proposal is both preposterous and unnecessary.'

'Mr Satyarnand, my wife is at her wit's end and I'm asking for your help. Surely there must be something you can do?'

'I have been led to believe you are an intelligent man, Mr Madison. I'm surprised you have not yet grasped the obvious.'

'Enlighten me!' snapped Rowan.

'Immigration, Mr Madison. Family reunification.'

'What?' If Rajiv Satyarnand had danced into his office dressed as a fairy and waving a wand, Rowan could not have been more stunned.

'Your government makes it difficult for Polynesian and Indo-Fijians to get a visa to visit Australia because of the problem of overstaying. However, rare exceptions are made in cases of hardship. I would not be the least surprised if Sitiveni Kefu now applied to emigrate to Australia to be close to his son, citing the court order and the severe financial penalty it imposed. Now, is there anything else I can do for you?'

'No ... no, thank you,' said Rowan. His mind reeled.

'Perhaps one day there will be something you can do for me in return. Good morning, Mr Madison.'

Rowan hung up and stared at the phone, his mind a whirl as all of the pieces of the jigsaw slotted into place. Siti didn't give a rat's arse about Junior: he was just the means to gain entry to Australia. Siti's motive was so obvious that Rowan was flabbergasted he hadn't thought of it before. With growing alarm, he also realised there was a good chance that Siti would not return to Australia with Junior as instructed. One, he probably didn't have the money for the return flight and, two, it might not be in his best interests. By flouting the conditions of the specific issues order, he would give Sandra grounds to have it rescinded, which would only serve to strengthen his claim for Australian residency. In the meantime, Sandra would go out of her mind with worry. He had no doubt that Siti would ultimately surrender Junior to Sandra, but only after sufficient drama had played out for him to make his point. Neither Sandra nor Junior deserved that.

But why was Siti so desperate to come to Australia? He grabbed the phone and rang Tiny. More pieces fell into place. According to Tiny, once Siti and his family had residence in Australia, his uncles, cousins, nephews and nieces could all apply to join them. They'd probably clubbed together to buy his air ticket. Why did they all want to uproot and come to Australia? So they could have TV, car, stereo, washing machine, health services and opportunities for a life far more sophisticated and privileged than was available to them in Fiji.

Armed with his new knowledge, Rowan raced out of his office, a man at last clear in his purpose. He nearly knocked a fresh replacement coffee out of Margaret's hands as he exited.

'Where are you going?' she asked in alarm.

'Back in time,' said Rowan.

Caroline and Sandy were ready to take Junior to the Airport Motel by eleven-fifteen, but their departure was delayed by a deluge of tears from his distraught sisters.

'I don't want Juni to go,' sobbed Rochelle. It was a refrain that had begun at six when she'd crawled teary-eyed into Sandra's bed. Sarah didn't want Junior to go either and had clung to him from the moment he'd woken up. She'd got out his cricket set and tried to play cricket with him, got out his football and tried to play soccer, rang every bell and flashed every light on his bus console. It was as if she wanted Junior to enjoy all his toys now, in case he didn't come back. Sandra had struggled to maintain a brave front but found the distress of the two girls heart-breaking. Her own tears had only made the situation worse.

They left late, at eleven-thirty, with Marion and Clive clutching two waving, crying girls on the driveway. Somewhere inside, Jenny was playing with the bus console, happy to finally have it all to herself. Sandra kept hoping they'd have an accident, nothing serious, but enough to delay them so she wouldn't have to give Junior away. Caroline drove impatiently, as quickly as she could without taking risks.

'You're going to have to stop crying,' Caroline said. 'You're not doing Junior any favours.'

'I know.' Sandra sat in the back alongside Junior's safety seat, stroking his hair and trying to fix his image in her mind. She dabbed her eyes with tissues. The tissues dried her tears but did nothing for the redness or swelling, or for the ache in her heart.

Caroline turned away from the airport towards Tempe. 'We'll be there in five minutes. For heaven's sake, pull yourself together.'

'Will you come in with me?'

'Of course.'

'I've got to tell him about the water purifiers, what Junior likes for meals. Oh God, I don't even know where to start!'

'I'll do the talking. You just chip in whenever you can. Okay? Now, chin up. Don't give that bastard any satisfaction.' They drove on in silence until Caroline pulled into the motel forecourt. The Airport Motel offered travellers budget accommodation. It was two storeys high and U-shaped, framing a car park and the smallest swimming pool Caroline had ever seen. The sign said NO DIVING and she could understand why. It would be impossible to dive in at one end without leaving your brains embedded in the other.

'You okay, Sandy?'

'Just fine.' There was a quaver in her voice and her hands had begun to shake uncontrollably.

'Have you got the room number?'

'Twelve.'

'Right,' said Caroline. 'Let's get it over with.'

'Oh God, Caro, I feel like I'm abandoning him! He'll never forgive me!'

'Nonsense. You carry Junior, I'll carry the bags. Now come on!'

Sandy unbuckled Junior from the car seat. 'I'm sorry, darling. I'm so sorry!' She kissed him and picked him up, holding him tightly against her chest.

'Come on,' said Caroline. 'It's five past twelve already.'

'Oh God!' said Sandra. She followed Caroline to the door, walking as though to her own execution. A lump came to her throat that she couldn't swallow. It felt so large, she could barely breathe. Caroline knocked. The door swung slightly on its hinges.

'Come on in. It's not locked.'

Caroline turned back to face Sandra, who'd stopped dead in her tracks.

'Rowan?' she said tentatively.

Caroline pushed the door wide open. The room wasn't much, just a bed, adjoining bathroom, TV, bar fridge and a bar with two stools. Siti sat on one, Rowan on the other. Siti held a bag of ice to his cheek, Rowan had a bag of ice resting on his right hand. They each had a beer.

'What the hell's going on?' said Caroline.

'Hi Caro,' said Rowan amiably. 'Hi Sandy. You're five minutes late.'

'What on earth are you doing here?' asked Sandra.

'Just having a chat. Our friend here has had a change of heart. He's decided he's not taking Junior to Fiji after all.'

'What?' said Sandra incredulously. She looked from

Rowan to Siti and back again, at the bruising around Siti's cheek and the swelling in Rowan's right hand, trying to take it all in and make sense of it.

'Payback,' said Rowan. 'None of your business. He was expecting you, he copped my right hand instead. Hardly fair, but effective, and long overdue. The important thing is, we've reached an agreement. You can relax, Sandy, Junior is not going to Fiji. He's not going anywhere but home. Okay?'

'Home?' Tears flooded Sandra's eyes, tears of gratitude and relief. But with them came an upwelling of anger. She had some unfinished business. She lifted Junior off her shoulder and cradled him so that he faced Siti. 'Look at him, you bastard. Look at my son!'

Siti refused, staring steadily at the floor.

'Look at him! Look at him now, because you're never going to see him again as long as you live.'

Siti glanced quickly at Junior and turned away again. 'So sorry, Mrs Sandra,' he said softly. 'So sorry to cause trouble.'

'You're sorry! That's it? That's all you've got to say?'

Rowan stepped between them. 'It's over, Sandy. Over. Just let it be. Take Junior and go.' He ushered her out through the door.

'What did you do?' asked Caroline. 'How did you get him to change his mind? For Christ's sake, Rowan!'

'I swapped Junior for a fishing boat. It's a long story. I'll tell you about it when we get home.'

Caroline stopped only long enough to pick up Jenny and give Rowan the sort of kiss women normally reserve for lovers. She made Sandra promise to ring her and left after suggesting to Marion and Clive that they followed suit. Sandra surrendered Junior to his ecstatic sisters, collapsed into a lounge chair and accepted a large gin and tonic from Rowan. He joined her with a scotch and sat on the sofa, an icepack bound around his injured hand.

'Are you going to tell me what happened?' she asked. Her gaze fixed on his hand. Rowan told her about his phone calls to Rajiv Satyarnand and Tiny.

'The motive was right under our noses the whole time,' he said.

'So what did you do? Just go around and punch his lights out?'

'That was a private thing between him and me. No, I simply made it possible for him to get in Fiji the things he wanted from Australia. Fiji has TV, cars and washing machines. All Siti lacked was the means to buy them.'

'So?'

'I made it possible for him to get what he wants. Siti is a boatman for Coralhaven, but given the choice he'd rather be a fisherman. That's what he does on his days off, goes fishing. That's what he was doing when he smashed my face. So I gave him cash and a bank cheque – an advance on money that will enable him to put a deposit on a reef fishing boat, not a game boat, but a twin-engined boat to take tourists out and catch bottom fish. He'd charge the tourists and sell the catch to Maurice. To get the rest of the cash, Siti has to sign a contract, which I'll send via Maurice, relinquishing all claim to Junior and rights under the court order. It's a sweet deal. Everyone wins. I even offered him enough to pay back his relatives.'

Sandra reached over and kissed Rowan gently. 'What you did, my darling, was sell your fantasy so I could keep Junior.'

'Something like that.'

'Why?' she asked softly.

Rowan put down his scotch. 'I've been doing some thinking,' he said.

'Yes.'

'A lot of thinking.'

'Go on.'

Rowan shuffled uncomfortably. 'Twelve months ago I chose the wrong option. Mike was right when he told me how my future could be, and I turned my back on it. He told me I didn't have the capacity to hate children, and I don't. I can't hate Junior or resent him any more. The little bugger crawled for me, for Christ's sake.'

'Yes, he did,' said Sandra cautiously.

'He only has to see me and his little face lights up. I only have to sit down and he climbs up onto my knee. I look at him now and see a child who is as much a part of this family as the girls. Almost as much.'

'Almost?'

'It occurs to me that the girls have a father but Junior is still deficient in that department. I was wondering if I'm not too late to put my hand up.'

Sandra's jaw dropped open. 'What?'

'I belong here. That is the one certainty in my life. The way things have been going, I've had to take a long, hard look at myself and admit a few truths. I've missed you every single day and I've missed the girls. I've missed having things the way they were. I want to come home, Sandy, if you'll have me.'

'Oh, I'll have you!'

Sandra thought she was all cried out but was proved spectacularly wrong. Tears flowed as though a dam had burst and there was nothing she could do to stop them. She thought she should say something but words seemed hopelessly inadequate. She just threw her arms around Rowan and held on. 'Welcome home,' she said finally. 'I thought this was going to be the worst day of my life but it's just the opposite.'

'It's a good day for me, too, Sandy.'

'You know, there have been times when I thought this would never happen, that you'd never come back, never accept Junior.'

'According to Caroline, anyone who didn't know us would just think he was adopted.'

'What?'

'You know, from overseas. Apparently overseas adoptions have become pretty commonplace recently.'

'Yes, they have,' said Sandra. 'You'd be surprised.' She had to smile. Rowan hadn't changed. He still had to find a justification for his actions, a means to salvage his pride, even if history had to be rewritten in the process.

'Of course, this raises another issue,' said Rowan.

'What do you mean?' A flicker of alarm crept into Sandra's voice.

'The family's incomplete. A boy should have a brother.'

'That can be arranged,' said Sandra.

'This time,' said Rowan, 'I choose the colour.'